Praise for Sean Dietrich

"I first read Sean Dietrich's work a few years ago when an email was sent to me with a persuasive argument that he should make his debut appearance on the Grand Ole Opry, the Nashville, Tennessee-based show that made country music famous. Convinced it was time he appeared on our stage and the world's longest-running radio show, I first met Sean backstage at the Opry in early spring 2023 on the night of his Opry debut. That evening, Sean received a standing ovation from the Opry audience before he'd even spoken a word or sang a note. The crowd was clearly there to see one of their favorite personalities make a dream come true. When Sean appeared at the Opry a second time, he followed Country Music Hall of Famer Bill Anderson, the Opry's longest-serving member ever. As Mr. Anderson stepped off stage and Sean prepared to go on, I encouraged Bill to stand side stage and watch Sean do his thing—tell tales of the South and tie them together with old-time favorites. Neither Bill nor anyone else in the Opry House was disappointed. In many ways, I'd describe Sean's latest work the way I described Sean's on-stage persona to Mr. Anderson that night. It goes without saying we'll be entertained. More specifically, we're introduced to characters we won't soon forget, we'll all likely both chuckle and tear up, and we could very well reflect on the purpose of our lives. I am convinced Mr. Dietrich has found his, both on the Opry airwaves and by sharing his written words, not the least of which are those in *Over Yonder*."

—Dan Rogers, executive producer,
Grand Ole Opry, for *Over Yonder*

"*Over Yonder* is a story of deeply complicated people having a deeply human experience. It's a love story for the tender-hearted, full of unexpected grace. Sean Dietrich brings to life a cast of Southern characters searching for meaning—and finding it in the most unlikely places. I hugged every single page."

—Laura Kate Whitney, Editor at Large, *Good Grit Magazine*

"A heart-pumping and heartwarming story of redemption—with car chases. This book was a sweet, sad ride, which is my favorite kind."

—Elizabeth Passarella, author of *Good Apple* and *It Was an Ugly Couch Anyway*, for *Over Yonder*

"Dietrich's latest gem combines his trademark wit and compassion. Using short, unadorned sentences, there is a timeless universality to the way in which he conjures ordinary people scarred by hardscrabble lives. His prose has a familiarity and gentle reverence for his cast members, allowing each their moment in the sun. Minnie's artistic coming-of-age is profound and uplifting, while Nub's life-changing decision puts him back in touch with his feelings and those of everyone around him. Reminiscent of his previous novels, and skillfully date-stamped in the early seventies, Dietrich's keen observations of his native Alabama underscore a natural love of life-affirming storytelling."

—Historical Novel Society for *Kinfolk*

"*Kinfolk* is the Southern story you've been waiting for. I absolutely loved this delightful and heart-wrenching story chock-full of both laughter and tears. In a small Alabama town where everyone knows your darkest secrets, and where the Grand Ole Opry is a balm to the soul, we meet a cast of endearing and quirky characters you won't forget. *Kinfolk* is a page-turning delight with Dietrich's trademark humor and heart-filled insight. In this wild ride we call life, Dietrich has a special view and one he shares with wit and kindness in turn. When a young girl working at Waffle House and a sixty-five-year-old man whose life is falling apart cross paths in Park, Alabama, no one in their world will ever be the same. *Kinfolk* is a novel about second chances, deep love, forgiveness, and the power of country music—all wrapped up in a lyrically told story."

—Patti Callahan Henry, *New York Times* bestselling author of *The Secret Book of Flora Lea*

"Sean Dietrich has a lovely, seasoned voice that's anchored by his deep understanding of the charm and depth of the South. *Kinfolk*, the latest in his oeuvre, is a heartwarming and well-told tale with lyrical writing that's as rich as my mother's grits casserole. I'm left satisfied, uplifted, and perhaps a little homesick too."

—Boo Walker, bestselling author of *A Spanish Sunrise*

"Sean Dietrich is a master at creating Southern characters who are relatable in their brokenness, hope, and perseverance. Laugh-out-loud colloquialisms bring sincerity and realism to small-town life. *Kinfolk* spins both a heartbreaking and heartwarming tale about family, redemption, second chances, and the power of love that moves us all."

—Jennifer Moorman, bestselling author of *The Baker's Man*

"The legion of fans who have already discovered Sean of the South's heartwarming Southern stories will be raving about this knock-out novel, and readers new to his work will find this tale strikes every perfect note. With relatable characters, comedic relief, sensory-rich descriptions, a dose of romance, and a fast-paced plot that keeps the pages turning, Dietrich has hit a home run with this one . . . a victory that would surely make The Incredible Winston Browne proud."

—*New York Journal of Books* for *The Incredible Winston Browne*

"Dietrich imbues plenty of Southern charm and colloquialisms in a read that will appeal to people of all genders, and especially to fans of small-town living. Readers who enjoy well-developed, realistic characters similar to those from Charles Martin and Lauren K. Denton will want to watch for more from this author."

—*Library Journal* for *The Incredible Winston Browne*

"Dietrich meshes mystery and romance beautifully in this moral tale about one man set on using what is left of his life to enrich the lives of others. Dietrich's fans will love this rip-roaring, dramatic inspirational."

—*Publishers Weekly* for *The Incredible Winston Browne*

"This poignant novel is about people, life, community, family, friendship, love, the day-to-day, even the mundane . . . Baseball fans and non-fans alike will enjoy this sometimes humorous, occasionally heartbreaking story about all that we hold dear, which gives us a timely reminder that we need to live in the moment, or life can pass us by while we aren't paying attention."

—Historical Novel Society for *The Incredible Winston Browne*

"Sean Dietrich has written a home run of a novel with *The Incredible Winston Browne*. Every bit as wonderful as its title implies, it's the story of Browne—a principled, baseball-loving sheriff—a precocious little girl in need of help, and the community that rallies around them. This warm, witty, tender novel celebrates the power of friendship and family to transform our lives. It left me nostalgic and hopeful, missing my grandfathers, and eager for baseball season to start again. I loved it."

—Ariel Lawhon, *New York Times* bestselling author of *I Was Anastasia*

"Sean's writing is infused with the small-town South—you can smell the exhaust of the cars cruising down dusty back roads, and you can sense the warmth of the potluck meal on your plate. Make no mistake. [*The Incredible Winston Browne*] is a classic story, told by an expert storyteller."

—Shawn Smucker, author of *Light from Distant Stars*

"Sean Dietrich has given us an absolute treasure of a novel. Moving, powerful, and dazzling, *Stars of Alabama* is a page-turning wonder of a story."

—Patti Callahan, *New York Times* bestselling author of *Becoming Mrs. Lewis*

"Dietrich is a Southern Garrison Keillor. Fans of the latter and former will be pleased."

—*Library Journal* for *Stars of Alabama*

"[*Stars of Alabama*] is a testament to inner strength and the good that can come from even the worst beginnings . . . Historical fiction and mystery readers will find this to be a very satisfying book."

—*Booklist*

"Sean Dietrich has woven together a rich tapestry of characters—some charming, some heartbreaking, all of them inspiring. *Stars of Alabama* is mesmerizing, a siren's call that holds the reader in a world softly Southern, full of broken lives and the good souls who pick up the pieces and put them back together into a brilliant, wondrous new mosaic full of hope."

—Dana Chamblee Carpenter, author of The Bohemian Trilogy

"Set during the Dust Bowl, this pleasing, ambitious epic from Dietrich brings together unlikely allies all escaping dire situations . . . Though filled with preachers declaring judgment and prophecies of the end-time, Dietrich's hopeful tale illuminates the small rays of faith that shine even in dark times."

—*Publishers Weekly* for *Stars of Alabama*

"Mysterious and dazzling."

—*Deep South* for *Stars of Alabama*

"Sean Dietrich can spin a story."

—*Southern Living* for *Stars of Alabama*

"A big-hearted novel."

—*Garden & Gun* for *Stars of Alabama*

"Sean Dietrich's *Stars of Alabama* is a beautiful novel, mesmerizing with its complex characters, lush settings, and lyrical language. It is, quite simply, Southern literature at its finest."

—*Southern Literary Review*

Over Yonder

Also by Sean Dietrich

FICTION

Kinfolk
The Incredible Winston Browne
Stars of Alabama
Lyla
The Other Side of the Bay

NONFICTION

You Are My Sunshine
Will the Circle Be Unbroken?
The Absolute Worst Christmas of All Time
The South's Okayest Writer
Caution: This Vehicle Makes Frequent Stops for Boiled Peanuts
Small Towns, Labradors, Barbecue, Biscuits, Beer, and Bibles
Sean of the South: On the Road
Sean of the South (Volume 1)
Sean of the South (Volume 2)
Sean of the South: Whistling Dixie

Over Yonder

SEAN DIETRICH

THOMAS NELSON
Since 1798

Published in Nashville, Tennessee, by Thomas Nelson. Thomas Nelson is a registered trademark of HarperCollins Christian Publishing, Inc.

Published in association with The Bindery Agency, www.TheBinderyAgency.com.

Thomas Nelson titles may be purchased in bulk for educational, business, fundraising, or sales promotional use. For information, please email SpecialMarkets@ThomasNelson.com.

Publisher's Note: This novel is a work of fiction. Names, characters, places, and incidents are either products of the author's imagination or used fictitiously. All characters are fictional, and any similarity to people living or dead is purely coincidental.

Any internet addresses (websites, blogs, etc.) in this book are offered as a resource. They are not intended in any way to be or imply an endorsement by Thomas Nelson, nor does Thomas Nelson vouch for the content of these sites for the life of this book.

Library of Congress Cataloging-in-Publication Data

Names: Dietrich, Sean, 1982- author

Title: Over yonder / Sean Dietrich.

Description: Nashville : Thomas Nelson, 2025. | Summary: "With the same dry humor and compassion for his characters as Fredrik Backman, Sean Dietrich's latest novel highlights the good of humanity and the light that's always just around the corner"—Provided by publisher.

Identifiers: LCCN 2025018850 (print) | LCCN 2025018851 (ebook) | ISBN 9781400235674 trade paperback | ISBN 9781400235698 | ISBN 9781400235681 epub

Subjects: LCGFT: Fiction | Southern fiction | Novels

Classification: LCC PS3604.I2254 O94 2025 (print) | LCC PS3604.I2254 (ebook) | DDC 813/.6—dc23/eng/20250603

LC record available at https://lccn.loc.gov/2025018850

LC ebook record available at https://lccn.loc.gov/2025018851

Printed in the United States of America

25 26 27 28 29 LBC 5 4 3 2 1

THIS BOOK IS DEDICATED TO MY DAD. THE LAST TIME I SAW MY dad, he was being arrested by the county sheriff's department. He would have served time in prison if he hadn't taken his own life in the interim before his trial. The circumstances surrounding his life were nothing like the circumstances of the character in this book. But people (people smarter than me) say that in novels you write the characters you know. And it became clear to me within the first few chapters of this book that I was writing my dad.

Daddy was a good man; he just didn't know it. He was a religious man—anyone honest enough to grapple with one's own religion is the most devout there is. He was a father, though he believed he didn't deserve the honor. He loved to smoke and yet was a fitness enthusiast and long-distance runner who often ate vegetarian. He was a hard guy to understand. He fit no mold.

My father was a blue-collar man with white-collar sensibilities and a neck that showed very red. An ironworker who listened to Bach. A stick welder who read Michener. He was funny. Kind. Sarcastic. Pensive. And he loved boats.

People were drawn to him. He coached Little League. He read books obsessively. He taught me to pray without speaking. He had more sorrow than any man I ever knew, felt pain deeper than anyone who ever lived, and he instilled in me that it was okay for a man to cry publicly. He had many nicknames, but the boys on my Little League team called him "Woody."

I never knew why.

Prologue

——

THE GIRL WAS DEAD BEFORE SHE EVER GOT TO THE HOSPITAL. Melinda could tell she was dead because the EMTs were unloading her slowly. They don't move slowly when you're alive. The killer had probably not expected the girl to be able to call an ambulance when the vomiting began. Odds are he had not expected the girl to call Melinda either. Melinda was praying the ambulance had arrived at the girl's apartment before the killer had.

When the ambulance pulled in, Melinda was waiting. She stood at a distance in the rain-slicked parking lot, beneath the vapor lights, smoking a cigarette in earnest, a pile of butts around her feet. She coughed between nearly every inhalation. The chemo had made her weak and wrecked her lungs. For the last hour she had been watching vehicles come and go from the ER entrance. She had come directly from work, which was why she still wore her Taco Bell outfit, minus the stupid obligatory visor. The corporate-approved shirt hung on her emaciated frame, tucked into faded black jeans that were size 0 but still a little too big on her wasted body.

Over the course of the last eleven cigarettes, twenty-two patients had entered the ER's sliding doors in varying states of disrepair. She had seen one gunshot victim. One stabbing. She saw parents rushing into the ER, tugging their kids by the hands, carrying their children in their arms. She had seen dozens of patients discharged too, wrapped in gauze, holding piles of paperwork, sitting in wheelchairs, marked with bracelets, doomed to wait for a ride. Or worse. Call an Uber.

The cigarette hissed when Melinda stepped on it. She trotted toward the entrance. Her boots clicked against the pavement. Her bleached, fried hair caught the moonglow, like an '80s heavy-metal band singer beneath the stage lights.

When Melinda got to the young woman, she felt tears swell to the surface. The EMTs told her to step back, but Melinda would not. It was her, all right. Her hair had streaks of Pepto-Bismol pink, like all the young kids were doing.

"Crystal!" Melinda shouted. "Oh my God, Crystal!"

"Ma'am, you're going to need to back away, please."

"What's wrong with my friend?" she shouted.

"Ma'am, please."

"We're roommates! You can tell me!"

Melinda flung herself atop the body. She pressed her cheek against the girl's forehead, which was as cold as a slab of marble.

"Crystal! No!"

The EMTs relented and gave her a moment. But after a few seconds, they gently removed Melinda from the deceased, albeit kicking and screaming. They wheeled the gurney past the ER doors, leaving Melinda on the sidewalk alone, mascara trails like two black spider legs crawling down her cheeks.

In her hand was the USB-C flash drive.

On her journey back through the parking lot toward her car, she could see a dark shape moving in tandem with her. She caught glimpses of him beneath the halide lights. He was moving a little too casually.

She walked faster.

So did he.

She slowed down.

He did too.

Her car was only a few feet away when he attacked. He was a big guy. Not tall but solid. Thick cowboy mustache in the shape of a horseshoe. Smooth head, shaved clean. She knew him. She had dated him once. They had both been members of the same organization. Just like Crystal had been.

He tackled her. He shoved her skull into the pavement as she hissed and swore at him. He pressed a knee upon her flailing left wrist, pinning her forearm to the ground.

"You thieving little Judas," he said.

He searched her pockets with both hands.

And this was his first mistake. The man was so busy searching her that he didn't see what was in her right hand and thus didn't know what to do when she stabbed him with it. She jammed the two prong-like electrodes into his rib cage, squeezed the trigger, and released 150,000 volts into his body.

He hit the pavement, unable to move, his face frozen in a silent cry. He sounded like he was choking on his own spit. She hit him two more times with the stun gun until the man had thoroughly wet his pants. She hit him one more time for Crystal's sake.

Then Melinda crawled off the asphalt, dusted herself off, and plucked the flash drive from his clenched fist. She lit her final cigarette, drew in a cleansing inhalation, and released a breath of fog into the autumn eve.

"Don't tread on me, Peter," she said.

Chapter 1

Inmates don't cry. They can't. If a guy cries inside, it's rare. And it doesn't last. Like a lunar eclipse. Over before it even begins. This is because crying gets you nowhere in prison. When they let you out of prison, however, you want to cry. You need to cry. You need it so badly it's frustrating. You want to experience the enormous release of celebrative emotion. You want to sob. Heave. Let go of all the accumulated sorrow. Fall onto your knees. Howl and scream. But you just stand there.

Your emotions are missing a few keys in the upper octaves.

Numb. That was how Woody Barker felt as he walked the long, sterile hallway toward the Receiving and Discharging desk. The corridor was gray and featureless, made of cinder blocks. After ten years inside, his hair was the same shade of white as his jumpsuit. And he was a lot leaner than he'd been back when he was fifty.

"This way," said one of the officers with a smile playing at the corners of his mouth. The officer used his key card to open a large, green steel door. "You get to see what's behind door number three today, Woody."

He was escorted by two officers whose faces were made of

wood. They were both young and solidly built, like pro wrestlers with badges.

When the green door opened, he wanted to weep. He truly did. But his tear ducts—thanks to years of disuse—wouldn't cooperate. He was like a Chatty Cathy doll missing its string. Or like the Stretch Armstrong dolls from his youth, whose legs had been overextended so many times that Stretch's crotch area had become purely theoretical.

Woody checked in with the R&D clerk. She gave him a small envelope containing his Social Security card, birth certificate, and a prepaid Visa with the rest of his inmate account money on it. They gave him some cash. There were purple watermarks on the money. He'd never seen these marks on US currency before.

"What's wrong?" asked the clerk behind the discharge desk.

"Money looks different," he said.

"Different how?"

"I don't know. Just different."

"If you don't want it, I'll take it."

His release clothes came in a plastic bag, courtesy of the Federal Bureau of Prisons. And in true BOP fashion, they were prodigiously crappy clothes. Dollar Store Polo shirt, brandless jeans, Nike knockoffs, and cheap underpants that bunched up in your main crevice like thong underwear made of cling wrap. When he emerged from the bathroom wearing his new clothes, tugging at the seat of his pants, he felt odd and out of place. The jeans were rough against his skin. His shirt smelled like plastic. He had also nearly forgotten how to tie his own shoes since he'd gone so long wearing rubber sandals.

"Don't you clean up nice?" said a female officer who was waiting for him outside the bathroom. The lady guard was imposing, with broad shoulders. The prison had started hiring female guards about five years earlier.

"I feel ridiculous in these clothes."

"How you think I feel wearing this every day?"

They made Woody wait for about an hour in R&D while they got his paperwork ready. He saw a guy in a nearby office making morning PA announcements. Woody was dumbstruck. He'd heard this man's voice reading announcements every morning for ten years but had never seen the guy's face. The guy came out of his office and shook Woody's hand.

Woody felt like he was meeting a celebrity.

Next, they led Woody to another waiting room, past electronic gates, steel doors, and chicken-wire windows. Finally, he was in the main lobby. The room had cushioned chairs. New carpet. *People* magazines on sofa tables. The CO and the lieutenant met him in the waiting room. Woody knew them both. But today they were acting differently. The decorum of authority was gone. In this room, they were all just guys. Just regular people.

"It's going to be a shock to the system out there," the CO said. "You take care of yourself, boss."

"Thanks," said Woody.

"And if you ever get lonely," added the lieutenant, "you can always come back, and we'll give you your old room."

The guards all laughed. But Woody wasn't certain whether he should join in or lower his head or what. You didn't laugh with an officer in Wallace Correctional.

After that, the guards fell into quoting many of the prototypical clichés you hear at funerals, weddings, and used car dealership grand openings. There is nothing more human than using a cliché to ruin a ceremonious moment.

"Just take it one day at a time."

"Live life to the fullest."

"Be a blessing to others."

"Don't sweat the small stuff."

"Take time to smell the roses."

"Remember, you're only as strong as the tables you dance on."

They all shook hands. Woody marveled at the firmness of their handshakes. He had not shaken another man's hand more than a few times in over a decade.

The doors of the Wallace Correctional swung open at 1:19 p.m. Woody walked out holding a plastic bag of belongings. His dad's truck was idling at the curb. His father's arm was hanging out the open window with the butt of a cigar cupped in it.

Nobody waved goodbye. Nobody did anything, really. He could feel the officers watching another former inmate exit hell on two legs.

And just like that, Reverend Woodrow Barker was a free man.

Chapter 2

———

THE BEAT-UP HONDA LOOKED LIKE A PORTA-JOHN ON WHEELS, only with more rust. The engine backfired and coughed black exhaust into the atmosphere, puncturing nearly visible holes into the ozone above. It had left a hundred-mile trail of sooty atmosphere all the way from Black Creek, Kentucky, to Knoxville. Caroline could hear a heavy grinding beneath the car each time her boyfriend shifted into third. It sounded like the vehicle was going to rattle apart into a heap of nuts and bolts on Interstate 40. The car had no suspension. There was a tetanus-rimmed hole in Caroline's floorboard; she could see the highway speeding beneath her.

The car was a '93.

The girl was seventeen and pregnant.

Caroline stared out the lace-like cracks of the passenger window's single bullet hole at downtown Knoxville as they rode past all the franchise chains that have transformed American townships into carbon duplicates of themselves. Her hair was the color of a carrot. She was 94 percent freckles. Her small, upturned nose, full cheeks, and cherub face brought to mind a character from the highly successful Cabbage Patch Kids product line.

Caroline lowered her book and tapped on the cracked window with the bullet hole in it.

"Pull over here," said Caroline. "I need to stop by Bath and Body Works."

Her boyfriend, Tater, glanced out the window at the shopping area's sea of cars glinting in the sunlight and snow.

"Bath and Body Works?"

"I need to get Selina a thank-you gift."

Tater ignored her. "We are not going shopping."

"It's not shopping. It's a gift."

"What does Bath and Body Works even sell?"

"Happiness."

He snorted. "We're definitely not going."

Tater wore a ballcap with a table-flat brim. Around his neck was a thick golden chain bearing a marijuana leaf medallion the size of a baseball glove. His bare torso was painted with a quilt of tattoos, which was why he was shirtless in twenty-nine-degree weather. There was a spider on his left pectoral. Buzz Lightyear was on his other one, flying in a victory pose as he plunged through outer space, hovering directly over Tater's right nipple as though it were Neptune.

He took a hit from his vape pen. "Selina can buy her own freaking perfume."

"She's covering my shifts."

"So?"

"So it's a way of saying thank you. She had to get a babysitter and everything."

He laughed. "She's stealing *your* hours. She should be buying *you* perfume."

He sped past Bath and Body Works.

"Are you serious right now?" she said.

Tater Bunson was indeed serious. Short men usually were,

and her boyfriend was barely five feet tall with shoes on. He wore a baby-hair mustache on his upper lip that was only visible in certain lighting. They had been together for a year, and it had not been a good year.

"Where's my next turn?" he said.

She looked at Tater's phone GPS. "It's right here."

Caroline was multitasking, calling out turns, but also reading a Richard Russo novel in her other hand. They shared one phone between them, and it belonged to Tater. Tater was the Keeper of the Phone because he was male. Caroline had never owned her own phone, and like most seventeen-year-olds, there was nothing she wanted out of life more than the latest model of Apple phone.

Tater spun the wheel right.

The car made a sound not unlike a Folgers can of rocks falling down a public stairwell. The Honda Civic EJ1 was a mutant vehicle, composed entirely of spare parts, forming a checkerboard of salvage-lot steel. The hood was primer gray, caked with clods of Tennessee dirt. The tires were a curated collection of four differently aged junkyard donuts. The spiderweb crack on the passenger window came from a .22 caliber bullet that had passed through the glass during Tater's last heated disagreement with his mom.

"Wait," said Caroline. "Why are you turning right?"

"You just said turn *right* here."

"No," Caroline said. "I said turn *right here*. You're supposed to turn *left* right here."

"What the hell, Caroline! Which is it? Right or left?"

She lowered her book and pointed out the windshield. "Can't you see the hospital on your left?"

He saw it all right. He saw North Knoxville Medical Center just as they were passing the exit.

Tater shouted a colorful word beginning with the sixth letter of the alphabet. He stamped on the brake and shifted into reverse in the middle of traffic. Soon he was heading backward in the intersection, moving against the flow. Horns blared. Cars swerved. Motorists extended hands from open windows and introduced Tater to the Tennessee state bird.

"Are you crazy? What're you doing?"

"Will you put down that stupid book and pay attention?" he demanded as they wheeled through traffic, butts first. "You're supposed to be looking at the GPS, not reading a freaking book while I drive."

Tater spun the wheel and screeched into the parking lot of North Knoxville Medical Center on two wheels. He barely avoided colliding with one Tesla, one Land Rover, and one little boy in a wheelchair.

The car came to a jarring halt, and Gary the goldfish's travel aquarium nearly fell off the dashboard. Caroline caught his temporary home with her foot. Gary traveled in a Hellmann's jar. Gary went everywhere Caroline went.

"We can't park here," Caroline said. "This is a handicap spot."

"Don't worry about it. Just hurry up."

"You've got to move."

"Relax. They won't do nothing to us. This is a hospital." He threw the gearshift into Neutral and yanked the parking brake to underline his point. Case closed. The male hath spoketh. Long live the male.

They just stared at each other.

She sighed, then placed Gary's jar into her backpack carefully, using library books to cushion the jar on all sides.

"I really think you should move the car," she said. "This is illegal, and it's not fair."

"It's not a big deal. I'm allowed to park here. My dad's on

full disability, and I'm a member of his medium family. It's legit, Caroline."

"*Immediate* family."

"Exactly."

Caroline kicked open the door and slung the backpack over her shoulder. She looked at Tater the way a kindergarten teacher looks with pity upon a kid who just pooped his pants in class.

"If you get a ticket, I'm warning you, I am going to be positively choleric."

"What the hell does that mean?"

"Let's not find out."

"Why don't you never speak English to me?"

"Sorry. I only speak English with members of my medium family."

Her own remark struck her as deeply hilarious. But she stifled her laugh because there was nothing Tater hated more than being laughed at, except for, perhaps, gainful employment.

"You think you're so much smarter than me," he said. "You and your stupid goldfish. Well, I got news for you—you ain't near as smart as you think you is. You're just sorry white trash like the rest of us."

"Well said, Stephen Hawking."

"Buzz off."

"Don't be upset because you don't know who Stephen Hawking is."

He slapped a hand on the dash. "Did you hear what I just called you, White Trash? Ain't no amount of reading that can fix being trash."

Unfazed, she leaned into the car and pinched his nipple hard enough to squish a cashew. "Put on a shirt. Your nips are turning blue."

"Dammit, Caroline!" Tater said, shielding his vulnerable areolas.

She fastened her hair into a ponytail and checked her face in the side mirror. Her state of dress embarrassed her. She was braless, wearing double T-shirts to make up for the lack of maternity undergarments. The overshirt was a Snoop Dogg T-shirt that belonged to her boyfriend, worn inside out so the world wouldn't see Snoop broadcasting his middle finger to the photographer. The shirt hung on her frame with all the charm of an unfurled parachute. But it was the only shirt that fit her pregnant body.

"I'm not skipping the water bill again," she said. "I'm done bathing outside in this freezing weather. I'm not paying your parking ticket. You're going to have to get an actual job."

Tater worked part-time for his cousin's start-up power washing venture. Business had been slow for the past three or four presidential administrations. Caroline, on the other hand, worked at the Super 8 off I-75. And she worked nights at Walmart stocking shelves.

"Now go find another parking place or so help me . . ."

He scoffed. "Or so help you what?"

"Don't tempt me, Tater. I'm serious."

"What're you going to do, leave me?"

She did not answer.

"You going to live under an overpass? Maybe a carboard box? You going to squat in some back alley somewhere and go to the bathroom against a brick wall? No, wait. I know. Maybe you could live behind Bath and Body Works."

Caroline was about to answer him, but she was worried if she spoke her voice might crack. Then she lobbed his iPhone at him. It was a direct hit. The phone bounced off his sternum, and he slammed the door behind her as hard as he could. The bullet-hole window crack grew three inches.

And she walked toward the hospital, crunching in the snow.

• • •

CAROLINE'S MOTHER'S HOSPITAL ROOM WAS NONDESCRIPT. WHITE walls. White floors. Vinyl upholstered chairs, torn and scuffed by too many visitors whose collective butts had squashed the cushions into pancake submission. Typical medical room decor. Corporate quaint. Like the interior of an IRS holding cell but with bedside toilets.

Caroline's mother was asleep in the bed. Her mother's boyfriend, Jack Jr., was sitting by the window, slumped in a chair, scrolling TikTok and watching a barrage of videos involving thong underwear. The room TV was blaring *Divorce Court* at a volume loud enough to change the migratory patterns of waterfowl.

He did not acknowledge Caroline's presence. When she approached the bed, she felt her composure start to fade. She had not seen her mother in a year. And things had changed considerably since her diagnosis.

Melinda Boyer was fifty-seven years old, but she looked *ninety*-seven today. She was bald, wearing one of those caps cancer patients wear. She had always been skinny, but now she was a ghost.

Her mother awoke slowly and focused her weary stare on the bouquet of white carnations Caroline carried in her hand. Then her gaze moved toward Caroline's midsection. The woman spoke with a slack jaw and labored voice.

"Oh my God, you're pregnant."

Caroline's emaciated mother struggled to sit upright and looked like she was going to break apart beneath the effort. "Who knocked you up? Please tell me it wasn't that idiot named after a potato."

"How are you, Mama?"

"How the hell's it look like I am?" Her mother snapped her fingers and held out her hand. "Did you bring them?"

Caroline reached into her backpack and withdrew a carton of Marlboro Blacks. Her mother yanked the cigarettes from Caroline's hand, then peeled the plastic packaging using her teeth.

"What about my lighter?" she asked, spitting plastic.

"All you said on the phone was cigarettes. I thought you'd already have a lighter."

Her mother fell back into her pillow. "Jesus, Mary, Joseph, and the donkey too, Caroline. You think they let me have a lighter in this place? Stupid, stupid girl."

The woman snapped her fingers at her boyfriend. "Jack Jr., go find me a lighter."

Jack Jr. wasn't paying attention.

So Caroline's mother threw the cigarettes at Jack Jr. They hit him in the face. "I said find me a lighter, loser."

Ah, *amor*.

Jack Jr. took several whole minutes to lumber to his feet.

"While we're young!" Melinda threw a sugar packet at him. Then a spoon. Caroline thought her mother would throw her entire meal tray at him too, but evidently Melinda was showing some restraint today.

Her mother had been with Jack Jr. longer than any other boyfriend. They had been on again and off again, at varying degrees of on- and off-ness, for several years. Her mom's boyfriend was cut from the same cloth as Tater, only older, with silver in his hair. He had a brown tattoo of a coiled snake on the back of his neck. The snake was supposed to be the timber rattler from the Don't Tread On Me flag but instead looked more like evidence of a healthy colon.

Caroline pulled a chair up to her mother's bed. The sound of *Divorce Court* filled the uncomfortable silence between them. TV had often done that when they were together. Like grout filling in all the cracks.

Caroline and her mother absently watched the screen, avoiding any actual talking.

Caroline muted the TV.

"Tell me how you've been, Mama."

"Oh, just wonderful," her mother said. "Look at me. Livin' the dream."

"Well, what's been happening?"

"Well, let's see. Last night we had a soufflé and a floor show. Tonight we're going to have an ice cream buffet and a sunset cruise. Geez, Caroline."

Nobody said anything. Her mother unmuted the TV, then coughed into a napkin. The napkin turned pink with blood. Pancreatic cancer was no way to go.

"When are they saying you can go home?" Caroline asked.

"They aren't."

"What do you mean?"

"I'm not going home. Least not through the front door."

Caroline looked into her lap. Her eyes began to get blurry with tears.

"I don't have long," her mother finally said. "I might not even have this week."

"Mama."

Melinda cranked up the volume. *Divorce Court* had turned into a wrestling match. They both watched the screen to keep from watching each other. Caroline thought daytime television represented about 80 percent of their relationship.

"But I'm glad you're here," her mother said, reaching out to touch her daughter's hand. "Because I need to talk to you."

"About what?"

They were interrupted when Jack Jr. entered the room. "Hey, no lighter, but I found a butane torch," he said, bearing a canister torch that was about the size of a thermos.

"Where did you find a butane torch in a hospital?" asked Melinda.

"The maintenance closet."

The torch had an electric ignitor switch. The butane hissed to life and a blue flame roared. Using this to light a Marlboro would have been akin to using a wrecking ball to secure a thumbtack. But any port in a storm.

Melinda Boyer removed the oxygen cannula from her face. She tossed back the sheets to reveal her bony frame. Her knees looked like soft balls attached to femurs.

The woman attempted to crawl out of bed and almost faceplanted. "Someone get me out of this bed. I need to smoke before I die."

Chapter 3

CAROLINE WAS THREE WHEN HER MOTHER WAS FIRST ARRESTED for possession. The incident happened in a Kmart parking lot. Caroline was too young to remember the entirety of it all, but she still recalled the highlights. She could remember, for example, riding in the shopping buggy as they exited Kmart. She remembered that it was sunny. Her red hair in pigtails. Her mother was pushing the buggy, singing to herself. Caroline was happy in the memory because her mother let her have a strawberry milkshake, back when Kmart served food.

She also remembered seeing all the cop cars parked around her mother's Pontiac Trans. She remembered the blue lights flashing, lighting up daylight. She remembered that her mother was messed up on something—meth probably. Maybe oxy. If you were the child of an addict, you always knew when your parent was high.

Her mom freaked out when she saw the cops. The woman lost all sanity—and she hadn't had much lucidity left to lose. Melinda Boyer let go of the cart and started running in the opposite direction. She had been just high enough to believe she could outrun cops.

The buggy with Caroline in it began rolling away, wheeling for the edge of the parking lot toward traffic. Caroline happily grasped her milkshake without knowing what was truly happening. She didn't know she was rolling toward a busy highway as she sipped away, the streaks of highway vehicles whooshing before her vision.

The buggy slammed into a curb, and Caroline shot out of the seat. The milkshake somersaulted through the air, landing on the pavement with a pink splatter. Caroline still bore a scar from where her lower tooth had punctured the skin above her chin. For weeks she could squirt milk at unsuspecting victims through a tiny hole in her lower lip.

That same week Caroline became property of the Tennessee Department of Children's Services and went into foster care. And it was only the beginning of what was to come.

Now Caroline wheeled her mother along the breezeway. Her mother was using the torch to light her cigarette and almost caught her gown on fire.

"Roll me over to those benches and tables," her mother said.

Foster care is a lot like a bad habit; once you enter the system, you're hooked for life. Most foster kids come and go from the system multiple times throughout their lives. Caroline went back into foster care three more times. She bounced between group foster homes like she was caught in a tragic pinball machine. Caroline's case was particularly complicated because she had medical issues. She was 80 percent blind in her left eye. She'd had three heart operations and eleven other surgeries. Nobody wanted a kid with medical issues. Not even her own mother, who caused all this to begin with.

When Caroline's mother got out of rehab the second time, Caroline tried moving back into her mother's trailer. She was fourteen at the time. Caroline thought it might work. But it didn't. One summer day, after a shower, she exited the bathroom wearing only a towel. Her mother's boyfriend du jour, Larry, was standing in the door, staring at her. His eyes were strange. His grin was menacing, and his hand was in his pants. Later that afternoon he walked into Caroline's room when she was changing her clothes. Caroline threw a lamp at him. Nothing happened, thankfully. But when Caroline's mother found out about this, she was horrified. The only logical solution in her mother's mind was to kick Caroline out.

So Caroline went back into foster care. She would technically remain in foster care until age eighteen. But at sixteen, she met a young man named after a starchy tuberous vegetable. The young man owned his own house, which his aunt had left him, so she moved in. Though they talked every once in a while, it had been a long time since Melinda and Caroline had been this close in proximity to each other.

Until today.

They were in the picnic area of the medical center, watching the snow fall. Her mother sat in a wheelchair looking into the iron sky. From this angle, Caroline could see Tater's Honda in the parking lot in the distance, crookedly parked in the handicapped space.

Melinda offered Caroline a cigarette.

"No thanks," said Caroline.

Her mother made a face. "Why? You quit?"

"I just don't want one."

Her mother looked at Caroline's tummy, then flicked her lighter. She pointed to Caroline's inner forearm. "You got a new tattoo."

The tattoo was a sunflower. The sunflower was adorned with cursive text: *Survive.* Her mother inspected the inkwork. "You design it?"

"Yes."

"*Survive?* What's that supposed to mean?"

A gaggle of nurses passed them. The medical staffers all stole glances at the frail woman on the breezeway, sucking smoke from the cigarette. Their looks of disapproval were palpable.

"It's not meant to be cryptic," said Caroline.

"What exactly do you think you survived?" asked her mother.

"Does it matter?"

Her mother didn't seem to care.

"You been by my house and fed my cats?"

"No."

"You said you'd go."

"Can't Jack Jr. feed them?"

"No. He's got the ankle bracelet thing."

"Then how's he even here?"

"He's been living in Knoxville for the last three months with his brother."

"He wasn't living with you?"

"We've had issues. Promise me you'll feed them."

Caroline stared into the parking lot at the Honda, puffing its blue exhaust. "I said I'll go. How many times do you want me to say it?"

Her mother seemed satisfied by her answer. She drew smoke inward, then exhaled it through her nostrils slowly. Melinda's face was harder and more angular than Caroline had ever seen it.

Melinda Boyer absently played with a necklace she wore. The gold pendant was the timber rattlesnake from the Don't Tread On Me flag. Same as on Jack Jr.'s neck.

"There's something I have to tell you," her mother said.

Her mother released another massive cloud, this one bigger than the former. Nicotine filled the air with the leathery, sweet smell Caroline had tasted in the womb. A smell she grew up with. A smell she both hated and enjoyed.

"Something to tell me?"

"Yeah." Her mother kept playing with the necklace. "And don't look at me like that, Caroline."

"Like what?"

"You can never manage to hide your disappointment in me."

"I'm not looking at you like anything."

"You are not my mother, Caroline."

The truth was, Caroline had always felt as though her mother were a sister. In many ways, a distant sister. Even from a young age Caroline had always seen herself as older than Melinda somehow.

Her mother released the gold pendant and was silent for a few moments. Melinda rolled her chair forward and touched her daughter's hand. It was such a small act. But it was maybe the most affection Caroline had ever received from the woman.

"You don't think I get it, Caroline? I screwed up your life. Believe me, I wish I could make it better. I wish I'd made different choices. Hell, I wish a lot of things. I know I made a mess of everything. I know I ruined your childhood."

Melinda gripped her hand. Caroline looked at the veiny hand clasping hers. The skin like tissue paper.

"Please, Care Bear. Try to understand me. Put yourself in my shoes. I wasn't always like this. I never meant to hurt anyone. Least of all you."

Caroline's mother hadn't called her Care Bear since she was a little kid.

"Mama, please."

"No, listen to me. I have something for you. Something important. Something that could change your life."

"Mama."

Her mother squeezed Caroline's hand harder. Caroline felt the bones in her hand pop. There were tears in her mother's eyes.

"Listen to me, Caroline." She held Caroline's gaze until the tears reached critical mass and began to fall onto her cheeks. Crying turned into heaving. Heaving turned into coughing. Coughing turned into choking. She was trying to speak, but nothing was coming out.

"Care Bear, I need you to forgive me."

Caroline did not respond.

Her mom took a deep breath, collecting herself, then flicked her cigarette into the snow. "Take me somewhere private. I'm done smoking. We need to be alone for what I want to say."

Caroline said, "Mama, there's hardly anyone around."

"Do as I say."

Caroline looked out at the parking lot. She saw a police car pulling up to Tater's Honda. The officer got out of the cruiser and walked around the Honda, examining the plates. Caroline watched the officer rap on Tater's window. Within moments, she could see the officer getting agitated, which was the classic reaction to social intercourse with Tater Bunson. Then the officer pulled out a pad and began writing a ticket.

Caroline reached for the butane torch in her mother's lap. "I'll take one of those cigarettes."

• • •

On April 2, 1865, the Civil War was only a week from its end, and the fall of the Confederate capital was imminent. Federal forces were closing in on Richmond. Confederate president Jefferson Davis and his cabinet were compelled to leave town quickly before their proverbial ass was metaphorical grass. At least that was how Caroline's mother put it when she told the story.

They were sitting behind the hospital, not far from the dumpsters. They were totally alone, and yet Caroline's mother was still whispering. Caroline was on her second cigarette, staring off into space, disgusted with herself but enjoying the small buzz.

"Are you even listening to me?" her mother said.

"I'm listening."

Jefferson Davis and the six members of his cabinet fled Richmond overnight, taking few belongings with them in their haste, along with the entirety of the Confederate treasury, which was upward of one and a half tons of gold and silver bullion. The money had been appropriated from various sources in the South, including banks and private donations, and from the seizure of Union assets. The cargo amounted to a pile of gold and silver so heavy it required iron-reinforced transport wagons. This was a payload too heavy for a modern-day Chevy truck to carry without completely wrecking the suspension. Which was why, Caroline pointed out, members of the cabinet should have unanimously agreed to purchase a Ford.

Her mother was annoyed. "Are you going to sit there and mock me or are you going to listen? This is important."

Caroline just closed her eyes.

The gold and silver were transferred via wagons, pulled by teams of Morgan draft horses. The cargo was guarded around the clock by a brigade of sharpshooters as wagons were hauled across the entirety of the American South on back roads, traversing hidden trails, hiding on local farms, resting in thickets. For a solid month, fleeing cabinet members and military escort lived in makeshift camps along the roadside, moving steadily southward, through Virginia, North Carolina, and Tennessee, until their capture in Irwinville, Georgia, on May 10. When federal forces came upon Davis, there were no wagons. No draft horses. No gold. They transferred Davis to Fort Monroe, Virginia, where he was imprisoned in a casemate cell, kept in close confinement, shackled by the ankles. For upward of seven hundred days, Davis was doggedly interrogated on the whereabouts of the gold and silver, but he maintained that the tonnage had simply been lost.

"Lost?" Caroline asked.

"The Yankees didn't believe it either," her mother said. "Think about it. How do you lose almost two tons of gold and silver?"

Even so, Jefferson Davis offered no explanation.

Davis was released on bail in 1867, after over two years of imprisonment. Following his release, he lived in Montreal and in London. He had been stripped of land, assets, and citizenship and died relatively poor compared to his former glory. The gold was never recovered.

"But," said Caroline's mother, watching a pencil-thin line of smoke drift upward from her splayed fingers, "it's still out there."

"How do you know?"

"Because I think I've found it."

Her mother's face was solemn.

Caroline waited a beat, then laughed. With undisguised disgust.

She took in her surroundings. The dumpster. Her mother. The pathetic reality of it all. Caroline looked at her cigarette, identical to the one in her mom's hand, and stabbed out her smoke like she was killing a spider.

"I can't believe what I am hearing," said Caroline. "I can*not* believe this. I came all the way to Tennessee for this?"

Her mother patted the air. "Lower your voice."

"Do you even care about me? Do you care about *anything* I've accomplished in my life? Do you care who I am? Do you have any interest whatsoever in anyone but yourself? You haven't even asked me how I'm doing. You haven't asked about my baby. You don't care about anything in my life."

Her mother wheeled backward. "This could change your life, honey." The woman lowered her voice to a whisper. "There is something hidden inside my trailer, something important, and I want you to have it. This could change everything for you. People have died for this."

"Are you kidding me right now?"

"Caroline, listen to me."

"Are you *freaking* kidding me?"

"Caroline."

"Buried treasure? Seriously?"

Caroline looked off. A sour cry still roiling beneath her hard surface. Then she looked at her mother with the most honesty she could muster.

"There's not enough gold in the world to make up for you not being there."

• • •

The Honda was parked at a Shell station. Tater sat in the front seat eating a gas station taquito that had been sitting on the roller grill since the Jimmy Carter administration. He was looking at his parking ticket with mild amusement. He ate while simultaneously administering inhalations from a raspberry vape cartridge. Tater was a big fan of combining the two flavors. Salty and sweet. Nutrition and carcinogen. The air-freshener fog exited his mouth and nose like two giant albino worms fighting free from his sinus cavities.

"Two hundred and fifty bucks," he said, eyeing the ticket.

"That chick fined me two hundred and fifty freaking bucks. You believe that?"

"That *chick* was a cop," she said.

He crumpled the ticket, threw it into the back seat, and passed the vape device to Caroline. She declined.

"Smoking just one won't hurt you. My mom smoked with me."

Caroline just looked at him.

She went back to her book, trying hard to be a hundred million light-years away from here. It was, however, impossible to be far away while trapped inside a Honda with Tater's rap music playing at an earsplitting volume. The volume knob to the stereo was broken, stuck in the wide-open position, requiring needle-nose pliers to operate. Thus, American rapper Pitbull was rapping in Español at a volume loud enough to qualify as a misdemeanor.

Caroline clicked off the stereo.

"Hey," said Tater. "I was listening to that."

"Gary doesn't like the noise."

Tater looked at the goldfish jar perched on the dashboard. Gary swam in circles, flicking his tail. She carried Gary everywhere. It was part of being a foster kid. You carried your possessions with you because you never knew when you might be on the move again.

"Fish can't hear music," said Tater.

"Yes, they can."

"Fish ain't got no ears."

"They absolutely have ears."

Tater wrinkled his forehead. He peered into the jar, squinting. Gary was opening his mouth and gills.

"Bull crap."

She closed her book. "You're eloquent, you know that?"

"How do they hear without ears?"

"They have internal ears connected to a gas bladder. They're tiny bones and hairs that amplify vibrations in their surroundings. It's complicated. I really don't have the energy to explain it right now. I'm sorry they didn't teach you this in high school biology."

"Ears connected to a bladder? Like for peeing?"

She sighed. "The movement of the swim bladder moves sensory cells in their head, and the fish's brains translate the movement as sound. In some ways, they can hear better than humans can. It's actually very fascinating."

If you were to have looked into Tater's eyes, you could have seen the back of his skull.

"Bull crap," he restated.

"Another excellent point." She grinned, then showed some teeth. "You should go into litigation."

"Flying planes?"

"Oh my God."

Caroline used this opportunity to feed Gary. Gary was pecking the food while Tater looked on in amazement. Tater had no idea, of course, that Caroline was demonstrating goldfish auditory perception. Gary heard the vibrations of food hitting the water, and that's how he knew it was time to eat.

"You really think Gary can hear Pitbull?"

Caroline nodded. "And he doesn't like the music, I can tell."

"Why not?"

"Because it's violent."

"You don't even know what they're saying. It's in Spanish."

"I speak Spanish."

He laughed. "Since when?"

She rolled her eyes. "Where have you been? We use Spanish at work all the time. Everyone I work with is a Spanish-speaker."

"Prove it."

She looked at him. *"Eres un zurullo."*

"What's that mean?"

"Means I love you."

He took another puff from his pen.

She cranked down her near-shattered window to let the vape escape from the hotbox. "Now hurry up and finish your taquito. I need you to take me somewhere."

Tater just looked at her. "I'm not going to that bath and body store for your stupid friend."

"Not there."

He wagged the vape device. "And I'm not going to Target either."

Caroline altered her demeanor. She leaned inward and gave him a big, disarming smile. "I have a feeling you'd change your mind if you knew what I was going to be buying."

He furrowed his brow.

"Because it's a surprise. For you."

Tater's whole mood changed. He looked both mystified by this and excited. He took a monster hit from the cartridge. When he exhaled, the interior of the vehicle looked like the inside of a bong.

"What kind of surprise?"

"You'll just have to wait and see."

A smirk crept onto his face. "You're getting me a PlayStation 5, aren't you?"

She said nothing.

"Aren't you?"

She batted her eyes.

"Caroline?"

She confiscated his phone and put the address into his GPS.

"No peeking."

Tater looked on with great interest as she entered the information. He was a little kid on Santa's knee.

"Is that a new necklace?" he said.

She touched the golden pendant on her neck. "No."

Chapter 4

FIVE HUNDRED AND THIRTY-SEVEN MILES SOUTH, A BARGE-LIKE houseboat sat moored in slip F-9. The *Ship Happens* was docked between one pontoon and one half-sunken sailboat named *She'll Get Over It*. Woody Barker was cooking tofu egg scramble in the galley. On mornings like this, it was hard to believe that only three months earlier he had been numbered among the 1.9 million incarcerated within the United States. Currently he bore the undistinguished honor of being one of six full-time residents at Bald Point Marina.

The marina was calm today, with a small army of outmoded leisure boats rising and falling among the reeds, rocking side to side like chess pieces on a fluid chessboard. The *Happens'* main cabin smelled like burning plant-based rubber. Woody added a spoonful of turmeric to the tofu for yellow color, then placed slices of Follow Your Heart cashew-based cheese atop the eggs and watched it *almost* melt. He used a spatula to move the "eggz" around the skillet, hoping they would begin to resemble something less akin to sautéed Silly Putty.

Elizabeth came padding out of the back bedroom. "I thought I smelled food."

Her black hair was in a ponytail. She was wearing his Willie Nelson Fourth of July Picnic '89 T-shirt and a pair of plaid pajama shorts that barely covered her thighs.

He looked up from the skillet and found it hard to speak.

"Where'd you find that shirt?"

"In your dresser."

"You went through my dresser?"

She tugged the T-shirt over her hips. It was a little small.

Woodrow Barker had been out of prison exactly ninety-two days. To be this close to a member of the female species was still surreal. He was used to solitude, mostly. Or being caught in a crowd that reeked of testosterone.

"My eyes are up here," she said.

Woody took out his frustration on the faux eggs. "It's just that nobody wears that shirt. Even I don't wear that shirt. Haven't worn it since I got it."

"Why not?" she said.

"Because it's a collector's item."

"You're such a dork."

His ex-wife was slender but not small. Fair but not pale. Brown-black eyes, bigger than average. She looked so different than she did when he went away. Now she had bangs. Her face used to be fuller. She was, however, still loose built and athletic. Still moving through life like a big kid on the volleyball team. Looking like a young woman caught in perpetual adolescence but approaching life with a soul that was older than his.

He stirred the tofu again. "Take it off."

She raised an eyebrow. "Right here?"

This line of thinking was already making him uncomfortable.

"Relax," she said. "I'm joking, Mr. Hefner."

He pointed to hallway. "There's a bathrobe hanging on the back of the bathroom door. Take my shirt off and use the robe, please."

A laugh escaped her mouth. "Surely you're not serious. You're really going to make me change?"

"I am serious. And don't call me Shirley."

His ex-wife let out a sigh, rolled her eyes, and traipsed away. Her heavy footsteps shook the *Happens*. The pots and pans hanging above the galley rattled beneath her stomping. She was not a soft-spoken woman; she was direct and animated. She rarely paused her train of thought long enough to let others find the on-ramp toward her conversational highway.

He could hear her in his bathroom, brushing her teeth. Humming to herself.

Woody plated their breakfast. Tofu eggs. Thick-cut, mesquite-smoked imitation vegan bacon. Dave's Killer bread, toasted, with Earth Balance butter substitute and scuppernong jelly from a lady at the farmers' market.

Elizabeth sat at the dinette, now clad in a terrycloth robe. She had not taken off the shirt; she had only put the robe on over it. A compromise. Her coworkers at the hospital called her the Colonel. A title that had nothing to do with an appreciation for Kentucky Fried Chicken. Elizabeth did what she wanted in life. Long ago, Woody used to introduce his then-wife to strangers by saying, "Elizabeth loves you and has a wonderful plan for your life."

Elizabeth took a bite of the bacon. "See? I told you. Going vegan isn't so horrible, now, is it?"

He lifted a piece of simulated pork. "Not if you like eating cooked plastic bags."

The Colonel had persuaded him to go vegan one week after

exiting Wallace. For his heart. He agreed to give it a shot. By week two he was having visceral dreams about cows. By week three he missed butter so badly he found himself whispering sweet nothings to dairy products in the supermarket.

They continued eating in quasi-quiet, only interrupted by the gentle voice of Willie Nelson emitting from an unseen Bluetooth speaker, singing about angels flying in dangerously close proximity to the earth. Their difference in age was so visible now that it embarrassed him. Prison years were harder on the body than regular years.

"I washed your dress," he said.

She didn't answer.

"It's in the dryer. The label said wash on cold water, dry on low heat."

"Thanks."

The night before, Elizabeth had come directly from some kind of party to the *Ship Happens*. She had been wearing a black gown so tight you could have read the laundering label through the fabric. She had, evidently, consumed a few too many Moscow mules and shown up on Woody's barge. When she threw herself into his arms, she begged to stay. Woody held her and wished he could have held her that closely forever.

There had been vomit on her dress and in her hair. He washed the garment after he put her in his bed. Woody ended up sleeping on the sofa.

"How did your cardiac appointment go yesterday?" she asked.

He shrugged. "Fine."

"You're not going to tell me?"

"Let's talk about something else."

The two dark eyebrows on her forehead furrowed. "Don't get defensive with me."

"I'm not defensive. I just don't want to talk about my heart right now."

Elizabeth used her fork to stab her imitation eggs. "I'm just concerned, that's all."

"Well, you shouldn't be. You're dating someone." He folded his toast slices like tacos and used his fork to shovel eggs onto the toast. "Besides, it was a minor attack. I'm okay. So you can put away the defibrillator."

She placed her fork on the table. "I just want to know what the doctors said. I think I'm entitled to that much. Rachel and I have been so worried."

Rachel was their nine-year-old daughter.

The beautiful woman on the other side of the dinette reached out and gripped his hand. He gazed at their hands. This woman had been his anchor to the real world for the past ten years. Her visits were the only things that kept him going. Her care packages had come every Wednesday, like clockwork.

"You haven't been yourself since you got out," she said. "You're lashing out. I feel like you're still inside Wallace. How much weight have you lost?"

"Will you just leave it alone?"

"No, I will not."

Woody quit eating and pushed his plate away.

Elizabeth gave him a wounded look, and he knew he had gone past the point of no return. You could feel it when things like that happened.

"I think this was a bad idea," he said.

Elizabeth held her stare. "You want me to leave?"

"You shouldn't be here. It's not fair to Jason."

Invoking the name seemed to bring new clarity to her situation. "Are you kicking me out?"

He said nothing.

Elizabeth released a sigh, then scooted out of the booth and walked into the galley to place her plate in the sink. She quietly walked into the hall, opened the dryer, and pulled out her clean dress, then went into the bedroom and closed the door.

Woody started to feel bad. He didn't want her to leave. It was the last thing he wanted, in fact.

When the bedroom door opened, Woody was standing in her way.

"Elizabeth, I'm sorry. I didn't mean you should leave right this second. Come back to the table. Let's eat our fake plant-based food like two adults."

She tried to weave around him in the narrow hallway, but he wouldn't let her get past him.

"Quit blocking me," she said. "I have to be at work in an hour. I need to go."

"Come back. Eat."

"No, I need to leave."

"Look. I'll tell you anything you want to know about my heart problems. I promise, I won't be a jerk. I'm just going through a lot right now. And I don't want to ruin your thing with Jason. I've stolen enough of your life as it is."

She smiled at him. "Please move."

He did not move.

She searched his eyes. He thought he saw her facade crack as she peered into him with her obsidian, girlish eyes. "Why won't you talk to me, Woody?"

Because the truth was, he could not talk to her. There was a noise gate on his mouth.

"Fine," she said. "Have it your way."

Elizabeth tried to move around him in the hallway, but he

stepped in front of her again. He caught her by the shoulder. "Please, don't go."

She placed both hands squarely onto his chest and pushed. There was no malice in it. It wasn't an angry push. It was more like a moody-kid shove. Almost playful. It wouldn't have been enough force to knock over a toddler. But it caught him off guard. It was enough to cause Woody's lanky body to crash onto the wooden floorboards with a loud *thud*. His head hit the wall. His legs crumpled. His arms splayed outward. He lay on the floor in the quintessential Wile E. Coyote pose, only with less dignity.

Elizabeth was mortified and rushed to him.

"Oh my God, Woody!"

She held him in her arms.

"I'm fine," he lied. "Really."

"Oh, God. I didn't mean to do that."

"It's not you. It's the new meds. They make me dizzy."

He sat up and felt something dripping on his upper lip. Something warm. He touched his nose, then inspected his palm to find it covered in bright red.

She touched his face. "What hurts?"

The world was spinning.

"Elizabeth, listen to me. I'm sorry. I'm sorry for every-thing . . ."

"Stop talking like that. Can you breathe?"

That was when he noticed that his feet were numb. The world felt like it wouldn't stop traveling sideways. And a stab-bing ache moved across his sternum, working its way into his neck. Then his jaw region. Then radiating into his left arm. He clutched his shoulder and tried to talk, but this required too much fortitude.

Then he blacked out.

• • •

ELIZABETH BARKER DID NOT KNOW WHAT HAD HAPPENED TO WOODY inside prison. He never spoke of his time there. It was like it had never happened. Every time the subject came up, he would go silent. But prison *had* happened. She could see prison in every movement he made. In his reactions. Prison was in the way he slumped. Prison was in his face. In his eyes. His matinee smile had been misplaced. So had his confidence.

The hospital machines were beeping. Woody was lying in the bed, eyes closed, electrodes snaking from beneath his gown. And Elizabeth was beside him, eyeing the crude tattoo on his left hand. Five dots, like the markings on dice. Four outer dots. One inner dot. She had no idea how he got the tat, nor what it was supposed to mean. There was another tattoo on his upper arm of a small cross, about the size of a thumbnail. She wondered if he had any more markings. She wondered what they meant. Before his accident, he had been expressly anti-tattoo. He even remarked on them when out in public ("Why would someone do that to themselves?"). And now he was painted. She didn't know who this man was.

Elizabeth had gotten someone to cover her shift after Woody's episode. She also told Jason she would not be able to go out for dinner tonight. He promised he didn't mind her postponing. He said he understood, seemed cool about it. But she wondered whether he was a little too nonchalant on the phone. There was no love lost between Woody and Jason. They were from different worlds. Opposite parts of the same Venn diagram, with Elizabeth's intersection firmly between them.

"Ma'am?" the doctor asked. "I'm sorry, but are you still listening to me?"

She was jolted from her own thoughts.

The doctor just looked at her. A moment passed. "Are you going to answer my question?"

"Sorry, what was the question?"

The doctor was shining a penlight into Woody's eyes. "I asked how often his nosebleeds happen."

She had been answering questions like this all morning as Woody slept. She was his mouthpiece. A role she frequently assumed. "I don't know," she said. "We only see each other when I drop our daughter off at his place for the weekend."

"They happen every couple days," Woody answered.

The doctor made a note.

Then the doctor looked at Woody intently and steepled his hands beneath his chin. Elizabeth knew that steepling was never a good sign. She was an RN. Doctors had a subconscious sign language they used. Hand steepling was bad. Chin rubbing was worse. The only thing worse than steepling or rubbing was when the doctor removed his glasses and drew in a breath. If a doctor did that, you were dying.

"Pull down your collar for me, sir," the doctor said, brandishing his stethoscope again.

Woody did not oblige. He just looked at Elizabeth. He made no move to pull down his collar. Something was making him hesitate.

"Sir, I need to see your chest."

Woody was alternating his gaze between Elizabeth and the doctor.

"Come on, old man," Elizabeth said, yanking down Woody's collar. "Show us your boobs."

She was shocked at the sight of Woody's bare torso, which looked leaner than it ever had. She could count his ribs. His sternum bore the ropy scar of two previous heart operations. But it was the tattoo on his upper abdomen in purple-black ink that moved her. Crudely written in large letters was the word *Lindsey.*

Elizabeth felt her heart shatter into hairline cracks. The tattoo was written in lopsided penmanship, almost like Woody had done it himself while looking in a mirror.

"This is one feisty woman," the doctor said with a laugh. "Is she your daughter?"

Woody said nothing.

"His ex-wife," Elizabeth said. "But thanks. I do yoga."

The doctor listened to Woody's chest, then pulled his gown back up. The doctor flashed a smile at them both, then he glanced at Elizabeth. "I suppose what I'm asking here is whether you're family or not."

"Oh, I'm family," said Elizabeth.

The doctor faced Woody.

"Do you want her here for this? This consultation is something only family members are allowed to be present for."

"We were married for thirteen years," said Elizabeth.

Woody straightened his collar. "Don't you have a kitchen that needs repainting?"

Elizabeth had been painting her kitchen all weekend. There were white flecks in her hair to prove it.

"I'm *not* leaving," she said.

The doctor grimaced. He was caught between a proverbial rock and a woman.

"Woody, I'm your ex-wife."

"And I'm a Capricorn," Woody said. "Both are irrelevant to HIPAA."

She directed her words to the doctor. "I'm staying." She turned to Woody. "Give your verbal consent."

A nurse entered the room and touched Elizabeth's shoulder. She had been a coworker of Elizabeth's before she moved to cardiology. The woman had never been very pleasant. Elizabeth gave her a white-hot glare indicating she'd better not get involved.

"Woody, if you don't tell them I'm not leaving, it won't be a heart attack that kills you, so help me."

Woody sighed. "She can stay."

The doctor's meeting was brief, but they covered a lot of ground. They spoke of his past operations. One operation was during infancy to correct a transposition of the great vessels. His chest was cut open at birth. Surgery took six hours. Woody's childhood doctor said he'd never play in Little League, never play basketball, and never be a Boy Scout. He did all three. Then the doctor asked about his most recent surgery seven years ago. The prison had released him for an aortic valve replacement.

Elizabeth remembered the surgery all too well. The Bureau of Prisons had dragged their feet scheduling the operation so that Woody almost died in due-process limbo. Elizabeth had to hire a lawyer. Finally, they shipped Woody off to UAB in Birmingham. The guards had said they would not let Elizabeth anywhere near him when they admitted him for surgery. But still, she was there. She sat parked in her car, positioned near the ambulance bay. She had waited all morning to catch a glimpse of inmate 7686647 wheeling past.

The surgeon installed a porcine valve in Woody's heart. A pig-heart valve. Some of the correctional officers gifted Woody little Porky Pig dolls, piggy banks, and rubber pig noses galore. Woody Barker's cell had the largest collection of pig paraphernalia in the state of Alabama.

"What did you notice most after the valve replacement?" the doctor asked Woody.

Woody shrugged. "Whenever I drive past barbecue joints, I break into cold sweats."

The doctor did not even blink. "Smoke or drink?"

"Sure. What do you got?"

"He doesn't drink," said Elizabeth. "And he only smokes cigars."

The doctor made a note. "There's not much of a difference between cigars and cigarettes."

"Said the guy who never tried a Cuban."

The doc made another note on his pad. "It says here you've lost six pounds since your last exam twelve weeks ago." The doctor flipped a page. "This exam was at Wallace Correctional? Is that right?"

"We went vegan when he was released," Elizabeth said.

We. Elizabeth loved to use the collective pronoun.

The doc made a note. "We're vegan, but we smoke cigars?"

Apparently the doctor did too.

"We're a hard guy to understand, Doc."

"It's only been three months," Elizabeth said. "But we've been making a lot of changes. We're thinking of trying some yoga."

The doctor rolled his chair away, then he resteepled hands beneath his chin. He looked directly at Woody.

"What do you do for a living, Mr. Barker?"

"I don't do anything for a living," said Woody.

"He's a retired priest," said Elizabeth.

This evidently came as a small shock to the doctor. People did not usually associate former inmates with the priesthood.

"I didn't retire," said Woody. "I was laicized."

The doctor furrowed his brows.

"Defrocked," Woody explained. "Fired."

Silence.

"He does handyman work now," Elizabeth said.

"Mostly for her."

The doctor nodded. He went on to explain that Woody had been losing weight because of poor blood flow to the intestines, which was preventing him from absorbing nutrients. He had no energy due to dangerously low cardiac output; not enough oxygen was reaching his brain or muscles. His lungs were working overtime to keep up. So were other organs in the body.

"He doesn't need to be working," the doctor said, more to Elizabeth than to him. "I'm forbidding him from physical exertion. He doesn't need *any* stress at this point, physical or mental." He looked at Woody. "It's unpredictable at this stage. Some days you might feel pretty strong and be able to run a marathon. Other days even a small argument with your wife could hurt you."

"Ex-wife," said Woody.

Elizabeth felt her eyes start to burn with tears as she watched the doctor. Because she knew what was coming next. She knew what the doctor was about to say, simply by the way he held his head.

"I'm going to shoot straight with you," the doctor said with a sigh.

Woody fell backward into his bed and closed his eyes. "I already know what you're going to say."

"How do you know that?"

"Because you're making that face."

"What face?"

"The sphincter face that doctors make. You're going to say I need another surgery of some kind."

A beat went by.

"I'm not talking about *another surgery*," said the doctor. "You don't need a new valve, Mr. Barker. You need a new heart. I'm recommending a transplant."

Then the doctor removed his glasses.

Chapter 5

————

"WHAT THE HELL ARE WE DOING AT A MATERNITY CLINIC?" asked Tater. "I thought we were going to Target. I thought I was getting a freaking PlayStation. You said it was a surprise."

Caroline threw up jazz hands. "Surprise."

He yanked his phone from her hands. "This is the last time I let you use my freaking GPS. You tricked me."

"It's not a trick. This is your gift."

He wrinkled his brow like he was looking at a clinically insane person who just tried to iron a hamster. "My gift is a maternity clinic?"

"The gift is a checkup for our baby."

The Crossroads Clinic was a free clinic. They did not have a maternity clinic in Black Creek, and they certainly didn't have a free one. Black Creek was a town so small both city limit signs were affixed to the same post. Black Creek's only qualified doctor specialized in vaccinating livestock.

Tater fished another vaporizer from his pocket and took a hit to calm himself. But the device was empty. He threw it out the window.

"You are not going in there," he said.

SEAN DIETRICH

"Not even for our baby."

"*Your* baby."

"I didn't put it there."

Tater's method of dealing with unpleasantness was not to deal with it at all. He had not acknowledged her pregnancy for months, not even when the baby began showing. He apparently believed Caroline's conception was the work of the Holy Spirit.

"You ain't going into a baby clinic," he said. "This is ridiculous. I ain't made of money. I just got a two-hundred-and-fifty-dollar parking ticket."

"For parking where I told you not to park."

"I parked there for *you*! Because you're *pregnant*!"

"At least now you admit it." She planted a kiss on his bare shoulder.

He smacked the steering wheel. "You think I can just squat out cash whenever you need it? We're going to have to work double shifts to afford that parking ticket."

By *we* Tater meant *she*, inasmuch as the power washing business was moving pretty slowly in the subzero Tennessee temperatures of late winter.

"It's a free clinic," she said. "It won't cost a thing. We're just wasting time arguing. I could be halfway finished with my exam by now."

His face hardened.

"You ain't getting out of this car." Tater kept his hand on the gear shift. He was wearing his toughest, most manly face.

Caroline wanted to jab that little vaporizer into a place where the sun shineth not.

The car was idling. She could see him chewing on the inside of his lip. He chewed his lip whenever he was uncomfortable. Which usually only occurred in the presence of peace officers or Amway representatives.

"You don't have to come inside," she said. "You can stay in the car, chill out for a few minutes. Take a nap. Play on your phone. It'll be quick, I promise."

Tater kept his hand on the gear shift. "We're leaving."

Caroline Boyer stared at clinic in the distance. "This doctor is going to look at *our* baby. He's going to make sure everything's okay."

"Ain't mine."

Her voice grew sharper. "I'm giving you one chance, Tater. You let me out of this car, or I will make you sorry."

Tater eased a foot onto the gas pedal.

The car inched forward. Soon they were moving at a steady clip through the parking lot. Caroline's blood pressure spiked. In one quick move, she opened the glove box and retrieved Tater's pistol. She trained the Glock on him, then pulled back the slide to arm the weapon, holding the gun sideways like they do in the movies.

Tater hit the brakes. The vehicle came to an abrupt halt.

He looked at her for a few moments with a quizzical grin. Then he began to laugh. He laughed until his face was the same color as his cold, granite-hard nipples.

"That gun don't shoot," he said. "I bought that at a yard sale for ten bucks. It don't fire."

"Then why did you buy it?"

"Um. Hello. Because it's a Glock."

Caroline looked at the weapon in her hands. The serial number had been filed off. She trained the gun on the floorboard. She pulled the trigger. The weapon discharged with a flash, and the pistol almost leapt right out of her hands. There was a new hole in the floorboards. The interior of the car smelled metallic and sulfurous, and Tater was already holding up his hands.

He shouted his preferred swear word at least four times,

screaming so loudly that his voice sounded like a little girl's on a Tilt-A-Whirl.

Caroline, however, was calm. Chipper, even.

"I am asking you nicely to let me out of this vehicle . . . with your blessing. Do you understand? It's very important to me to have your blessing."

"Asking nicely? You almost shot me in the crotch!"

So she adjusted the aim of the weapon to the aforementioned anatomical region.

"Your blessing, please."

Tater threw the car into Neutral and yanked on the parking brake. "Fine. You have my blessing. Just put the gun down."

She pressed the muzzle closer. "You don't sound like you mean it."

"I said you have my blessing, all right? Here's my blessing! You're blessed, okay? Bless you! Be blessed!"

She smiled and clicked on the safety. "Thank you." Caroline kneed open the door, then tucked the Glock into her rear waistband.

"Bless you too, Tater," she said. "And the horse you rode in on."

Then she walked inside.

• • •

WOODY STEPPED OUT OF HIS SHOWER USING THE BACK OF THE TOIlet for support. They had discharged him a few hours earlier. Well, more accurately, Woody discharged himself. Against the doctor's advice. Although, admittedly, there was nothing more the doctors could do. Plus, the average cost of staying in an American hospital was three grand per night. And Woody did not have health insurance.

Adios.

His muscles strained to hold his body weight as he wiped

steam from his bathroom mirror with a quivering hand. His reflection looked ancient. His cotton hair bore no traces of auburn anymore. He looked like he could land the role of a protagonist in *Cocoon*. His neck was gaunt. The skin around his belly sagged from where he'd lost weight too quickly. To his own eyes, he looked meaner than he remembered. He didn't *feel* any meaner, but his face looked it.

An inmate undergoes nonstop bombardment of emotional violations. You live in a cell. You exist in an obscenely structured world that makes no logical sense. You urinate on command. You are disciplined. Publicly chastised by guards half your age. Belittled. Constantly threatened by fellow inmates. Harmed by fellow inmates, both emotionally and spiritually. When you leave prison, you do not have PTSD. You have TSD. The only thing that changes is the color of the walls.

Prison makes you mean.

He pressed a hand against his sternal scar. The hot shower had made his heart beat in a weird pattern. Hot showers were havoc on weak hearts. So were caffeine, sodium, alcohol, and pretty much anything else that made life grand. Most mornings he played the mental game Caffeine or Mitral Valve Prolapse? He knew he should give up coffee, but after ten years of drinking crappy coffee, it was one of the vices he was willing to indulge.

Elizabeth knocked on the bathroom door. "You okay in there?"

"I'm fine."

"Need anything?"

"No."

"Let me know if you need any help, okay?"

She cracked open the door and peeked in on him. He was naked, so he hid himself from her. Her face was impish and happy. "You don't have anything I haven't seen before, old man."

He shut the door.

A muffled catcall came from behind the door. Her disposition had been a little too upbeat. Which only proved how worried she truly was.

He stood before his vanity mirror, wrapped in a towel, opening pill containers, one by one, swallowing his pills dry. He hated taking pills. It was a process that took about ten minutes four times per day. That equaled forty minutes per day. Forty minutes times seven days totaled 4.7 hours per week. In a year, that came to 243 hours of pill taking. Which is the annual equivalent of ten twenty-four-hour days. He had never gotten used to the regimen of constant meds. Doctors told him it would become the New Normal. But there was no normal.

His phone vibrated on the sink.

It was Elizabeth.

He answered the phone with a sigh.

He could hear the delay between the phone voice and her actual voice outside his door, like an echo chamber.

"You okay in there?" she said.

"Liz," he said. "If anything newsworthy happens in here, I promise you'll be the first to know."

"I just want to help."

"Then call United Way." He hung up the phone.

Woody sat on the marine toilet and put his head in his hands. He massaged his face. His eyes ached. There was a dull pounding in his head. The steam made him short of breath.

The phone vibrated again.

He silenced it.

It vibrated again.

Woody answered the phone. He angrily pressed the phone against his face and was about to tell Elizabeth exactly where to go. But when he heard the voice on the phone, he stopped.

It was not Elizabeth. The voice was a female voice, but older. A thick Alabamian cadence. A familiar no-nonsense tone. And a million-and-one memories hit him at once, like rainfall. Like video recordings in his mind set on endless repeat cycles, he saw recollections of his idyllic youth. In his mind he saw a tomboy in lace, with a spark of devilment in her eyes. He saw the face of his first wife.

"Hi, Woody," said the voice of Melinda Boyer.

Chapter 6

———

ELIZABETH DIPPED HER SHRIMP INTO THE LIME-BASIL vinaigrette and watched Woody stare at the limp, colorless, existentially dead veggies on his plate. They were at the Andrew's Seaside Bar and Grille. The sun was setting over the bay. The orange water looked like a mirror. It was March, but it already looked like summer.

Woody sat at the table across from her, still wearing his hospital bracelet. Their daughter, Rachel, was beside him, playing on her phone, wearing the zoned-out face of a kid caught within the electronic stupor of the Great American Technological Attention-Deficit Disorder.

All night people kept stopping by the table to say hi to Elizabeth. Mostly people were asking about her upcoming wedding with Jason Cordell. They asked how Jason was doing. They gave their congratulations. They all seemed to give Woody mild glares of disapprobation, which came as no surprise to Elizabeth. People knew where he'd been for the last ten years. Although few of them, she figured, knew what the word *disapprobation* meant.

"Why aren't you eating?" Elizabeth asked.

"Because this isn't real food," he said.

"You need your strength."

"I'm not going to get it eating broccoli." He looked at her plate. "How come you're eating shrimp? You're the one who started this whole vegan thing."

"I'm not vegan. I'm pescatarian. I can eat fish."

"You just invented that."

"No. The Native Americans invented it."

"Well, I want to be pescatarian."

"Eat your broccoli or you're going to be hungry."

Woody pushed his plate away and lit a cigar. Dinner guests on the patio looked at him like he'd just strangled a puppy.

"You're not supposed to smoke out here," said Elizabeth.

"This is a bar."

"Smoking laws have changed in ten years," she said.

Woody turned his cigar in the open flame, puffing.

"I'm sixty years old. I grew up in an age when you could smoke in airplanes, Waffle Houses, and on elementary school playgrounds."

Elizabeth said, "You could add ten years to your life if you gave up smoking."

He looked at the cigar wistfully. "But that decade would have no smoking in it."

Elizabeth was unfazed. She had made a personal vow in the hospital. She would remain as bubbly as possible. Obscenely cheerful. Disturbingly optimistic. She would be so positive she would make Santa Claus look like a jerk. As a nurse, you learn that people absorb other people's energy.

"I'd say we were all very lucky today," said Elizabeth in her most Pollyanna tone. "Wouldn't you?"

Woody just stared at her. "Not the first word that came to mind, no."

"Aren't we lucky, Rachel?" said Elizabeth, looking to her daughter for moral support.

Her daughter was busy thumbing away on her screen. What was she even doing on that stupid phone? And how important could it be? She was only nine. When Elizabeth had given Rachel the phone, she had put strict rules in place. But the borders of such rules were getting hazier by the day.

"No, I mean it," Elizabeth said. "It's a good thing I was there with you. If I hadn't been at your place, who knows what would have happened?"

"I'd be hanging out with Elvis right now," he said.

"Who's Elvis?" his daughter asked, still glued to her device.

"Elvis was the king of rock and roll," he explained. "Are you honestly saying you've never heard of him?"

Rachel frowned. "I literally thought the king of rock and roll was Michael Jackson."

"Michael Jackson is literally a weenie."

"Dad, Michael Jackson is dead."

"May his weenie soul rest in peace. Literally."

On cue, Rachel was navigating YouTube to fact-check claims about Elvis. Soon the phone was showing a video of Elvis Presley in black-and-white, gyrating his hips, dancing across a stage.

"This guy's weird," said Rachel, turning up the volume. "He doesn't look like the king of anything to me. Why does he dance like that?"

Woody shrugged.

That was when Elizabeth reached across the table to take the phone from Rachel's hand, but Rachel, being a nine-year-old, high on the body's own natural performance-enhancing drugs, was quicker than her mother and evaded her grasp.

Mother and daughter had a brief stare-down.

Elizabeth gave her daughter a glare that was powerful enough to kill small woodland creatures. "Put it away."

Rachel placed the phone face down on the table.

They ate in silence for a few minutes.

Elizabeth watched her ex-husband poke around at his broccoli and tried not to remember the fear she experienced when performing CPR on his lifeless body before he started breathing again. The experience of holding his frailty had changed her. Deeply. She wanted him. She needed him.

"I don't think you should be living by yourself anymore," said Elizabeth.

Woody stopped stabbing at his food.

"I'm serious," Elizabeth said. "If you're going on a transplant list, they're going to look at your family, your support system. I think you need family around you. We tell stroke patients all the time that isolation increases risk by 60 percent."

"I didn't have a stroke."

"The percentage is higher with cardiac. Loneliness is bad."

"So I'll join the Freemasons."

"You need us. For the last three months you haven't done anything but run power tools on that boat, fixing God knows what. When was the last time you shaved? You've got a full beard."

He touched his face. "It's called a stubble beard, for your information."

"You could've hit your head and bled to death if I hadn't been there."

"You pushed me."

Elizabeth leaned forward. "You were in congestive heart failure, laying on the floor, not breathing. I didn't do *that* to you."

He puffed plumes of smoke. "I think you mean *lying* on the floor. Lay is transitive."

Elizabeth's eyes turned into flames. A monstrous boat with four outboard motors sped past the patio. The air was polluted with the music from its massive stereo. Rap of some sort. All the diners in the restaurant looked at the boat going by.

"I'm trying to help you," Elizabeth said.

"How could I forget."

Elizabeth looked at her daughter, who was back on her phone again. And it made her yearn for simpler days. Back when there was no internet. No iPhones. Back when a girl's most important possession was her bicycle. How had we traded in such unspoiled days? Elizabeth glanced around the restaurant. Nearly all patrons were on their phones, scrolling. It was like living in a world of zombies. She regretted ever giving Rachel that phone.

She asked, "Did you know that when we were kids, 70 percent of American kids rode bikes?"

Woody leaned back in his chair and crossed his arms.

"Today?" Elizabeth said. "Today it's only 9 percent. Am I the only one who thinks that's sad? What happened to us?"

Neither Woody nor her daughter answered.

Elizabeth reached across the table and yanked the device from her daughter's hands.

"Hey!" said Rachel.

"You don't need a phone to digest food," said Elizabeth.

Rachel copped an attitude and pushed her plate away. "I don't even like this shrimp. It literally tastes like butthole."

Elizabeth's voice hit a new pitch of dismay. "Watch your mouth. And quit saying *literally*. You're not even using it right."

"No, I tasted the shrimp," said Woody. "In this case, she's right."

Elizabeth was about to say something else when she noticed two older people walking into the restaurant. A couple. Man and woman. Silver hair. Dressed in obligatory Tommy Bahama colors. While the couple drew handshakes and backslaps from nearby customers, Elizabeth's whole body went cold.

"What's wrong with you?" asked Woody.

Elizabeth didn't move. "Don't look behind you."

"Why?"

The older couple was making their way directly toward Woody's table. She knew they were unaware that Woody was here, because if Lindsey Holcomb's parents had known he was here, they would either refuse to come inside or set his truck on fire in the parking lot.

"Tricia and Leo Holcomb are here."

Elizabeth could see the color of Woody's face change, although his expression registered no reaction. Still, she could feel his body temperature drop.

"I need to get out of here," he said.

"It's too late."

He was already scooting his chair out.

"Woody, you can't leave, not yet . . ."

Before Elizabeth had even finished speaking, a sequence of events was already playing out.

Lindsey's parents were moving past the table. In slow motion. The older couple spotted Woody. They both stopped walking. Three deer, caught in high beams. The husband and wife glowered at Woody, who stood, paralyzed.

"Hello, Tricia," Woody said. On his feet. Then he nodded toward her husband. "Leo."

The older woman became a statue. The restaurant seemed to fall quiet. Tricia Holcomb's face contorted with tears. Her eyes turned red, and her chin started to tremble. Elizabeth watched the woman's sorrow morph into rage. The rage seemingly swallowed her whole, turning her lip upward in a snarl. Then Tricia Holcomb drew her arm back and slapped Woody across the face. Hard. Elizabeth could feel the impact from where she sat.

Woody lowered his head.

"You scumbag," her husband said.

And the couple left.

Chapter 7

———

Iт was night. Caroline's mother's singlewide trailer sat surrounded by vacant pasture, covered in a duvet of snow, with an impressive graveyard of dead appliances smattering the landscape. The sun was setting, and it had started to snow again. The air was so cold it hurt to breathe. Mount Le Conte stood in the distance, looking over the world like a mother hen guarding her chicks.

Tater parked the Honda beneath a giant tree. He marveled at the trailer home. "This is where you grew up?"

"Sort of."

He looked at the scene outside his windshield. "This is a craphole."

"You should totally go into poetry."

She got out of the car into the chill air and shut the door with a creaky slam. "Stay in the car. This will only take a few minutes."

"I'm not staying here. I'm going inside. It's cold and I'm hungry."

She leaned into the Honda. "I really do not want you going inside that trailer, do you understand? This is hard for me. I don't even want to be here. It brings back bad memories. Just stay in the car. I won't be long."

Caroline marched through the snow toward the woodshed. Her hand rested on her belly. The doctor said she was at thirty-six weeks, which left only a month before showtime.

On her journey across the snowy yard, she felt memories suffocate her. Good memories, bad ones, and all the sad ones between. The place hadn't changed since her early days. She found the old swing set and touched it, replaying the sunny afternoons she spent on the contraption.

A welcome committee of cats rushed from beneath the trailer to greet her. She found a bucket of cat food inside the shed, where Jack Jr. told her it would be. She scattered handfuls of frozen food on the snow-covered deck. The cats swarmed the food like prison camp victims. Screaming at her with little voices. Wrapping themselves around her ankles. Her heart broke for them. Her mother had asked the neighbor to feed the cats, but she didn't trust that floozy to remember. She'd been right too. Their little bodies were ribs and fur.

More cats emerged from the rooftop of the shed, from tree limbs, from the innards of old appliances. There must have been forty cats or more.

A gray cat was bumping into obstacles, walking in zigzag patterns, running headfirst into anything in its path. It was small compared to the others.

She lifted the cat into her arms only to discover that both its eyes were missing, both eyelids scarred shut. It was purring like a tiny washing machine. Crying loudly at her.

"Aw," she said. "You can't see."

The cat was male. She took him away from the other cats and fed him privately, making sure no other cats stole his food. The whole feeding ordeal took about thirty minutes. When they finished eating, most of the cats took off. She put the bucket of food back into the shed and closed the huge wooden door behind her.

When she got back to the Honda, the engine was not running. And the door to her mother's trailer was open.

• • •

SHE FOUND TATER IN THE LIVING ROOM, EATING CHILI CHEESE FRItos, watching television on a flatscreen that was roughly the size of the Lincoln Memorial. The brilliant colors were bright enough to be seen from Canada.

What was it with poor people and nice televisions?

"They got a PlayStation," Tater said with overtones of what could only be described as rapture. "It's only a Four, though," he said, a little crestfallen.

"I finished feeding the cats," she said. "I'm ready to go now."

But the wireless gaming controller was in his hands, and he was already firing up the console. Tater's size 6 feet were propped on the coffee table. He was working on his third can of Natty Light.

"Get off the couch," she said. "I want to leave. I don't like it here. This place brings back too many memories."

He cranked up the volume. "Tough titty."

"Tater. Come on."

"I'm tired. I'm not driving back to Black Creek tonight. We're staying here. It's free. Plus, they have *Grand Theft Auto*."

She stepped in front of the enormous TV screen. The screen was so large she looked like someone delivering the weather forecast before a green screen.

"Please respect my feelings. This is very difficult for me. I don't want to be here. I really want to go home."

"You going to shoot me in the crotch again?"

• • •

THE SNOWFALL WAS PICKING UP TEMPO. ONLY HALF OF THE lighting fixtures in the trailer had working bulbs. There was no running water because her mom hadn't paid the bill. She tried the faucet in the kitchen, but it didn't work. She tried the faucets in the bathrooms. Nothing. There was a five-gallon bucket of drinking water in the laundry room with a ladle and dead bugs floating atop a modest film of scum. This was how her mother lived.

"There's no water in this trailer," she told Tater.

He shrugged and kept playing his game. "I'm used to it."

"We won't be able to use the toilets," she said.

"Too late. Stay out of the hallway bathroom for a while."

Caroline wandered through the trailer, trying not to touch anything. The domicile was a sad shrine to her mother's even sadder life. A pigsty. Proving her mother's neglect was capable of reaching new lows.

Caroline clicked on a lamp in the master bedroom.

The room flickered orange. The bed was unmade. Throw pillows galore. Cubical furniture made of particle board. Pictures askew on the walls. Lots of pictures. The images were Caroline's artwork from years gone by. Drawings, paintings, watercolors, and gouaches hung like wallpaper across a paneled wall. Every inch of vertical space was covered with Caroline's art. Some pieces dated back to Caroline's first-grade year. Others had been created when her mom was in rehab. She moved closer to a picture drawn in crayon. A little-girl stick figure holding a woman stick figure's hand. There was handwriting on the bottom: *Mommy*.

Her mother had never acted interested in her art before. She never knew her mother even cared about her creative side.

Caroline flipped on the light to the bathroom. Plastic tub and shower. The sink was olive green, à la 1970. The room smelled like decades of burnt hair and Aqua Net, mingled with a fine bouquet of Philip Morris.

She opened the cupboard. The cabinet was a mess. All the

contents disrupted. Beneath the sink was a shipload of cosmetic supplies and all the usual female things, heaped in a pile. Caroline closed and locked the door to the bathroom. She stared at the vanity for a few minutes. This had been her mother's hiding place, where she had always kept her stash. Addicts don't realize their secret hiding places are not all that secret. Caroline knew she shouldn't, but she removed the items in the vanity cabinet, one by one, placing containers of various lotions, moisturizers, and perfumes on the floor. When the cupboard was empty, she pried up the false bottom using the handle of a toothbrush. She removed the plywood and peered inside the cavern beneath the vanity. She expected to find a glass pipe stained with sticky carbon. But she found nothing.

Unsatisfied, Caroline got on her knees and reached into the depths of the cavern beneath the cupboard to feel around. Something was back there. Whatever it was, she knew for certain it wasn't good.

Stupid, stupid girl.

Chapter 8

THREE MILES AWAY, PETER TABARES WAS SLOWLY WALKING across his property with a distance measuring wheel. It was getting dark outside. The sun was setting. The sky was a smear of pinks and peaches, with Purple Mountains Majesty in the distance and a gray pasture in the foreground.

He was stepping off the perimeter of his land, tucked in the valley of the Smokies. Wheel pressed to the earth, bouncing over rocks and mud. The man was thickly built. Heavy. Not overweight, but right on the cusp of being fat. Blue-collar fat. The kind that looked like muscle to the untrained eye. His head was shaved bald because his current girlfriend said Smooth Scalp looked more badass than Fringed Egg. He wore a thick horseshoe mustache to make up for the casualties of male pattern baldness. And he wore cowboy boots to elevate himself off the ground, transforming his five-eight frame into a mammoth five-nine-and-a-half.

He pushed the measuring wheel along, counting off footage for a new electric fence he was going to install. He had been walking for an hour, and he still wasn't even close to having measured the eastern leg of his property line. Still, it was a necessary effort since he trusted measuring wheels more than laser-operated

distance calculation devices. He was going to build a house here.
An off-grid cabin. A bunker would be located on the south side of
the property. The barn would sit on the eastern edge. He would
grow his own food or hunt it. When the hard times came—and
they would come—his organization would defend the final rem-
nants of what used to be America.

The organization was financed by running drugs. Not street
drugs. Pharmaceuticals. Reporters usually focused on the Big
Four: coke, opiates, meth, pot—although fentanyl was contend-
ing for a place on the list. But the windfall was not in the street
drugs; it was in the trillions of little pills ordinary Americans took
every day. Blood pressure meds, cholesterol meds, anxiety meds,
and so on.

Peter had his hands in other industries as well. He owned a
junkyard in Arkansas that bought illegally acquired vehicles and
sold auto parts on eBay Motors. He owned an operation that re-
furbished stolen iPhones. He operated a trucking business, based
in Texas, that smuggled goods across the Mexican border.

It was through his trucking business that he met a man from
south Texas. The guy was older. Loud-spoken. Tough. A stereo-
typical Texan male, complete with bowed legs. The two were
temporary partners in a pretty haul of textiles from La Ciudad.
One night after they had consumed a few too many *chelas*, Peter's
partner told him a story involving the most coveted mineral known
to man. An enthralling epic dating back to the War of Northern
Aggression. A tale involving disgruntled generals, Confederate
presidents, lost love, war and peace, and two tons of minted bullion. Then the man removed from a safe a small flash drive and
popped it into his laptop to share the excitement of the newfound
secret.

They never found his partner's body.

The storage drive had been in Peter's possession for less than forty-eight hours before his ex-wife stole it. She was young and impulsive. And now she was no more. But the flash drive was nowhere to be found. He was certain that Melinda had it, but they had ransacked her trailer and come up empty.

When his phone rang, he was surprised. He had limited cell service out here. If any. This, too, was a major selling point for a guy who wanted to live off-grid. He looked at his phone with genuine amazement. He had never expected it to ring.

He stopped walking, used his spray can to mark the patch of earth, made a note on his notepad, and dug the phone from his pocket. He looked at the ID on the screen. It was one of his guys.

"Go ahead," said Peter.

"Someone's at her trailer," said the man.

He looked at the sun setting over the Tennessee hills. "When?"

"Few hours ago."

"Who was it?"

"There's two of them. Girl and a guy."

"I asked *who*, not how many."

"I don't know who the guy is. Think the girl is the daughter." Peter spit.

The cold mountains framed the oldest continually occupied town in Tennessee (pop. 158). A town that predated the American Revolution by over one hundred years, when a religious sect from Pennsylvania settled here.

"Melinda's daughter lives a long way from here. Can't be her."

"Got to be her. She looks just like her mom. Except she's not as hot."

Peter subconsciously touched his rib cage. The last time Peter had seen his ex-wife's best friend, she had shoved a stun gun against his torso and almost stopped his heart. He spent two weeks on the sofa watching Netflix.

She had not been back to her trailer in over a month. He knew this because after searching her place thoroughly, he had installed eight wild game cameras, trained on the mobile home. No living thing came within two hundred yards of that trailer without a notification.

"The cameras are too far away to pick up sound," said his man, "so I couldn't hear what they were saying. But I can see them in the video. They're both pretty young. You think they have it? You think she gave it to them?"

"Are they still there?"

"Yeah."

"If Melinda's daughter is in town, Melinda must be dead."

"She's not dead. Not yet. She's still in ICU. I think the girl's just feeding the cats or something. That's all I saw her do so far. Now they're in the trailer. I thought you'd want to know."

"Keep an eye on them."

"Should we try to establish contact with them?"

Peter removed the phone from his ear and checked the signal. He had one bar of reception. "Yeah. Go over and say hi."

Chapter 9

————

THE FAIRVIEW RETIREMENT HOME WAS A BRICK RANCH BUILT IN the early '60s, converted into a nursing home in the gaudy '70s. The siding was fever-blister pink, hiding four or five thousand layers of lead-based paint beneath it. The windows were cloudy with mildew, rusted shut. The roof was the color of Alabama black mold.

The lady at the front desk buzzed Woody through the doors. He was immediately standing in the lobby beside an old upright piano, a fake palm tree, and a corral of parked walkers. Various elderly persons littered the lounge area, congregating in communal clots, their wheelchairs forming tight social circles. Many were watching TV. Some were watching Woody, ruffling their brows, trying to figure out whether Woody was one of their relatives. Other residents were playing games in the game room. Games like solitaire, checkers, Cards Against Humanity.

"How are things tonight?" he asked the nurse.

"Lively," said the nurse. "They're rowdy, can't you tell?"

"How's the Major been?"

Shrug. "*Lonesome Dove* has been on Pluto TV all day. We've

had so many complaints about the volume, I've disconnected the phone."

Woody shook his head. "'The reason men are so awful is because some woman has spoiled them.'"

The young nurse raised an eyebrow and gave him a perplexed look.

"I guess you've never read the book," said Woody.

"Guess not."

Woody walked the long hallway toward the rearmost room. There was a sign outside the room's door that read "Knock Slowly, We Need to Put on Our Pants."

Woody knocked.

There was no answer, only the blaring of a television. He cracked the door and peered inside.

"Hello?" Woody called out, knocking on the doorjamb.

Woody saw an elderly man seated in a recliner with two cats in his lap. The chair was positioned as close to the television as it could be without touching the plasma itself. A prescription drug commercial disclaimer was rolling at full volume. (*Zambara may cause diarrhea, vomiting, or the growth of a third leg from a crucial bodily orifice. Zambara should not be taken by people who are pregnant or nursing, by anyone who has a baby, or by anyone who has ever been a baby. Zambara is in no way responsible for anything that happens to you while taking Zambara . . .*)

The old man was slumped in his chair, sleeping, with a tumbler of whiskey in his slack hand. The tumbler looked like it had already tipped over and spilled on one of the sleeping cats.

Woody found a remote lying on the floor beneath the man's chair and turned the volume down. The drastic volume change was noticed by the resident of the chair who, throughout Woody's childhood, had always found sleep impossible unless he was seated before an audio device louder than a nuclear weapons field test.

The old man stirred in his chair. "I was listening to that, dammit," the man said.

"So was everyone else in the county, Dad."

• • •

"WAIT," SAID AMOS. "YOU HAVE *ANOTHER* DAUGHTER?"

Amos Barker was eighty-six years young and wholly incapable of using an indoor voice. This was because he'd spent too many hours in the cockpit of a M48 Patton firing 90 mm guns at the Vietcong. Everything he said was shouted. Even his whispers.

"You're lying," his dad said.

Woody shook his head.

"How'd you manage to get someone pregnant while you were in the clink?"

"This was before I went away. A long time before I went away."

Woody and his father sat on the little covered porch attached to his dad's unit. The porch was cluttered with cat bowls and litter boxes. Several orange cats were looking at him with soul-stealing eyes from their perches in the corner. The old man sat on his patio chair and avoided eye contact with the throng of cats that had all arrived at this nursing home with other residents before emigrating to Amos's quarters, where a twenty-four-hour cat food buffet awaited them.

Woody sat in a plastic wicker chair with his head leaning back. His father had tried to force him to imbibe three fingers of Wild Turkey Rare Breed Rye, but Woodrow had to reexplain to his dad, for the sixteen billionth time, that he'd quit drinking.

"Quit drinking?" he said. "Why?"

"Dad, I have to tell you this every time I visit. It's a personal choice."

Shrug.

It was not Amos's bad memory that landed the old ironworker

in Fairview Retirement Home. It was his stainless steel hip, the steel rod in his leg, his two titanium knees, the screws in his ankles, the steel cervical plate in his neck, the fusion of L4, L5, and S1, the insulin pump, the pacemaker, and the Kevlar hernia mesh. Rumor had it that beneath Amos's skin, he was the Terminator.

"How'd you find out?" asked Amos.

"Melinda called. This morning. She told me."

"She sure waited a helluva long time to get that off her chest. Why's she telling you now?"

"She's dying."

Amos grunted. "Women."

They were looking into the night sky. A plane flew overhead and filled the air with a low rumble.

"What's the girl's name?"

"She didn't tell me. Or if she did, I was in shock and couldn't process anything else." Woody ran his hands across his stubble. "I don't know how this happened."

His dad laughed. "You want me to walk you through it?"

"Dad. Please."

"Boy meets girl. Boy kisses girl. Boy says, 'Hey, let's play hide the—'"

Woody held up his hands. "I know how it happens. What I'm saying is that this was a long time ago."

"Couldn't have been that long ago. You're still a young man."

"Dad, I have my AARP card."

"Dang liberals."

Amos Barker wore a thick Carhartt and was bundled with a tartan scarf. His lower half was covered with a furry blanket that bore multiple photos of Rachel printed on it. The blanket had been a Christmas gift and ruined the Major's hardened image completely.

"How old is this girl?"

"Seventeen."

The ice in Amos's glass made a clinking noise when he sipped. The Major was doing the mental math. When he had solved the equation, he looked at Woody.

Woody bowed his head. "I know."

"You were still married."

"It was during our rough patch. We were separated at the time."

"Well, that makes it all better."

Silence.

"Another daughter," said Amos. "Crime in Italy, would it have killed you to have at least one son for your old man? I'm dying in a cloud of estrogen over here."

Woody leaned back in the wicker chair and massaged the bridge of his nose. His eyes hurt. His neck hurt. Everything hurt.

"I don't know what to do," said Woody. "I can't even figure out how to live my own life right now. I definitely *don't* need another daughter."

"No arguments from me. You're a worse father than even I was. And *that* took real effort."

With that, the Major shot to his feet and lumbered to the edge of the porch, leaning on his three-pronged cane for support. Woody could hear his dad unzip and begin making water. He had a perfect shot of his father's backside as the old man performed his necessaries while traffic on Highway 39 passed by.

"Dad, you should do that inside."

"No, I like my carpet too much," he said, midstream. "Where is Melinda now?"

"East Tennessee."

"How'd she get up there?"

"I'm not sure. But I'm going to visit her, so I'll find out more soon."

His father rezipped with a grand flourish. The old man turned to face his son. "When are we leaving?"

"No, Dad. I'm sorry but—"

"What's our ETA?"

"Dad, listen, I've got a lot to think about. I really need to do this alone. And I'm not leaving until tomorrow morning anyway."

But the old man had already tugged open the sliding door of his porch and tottered inside.

"Shut up and help me pack my CPAP machine."

• • •

CAROLINE PUT HER HAND DEEPER INTO THE CAVERN BENEATH THE vanity in her mother's bathroom, reaching past a confetti of mouse droppings and dead cockroaches. She covered her nose and mouth with a towel and removed the insulation beneath the vanity. Soon she was up to her armpit in fiberglass, digging around, trying not to think of the wildlife that might be lurking in this air duct.

She used her hand to feel around but couldn't find anything. Her mother used to hide things in this duct. On two occasions, this cavern had gone overlooked by officers with search warrants. But there was nothing here, apparently. Caroline was about to give up when she felt something.

It was small.

About the size of a deck of cards.

And it was a little too far away to reach. So Caroline inserted a toilet brush into the duct cavern and used the brush to drag the object toward her. It was a small tin box, about the size of an Altoids container. There was a yellow flag sticker on the box with a coiled timber rattler on the front that matched her necklace.

Caroline opened the box. Inside was a small flash drive. About the same size as a Cheez-It. It was blue with *Samsung* printed on it. The drive had a small plastic cap covering the USB-C connector.

Then came a loud knock on the bathroom door.

"Caroline! Open this door!"

It was Tater.

"I'm in the bathroom!" she said. "A little privacy."

"You said we weren't supposed to use the toilets."

Caroline moved to the door and cracked it a fraction of an inch. "Since when does anyone listen to me?"

Tater's face was pale. "You need to get out here, now," he said in a panicked whisper.

"What's wrong? Why?"

"Because the police are here."

• • •

THE TRAILER INTERIOR WAS DARK EXCEPT FOR THE BLUE LIGHTS from the cop car filling the den. Caroline peeked out the blinds, using her pinky to separate the shades á la Mrs. Kravitz. Tater moved toward another window, back pressed against the wall.

"What do you see?" he whispered.

"Shut up," she mouthed. "These walls are thin."

"I only see one car out there," he whispered.

She placed a hand over his mouth. "Shut. Up."

The headlights were stabbing into the rural darkness. The emergency light bar was on. The door to the cruiser finally opened. The man who stepped out wore jeans and boots and a barn jacket. He was not dressed like a cop, but he walked like a cop. Part gunslinger, part high school football coach.

She spoke directly into Tater's ear. "How long has he been parked out there?"

"Maybe five minutes. He's just been sitting out there with his lights on."

"Why didn't you tell me?"

"I've been calling your name. How could you not hear me?"

Caroline gestured to the television. "How could anyone hear over *Grand Theft Auto*?"

The cop knocked on the flimsy door, and the mobile home's interior shuddered beneath his fist. The knock was not a polite *tap, tappity, tap*. It had some authority to it. It was *boom, boom, boom!*

Tater said, "What should we do?"

She used both hands to shove him toward the door. "You should answer the door, idiot."

"No way." He scurried away. "I ain't answering that door. I've been smoking weed."

"Are you kidding me?"

He pointed to the living room. The coffee table was littered with paraphernalia.

"Are you *kidding* me?"

Tater threw up his hands. "You said make yourself at home."

"I never said that. I said I didn't want you to go inside."

"Same difference."

Caroline took a full minute to gather herself. She placed a hand on the knob and swung the door open. The icy Tennessee air hit her face. The cop grinned at her. He was enormous. His arms were bigger than most people's legs. He had a chest the size of a whiskey barrel. His face was windburned and red; bits of snow clung to his hair.

"You must be Caroline."

Caroline could smell skunk-like weed fumes exiting the trailer behind her. She smiled like Tammy Faye Bakker.

"Yes, I'm Caroline. What's going on?"

"Sorry for the flashing lights, but this is kind of an emergency, and I wanted to make sure you answered the door. Sometimes people don't answer the door unless they see the lights."

Tater stepped onto the porch. "'Sup."

The officer studied Tater for a flickering instant. Her boyfriend's eyes brought to mind one who recreationally snorted pepper spray.

"Well," the officer went on, "I'm sort of the neighborhood watch patrol around here—if you can call this a neighborhood. I got a call when you pulled up. People haven't seen anyone at this house for a few weeks, and nobody recognized your car."

"It's a Honda," Tater explained.

Caroline turned to face him. "Thank you, Taylor. Maybe you should go inside and play your game."

"No, I'm cool."

The man glanced at Tater, then back to Caroline. He gestured to the idling cruiser behind him, and Caroline noticed the small rattlesnake tattoo on his wrist.

"Sorry if I scared you. I would've called, but I know Melinda's been in the hospital. Anyway, this is just a courtesy visit, checking to make sure everything is okay."

"Do cops ever make food deliveries out here?" asked Tater.

Caroline nonchalantly rested her heel atop Tater's toes and put her weight down on his brittle bones.

"Ow," said Tater.

"That car might not be safe to get you around up here," said the cop, nodding to the Honda. "Roads are covered in ice. You'll never make it into town driving that."

Something in the way the man spoke made her stomach uneasy. There was an authority to his voice but not the kind you normally hear from cops. It was darker.

"If you need anything, I have four-wheel drive. I can give you my cell."

"I think we'll be okay," Caroline said.

The man nodded. Then he looked Tater up and down with a stony glare, moving only his eyes. Flicking them from Tater's head to his toes. The granite eyes met Caroline's again.

"Well, if you two change your minds, I'll be keeping an eye out."

Chapter 10

———

WOODY AND HIS DAD WERE PASSING THROUGH MONTGOMERY doing seventy-five. The sun was bright, and it felt later than ten. More like noon. The Major browsed radio stations, spinning the dial back and forth, grumbling about every station he landed on.

"This is Montgomery," the Major said, "home of Hank Sr. You'd think there might be a decent country music station on the radio."

No such luck. Only modern bro-country songs about cold beer, pickup trucks, and of course, boobies. The international music of grown men stuck in high school. The song playing was "Body Like a Back Road." The cringe-inducing lyrics sounded like they had been written by a prepubescent horndog with a loose understanding of basic English syntax.

His dad clicked off the radio. "Body like a back road?"

"Guess that's better than a frontage road."

After three hours of interstate, Woody's brain was numb from driving. It had been a decade since he'd sat behind a wheel for this long, and he was out of driving shape. His reaction time was a little off. He was pushing the envelope being out here on this interstate with all this snow.

By hour four, they were crossing into Birmingham and the weather was getting bad. It was so windy Woody had to fight the wheel to stay in the right lane. Snow cascaded all over the road, obscuring the dotted lines and causing some cars to move to the shoulder and use their hazards. Woody's hands were trembling.

He pulled over to get some coffee at a Shell station. Woody and the Major walked inside, got snacks, paid for the coffees, then braved the snow on the way back to the truck. At least another inch had fallen since they'd pulled over.

"I don't know if I can keep driving, Dad."

The Major just looked at him. "What's wrong?"

"I haven't been behind the wheel much since the accident."

The cab fell silent.

The whistling wind surrounded them. His father's face held a modicum of compassion, which was seldom seen in men of the Eleventh Regiment. His father rested a heavy paw on his shoulder. In a small, tender voice, his father said, "I'll bet you probably pee sitting down, don't you, Nancy?"

The corners of Woody's mouth turned upward. This was as close to paternal bonding as they would ever get.

They were driving again.

His dad passed the time reading a *Cowboys & Indians* magazine until they hit Birmingham. The Major did not read anything quietly to himself but felt the need to announce every tidbit he discovered.

"Did you know Kevin Costner's marriage broke up because he had an affair with a hula dancer?"

Woody felt his eyes roll slightly.

"Hey, look on the bright side," his father added. "Least you didn't have a daughter with a hula dancer."

"Small blessings."

His father lowered the magazine. "You know, you're supposed to watch their hands."

Woody faced his dad. "Whose hands?"

"When I was in Hawaii after the war, they said you're supposed to watch the girl's hands when she dances the hula. She tells a story with her hands."

Woody's nod was so slight it was invisible.

Amos went back to reading. "I never saw no soldiers watching her hands."

The iridescent highway line sped past them in the darkness. Woody tuned his dad out. He found himself thinking about his old life. Before prison. To think of pre-prison life was suicide when you were inside. When you were outside, it was painful and humiliating, for you were viscerally confronted with everything prison had taken from you. Not just the big things. But the little things as well. The little, almost unidentifiable attributes and nuances of yourself. Things that used to make up your personality. Things that were gone now.

Ten years ago, Woody's life had been all about the church calendar. His whole life revolved around The Schedule. There was Saint John's elementary, connected to the church. There were endless emails. There was paying the bills, managing the church website, taking care of payroll, working on sermons. Finance meetings, budget planning meetings, outreach strategy meetings, vestry meetings, congregational discernment committees, school meetings, private counseling meetings. He also visited the hospital three times a week, coached the at-risk Little League team, and led the seniors' Bible study. After a workday, he'd visit the parsonage, where Elizabeth had supper waiting, choke down his meal, then trot across the street to unlock the church for choir practice, Alcoholics Anonymous, Al-Anon family groups, or any other program that used the church building. He had been a good priest. But he had been a crappy husband.

He looked at his phone in the cupholder. He could see the phone screen lighting up every few moments. He knew his screen would show dozens of new notifications from Rachel and Elizabeth. New texts. Humorous, animated GIFs. Funny memes. The two females in his life kept his phone constantly buzzing. They were trying to make him feel involved in their lives. They were trying so hard, and he was so grateful for their effort. But in a few hours, they would start to wonder where he was. Woody looked at his watch. It was only a few hours before Elizabeth would bring Rachel over. She would soon be wondering why a man who'd just suffered a cardiac event wasn't at home.

The phone started vibrating in the cupholder again.

Woody ignored it.

His father lowered the magazine and stared at the phone.

The screen was glowing, the phone humming against the cupholder.

"Aren't you going to answer that?" asked his dad.

Woody just kept his eyes on the highway.

• • •

THE NEXT-TO-LAST ROOM AT THE END OF THE HOSPITAL HALLWAY: Room 327. Getting here was like navigating through a miniature New York City, hopping elevators, doubling back, weaving through a labyrinth of corridors, crossing busy intersections. Woody's dad was complaining about his feet hurting, cussing beneath his breath about how GD fast Woody walked through the hospital. But Woody was not listening. His mind was somewhere else. The whole atmosphere seemed to be thrumming with deep emotion. He had not seen Melinda in eighteen years. His whole life felt as though it were coming to a head.

Finally, Woody stood before the oaken hospital door. The card on the room's nameplate said *Boyer*.

He drew in a deep breath and tried to calm his nerves. His hands were shaking. His knees felt like spaghetti.

"Cripes," said his dad. "We didn't walk this fast in the army." The Major leaned against the wall to catch his breath. Woody had been praying silently. He finished by crossing himself and taking a deep breath.

Amos Barker looked at the ceiling. "How the hell did I end up raising a preacher? Where did I go wrong?"

Woody did not dignify this remark.

"What are you praying for?"

"I'm just nervous."

"About what?"

"Can you give me a break? I just got out of a medium-security correctional institution. I need a moment."

The Major let out one scoffing laugh. He put a hand on the doorknob and tossed open the door.

"Dad!"

"Dad yourself. If you ain't man enough to go inside, I am."

Woody did not know what he would find when they opened the door. He didn't know what she might say or how she might look. He didn't know what bits of their own history they would need to discuss.

As it happened, what they found wasn't Melinda at all; it was the chaplain. Smiling warmly at them as though he had been expecting them.

"You must be Woody," the chaplain said, extending his hand. The chaplain pumped the Major's hand next. "It's a pleasure."

"Mutual, I'm sure," said the Major.

The chaplain was a robust man who had apparently gained some weight since the picture on his ID lanyard had been taken.

He said, "Melinda has been moved to ICU. She said you were coming. I thought I'd wait here in case you got lost."

Soon the chaplain was leading the way to the ICU. Woody and his dad followed. The Major was once again swearing gently beneath his breath about the pace the chaplain kept.

"She hasn't quit talking about you since you called," the chaplain told Woody.

"Well," said Woody, "she called me."

The chaplain's face was neither warm nor cold. Kind but distant. The face of a professional spiritual person. You learned how to make this face after your first few years on the job. Woody had a face like that in his repertoire too.

"Either way," said the chaplain, "I've heard a lot about you, and I believe she's going to be very glad you are here. All she's done is tell old stories about when you were young."

They arrived at the elevators. The chaplain mashed a button on the wall.

"How is she?"

"Struggling. Her oxygen level is dropping. They said they don't expect her to last the night."

Woody looked off.

He expected something to happen in the tears department. If for no other reason than for old time's sake. But Woody's eyes did nothing. And worse, he didn't feel anything.

The elevator doors opened. They all stepped inside to join a gaggle of young women in scrubs. The chaplain pressed the button for the second floor while Woody's dad made a serious attempt at flirting with women who were fifty years his junior.

When the doors opened, everyone deboarded except Woody.

The chaplain leaned against the edge to keep the doors open, reached back in, and patted Woody's shoulder. "We're here. We have the species ready for you. So whenever you're ready to do it, just let me know."

Woody felt his insides sink.

"Species?" said the Major.

"The bread and wine," explained the chaplain. "For last rites."

Woody collapsed against the elevator wall. This small space reminded him of a place he didn't want to remember.

"What species?" said Woody.

The chaplain asked, "You're here for the viaticum, correct? She requested for you to do last rites."

Silence.

"What?" asked Woody.

"I'm sorry, I thought you already knew. I thought that's why you came."

"I don't do last rites anymore, Father."

The chaplain placed his hand back on Woody's arm. "You do tonight, Father."

Chapter 11

———

THE STATISTICS WERE FRIGHTENING. THERE WERE 3,800 PEO-ple in the US awaiting heart transplants. Fewer than 1,700 people annually receive a transplant. Do the math. Each year an unlucky 2,100 people would sit on the list. Most of them died. Others spent the remainder of their lives checked into hospitals, living on machines.

Elizabeth read all this information while feeling a sense of heaviness fall over her. It was a slow night at Gulf Beach ER. She had been texting Woody all day without response. He was ghosting her—that was what her daughter's generation called it. Ghosting. Elizabeth's generation just called it being a big old butthead.

She leaned back into her chair and sighed.

Namely, because to receive a heart transplant in America, you must jump through more hoops and cut through more red tape than if you were trying to buy a stealth bomber. It all started with the application. Simply applying for a heart transplant was like signing up to be an astronaut. A team of doctors and professionals evaluated you. You were interviewed by a cardiologist, a cardiovascular surgeon, a transplant coordinator, a social worker, a dietician, a family therapist, a case worker, a financial analyst, a psychiatrist, psychologist, and two of the original Jonas Brothers. The team dove into every aspect of your life. First, an assessment of your finances. This is America; you pay to play. Then came the physicals. Then came the psych evaluations. Oh, and you couldn't be a smoker.

Elizabeth looked at the screen, lost in a kind of morose daze. Woody didn't have a shot in a frozen-over hell.

She did not notice that her boyfriend was standing on the other side of the computer monitor until she heard him clear his throat. Jason Cordell was dressed in his Class B tactical uniform. Duty belt slung low on his hip.

"You scared me," she said. "I didn't see you there."

"Penny for your thoughts?" asked Jason.

Her eyes were warm. "They're not worth a penny."

"Sorry. I don't have half a cent." He took off his GBPD ball cap to reveal a mass of sweaty hair. He ran his fingers through it. "You look like someone shot your dog."

"I think someone just did."

"You don't have a dog."

"Well, if I did, this is how I'd look."

Jason leaned onto the horseshoe desk. "I'm sorry, Liz. I'm afraid I'm losing track of this metaphor."

Jason's hair sort of fell over his eyebrows. Like one of the Beatles. He was in his early forties. Handsome. All Elizabeth's female employees were crazy about him. Especially the younger ones. Although, to be fair, her female staffers were crazy about any male with a pulse, including but not limited to UPS delivery-men or those who read the gas meter.

"Are you going to tell me what's up?" he asked.

"No."

Jason came around the desk and held her hand. He was

looking into her, not just looking *at* her. Officer Jason Cordell always tried so desperately to be in tune with her. Sometimes he tried too hard.

"It's his heart transplant," she said. "I think I'm figuring out that he doesn't qualify. He's probably not going to make the list."

Jason made a face. "Are you sure?"

"He is a sixty-year-old former inmate who smokes. He has no support system, no income, and no in-home care. I talked to a cardio nurse friend today; she said it's pointless to even apply."

"You can't lose hope."

"Actually, I can. And I think it's necessary that I do."

Elizabeth started chewing her thumb. It was a bad habit from her youth and caused her thumb tip to resemble the tip of a baked hot dog.

Jason lowered himself to her eye level. He touched her face. "You have paint on your face. Do you know that?"

She wiped her cheek.

"Little white flecks," he said. "They're everywhere."

"I've been on ladders all day."

He used a thumb to wipe something from her chin. "I've told you. You don't have to repaint my kitchen just because you and Rachel are moving in. I liked the old paint job just fine."

"I'm not painting for you. It's for me. For us. I want a fresh start. I want everything to be brand-new. I want my life to feel new again. I want a clean slate. We both deserve that."

He wrapped his arms around her.

Jason kissed her, and she felt her body tighten a little. Jason pulled away and looked into her dark eyes.

"Are you okay?" he asked.

"I'm great."

Chapter 12

MELINDA'S EYES WERE CLOSED, HEAVY BENEATH THE WEIGHT of medication. They had just removed her breathing tube. Machines were beeping. Compressors hissing. Everyone in the room was watching Woody, waiting for him to do something. Melinda's boyfriend was standing outside the door playing on his phone.

"Are you awake, Melinda?" Woody asked.

She nodded. "Yes." Opened her eyes.

"Are you ready for this?"

"I think so."

In third-century Rome, Christians were killed for sport. They were flayed alive, burned as living torches, locked inside barrels full of protruding spikes and rolled down hills, attacked by dogs. On the eve of their deaths, local churches sent secret messengers to prisons and work camps to celebrate the Last Supper with the inmates. The messengers would carry bread and wine with them. Visiting prisoners was a death sentence for the messengers, but it didn't stop them from volunteering by the droves.

Tarcisius was one such twelve-year-old boy. He was ordained as a minister and sent to the prisons with bread and wineskins tucked in the folds of his cloak. On the way, a gang attacked and killed him. They left him lying in a puddle of blood and confiscated his bread and wine. Bread and wine for last rites would later, in the sixteenth century, come to be called "viaticum"—literally, provisions for the journey. If you've ever wondered why children are elected to carry bread and wine during a liturgical Eucharist, now you know.

Right now, Woody felt about as competent as a twelve-year-old boy. He had not performed the role of celebrant in over a decade. But somehow he remembered the recitations. Some things never leave you. He remembered the inflections. He remembered to pause in all the right places. He remembered it all.

"Do you need a book?" the chaplain asked.

"No," said Woody.

He moved toward the bed and rested his hand on the rail. He closed his eyes.

"Wait," said Melinda. "Where's Caroline?"

The chaplain said, "Jack Jr. couldn't reach her. He left a message on her boyfriend's phone."

"I want her here for this."

"We need to do this now, Melinda," said the chaplain with a soothing voice. "There isn't a lot of time."

Then he nodded to Woody.

Everyone in the room bowed their head. The former inmate found a timbre of voice that originated deep in his chest. A voice he had not heard with his own ears in a long time. The words seemed to fall from his lips without even trying.

"Almighty God, look upon this your servant, lying in great weakness, and comfort her with the promise of life everlasting, given in the resurrection of your Son, Jesus Christ our Lord. Amen."

A round of "amens" from the room.

He recited the Sursum Corda. The Doxology. He blessed the sacraments. He placed a wafer into Melinda's mouth. And so began the ancient custom for which so many died.

"The body of Christ. The bread of heaven, keep you until everlasting life."

The chaplain passed Woody a chalice draped in white cloth. He lowered the rim to Melinda's lips. The wine flowed into her mouth, but most of it dribbled onto her hospital gown.

"The blood of Christ. The cup of his grace, his salvation, and his mercy unto all. Unto you. And unto me."

Melinda began coughing. It looked like she was about to choke on the wine. A nurse stepped in and wiped her face.

Melinda spoke between wheezing. "I'm sorry, Woody."

Woody touched Melinda's face. Her skin was warmer than he expected. He closed his eyes. "May the Lord Jesus Christ lead you on the way to everlasting life, Melinda. May he lead you into the everlasting peace of eternal union."

The chaplain made the sign of the cross.

Two nurses crossed themselves.

The Major jingled the change in his pockets.

Melinda reached out to hold Woody's hand. She clasped it between both of hers. Her fingers were pure bone. But in her eyes he thought he saw a flicker of peace. Behind the mask of death, he saw the young woman he fell in love with so long ago. And in her eyes Woody saw himself. Not as he was today. But the way he used to be.

"Promise me you'll take care of her, Woody."

He squeezed her hand.

"May you find the forgiveness and peace Christ has brought. And may the Lord God watch over me and thee while we are absent from one another—*Mizpah*."

"*Mizpah*," she whispered.

At that moment, a red-haired young woman entered the room, clutching the straps of her backpack. She was very beautiful. She was very pregnant.

And she looked just like her dad.

. . .

THE MAJOR DUG A CIGAR FROM HIS POCKET. HE HAD BEEN CUTTING back lately. He was a big believer in moderation. He restricted himself to smoking only one cigar at a time. And it was his policy never to smoke while sleeping.

Woody and his dad were standing outside of North Knoxville Medical Center, watching the snow fall. The aftershock of Melinda's death was still heavy in the air.

Woody's dad handed him the pack of De Nobilis. Woody removed one, wet the tip with his mouth, then bit the end. He sat on the bench near the hospital entrance beside his dad, caught in a daze.

"I always liked her," said the Major. "She had a lot of sass."

Woody smiled. "She had plenty."

Melinda Boyer's family had moved into the parsonage when Woody was four years old. Her dad was the priest of Saint John's. Melinda was the quintessential preacher's kid. Buck wild. Mischievous spark in her eyes. Kiss-my-grits attitude. Always in trouble. Woody and Melinda were joined at the hip from day one. They passed an entire childhood among the creek beds, climbing trees, or seated on the saddles of Schwinns. He had never even considered that Melinda was a real girl until they hit their teenage years and hormones got involved. She was his first couple-skating partner. His first summer love. His first kiss. His first wife.

It was Melinda's dad, Father Roger, who baptized him when Woody was sixteen. Woody's family had not been religious. It was

Melinda's father who took Woody under his wing while Woody's father worked double overtime on ironworking crews.

Woody flicked his lighter and got his ember started. He passed the lighter to his dad.

"Do they let you smoke inside prison?" asked the Major.

"Only in the movies."

"That's unconstitutional."

"Take it up with the BOP."

"Not even just a cigarette?"

Prisons in the US banned smoking. If you were caught smoking, you faced serious disciplinary action. Emphasis on *caught*. There was a thriving underground tobacco trade inside. Inmates smoked "pinners": tobacco rolled in toilet paper. They contained just enough nicotine to piss you off.

"I couldn't make it inside," said the Major, eyeing his cigar.

Woody removed the phone from his pocket and dialed Elizabeth's number. He wandered away from his dad for privacy. The phone rang, but no answer. He looked at his watch. It was late, after eleven. He dialed again. Nothing.

"What did you expect?" asked his dad. "You never answered her calls."

"Funny. I don't remember asking your advice."

"See? That's your first mistake."

Woody dialed Rachel's cell. This time there was an answer. Only it wasn't Elizabeth or Rachel. It was a man. Strong and confident.

"Is this Jason?"

"I'm sorry," said the voice. "Who is this? This is a nine-year-old's phone."

"This is the nine-year-old's dad."

The man's voice changed from police officer to buddy-buddy. "Woody? I'm sorry, man. Your name didn't show up on the screen, my mistake. Listen, Rachel's asleep right now. You want to talk to Elizabeth?"

"Only if she's nearby."

"Well, I'm watching her stand on a ladder right now. And I hate to get her off the ladder because I kind of like this view."

Woody felt a stabbing ache inside him. It hurt more than he had anticipated.

"Hold on," said Jason with a laugh. "I'll get her for you."

"Thanks."

Woody heard more laughter in the background. Indiscriminate voices talking playfully with one another. Life is a party.

Elizabeth said hello.

"Little late for a sleepover, isn't it?" said Woody.

"We're repainting Jason's kitchen."

Woody drew in smoke and released it. "Is that what they call it these days?"

"Did you call to inquire about my personal habits, or are you calling to be a horse's ass?"

"I haven't decided."

Woody looked at his dad, leaning against the wall. The old man was picking his nose with his thumb.

She said, "You're in no position to get mad at me when you haven't answered my texts all day."

"Do you leave a toothbrush at his house?" Woody said.

She was whispering now. "Listen to me. What I do with my private life is none of your business."

"It's my business if you're doing it on the kitchen table in front of our daughter."

"Oh my God. I'm hanging up now."

Woody felt the greenery of jealousy consuming him as he watched interstate traffic go by in the distance. Snow was falling heavily. He had not felt this kind of covetousness in so long that the sensation was almost foreign. It was confusing. He didn't know what to do with the resentful envy that was eating him alive.

"There's no need to be like this," she said. "Jason is trying to be part of our family. He just wants in."

"Yes, he certainly wants to get into something."

"You have ten seconds to get to the point or I'm hanging up."

Woody looked into the sky at the stars above. He flicked his cigar into the snowy parking lot. He tried to figure out how he was going to tell her he had a daughter with a woman she hated. But no words came to him. There had been no love lost between Melinda and Elizabeth.

"Are you okay?" she asked.

"I honestly don't know."

"Where are you?"

Pause.

"Knoxville."

This was met with a hush.

"I'm kind of going through a lot right now, Liz. I need to talk to someone, and I don't know who else to call. I don't have anyone who will listen to my—"

They were interrupted.

It was Jason. She gave him a quick answer. Her voice was wifey. Feminine. Happy. Without the maternally nagging overtones she used on Woody.

And that was when it sank into Woody's brain fully. He hadn't seen the truth quite as plainly as he did now. But the fact was, Elizabeth Barker was not his. She hadn't been his in ten years. Not really. In her kindness, she had maintained the illusion for his sake. Suddenly, Woody felt thoroughly and everlastingly stupid.

He hung up the phone and lit another cigar.

Chapter 13

———

THE FUNERAL HOME SAT OFF THE INTERSTATE IN A LARGE PAS-
ture framed by mountains, graced with a temperamentally
gray sky. It was a pole-barn structure, similar to a cattle auction
warehouse, except for the homemade painted plywood steeple
on the roof.

The casket was nice. Nicer than Caroline expected. Red oak.
Gold hardware. The lining was purple satin. Her mother was
wearing a gold, lowcut dress Jack Jr. had selected. The funeral
director told Jack Jr. the neckline was too low. The morticians
tried to talk him out of it since this was a celebration of life service, not a two-for-one special at the Bazoom Room. But Jack Jr.
insisted this was her mother's favorite dress. So the morticians
made it work. The blond wig on her head, the final touch, made
her mother look as though she had died while performing a Dolly
Parton tribute routine.

Oh, what cosmetic atrocities are committed in the name of
open-casket funerals.

Jack Jr. stood beside the coffin, weeping. "They did a good
job on her."

Caroline stared at her mother and wondered whether she and Jack Jr. were looking at the same remains.

Jack Jr. wiped his face. "I don't know what I'm going to do without her. I don't know how I'll survive."

"You'll keep going," said Caroline.

Jack Jr. looked at her. "I'm not strong like you."

Caroline pulled him close. "I'm not strong. I'm just dumb."

Jack Jr. held her tightly and sobbed. He reeked of weed and aftershave, and his pupils were the size of a single atomic particle.

The service was poorly attended. Eight attendees altogether, not counting Jack Jr., Tater, and herself. There was no preacher. There was no eulogy, no prayer, no sermons. Like many addicted persons, her mother's world had grown so increasingly small and isolated that very few could mourn her.

On the front row sat the two men Caroline had met in the hospital: Woody and Amos Barker. They kept staring at her when they didn't think she was looking, but she saw them gawking. The men wore neckties and slacks. They hadn't moved from their spot on the front row all morning. Caroline had not spoken to them. Not even once, because they were weird. She had no interest in talking to a couple of strangers who had introduced themselves as her mom's friends. She was not about to listen to some memory they had of Melinda that would require her to slap on a plasticized smile and pretend the woman in the casket hadn't robbed Caroline of her childhood.

When the visitation was over, the older man began limping his way to her. The younger man waited by the door, staring out the window.

The man named Amos took her hand, lifted it to his mouth, then kissed it with his dry lips. "I know you're busy today, sweetheart. But if you have the time, we'd like to buy you a cup of coffee and talk."

She noticed the middle-aged man watching.

"Coffee?"

"You drink coffee?"

"Yes. Where?"

The old man pointed to the IHOP across the street. The cerulean roof was visible through the funeral parlor window.

"We'll have a booth in the back."

"Uh . . ."

"It would mean so much to us."

"Well, I . . ."

"We'll be there waiting."

Caroline watched the funeral parlor staff start to move through the chapel aisles, picking up trash and straightening chairs. They were already closing the place down.

"It's just . . . I'll have to ask my boyfriend if I can go."

The old man smiled. "Or you could just tell him."

• • •

CAROLINE AND TATER HELPED JACK JR. OUT TO HIS TRUCK. Caroline put her arm around his waist and muscled him through the parking lot.

"Come on," she said to Jack Jr. "Let's get you home. You need food on your stomach. You haven't eaten all day."

"What about me?" said Tater. "I haven't eaten all day either."

"Can we worry about you later?" she said.

"I don't see what the big deal is. He's just a little stoned."

Caroline helped Jack Jr. into his enormous Chevy Silverado. The tricked-out truck featured LCD television screens embedded in the back seats, a stereo system that was barely legal, and a pair of rubberized bovine testes dangling from the trailer hitch.

Jack Jr. sat slumped in the passenger seat with his head pressed against the window. He was drooling.

"Caroline," he muttered, his voice garbled with thick spit. "What am I gonna do without my baby girl?"

"You'll figure something out."

"My baby girl!"

"Try to breathe."

Jack Jr. reached out his meaty hand and grabbed her necklace. His lazy eyes focused on the pendant. "Where'd you get this?"

Caroline said nothing.

"This isn't yours."

She removed the necklace from his hands.

Caroline slammed the door on him. She placed the truck keys into Tater's hand and said, "Do *not* let him drive this truck. Make sure he gets home safe and don't speed. There are cops all over this area."

Tater looked at the keys. "How are *you* going to get home?"

She pointed to the Honda. "I'll take the Rolls."

He laughed. "You're kidding me."

She didn't even dignify his remark. She held out her hand. "Give me your keys. I don't have energy for this."

"You're crazy. You're not driving my car. That's a classic. Get in the flippin' truck, woman."

"Or you could just tell him."

"I pay the insurance on that car," she said. "Now give me your keys."

Tater did no such thing. He only laughed, then began crawling into Jack Jr.'s truck. "Get in. We're leaving."

"You're *seriously* going to do this to me?"

"Get in."

"Or you could just tell him."

"On the day of my mother's funeral? You're going to do this?"

"Go to hell, Caroline."

"What am I supposed to do, walk home in the snow?"

Tater nestled into the truck's driver's seat. "You can either ride home with me or you can stay here. Your choice. You're not driving my car, Stevie Wonder."

"You owe me better than this."

"I don't owe you jack."

"I'm carrying your son."

Tater's mouth quit moving. His eyes moved to her belly. He held his gaze there. If he had a morsel of humanity in him, she had touched it.

"My what?"

"Your son."

He was still for a few moments. Then he reached into his pocket and handed her the keys. But not without issuing a stern warning first.

"Be careful with my freaking car," he said, gripping her wrist.

She tugged her wrist free. "I'll be sure not to scratch it."

Chapter 14

CAROLINE ENTERED THE IHOP WITH A BLAST OF SNOW AND cold air. The teenage hostess greeted her without even looking up from her phone.

"How many?" said the hostess.

"I'm meeting someone," said Caroline, already standing on her toes, scanning the dining room full of heads.

The carpet in the IHOP was bacterial-infection green. The walls bore evidence of a lifetime of deep-frying. The music overhead was Reba, singing about hard times as only a redheaded cross-eyed millionaire could. There was a chalkboard next to the hostess station. The breakfast special was "Frinch Toast." You had to love Tennessee.

Caroline found them in the back. She walked across the restaurant and slid into the booth next to Amos Barker, across from Woody Barker, without saying anything. She plopped her backpack onto the floor beside her and took off her mittens. They both looked at her with a kind of happy, astonished stare.

"You came," Amos said, sipping coffee.

"I like coffee," she replied.

"There are a lot of other places to get coffee," said Woody.

"Yeah," said Amos. "But none of them have *Frinch* toast."

Woody looked at Amos. "I wish you hadn't invited her." Then he looked to her. "I'm afraid I won't be very good company today. Maybe we can talk later. Maybe you should choose another table."

Amos gave Woody a look that could have melted steel. Caroline removed her jacket and rolled it into a ball beside her.

"No, thanks. This table suits me fine."

Woody sighed. "It's just that today's been a long day for me."

"Really. Well, I wouldn't know what that's like."

The old man laughed and patted her knee. "Hey, I like this kid."

Woody went back to staring at his menu.

Amos whispered loudly, "Don't let him bother you, sweetie. Woody is what they refer to in the zoological community as a turd." The old man laughed at his own remark, then draped an arm around her and pulled her close. "She's cute!"

Woody glanced up from his menu long enough to flash annoyance.

The waitress came. A wholesome-looking girl. High school age. Perfect teeth. Perfect eyes. She probably had two working parents, one-point-five siblings, stuffed animals on her bed, and a dog named Bella or Luna.

Caroline ordered coffee. Black. That was all she planned on ordering, but before the waitress could get away, the old man stepped in and ordered Caroline a large breakfast without even asking whether she wanted one or whether she was hungry. He ordered eggs, toast, pancakes, the works.

"Why did you do that?" Caroline asked as the waitress walked away.

He patted her knee again. "I'm eighty-seven years old, sweetie. Not everything I do makes sense."

Caroline excused herself from the table to refill Gary's jar with fresh water from the ladies' room. When she returned, she placed Gary's Hellmann's jar on the table beside the napkin dispenser. Gary swam around, whipping his tail, looking energized and refreshed. The two men ogled the fish on the table.

"Nice fish," Amos said.

"Thanks."

"You carry a goldfish everywhere you go?" asked Woody.

"Not everywhere," she said.

"Good for you," said Amos. "You have to set your boundaries."

After a few conversationless minutes, the waitress placed hot breakfasts before them all.

Woody used a fork to cut his "Frinch" toast, then drowned it in maple-ish syrup. The old man was tucking into a plate of eggs and bacon as though he had not eaten since the reign of Nixon. And Caroline was realizing how famished she was as she got to work on her food.

"Are you going to tell us why you have a goldfish at the breakfast table?" asked Woody.

"Leave her alone," said Amos. "It's her emotional support fish."

Woody looked at the fish. "What's its name?"

"Gary."

"Why Gary?" said Woody.

"Why's your name Woody?"

Amos salted his hash browns. "Because the twenty-eighth president was the greatest military leader of our time. God rest his soul."

Woody reached into his coat pocket and removed a folded manila envelope. He tossed the envelope on the table between them. Caroline stared at the envelope. She wiped her sticky hand on a napkin, then used her thumb to open the package. Inside was a stack of photos. The images were snapshots of her mother's youth. Faded images of Melinda from another era. Out-moded fashions, corny hairstyles, dated eyeglasses. Woody was in many of the photos too. In the later photos, Woody was wearing a white clerical collar. His hair was red in the photos, just like Caroline's.

She held the picture closer.

One of the photos showed a wedding. Woody was a younger man in the image, with more meat on his bones. He was wearing a wash-and-wear tux. In the image, her mother was locking arms with Woody, dressed in a '90s-era miniskirt wedding dress. She did not look like an addict in this picture. She looked like Miss Small Town. And a weighty realization fell upon her.

"You were married?" she asked.

"Eleven years."

"And you're a priest?"

"Was."

"I thought priests couldn't marry," said Caroline.

"Believe me," said Amos, "judging from this idiot's track record, they shouldn't."

She looked closer at the photo and felt herself getting light-headed. The room was moving sideways, and she was nauseous.

"Deep breaths," Amos said. "Don't pass out on us, darling. We don't know the first thing about raising goldfish."

Caroline looked at the old man, then to Woody.

"You're my dad?"

Woody's eyes were on the table.

Amos took a sip. "And she's smart too."

Chapter 15

CAROLINE PULLED THE HONDA INTO THE DRIVEWAY AT NINE o'clock in the evening after spending the afternoon driving around with neither destination nor objective in mind. Her eyes had been giving her problems in the dim, overcast weather. She had nearly caused not one but three separate traffic accidents. More from lack of practice than lack of ability, but still.

A special education teacher from the state had visited school twice a week to teach Caroline to drive because of her disability. She had learned to use visual cues to judge distance, to move her head from side to side to maintain a broader range of vision.

But it had been a while since driver's ed.

Jack Jr. and Tater were in the yard, seated before a roaring bonfire of automotive tires sending purple flames into the night sky, stinking up the tri-county area with the smell of sulfur and synthetic rubber. Tater was scrolling TikTok. Jack Jr. was also playing on his phone, watching *Is It Cake?*, the hit streaming series wherein cake artists create replicas of handbags, sewing machines, and musical instruments.

"Where the hell have you been?" Tater shouted, rising from

his seat. His speech was inarticulate, devoid of edges and consonants. The words seemed to flop out of his mouth.

Caroline ignored him and walked toward the trailer. She couldn't find words to respond to him. She had been through too much today.

"Caroline!" he called out. "I'm talking to you!"

Tater tried to follow her but fell over.

Jack Jr. laughed.

She paid the two drunk men no attention and instead went to feed the cats. Then she walked inside, let the screen door slam, and prepared supper for the guys because she knew they had not eaten all day.

Soon they sat before the fire, eating SpaghettiOs from coffee mugs in absolute silence.

After supper, Jack Jr. staggered inside for a few moments. She heard him rummaging through the cabinets, muttering to himself. He reemerged on the porch holding a bottle of port wine, declaring that it was time to celebrate the memory of Melinda Boyer.

Jack Jr. poured the wine into coffee mugs. The cups were old and stained from years of use. Jack Jr. was first to toast. He made a speech that contained words that were incomprehensible except for smatterings of the F-bomb. The guys drank to Melinda. Jack Jr. downed his glass in one swig and lost consciousness. Tater took a slug from his cup. Then he offered the wine to Caroline.

"No thanks." She shook her head. "I don't want any."

"Come on, Caroline. A sip won't hurt."

"No. I don't want any wine."

Tater pressed his mug toward her, sloshing wine over the rim. "Do it for your mom. She'd want you to celebrate her life."

"I can celebrate her life without drinking wine. I'm pregnant."

Tater wrinkled his face comically and looked at Jack Jr. for moral support. "And?"

"And being pregnant means I can't drink."

Tater was growing increasingly agitated. "Even one sip?"

She shoved him away. "I don't even like wine."

Tater pushed her back. He told her to drink it. It was no longer a request.

"I said no."

Caroline turned to go inside, but Tater chased her. Caught her in a headlock.

"Get off me!" she yelled.

Tater was already spinning her around, her head beneath his sweaty arm, as she swatted at him with both hands.

"Let me go!"

Tater laughed wildly. Jack Jr. woke up and returned to scrolling on his phone.

And then time began to slow down. Maybe it was because of the funeral. Funerals do funny things to people. Or maybe it was because she had just met her biological father and grandfather. Maybe it was because a lot of life had happened in the past few days. Either way, looking back, Caroline would later realize the choice she was about to make changed everything.

It began when the blind cat wrapped himself around Caroline's lower leg. The cat was purring, begging for food.

In one swift motion, Tater released Caroline, then stooped to pick up the cat. He pitched the cat against the side of the trailer like he was passing a football. The cat's little body crashed against the sheet metal trailer. The cat screamed. And when the animal hit the ground, it scurried off, running headfirst into every obstacle in its way.

Caroline felt a great heat building inside her, rising to the surface. She rushed toward Tater, screaming at the top of her voice.

She was imbued with a strength she never knew she possessed. She knocked the mug from his hands. The cup flew through the air. Red wine went airborne, like a bouquet of roses.

Tater was too stunned to react.

She hit him. Not once, but twice. Three times. Four times. Five. Six.

Tater was not passive for long. He used the back of his hand to strike her. He connected with her cheekbone with a blow so stiff it knocked her backward.

"Don't you ever touch me again!" he screamed.

Then he crawled atop her and began cuffing her face. Over and again. He was small but strong enough to keep her pinned to the ground. The next thing she knew, he had come up with a wine bottle and was shoving it between her lips and pouring.

"Drink it!" he shouted.

She gagged on the wine as he wedged the bottle's mouth between her closed lips, pressing her skull into the hard earth. Bitter gall drained all over her face, into her eyes, and up her nostrils. Crimson ran over her new funeral clothes. All over the ground. All over her hair.

When he had emptied the contents, he lobbed the bottle into the darkness. She heard it thud in the weeds.

Then Tater grabbed the pendant of her necklace and yanked until the necklace snapped off her neck. He wobbled up the steps into the trailer and slammed the door behind him. The last thing she heard him say was, "White trash."

Chapter 16

IT'S WEIRD HOW CERTAIN THINGS STICK WITH YOU. THE FIRST time anyone ever called Caroline white trash, she was twelve. One of the boys at school said it. This boy was not the brightest bulb on the Christmas tree of life—the proverbial wheel was spinning, but the hamster was dead. But it stuck nonetheless. He said it during physical education class. That godless period in childhood when kids are compelled to wear a uniform consisting of butt-hugging nylon gym shorts, dorky white tennis shoes, and a sausage-casing white T-shirt. Everyone, even international supermodels, looks like a schnoz-whistle in a gym class uniform.

On the back of Caroline's gym T-shirt, a qualified parent was supposed to have spelled her last name with vinyl, iron-on, alphabet letters. It was a simple procedure. Line up the letters; iron them on. Everyone else's parents had no problems with this task. But purchasing heat-transfer lettering from Hobby Lobby was a bridge too far for Melinda Boyer. Instead, her mother spelled Caroline's name on the T-shirt with black Sharpie marker. It bears mentioning that it is extremely difficult—if not impossible—to write on cotton-polyester blend with a Sharpie. The material moves beneath the marker. So the surname BOYER came out looking more like BOV8K$, as though the name had been crafted by a drunk. Which, of course, it had.

Plus, her mother bought the wrong size T-shirt, so the shirt clung to Caroline's developing figure like a layer of latex paint, showing every imperfection of her chubby adolescent frame. Caroline did not own an adequate bra because her mother refused to acknowledge that her daughter was becoming a woman. So she wore a trainer that dug into her skin, making huge divots beneath the shirt.

The boys had a field day with her. They called her horrible names. They made lewd gestures. The nicknames mutated from "Miss Nipple" to "Quarter Pounder," and finally they settled on plain old "White Trash."

The only ones who don't believe there is a fixed social hierarchy system in this country are the ones located at the top of such a system. The American caste system can operate under many names: racism, classism, sexism, elitism, ageism, colorism, homophobia, Latinophobia, fatphobia. But it's all the same thing.

Until that moment in gym class, Caroline had never known she was white trash. She had heard the term before, yes. But she never applied it to herself. She had always thought she was a regular person. Until the other kids started calling her White Trash, she hadn't truly understood who or what she was. A mouse doesn't know it's a mouse. A bird doesn't realize it's a bird. It just is.

She began to assess her life, and things began to make sense. The bullies were right. She was indeed one of the few unfortunate kids in the middle school without running water, without food in the fridge, without real shoes, without a laptop or Wi-Fi or anything technological save for a digital watch. For crying out loud, her mother didn't even have a home phone. Or an operational toilet, for that matter. She was the only kid without a smartphone in her class. How bad off did you have to be not to have a phone? Even homeless people had Facebook accounts. Oh, what Caroline would have given for even a flip phone. Or a beeper, for God's sake. Anything would have been better than nothing. But nothing was what she had.

Caroline was thinking about all this as she quietly exited her mother's trailer before sunrise. She had taken the cash from Tater's wallet. Her eye was blackened, her lip was busted, and there was the scent of blood in her swollen sinuses. There was a cat in her arms. Backpack over her shoulder. Goldfish in a jar. A necklace repaired with Scotch tape dangled around her neck. The flash drive in her pocket was poking her in the leg, its outline visible through the stretchy fabric of her yoga pants.

The young woman gingerly closed the door behind her. She stepped into the Honda Civic, wedging herself tightly behind the wheel. Caroline felt like a pregnant African bush elephant climbing into the cockpit of a go-kart.

She took a deep breath.

The blind cat was already curled up and sleeping in the passenger seat where she had placed him. She was wearing her mother's clothes. A black sweatshirt with holes in the sleeve cuffs where her mother presumably hitched her thumbs. She had no way of washing all the wine from her skin and hair, so she had done her best to rinse herself using a bottle of water she'd found in Tater's car.

Outside, the first pangs of gray were peeking behind the Smokies. She wasn't sure she was doing the right thing. If she was doing the right thing, why was this so frightening? She was waiting for the warm feeling that accompanies good decisions, but it wasn't coming. She just felt lost and alone. And most of all, she felt different from the person she had been twenty-four hours earlier. Now that her mother's remains were dust, everything was different. Nothing was ever going to be the same again. This was the beginning of the rest of her life.

Caroline turned over the engine. The motor sputtered to life. The icy morning air filled with blue exhaust. She looked at her own reflection in the mirror. She touched her battered cheek and probed her split lip. She stamped the clutch, moved the gearshift.

And White Trash drove away.

• • •

THE BEST WESTERN'S AUTOMATIC DOORS PARTED WHEN CAROLINE walked in. She was rattled from the drive. Her good eye was swollen, which made it hard to concentrate. But not too bad to drive.

There was a continental breakfast going on in the hotel. Guests were waiting in a long line for their granite bananas, fake eggs, and oranges shriveled like shrunken skulls. The first person she saw was Amos, fixing a plate, shambling through a line of hotel guests, using his three-legged cane to help them hurry through the line.

Caroline could see a kind of mild shock registering on everyone's face. She must have looked worse than she thought. Woody came to her first.

"What happened to you?"

"I fell."

His eyes went to the cat in her arms. Then the backpack, which was bursting with clothes she had confiscated from her mother's house.

"Bad fall," he said.

"You have no idea."

They found a table in the dining area. Amos scooted his chair so close to her that their legs were touching, and he dedicated himself to rubbing her back.

"I'm sorry about the way things went yesterday," she said. "I really am."

"No, you're not," said Woody.

A beat went by.

"And you shouldn't be," Woody added. "You should feel angry. You deserve to feel angry."

"Hell," said Amos. "I'm angry, too, right now."

"Why?" said Caroline.

"Because you look like you stood in front of a train."

Woody stirred his oatmeal and blew on it. People started to fill up the dining area, sitting together, happily carrying on morning discussions over their complimentary inorganic matter. The guests kept stealing glances at her goldfish and her cat. Sometimes she felt ridiculous. This morning was one of those times.

"You aren't going to tell us what happened to your face?" asked Amos.

"No."

Woody tapped his spoon on the rim of his bowl. "Then what did you come here to talk about?"

She adjusted herself in her chair. "I want you to take me with you."

Amos quit rubbing. Woody wiped his chin with a napkin. Nobody spoke for a few moments.

"You didn't want anything to do with me yesterday," said Woody.

"I have money. I can help with gas."

"Why don't you start by telling me who did that to your face?"

She looked down. "I told you, nobody."

"And where is Nobody right now?" said Amos.

"I just want a clean start. That's all."

Woody sipped. "This isn't the Disney Channel, kid. It doesn't work that way."

"I have my own money. I won't be any problem."

Woody began eating his oatmeal in earnest. He washed each bite down with routine sips. "Why don't we start from the beginning and see if we can try a little honesty." He looked at Caroline. "What do you say?"

She nodded.

Amos was still rubbing. "You just take your time, sweetie."

Woody was looking directly at her. "Now, last night you wouldn't have peed on us if we were on fire. Suddenly you show up with a bloody lip and it's 'take me with you, Daddy'? It looks and sounds to me like you're in trouble. Is that true?"

"I honestly don't know anymore."

"Of course you don't, baby," said Amos.

"That's fair," said Woody. "But how do we know you're not going to brain us with a stick half a mile down the road and steal my truck?"

"I don't have a stick," she said.

"What about your boyfriend?" asked Amos.

"He doesn't have a stick either."

"And what's he think about you leaving?" asked Woody.

Caroline shook her head. "I didn't ask him. I just wanted to get out of there."

"I'm sorry," said Woody. "But the answer is no."

"No?"

"No, you can't come with us."

"What?" asked Amos. "She's your daughter."

Woody was talking to the old man now. "She's a minor, in foster care. We can't just remove her from the state. There's a legal process to this. Tennessee courts could charge me with kidnapping. And believe me, the last thing I need is trouble with the law."

Amos made a raspberry sound to indicate the level of respect he had for the law.

Caroline's gaze fell downward.

"I've been living with my boyfriend since I left my last foster home, and my foster parents know that. They've never said a word about it. I don't think anyone in the system even knows where I am. Nobody gives a crap what I do or where I go."

"Believe me," Woody said, "the courts give a crap about everything."

She was pleading now. "I age out of the foster system in three months. By then it won't matter. I can do whatever I want."

"So call us in three months."

Caroline absently touched her bruised cheek. Her eye felt swollen and hot. Thank God it wasn't her good eye Tater had blackened, or she wouldn't have been able to see well enough to drive. The throbbing spread all the way to her ears.

"You're a priest, right?"

"I'm not a priest."

"In the hospital," said Caroline, "you gave my mom Communion."

Woody tilted his head back. "And . . . ?"

"Well, isn't a priest supposed to help people?"

His chest rose and fell with a sigh. "Help, yes. Break the law—not since I last checked."

Caroline said, "'For I hungered, and ye gave me meat; I was thirsty, and ye gave me drink; I was a stranger, and ye took me in.'"

Woody's eyes met hers.

"Yeah," he said, "that's not gonna work either."

Chapter 17

———

Elizabeth stood before a trifold mirror with her mother behind her eyeing Elizabeth's white gown, scrutinizing each fold of her garment, wrinkling her mouth at this and that, her fist fixed firmly beneath her chin like she had been sculpted by Auguste Rodin. Her mother took the hemline between her fingers, then traced her hands up Elizabeth's hips and waist. She grabbed the fabric around Elizabeth's bust.

"Chest needs to come in a little."

Her mother pulled the material tightly across her bosom. "You could fit a three-year-old in the bust of this dress. This is the wrong one for you."

"I like the cut of it," said Elizabeth.

Her mother stood back at a distance and observed again. "No. I think I like the last one better. This is too sassy."

"Sassy isn't bad."

"Sassy is bad on the day of your wedding."

"What about on the day of your second wedding?"

Her mother ignored the remark. Denial was not a river in Egypt in Elizabeth's family but the guiding principle on which the family had been established.

The phone in Elizabeth's purse rang. She walked toward the

sound, trying to maintain her balance in the heels that were tall enough to interfere with commercial airline traffic.

"Don't answer that," said her mother. "You're busy right now."

"It's Woody."

"Then definitely don't answer that."

Her mother had disliked Woody Barker from the moment she met him. From the day, so long ago, when her twenty-three-year-old brought home a forty-one-year-old world religion professor for supper. Surprise, Mom.

Elizabeth answered.

"Sorry to bother you," Woody said, "but do we still have an air mattress?"

"I think so. Why?"

"Just wondering."

"Who's it for?"

"An old friend. Can I borrow it?"

"I'll leave it at your place this afternoon when I drop off Rachel."

Long sigh. "About that."

Elizabeth looked at her mother, who was listening to every word with an intensity often associated with Soviet espionage. Elizabeth held one finger up to her mother, then walked into one of the empty dressing rooms and shut the door.

"I can't watch Rachel tonight," he said.

She sat down in a chair and fell into the massive folds of her dress. It had been almost a week since Rachel had seen this man she was just getting to know. And already, three months into their blossoming relationship, he was bailing on her.

"Woody, I was counting on you. You know I go to work at four today. I don't have anyone to watch her."

"I know. I'm sorry. I'll pay for the babysitter."

"It's not about a babysitter. Rachel was looking forward to this. She's waited her whole life to get to know you. This is huge for her. Are we still on for Friday?"

"Yes, but . . ."

Elizabeth kicked off her heels and massaged her aching feet.

"But what?"

"Well, I've been doing a lot of thinking over the last few days."

"I thought I told you to quit thinking."

She could hear him smoking on the other end.

"Yeah, well, I don't think I'm doing your social life any favors, and I don't think me being around is giving you or Rachel a fair shot with Jason. He deserves a real chance to be her dad. That's not going to happen as long as you keep organizing playdates with a convicted felon."

"Quit talking like that. You're Rachel's dad. Jason knows what he's getting into."

"Rachel deserves a lot better than watching her dad get spit on in public. And so do you."

"Who cares about the public."

Elizabeth looked at herself in the mirror. She did not look like a bride. She looked like a middle-aged soccer mom in a wedding dress.

"Okay," said Elizabeth. "So are you're telling me you want to be done with us now? Simple as that? After ten years of getting lawyers to fight for your release, after we sued Wallace for medical negligence, after we *got your sentence commuted*. Now that you've finally been set free, we're finished?"

"Not finished. No. But I think it's time."

"Time for what?"

Sigh. "Time for me to return the favor and set you free."

. . .

Tater sat in the police station watching the officer shovel paper from one side of his desk to the other. He was surprised to see so much paperwork being used in a police station. This was the twenty-first century. Or maybe it was the twentieth century. He honestly couldn't remember which. Either way, he thought everything had gone paperless. Apparently he was wrong.

He remembered sitting in a similar station with his mother long ago. He was maybe six or seven. His mom called 911 to report a domestic disturbance in her household. The cops came and removed his mother, along with Tater and his little brother, Miller. Tater and his brother sat in the police station all day with their battered mother, playing with coloring books, eating microwave popcorn, while Tater's mother filed a report against their daddy.

"Are you Taylor Bunson?" asked the officer.

Tater stood from the bench in the hallway. "That's me."

The officer said the Honda Civic EJ1 had been recovered in a Best Western parking lot. The keys had been in the glove box. The car had been left unlocked. It had a full tank of gas.

"And you say you think you know who stole it?" asked the officer.

Tater glanced through a dividing window into a cluster of cubicles in the next room. He could see a woman on the other side, waiting. She was about his age, sitting on a chair, a few kids with her. And she was pregnant. Her hair was a mess. Her clothes were rags. Her face was bruised.

"No, I don't think it was stolen," said Tater. "I think this was all just a misunderstanding."

"Sounds like more than just a misunderstanding to me."

Tater thought back to the events from the night before. He felt the burden of his own humiliation settling on him.

"It was a friend who stole the car, so it's no big deal."

The officer raised an eyebrow. "A friend?"

"My girlfriend, actually. We kind of got into a fight."

The policeman nodded like it was all making a lot more sense now. The officer tossed the stack of papers onto his desk and folded his hands.

The pregnant woman in the other room was crying before a gaggle of officers surrounded her. A female officer was now sitting beside the woman and consoling her.

The officer said, "It's a felony, stealing a car. You realize that. You have rights here, Mr. Bunson. This was a criminal act, girlfriend or not."

Tater shook his head. "No. It's all good."

The officer waited. "Is it?"

"Yeah. It's fine."

The policeman got a pen from a jar on his desk and clicked it. "What's your girlfriend's name? How about we start there and see where it leads us."

Tater shook his head. "No. I don't want to do that."

The officer apparently got the message and let out a deep breath. "I can't help you if you don't give me something to go on."

"I don't need help. I just want my car back."

The young woman was being led away by the female cop. Her two children were holding hands, following behind the young woman.

"All right, you're the boss," said the officer. "Let's make a copy of your driver's license, and you should be good to go."

The officer spun to and fro in his office chair, making a copy of this, a copy of that. Then the officer reached into an envelope and withdrew a set of car keys. He handed them to Tater, who placed them into his pocket.

When Tater stood to leave, the pregnant young woman in the other room was watching him through the window.

But he was avoiding her eyes.

Chapter 18

———

WOODY BELIEVED THAT EVERY PERSON WAS GIVEN ONE ADVEN-ture in their lifetime. The kind of adventure that changes a person's life. The kind of experience that pierces you, reaches into your core, withdrawing your heart from the cavern of your chest, causing you to examine yourself, causing you to grow. This adventure makes you more human than you ever thought you could be. And it happened when you least expected it. Where it took you was a mystery. But the end result was always the same.

His Ford Ranger sped down the interstate doing an easy seventy-five. Caroline was sitting in the middle, reading a book in a curious position, holding the book far away from her face. Woody's dad was in the passenger seat, sleeping with his head pressed against the window, a string of drool running down his chin and onto his shirt. The gray cat was sleeping in the Major's lap. Gary was on the dashboard, his packet of fish food and bottle of aquarium pH stabilizer beside his jar. They were a mobile PetSmart.

Throughout the entire ride, Caroline had not said more than three words. But Woody watched her when she wasn't looking. He studied her profile, her mannerisms, her body language, her reactions to the world around her. The way she held her head. The way she closed one eye to read. The shape of her nose. The roundness of her youthful features. The way she licked her thumb and forefinger before she turned a page. The way she breathed through her nostrils with a slight sinus whistle.

"Who's going to miss you back home?" Woody asked the girl beside him.

The beautiful mass of red hair shook her head. "Nobody."

"I find that hard to believe."

"My boss will be mad, but that's about all."

"Should we call him?"

"Sexist much? And no, she'll figure it out."

She went back to reading. Her nose was almost grazing the pages.

They passed a few billboards. Cracker Barrel. McDonald's. Chick-fil-A. The Big Three. The interstate was littered with advertisements. One of the most jarring things about leaving prison was all the advertisements. Ads on every flat surface, digital platform, and billboard. Product names plastered on people's clothing. On their shoes. On the bands of their underpants. And ads kept multiplying exponentially as though they were having wild billboard sex every night when the world was asleep and making new ad babies.

"Won't your boyfriend miss you?"

She gave a small, almost nonexistent shrug.

"He the one who did that to your face?"

"I told you, I fell."

"Down a cliff?"

Caroline turned a page.

"I don't mean to harp on it, but you can usually tell whether someone has fallen or not. Your palms are almost always scraped after a serious fall. Especially one that's bad enough to show on your face. It's an evolutionary thing. Your brain gets your hands involved."

"Thanks. I like Wikipedia too."

Woody smiled.

The girl began reading again, holding the book close.

"You're going to strain your eyes."

"Eye," she said. "I'm 80 percent blind in this eye."

"How'd that happen?"

She turned a page. "I was a crack baby."

He looked at her. "Are you serious?"

"The more PC term is drug-addicted infant."

Woody stared out the windshield. He thought about infants he'd seen in the NICU when he was a hospital chaplain in Maryland. He remembered especially the infants suffering from maternal drug-use withdrawal. Neonatal abstinence babies, they called them. The babies had seizures; they cried all the time, using a different pitch than other babies.

She put the book down. "I wouldn't steal your truck, by the way."

"You're too kind."

"No, I mean I'm a horrible driver. I mean, I have my driver's license, but I don't drive much. My boyfriend doesn't like it. I just thought you should know."

"Well, now I know."

"I also have heart issues," she said.

Woody flicked his blinker and changed lanes. "Issues?"

"It's aortic. I had a prosthetic valve replacement to fix it about seven years ago. It's called a congenital condition. That's just medical speak; *congenital* just means I was born with it."

"I'm familiar."

They passed a highway sign with a geographical outline of the sixteenth state that read "Now Leaving Tennessee."

"Anything else I should know?" he said.

Caroline reached into her backpack. She removed a black Glock 9 mm pistol and placed the firearm on the bench seat between them. The safety was on.

"You can have this," she said. "It's not mine. I stole it."

Amos spoke without opening his eyes. "Well, aren't we all just one big happy family."

. . .

BUC-EE'S COUNTRY STORE AND GAS STATION IN ATHENS, ALABAMA, was about the size of a residential school district. There were acres of gas pumps. There must have been two hundred cars and ten times as many people beneath the overhang, pumping gas, eating ice cream, wearing beaver hats, posing for selfies. The man at the pump in front of them was applying a bumper sticker that read "I Heart Buc-ee's Bathrooms."

Woody jammed the parking brake and killed the engine.

"Welcome to heaven," said Amos.

"I've never seen a gas station this big," she said.

"I envy you," said Amos. "Wish I could relive my first time."

Woody jumped out and slammed his door. "The Major likes it here, in case you can't tell."

"It's like being on a cruise ship, except they have beef jerky."

Woody said, "I've got to go pay the water bill. Meet you both back here in ten minutes. Caroline, you have my number in case you need to text me?"

"I don't text," she said.

Woody just looked at her. "You have a religious objection to phones?"

Caroline shook her head. "No, I just don't have one."

"No phone?" said Amos. "Even homeless people have phones."

"Okay," Woody said, "then just shoot your pistol into the air if you need me."

"And let's try not to get lost inside," said Amos. "There's a lot to see. Now get this cat out of my lap and help me out of this seat. My legs are stoved up."

Caroline was not prepared for the full-frontal Buc-ee's experience. Walking into a Buc-ee's was a lot like attending a Tim McGraw concert, only with less teeth. Caroline escorted the eighty-seven-year-old across the store, taking it all in. Buc-ee's was a veritable wonderland of commercial retail space, fast food, and general consumer effluvia that you find at gas stations, only more of it. There were customers from all walks. Rich and poor. Old and young. Wearing anything from Mennonite skirts to thong bikinis.

She and Amos parted ways when they got to the restrooms.

Woody was just emerging from the men's room. "I'll help the Major navigate back through the gauntlet. We'll meet you at the truck."

"Try the fudge," said Amos. "It will change your life."

The restroom was even larger than the sales floor. There were enough stalls to accommodate the urinary needs of the People's Liberation Army of China. And the facilities were so clean you could almost see your reflection in the floor.

She walked up to the sinks. She removed an empty Hellmann's jar from her pack, unscrewed the lid, and filled it with water. She emptied a packet of aquarium pH powder into the water to neutralize the chlorine and fluoride, then gently swirled the water with her finger. After a few minutes, the new water was ready. She scooped Gary from the old jar and plopped him into the new one.

Caroline stared in the mirror. Her gruesome face caught her

off guard. The bruise on her eye was darker than it had been this morning. Her hair reeked of bitter wine. Her lips were even more swollen. She touched her face and felt a wave of humiliation engulf her.

She stared at the redheaded fool. How had this happened in her life? How had she given someone the permission to degrade her like this?

She placed Gary back into her backpack and used one of the restroom stalls. She washed her hands, then used the hand dryer, which was powerful enough to remove skin. She exited the bathroom and wandered through the store, clutching her backpack straps, weaving through clots of customers, hoping nobody would look at her battered face.

When she got to the doors, a bald guy with a thick horseshoe-shaped mustache who was walking inside rushed to hold open the door for her. She walked through the open door and gave him a sincere thank-you.

He gave a dark smile at her as she passed.

"I like your necklace," he said.

Chapter 19

———

THEIR HOTEL ROOMS WERE AT SEPARATE ENDS OF A LONG
hallway with a patterned carpet so hideous it was almost
a violation of human rights. Despite that, it was decent hotel.
Much nicer than the Super 8 where Caroline worked, where most
rooms bore traces of bodily fluid stains on the walls, furniture,
and ceilings.

They all got off the elevator and stood in the hall, everyone
holding their luggage. Amos was cradling the cat against his chest,
stroking its head. Woody had paid fifty bucks extra for the animal.

"Good night to all," said Amos.

"Good night, Dad."

Before Amos headed to his room, he kissed Caroline on the
forehead. Caroline didn't really know what to say. Amos shuffled
down the hall, still carrying the cat and talking to it.

"Are you sharing a room with him?" she asked.

"Are you insane?"

They stared at each other for a beat.

"He took my cat," she said.

"Yeah, sorry. That's not your cat anymore. Dad owns every
cat in South Alabama."

They said good night and parted ways awkwardly but politely.

Her room was nice. Two queens. Both beds facing a window that was overlooking the distant skyline of Birmingham. There was a flatscreen television with a welcome screen that said, "Hi, Caroline!"

She clicked on the bathroom light. The vanity counters were slabs of white granite. The shower looked like a glass-enclosed time machine. You could have fit a Brazilian water polo team in the tub.

She spent a full forty-five minutes beneath the scalding showerhead, letting the torrent of water wash the trauma off her skin. It had been almost a week since she'd used a real shower. Then she donned a complimentary robe and watched television with Gary. *SpongeBob SquarePants* was playing. It was perhaps the greatest show of the twentieth century, created by Stephen Hillenburg, a marine biologist who demanded the show end after its third season, claiming the show had run its course, but Nickelodeon refused, so Hillenburg left the show and *SpongeBob* turned into crap. The first three seasons, however, were nothing short of flawless.

The things you learn in books.

When *SpongeBob* was finished, she scrolled television channels, trying to turn her brain off and forget everything that had happened within the last week. Trying to forget how far away from home she was. She had never left the state of Tennessee before. She had never ventured any farther south than Lenoir City.

She hadn't realized she had fallen asleep until a knock at her door awoke her. It was a heavy knocking. With some authority behind it. Her eyes lazily opened.

Knock, knock!

Caroline forced herself off the bed and lumbered to the door, tightening the belt on her bathrobe.

"Who is it?" she asked.

"America's favorite TV dad."

When she opened the door, she found Woody Barker standing there holding big plastic shopping bags.

"I see you're settling in," he said. Woody extended a plastic bag that bore the name *Carrabba's* on it. "I didn't know what you liked to eat, so I ordered you a little of everything. Hope you like chicken marsala." He also presented her with several Walmart bags.

"What's all this?" she asked.

"Just a few things you might need."

She looked at the bags in her hands.

"You didn't have to do all this. I'm not comfortable accepting charity."

"You're going to be uncomfortable a lot then."

He flashed a low-wattage smile. "Just try not to stay up too late. Big drive tomorrow. There's an ice pack in there. Use it on your face to keep the swelling down."

Woody started to walk away, but she called after him.

He stopped and turned to face her.

"I don't know how to thank you."

"You'll never have to."

• • •

CAROLINE ATE ON THE BED, WITH BATH TOWELS SPREAD BENEATH herself to catch spillage. To be polite, she forced herself to eat her salad. The dessert was tiramisu; no politeness was required to eat that.

After supper, she dumped the contents of the Walmart bags onto the bed and rifled through them. Inside were clothes. Shirts, pants, and maternity wear. Blouses, jumpers, even a pair of jeans with an elastic waistband. Until now, she had not owned a single pair of maternity panties. Now she had four. She didn't know there were males walking the earth who even knew about such things as maternity underwear.

Also inside the bag were shoes. Tennis shoes: white, with pink designs. Amazingly, they were her size. There were socks: three different colors in a multipack. There was an all-in-one toiletry kit, complete with nail clippers, nail file, and two colors of nail polish. There was deodorant, bodywash, and shampoo. And in the bottom of the Walmart bag was another plastic bag, marked AT&T. Inside this bag was a small white cardboard box about the size of a brick and almost as heavy. She removed the box and noticed the Apple logo on the front. Her mouth gaped open when she saw the image of an iPhone printed on the package. She dropped the box. She covered her face with both hands like she was praying. And hot tears fell down her cheeks.

. . .

THE NEXT MORNING CAROLINE FOUND THE GUEST LAUNDRY SERVICES. It was just past the fitness room, where obsessive-compulsives were already on their hamster wheels, doing penance for eating carbs. The laundry room door didn't have a card-key lock, so she walked right in. There were two washing machines and one dryer.

She set the plastic bag on the floor, opened the machine's hatch, and removed the tags from her Walmart clothes with her new nail clippers. She wadded the clothes into a heap and punched them inside the machine, then selected the largest load setting. Caroline placed quarters into the slots and pressed the button. Laundry soap was two dollars, but thankfully someone had left a jug of Tide sitting on the shelf. Small blessings.

She started the washer, then hoisted herself onto the vibrating machine and swung her feet while she played *Bejeweled Blitz* on her phone.

The smells of the complimentary hotel breakfast were fanning through the hotel. She heard voices passing by the laundry room. Old voices. Young voices. Happy voices. Tired voices. Chatty guests on their way to breakfast. Usually she was the one pushing the maid's cart, greeting these guests, asking whether they were checking out.

Her stomach gurgled at the thought of food. She finally withdrew herself from the rapture of her game, clicked off her phone, and decided to go to the lobby. Caroline leapt off the washing machine, tucked her phone into her back pocket, and checked the washing machine. But she never made it out the door because a smooth-scalped man with a horseshoe mustache was entering at the same time she was exiting.

Chapter 20

WOODY BARKER WAS FILLING HIS FOURTH CUP OF COFFEE when he saw Caroline wander into the laundry room at the end of the hall. She was already wearing the new rust-colored maternity jumper he'd bought from Walmart. The color went well with her red hair. Woody's mother would never let him wear anything rust colored when he was a boy; she said it clashed with his hair. But Woody disagreed. He felt rust belonged as the fourth member of the trifecta of appointed redheaded apparel colors: green, white, and blue.

Caroline had been too busy staring at her phone to notice him. Which both warmed him and scared him.

Woody knew that phones were the downfall of modern civilization. Not only because of what phones were doing to our brains (an average American checks their phone three hundred fifty times per day) but because of what smartphones were doing to our mortality rate. Phones were dangerous. Upward of 1.6 million automotive crashes per year were caused by phones. And last year texting while walking resulted in eleven thousand injuries and five thousand deaths in the US alone, with 70 percent of those injured being women under age twenty-five. Not to mention what they do to your focus and attention span. You become so accustomed to switching between tasks that during normal activities, your lizard brain says to you, out of a blue sky, *You need to check your phone.*

But here's the thing. You needed a phone to function in this world. You need a phone to do everything from paying your power bill to scheduling a hair appointment. And you can't pull over and buy a map at a gas station anymore because they don't sell maps. Everyone uses GPS.

He topped off his cup. The coffee had already started to sour his stomach. He'd spent half the morning vomiting in the toilet because of the new meds to stabilize him in hopes of a transplant. He was reading a complimentary copy of *USA Today* when a man wandered past him, heading down the hall. The man had a thick cowboy mustache. A Saint Louis Cardinals T-shirt. Ostrich skin boots. Woody noticed the man's determined gait before noticing anything else. Like he had somewhere to be. It wasn't a hotel walk. The man's walk was an airport walk. A subway station walk. Quick and purposeful.

Woody put down the paper and watched.

You learn to identify troublemakers when you live with them in a giant concrete box. You learn to see them before they see you. It's self-preservation. You learned how to stay away from trouble-makers. Their swagger was unmistakable. A limber gait. Torso erect. Hands and arms loose. An invisible chip on the shoulder. Woody also noticed the irregular bulge in the man's lower back, beneath his shirt, just above the waistband.

The man reached the end of the hall and entered the laundry facility.

Woody took a sip of his scalding coffee. It was so hot it burned the roof of his mouth, but he managed to swallow it. It felt good going down and actually seemed to be settling his stomach.

Woody found it odd that the man had not been carrying a laundry bag. No dirty clothes either. No laundry soap. Also the man had pulled the door shut. Which was also unusual. Most people let a hydraulic door close behind them on its own.

Woody waited for someone to reemerge. It was basic human behavior.

A seventeen-year-old girl would not have wanted to share such a tiny room with a middle-aged guy. Too awkward. Too weird. She would have exited first. Unless, of course, the guy was just picking up his clean laundry. In which case, the guy would have taken a total of thirty seconds to grab his clean clothes and come out. Guys were not big folders.

And even if he had been a folder, Caroline would not have stayed to watch him fold; that would have been double creepy.

Someone should be coming out of the small room.

But nobody did.

Woody checked his watch. One hundred and twenty-three seconds had gone by, and Saint Louis Cardinals guy was still in there.

Woody stood up and made his way toward the laundromat.

• • •

WOODY QUIETLY UNLATCHED THE LAUNDROMAT DOOR AND FOUND Cardinals Shirt Guy had Caroline pinned against the wall with his elbow compressing her throat. The man had nearly lifted her off her feet and only her toes were touching the ground. "Where is it?" he growled at her. "Tell me."

Woody whistled at him. Like calling a horse. The man turned, but only for a split second. It was all the time Woody needed.

"Howdy, Tex," said Woody.

The guy turned to look at Woody just in time to see a wall

of blistering coffee flying into his open eyes. The coffee hissed against the man's skin as he screamed. The guy released Caroline and clutched his face and let out a deafening roar.

Woody boxed the man's ears, then used the butt of his palm to deliver a shot to the larynx. It was dirty fighting, but it was the only fighting style Woody had learned.

The man fell to his knees. Woody placed his own knee on the man's shoulders and forced the man's arm behind his back in a rear wristlock, but the guy rolled from beneath him and somehow gained the upper hand.

Cardinals Guy leapt to his feet and tackled Woody, pressing Woody's birdlike shoulders against the floor. He started slamming his fists into Woody's face. Woody felt his nose sustain full impact. His chin took the next hit. Then his jaw. Then he heard something give way in his cheek area, and it sounded like crumpling potato chips.

"Stop it!" shouted Caroline.

The man just kept pommeling Woody.

"Please, stop!"

Caroline threw open the door and shouted for help.

One of the first things you learn in prison is that you are not made of paper mâché. Prison fights happen daily. Hourly. Minutely. They are rarely over material goods; they're about prison politics. Respect, fairness, loyalty, or what's playing on the rec room TV. The thing about getting hit: It doesn't hurt as bad as you expect. A lot of new guys are afraid of getting hit. They abandon the fight early because they don't want to get messed up. But if you lean into it, you realize it's not the end of the world. He'd almost forgotten how it felt to be hit. It hurt. But in a familiar way. It was almost like meeting an old friend.

He threw a knee into the guy's groin. The man let out a

moan, but wasn't hurt enough to let up. The guy was built like a beer keg. Arms like sequoias. Shoulders like an oxen yoke. The man reached into his waistband and removed a pistol. He placed it beneath Woody's jaw and jammed it upward into his hyoid bone.

The guy said, "Wrong move, old man."

Woody spit blood. "Respect your elders, sonny."

In one quick move, Woody used his thumb to dig into the guy's eye sockets. When his thumb was inserted into the eye socket and touched the soft flesh near the corner of the eye, Woody pushed even harder, until he felt the eyeball give way. Like mashing a strawberry. The guy screamed like a mezzo-soprano. There are other things you learn in prison too.

The guy's body finally went limp. Woody dropped him. The man wallowed on the floor, clutching his face. He was whimpering now, making animal sounds.

"You okay?" he said to Caroline.

Woody's world was turning black around him. Everything was spinning.

"I'm all right," she said.

Several men entered the laundry room. Caroline's attacker continued rolling on the tile, moaning.

"What in the world is going on in here?" said a guy in a polo shirt, a gilded badge on his shirt bearing his name and the hotel logo.

People were shouting. Others were tending to the hurt man on the floor.

Woody touched his battered nose. It was numb with pain. His whole chest fluttered. His limbs were becoming heavy. He was lightheaded. And he couldn't breathe. He closed his eyes for a moment and felt that he might tip over. He could hear

Caroline talking to him, but her voice seemed to be coming from all around him. Like an echo chamber.

"Are you okay?" said Caroline.

"I've changed my mind," he said. "You can have your gun back."

Chapter 21

———

A ND MAKE SURE YOU EAT ALL THE FRUIT I PACKED FOR YOU," said Elizabeth. "Not just some of it. You need the fiber."

The car line at Saint John of the Cross Episcopal Elementary was long, with vehicles backing up into the main highway, stretching northward through town, approaching Canada. Elizabeth was about to drop off Rachel for school, delivering her pre-school briefing. Today the fourth-grade class was going on a field trip to the Wildlife Center in Mobile. Elizabeth was reminding her daughter to apply the SPF 2,950 sunscreen she packed, eat *all the fruit* in her lunch bag, and use the bathroom *before* boarding the bus so Rachel didn't suffer a humiliating event like on the last field trip.

Elizabeth's diatribe was interrupted when her phone rang. It was Woody. She answered the phone quickly.

"Hey," she said. "Can I call you back in two seconds? I'm in the carpool line."

The voice was not Woody's.

"Is this Woodrow Barker's wife?"

It was a man's voice. Official sounding.

"Yes," she said. "Well. I mean, no."

"Ma'am, this number was in his phone under 'wife.' I need to speak with his wife, please."

"I'm his ex-wife. Who am I speaking with?"

"This is Robert, Metro EMS, Birmingham. Do you know how I can get in touch with his current wife?"

Elizabeth was watching Rachel, who was still sitting in the passenger seat. The little girl was sorting through the fruit in her lunch bag like she was handling jars of warm sputum.

"He doesn't have a current wife. What's going on?"

"He's fine. He's just got some cuts and bruises."

She shifted the phone to her other ear. "What?"

The man broke up. The static voice said, ". . . most likely a heart attack, but he's coherent, and he's refusing treatment so . . ."

She spoke loudly into the phone. "You're breaking up. Heart attack?"

More static. "Apparently he got into a fight."

Elizabeth was mute for a few moments. Staring out her windshield.

"Who was he fighting with?"

"I'm sorry, ma'am, your phone keeps cutting out."

"I asked, *who was he fighting with?*"

"Sorry, ma'am, I can't hear you, but we're on our way to UAB. You can see him there if you want. He keeps asking for someone named Elizabeth."

"That's me. I am Elizabeth."

Another crackle of static.

"Hello? Are you still there? Is he going to be okay?"

"Yes, ma'am," the voice replied. "He's going to be just fine. He's a hoss. You should see the other guy. Don't worry about him. He's got his daughter beside him."

Chapter 22

WOODY'S DAD HAD TAKEN A PICTURE OF HIS FACE AND SHOWED it to him on his phone. His face was a rainbow of reds and violets and blacks. His nose was an eggplant. The officers had been questioning him all morning in the ER, and they kept calling him Father, probably because he still carried clergy identification in his wallet.

Woody could hardly focus on a single train of thought. He knew his mind was wandering because he had a concussion. Other symptoms were dizziness and vomiting. Both of which he also had. He had learned a lot about concussions over the years.

The ice pack against his face was making his headache worse. He wasn't able to give the police many details. His clarity was coming back to him, albeit slowly. And the officers realized they were only making things worse by asking questions. They wrapped up their interview and let him alone. They went outside to question Caroline next.

Woody leaned back into the bed and closed his eyes. Another hour disappeared, but it felt like only a couple seconds. He wasn't processing time in a normal way. Time seemed to rush forward, then slow to a mere crawl.

When he opened his eyes again, the clock said he'd been

asleep for two hours. The whole world felt vaguely like a dream. He wasn't even sure whether he was technically awake.

Beside his bed, Caroline was sitting in the chair. He could see her pinkened eyes. She had been crying.

"Do I look *that* good?" he said.

"They said you might have had a heart attack."

He shook his head. "Yeah, but I didn't."

"How do you know?"

"Because I took nitroglycerin pills, and I felt fine in the heart department. I know what a heart attack feels like; that wasn't it." He removed the ice pack from his head; it was melted. "I was low on oxygen, that's all. I passed out. Where's the Major?"

"Who?"

"The octogenarian."

"Your dad's in the cafeteria. They have an ice cream bar."

"We'll never see him again."

Woody used his hands to sit upright. His head felt like a bowling ball. He used his tongue to probe his teeth. His front teeth were loose but still holding. His jaw, however, felt like a mule had kicked him with its hind legs.

"They said you popped that guy's eyeball out of its socket."

Woody shrugged. "He was a Cardinals fan."

He realized he was seeing double.

"Where did you learn to fight like that?"

"Seminary."

He looked out the sliding glass door of his room. The police were still outside, gathered in a little cluster. They were having a long discussion, comparing notes. Talking into radios, pushing buttons on iPads. Wearing chest-mounted cameras.

He looked at her.

"Are we finally going to talk now?" he asked. "You going to tell me what that was all about?"

"I told the police all I know."

"Great, now how about telling me."

She shrugged, stammered, and kept looking away. "Some guy came into the laundry room and attacked me. I don't know anything else."

He nodded. "Perfect. Now can you practice saying that without staring at your shoes?"

"I'm being honest with you."

"You were attacked in broad daylight. That man defiled my nose. You're carrying a firearm without a serial number. So I'm going to need you to put on your big-girl pants and explain to me exactly what's going on."

Woody swung his feet off the bed and forced himself to stand. Blood rushed from his head and he felt dizzy. He also needed to vomit.

"Are you hurt?" she asked.

"I'm going to pretend like you didn't just ask that."

She came to support him as he struggled to his feet.

"Start talking," he said.

Caroline fell into default silent mode.

He folded his arms and waited. They had a blinking contest. Which was fine. Woody was good at blinking contests. He could go a long time without blinking. Yes, it hurt a little, but victory was sweet.

"It's a complicated story," she finally said.

"It's okay. I'm smart."

She went quiet again.

"I don't want to talk in here," she said.

He flicked his eyes around the room, then yanked the heart monitor electrodes and suction cups from his hairy chest. "Have it your way. I'm discharging myself, and we get to continue our fantastic road trip of discovery and paternal bonding." He tore

another sticky pad from the freshly shaved patch on his chest.
"How bad of a driver are you?"

"What do you mean?"

"I wasn't speaking Greek."

"Well, I have my driver's license."

"That's not what I asked."

Chapter 23

——

WHEN AMOS BARKER JOINED THE ARMY, HE WAS A TWENTY-year-old without a single strand of chest hair and a high-tenor voice that hadn't dropped. He'd had exactly one girlfriend in his entire life. She didn't want to marry him because he had no money and even fewer prospects at being successful. And in Hamilton, Alabama, back in the 1950s, girls did not marry for love; they married for status. When Sandra Sue Minson broke his heart, she did it gingerly. She explained herself in the front seat of Amos's '48 Fleetline. She was trying to let him down easy, but instead Sandra spoke to him as though talking to a toddler.

Two days later, Amos was in an army recruiter's office, sign-ing his name to a piece of government paper, listening to the official army spiel about how great the US Army was. In those days, the army highlighted world travel as their main selling point. The recruiter told Amos he would visit the finest beaches on the globe, eat the most exotic foods, and kiss the prettiest international girls, all on Uncle Sam's dime. A week later, he was in a bus that smelled like sweaty feet, bound for boot camp at Fort Knox, Kentucky, Armor School. One year and three months later, he was snugly seated in the driver's seat of an M48 Patton with the Eleventh Armored Cavalry.

Driving became his life. Driving was all you did as a tank operator.

It was misery. Temperatures inside the tank could reach 130 degrees Fahrenheit. You spent weeks breathing in ammunition smoke, diesel fumes, and the smell of your four crewmen's armpits. The exhaustion from sleep deprivation was overwhelming. Each hour of tank operation required about three hours of maintenance. So when you weren't driving, you were lifting or hauling something made of steel. The US government claimed both of Amos's knees, two of his spinal discs, and three-quarters of his hearing.

The Ford was doing eighty-eight down the interstate with Caroline behind the wheel, using a two-hand grip, constantly swinging her attention left and right, like she said her driver's ed instructor had shown her. She looked like a dog watching a tennis match.

Currently, Amos Barker sat in the center of the bench seat beside her, talking her through the finer points of interstate combat. Woody sat in the passenger seat half conscious, with an ice pack pressed against his face.

"You don't have to drive so fast," Amos said. "I think we've all had enough thrills for one day. How about keeping it below eighty-eight?"

"Why aren't *you* the one driving?" Caroline asked. "You're obviously a better driver than I am."

"Honey, I'm on enough medication to tranquilize an elephant. Now, slow down; I don't want to die young."

"But you're not young."

"I've decided whatever age I am is the new thirty."

Caroline reduced speed and fell in behind a truck in the left lane. It was an Amazon truck doing seventy. She was eating his bumper.

"And you might not want to ride that truck's ass so hard. If this guy taps his brakes, they'll be burying us in Amazon crates."

"Sorry."

Amos patted her thigh. "Quit apologizing to me."

"Right," she said. "Sorry."

Amos used to drive a lot. He loved driving. Back in his childhood, families used to get in the car and go for drives. It was an American pastime. But when he hit eighty-four, he fell. One brain surgery later, his driving days were over.

"I have to use the restroom," said Amos. "Pull over at the first exit."

"Okay."

She flipped her blinker and took the off-ramp with incredible poise.

"Where do you want to go to the bathroom?" she asked.

"A toilet would be nice."

Both of her hands were still firmly affixed to the wheel. "I mean, where should I pull over?"

"Sweetie, I have a prostate the size of a cantaloupe, so anywhere will do."

"Find somewhere to eat," said Woody, his voice muffled with the ice pack. "I'm hungry."

"Where do you want to eat?"

"Your choice," said Woody.

When they got to the edge of town, Caroline pulled into a McDonald's parking lot.

"This is where you want to go?" Woody asked. "Out of all the places in this town, you chose McDonald's?"

"Why? You don't like McDonald's?"

"No. McDonald's is good."

"Park this truck right now."

"I can choose somewhere else."

"No, this is fine."

"Park this truck or we're all going to drown."

Caroline swung the truck wheel into a parking space with the screech of rubber. The front tire slammed into the parking barrier and the grille rammed the thirty-minute parking sign. Amos flew forward out of his seat and almost collided with the windshield.

"I'm so sorry," said Caroline.

"Everyone all right?" asked Woody.

Amos crawled back into his seat. "Good news is, I don't need to use the bathroom anymore."

• • •

THE THREE OF THEM ENTERED THE UNIQUELY AMERICAN INSTItution that smells of hydrogenated soybean oil, shoestring-cut Russet potatoes, and Pine-Sol, and waited in a short line. The young cashier watched them all approach the register. The young man behind the register was intently looking at Woody's beat-up face.

"Cut myself shaving," Woody explained.

The cashier turned to Caroline, who also had a black eye, a busted lip, and bruised cheeks. "I was the one shaving him," she said.

Woody ordered a Big Mac. Amos ordered the twelve-piece chicken nuggets. Caroline ordered a kid's meal with double fries, an order of nuggets, a large chocolate McFlurry with Oreos, Heath crumbles, Butterfingers, and one hot apple pie. "And," she added, "I'll have a Mountain Dew."

The cashier gawked at her tummy. "How many months along are you?"

She smiled. "Oooh, I like this game. Is it my turn to comment on your body?"

Amos was smiling. "No flies on her."

They found a table in the back. Caroline decimated the kid's meal. Then she started in on Amos's fries. The old man watched in wonder as she ate.

"Slow down," said Amos. "You're going to choke."

She took a pull of her McFlurry. "I'm building a human."

"You sure you're not building triplets?" Woody opened his burger and looked at it. After a few seconds, he pushed his burger away, untouched.

The Major wore a quizzical expression. "Not hungry?"

"Chewing hurts too bad. Plus, I shouldn't be eating beef or cheese. I'm supposed to be vegan. I promised Elizabeth."

"Vegan?"

"We're from the planet Vega."

"I know what a vegan is," said Amos. "But why?"

"I have a deeply emotional connection to dairy cows."

Caroline looked at them both. "Are you two always such smart alecks?"

Woody and his dad exchanged glances.

"Yes."

He watched Caroline eating the fries. "Why did you order the kid's meal?" he asked.

"Why not?"

"Well, for starters, you're an adult." Woody gestured to her meal.

"There's no rule for Happy Meals. You don't have to be a kid to order them."

"Maybe not, but you clearly eat more than one of Ronald Mc-Donald's Crumb McSnatchers."

She paused to lick a finger. "I have a kid inside me."

"I would ask how far along you are, but I don't want you to neuter me like you did the cashier."

"Nine months. When I was in foster care," Caroline said, "we came to McDonald's every Friday. All the fosters got free meals at McDonald's, so it was a big deal. It was like getting out of prison for us."

"How long were you in foster care?" Amos asked.

"All my life, off and on."

"Where was your mom?"

"Rehab, usually. Or off living with some guy. I lost count how many boyfriends she had after the fifth one. DCS kept sending me to live with Mr. Butch and Miss Anne Ryans over the years; that's where I lived the longest. They were weird. They made you read the Bible every day, you couldn't wear shorts or skirts, you couldn't cut your hair, and if you said the words *gosh* or *jeez*, you got whipped with a skinny stick. Really religious. There were fifteen or sixteen fosters in their house at one time."

"Fun people."

She laughed. "They were pretty cool, mostly. Mr. Butch knew we loved going to McDonald's, so he never skipped. I have a lot of memories in dining rooms like this."

Woody smiled. "You are a McDonald's evangelist."

"I guess."

"You could have gotten more than one Happy Meal, you know."

She shrugged. "One is enough. It just reminds me of Fridays. Fridays were everything to me."

"Because of Happy Meals?"

"No, because Fridays were like having a real family."

Woody's heart began to ache. And this ache had nothing to do with an aortic valve.

Chapter 24

"WELCOME TO GULF BEACH, ALABAMA." THAT WAS WHAT THE sign said. It was a bas-relief carved cedar slab that read "Voted One of America's 100 Best Small Towns." Woody always had wanted to know what the other ninety-nine towns were. What was the criterion of being elected one of America's best small towns? What made Gulf Beach better than, say, Stowe, Vermont? Or Avalon, California? Or Valentine, Nebraska? Who made the final decision? Was it a vote? Woody wanted to know about the democratic process involved. He had questions.

When Woody was a kid, Gulf Beach had been a remote place of white dunes, sea oats, block houses, cedar-shingled beach shacks, mildewed fishing boats, and mom-and-pop joints without A/C. There was one barbecue place. Two seafood shacks. One supermarket called the Jitney Jungle that closed for one month each January. It was a small town. There were nine hundred residents in the winter.

If that.

Today, however, Gulf Beach was Six Flags over Jimmy Buffet. Everywhere you looked there were fourteen-story condos, hundred-acre entertainment complexes, Publix supermarkets, and scores of T-shirt shops selling everything from live alligators to custom groinal tattoos written in Sanskrit. The population of Gulf Beach was currently 310,000. An estimated 4 million tourists moved through the county every year, resulting in $2.9 billion in direct spending. Woody's hometown had been replaced with a land-based Carnival cruise ship.

Caroline was driving slowly through town but not saying much. There was a lot to see. When she caught her first glimpse of the beach, she oohed and aahed. She said it was the first time she had ever seen the beach.

Next, Woody directed her down Clearfield Avenue, where all the historic houses were located. People waved at him. Amos explained briefly to her who the waving people were, whether they were related and why they were insane.

They drove by the little hospital where Woody had been born. And the old Episcopal church.

He pointed through the windshield. "And there's Saint John's."

Saint John of the Cross Episcopal stood proudly in a large copse of magnolias. It was small, as churches go, although the steeple was tall and could be seen from the interstate. The white board and batten were freshly painted. The red door was bright, traditionally signifying that all travelers were welcome inside no matter their race or creed as long as they weren't Democrats.

"You were the priest here?" she asked.

"Once."

"Why not anymore?"

Amos cleared his throat and changed the subject.

When they arrived at the Bald Point Marina, she pulled into the gravel parking area. There weren't many cars around. There were only six full-time residents at Bald Point. Each month renters had to chip in, paying above and beyond their annual slip fees to keep the place going. But they did it cheerfully because Bald

Point represented the Old Gulf Coast, and if this land went to market, some godless real estate developer would sweep it up and build a nightclub, a strip bar, or worse, a Chipotle.

"What is this place?" Caroline asked.

"Home sweet home."

"You live here?"

The *Ship Happens* sat in the distance. She was bare wood with two old paddle wheels, blackened with age. She looked like a defunct cargo riverboat because that was what she was.

Caroline put the truck in Park and stared at the boat. The young woman looked at Woody with a flicker of excitement in her eyes. A flicker he had not seen before.

"You actually live on the ocean?" she asked.

"No," said Woody. "I live on the bay."

"Aren't they the same thing?"

"Only if you're from Tennessee," said Amos. "Now, everyone get out of the car. I can't feel my butt cheeks anymore."

Everyone piled out of the truck onto weary legs. Woody stretched his sore body and noticed someone sitting on the sundeck of the *Happens*. Elizabeth. The black-haired woman was striking, even from a distance. The vision of her was arresting not only to his heart but to his spirit. She was a Renoir come to life. One part woman, the other part permanent girl.

Elizabeth descended the gangway, debarking the *Happens*, with Rachel in tow. She walked toward his truck quickly, and by her gait, Woody knew she was clearly not in a beautiful mood.

"Who's that?" Caroline asked.

"That," Amos said, "is General Tecumseh Sherman."

Chapter 25

―――

S HE LOOKS JUST LIKE YOU," ELIZABETH SAID.
He sat on one of the loungers on the topmost sundeck.
It was just the two of them. Except for all the power tools and
extension cords.

"I know," he said.

"She looks more like you than Rachel does."

Woody did not respond.

Elizabeth was sitting on a lounge chair, facing him, her knees
pressed so tightly together she could have cracked diamonds.

"So that's what you were doing in Tennessee? Meeting up
with your daughter?"

"Knoxville."

"But you got beat up in Birmingham."

"I get around."

She used a pinky to dab her eye. Woody could not tell if she
was crying or fixing her makeup. Or perhaps both.

"And why did this man attack you?"

"No idea."

"Surely you must know something."

He shrugged. "Jehovah's Witnesses can get very angry. And don't call me Shirley."

A seagull landed on the railing. Woody often fed them while working on the sundeck, which made the *Happens* a popular spot in the seagull community. Which was also why the sundeck was littered with prodigious smatterings of seagull gratitude.

"Do you always have to be such a smart ass?"

"I'm not so sure about the smart part."

They could hear the happy voice of Rachel below deck. His nine-year-old daughter's footsteps resounded throughout the vessel like falling cinder blocks. The kid did not know how to do anything softly. It was the first time he had seen her this animated. Apparently she had always wanted a big sister.

"So," Woody went on, "did you and Jason finally get your kitchen repainted?"

She whipped her eyes at him. "Do *not* start with me. Especially when you were across the country visiting your baby mama." Elizabeth got up and walked to the edge of the sundeck to look at the bay.

The seagull was squawking at him. *Get in line*, Woody thought.

More than anything, he wanted to rush toward Elizabeth, take her in his arms, and feel her against him. He wanted to breathe her in and tell her everything. To tell her that she was his reason. To tell her about the numerous nights in his cell; dark nights, when he had entertained the idea of securing his own eternal peace. To tell her that it was always her lovely face that brought him back.

"So what happens next?" Elizabeth asked.

He held out both hands. "Playing it by ear."

"You're just going to, what, let this girl live with you?"

"Her name is Caroline."

Silence.

"You need to take a paternity test," she said.

"I think you should go look at her again."

He removed a cigar from his pocket. Elizabeth watched him light the smoke with disgust. She shook her head slowly as though she were trying to wish the cigar away. And him.

"I don't get it." She touched her chest. "You're cutting me out of your life, but you're going to let her in?"

"She doesn't have a Jason."

Woody wished he could've swallowed the words before they had been said. And yet he felt sour bile rising to the surface. Elizabeth had waited exactly three days after his release to tell him she was seeing someone.

"You can't let her live here. She's a stranger."

"Okay. Should I drop her off at Walmart with a tin cup and a cardboard sign saying, 'Anything helps'?"

She looked away.

"Did you ever think to ask me what I thought about this? I'm still in your life, you know."

"For how long? I have no life. I'm dying, Liz."

"Why do you keep saying that?" Elizabeth closed her eyes. She was definitely crying now.

"The paramedics called and said you'd had a heart attack in Birmingham. You wouldn't return my calls. You wouldn't text." She was yelling now. "I had no idea whether you were lying in a bed with a tag on your toe. I'm trying to help you. But I can't do this anymore, Woody. It's not fair."

"Is this the part where you tell me you want a divorce?"

She swore at him through tears.

The seagull flew away.

"You're in no position to take on raising a kid. You can't even take care of yourself. You've only been out for a few months. Your life is a wreck. This boat is a wreck. There are tools everywhere. This is no place for a kid."

"Caroline is not a kid."

"News flash: She's *carrying* a kid. Do you know how much it costs to have a baby?"

Woody thought back. He remembered exactly where he was when they told him Rachel had been born. He was working in the prison laundry room, washing linens and bath towels, soaking them in a vat of bleach and lye to kill the parasites.

"Put yourself in her shoes," Woody said. "This young woman has nobody but me. She needs me. You don't."

Elizabeth moved toward the stanchions and looked out at the water. She wiped her face a few more times, then drew in a large breath. Woody knew what questions were coming next. He braced for them.

"How old is she?" she asked.

"Does it matter?"

"How old?"

"You served me divorce papers eighteen years ago. If you'll recall, the sheriff came to the parsonage and put the papers in my hand."

"How. Old?"

"Irreconcilable differences, that's what the papers said. You don't think that hit me like a bolt? You said you were done with me; you said all I did was work. Your mother told me you were already seeing someone else."

"Tell me how old she is."

"Seventeen."

Elizabeth just looked at him. "I have to go."

Chapter 26

———

WOODY AND ELIZABETH HAD ELOPED. IT WAS ALL WOODY'S idea. He had not wanted a church wedding. He'd been to enough church weddings. He wanted something simple. Something easy. She agreed inasmuch as the idea of having bridesmaids and banquets always seemed so juvenile to her. She didn't have anyone to *be* her bridesmaids. In high school she had been largely friendless. In college it was the same thing. Instead of slumber parties or joyriding with the girls, Elizabeth had preferred to go antique hunting, or finding estate sales in the paper, or looking for vintage wear.

Her mother hated this. She wanted her daughter to be normal. Whatever *normal* was.

Elizabeth shut the car off.

She had pulled onto the sandy shoulder of the beach highway. It was dark. Rachel was at her mom's tonight, and Elizabeth was scheduled to work the late shift.

The night was cool but not cold. The moon was shaped like a volleyball, staring at her. She took off her shoes, rolled up the pantlegs of her scrubs, and walked to the shoreline. She stood in the gulf water up to her ankles. Each new breaking wave washed ut the sand from beneath her feet, lowering her another inch

out the sand from beneath her feet, lowering her another inch into the water.

After working for several years at an antique store, she enrolled in community college when she was twenty-two. In the college's four-year nursing program. College was not easy for Elizabeth. It wasn't that she was stupid; it was that she found it hard to care about all the classes the college forced her to take before she could approach her actual degree. It was just a way for colleges to bleed students of more cash, making them read books written by dead Russian guys, forcing them to plot vectors in three dimensional spaces, and compelling them to memorize meaningless words such as, for example, *cosine*.

The electives were even worse. She tried pottery, but the teacher was a weird, pervy guy who would sit behind female students like Patrick Swayze from *Ghost*. She took a photography class. The professor said Elizabeth's artistic style could loosely be referred to as Kmart Senior Portrait. But during her second year, she took a world religion class on a whim. She wasn't religious. Her parents weren't religious; they were just Methodist. But something drew her interest.

The course was taught by a priest. He was fortyish, shaggy hair, honest face. Cigar burns on his trousers. There wasn't anything about him she didn't like. He was a hopeless wisecrack. He was clever. He made the entire classroom laugh. He spoke about the Dharma of Buddhism. Taoism. The Five Pillars of Islam. Catholicism. Tribalism. Animism. And all the other -isms. His lectures were passionate, moving, and on occasion he would work himself into tears.

It was Elizabeth who asked him on their first date. She walked into his office, bold and brazen. She sat down and said that she had been thinking a lot about it, and, well, she wanted to take him out to dinner because she really thought they could be great friends.

His reaction was to laugh at her, not diminutively, but kindly. "You want to take *me* to dinner?"

"As a friend."

He turned her down. Twice. But he agreed to lunches together in the common area. They did become friends. Close friends. They talked to each other. Really talked. Soon it was more than lunches. They spent hours on the phone. Hours in secluded restaurant booths. Each day they passed each other in the hallways, and she would say something witty to him and he'd respond in kind. In public they mostly communicated in phony insults, with lots of smiles.

"I didn't come here to be insulted," he'd say in the hallway as they passed.

"Well then, where do you usually go?" she'd say.

They were Burns and Allen. Say good night, Gracie.

Elizabeth walked farther into the water. The water was lapping against her bare shins, saturating her scrubs bottoms. The icy temperature was making her lower legs numb. But it felt nice to be numb. Numb was good. She could see a few boats in the distance. Big yachts, their running lights on. Who actually lived aboard those things? And what the heck did they do all day?

One day she arrived early to world religion class and Woody wasn't there. Someone else was teaching. Some fat guy with a goatee. They said Woody had been promoted from supply priest to head priest. They were giving him a church in Lubbock, Texas. He had resigned from his post at the college, effective immediately.

And so it was that same evening she showed up on Woody's porch on Campbell Street. It was raining. And Elizabeth was drenched. Looking back, it could have been a romantic scene from some straight-to-DVD Nicholas Sparks movie. Only it wasn't. Instead, it was awful. Her pink rayon top was soaked so that it was translucent. Her skirt was ruined. Her shoes were falling apart. Woody answered the door to find her sopping wet, trying to cover herself so he couldn't see her undergarments. "You son of a nutcracker!" were her first words to him. "Why didn't you tell me you were leaving?"

So things were going great.

Within ten minutes, Woody had delivered her back to her parents' house wearing a pair of his cowboy-print pajamas and a terrycloth robe. This went over swimmingly well with Elizabeth's mom. The next month, Elizabeth moved to Lubbock, got an apartment, and took a job waiting tables at a Mexican joint. She enrolled in South Plains College. They were married eight months later.

She reached into the pocket of her scrubs for her phone to check the time. What had happened to the girl she used to be? Where was that girl today? Did the girl just disappear? Did Elizabeth suffocate her with adulthood? Where had all that innocence gone? How had her experiences taught her to be so cynical and cautious? Why did she hurt so badly inside right now? And how could she make it stop?

She went to her phone contacts and made a call. Jason answered.

"Did I wake you up?" she asked.

"No." His voice was groggy. "Long day. What is it, babe?"

She stared at the black gulf.

"I want to elope."

Chapter 27

—

THE BLACK TOYOTA SUV SAT PARKED AT THE GULF BEACH Walmart. Idling. Air conditioner running. Tourists came and went by the hundreds, doing their shopping for spring break week. It was easy to separate the tourists from the locals at Walmart. The tourists were the only ones not wearing employee vests.

Peter watched the tourists walk into Walmart. There was real purpose in their strides. They entered empty-handed and left with a Vesuvius of food in their carts, along with an overflow of cheap beach paraphernalia to last them for six days of unmitigated condo-induced orgasm.

Peter lowered his binoculars. He'd gotten out of police custody early that same morning. Within two hours, he had spoken with his contacts, who told him Caroline was last seen in the front seat of a beat-up Ford Ranger, heading for Gulf Beach, Alabama. Within three hours, Peter was traveling ninety on I-65 with three other men in the vehicle armed with a license plate number and a general route.

An eye patch covered one of Peter's eyes, a trail of eye fluid seeping from beneath the patch. But at least he would not lose the eye. The doctor said it would heal. Peter's pride, however, was another matter entirely.

"Americans consume more than we produce," he said to his fellow patriots in the SUV. "Did you know that?"

The rest of the guys in the vehicle did not know. Nor did they care. They were too busy checking out the girls walking in and out of Walmart.

"In China, they don't have this problem," Peter said. "The Chinese produce more than they consume. So do Canadians. Even Mexico produces more than it consumes."

One of the guys said, "That must be why so many Mexicans swim across the Rio Grande."

Everyone laughed.

Everyone except Peter.

"Our nation is losing its power status because of how much we *consume*. Do you understand me? This country will go under not because of war, not because of foreign attack, but because we have to have our flatscreens and dryer sheets."

"Hey, I like dryer sheets."

Laughter.

"You wouldn't understand," said Peter. "You can't see the forest because you're too busy cutting it down."

They were all looking out the windows. The young guys had high-powered SLR digital cameras. But Peter used old-school binoculars. Which might as well have been a telescope with his bad eye.

The first thing Peter should have done when getting the USB-C drive in his possession was make a copy of it. The golden rule in his business was back *everything* up, and he had violated this rule. To make matters worse, he hadn't had a chance to look at the flash drive before Crystal swiped it, so he knew almost nothing about the contents, which infuriated him. Being kept in the dark was not Peter's preferred position.

"Here he comes," said one guy.

Peter and his comrades trained their lenses and 30mm binoculars at the Walmart door. An older guy emerged from Walmart pushing a cart full of plastic bags. His face was bruised. He was looking through the bags as he walked. Checking the receipt.

"*He's* the one?" asked one of the guys. "That's the one who popped Peter's eyeball out?"

"I thought you said he was a fighter."

"He don't look like no fighter."

"Where's the girl with the goldfish?" asked a young guy.

Peter squeezed his binoculars so hard the lenses creaked. "Everyone take your pictures and shut up."

The sounds of the camera shutters filled the vehicle with clicking and chattering. They watched the man step into a clap-trap truck. The tailpipe coughed a cloud of exhaust.

"What do we know about him?" asked Peter.

One of the guys flipped through a stack of printed pages.

"He was married to Melinda for eleven years. He did a dime at Wallace Correctional Facility outside Mobile. Spent four months in an infirmary after breaking another inmate's jaw. It says here that he is a former priest."

The car went silent.

They all watched the former priest roll down his window. He flicked a Zippo and began puffing on a cigar.

"*He* did time?" asked Peter.

"A priest?"

"I cannot believe that a priest kicked your ass," said one troublemaker.

The others stifled laughs. But not successfully. Peter put the binoculars down. He flashed his liquid gaze at the kid who made the remark, and the whole car got quiet.

"You're pretty funny," Peter said to the troublemaker.

The kid was eyeing the floorboards, showing signs of contrition. Nobody breathed.

Peter slowly withdrew the .45 from the pancake holster and weighed it in his hand. The 1911 was a heavy gun, much too big to be carrying as a concealed weapon. At thirty-nine ounces, it was almost twice the weight of commonly carried pistols. But it was an American gun. Designed by John Browning. A patriot.

"I like to laugh," Peter said.

"Hey, man, I was just kidding."

"No, really," Peter said. "I love a good joke. Sometimes I like to tell a few myself. Sometimes I joke around." Peter was smiling as he attached a suppressor to the muzzle, turning the device along the threads. Contrary to what you see in Hollywood, a suppressor does not mute gunfire. But it will muffle it enough so that it sounds like a slamming tailgate or a shutting car door. Although a suppressed gunshot in close quarters will still make your ears ring for three days.

"Geez, Peter. Look, I'm sorry. I was just, you know, being funny. I didn't mean anything by it."

Peter nodded. "I know."

He pressed the barrel against the kid's thigh. He pushed the metal into the boy's quadricep so hard he could feel the boy's femur. The kid started squirming and shouting.

"I was just joking, man!"

The discharge of the weapon made everyone momentarily deaf.

Which was why nobody heard Peter reply, "So was I."

Chapter 28

CAROLINE AWOKE TO THE SOUND OF POWER TOOLS FOR THE fifth morning in a row. A high-pitched whining sound that emanated throughout the boat. She sat up in bed and stretched her arms. The sound was coming from the sundeck. This was followed by a heavy, rhythmic banging that made pictures on the walls quiver.

She crawled out of bed. She was *not* ready to get up. The vista from the bedroom's sliding glass doors was arresting. The sun was suspended high in the cloudless sky. She had a pristine view of open bay water, just beyond the marina. The legs of land jutting into the navy water were littered with forest and reeds. There were sailboats in the distance. White sails like tiny triangles on the horizon.

The howl of power tools sounded again. She looked at the ceiling, watching the light fixtures wobble. Soon the whole boat began to rise and fall, rocking side to side. It had taken six days to find her sea legs. At first, the nonstop motion made her feel almost nauseous. After day two, her legs adjusted. After day three, her stomach was fine.

Caroline tugged on a T-shirt and pajama bottoms. She looked

at herself in the mirror. Her tummy was bigger than it had been yesterday, if that was even possible. She was four pounds heavier too, according to Woody's digital scale. But then, she had been eating much better lately. She had never realized how devoid her life was of fruits and vegetables until now. Elizabeth had not allowed Woody to have any junk food on the boat. Only fruits and veggies and legumes and various kinds of grains and granolas. Instead of losing weight, like she would have thought, she began to fill out a little and develop a healthier glow.

Caroline went to the closet. She slid the louvered door, teak maybe. She squatted and lifted the door off its track. Nestled into the aluminum track was the flash drive. The groove was a perfect fit for the drive. She tucked it into her bra.

The cock-and-bull story she'd fed to Woody about her attacker had nothing to do with the flash drive. She'd blamed everything on her ex-boyfriend and his loser constituents; a concocted story of abuse and stalking and all the other elements that make Lifetime movies so captivating. Although the more Caroline talked, the less it sounded made up. She almost cried during the telling and wondered whether the emotion was real or false.

She padded into the kitchen to feed Gary. When she opened the pantry doors, food was sliding off the shelves from all the sea motion, threatening to spill on the floor. Gary's jar of food was on the bottom shelf.

Caroline unscrewed the lid to Gary's container and went to the kitchen window where his carrier usually sat. But when she got to the window, Gary's small aquarium was not there.

Gary wasn't in the dining area. He wasn't in the den either. She checked the whole boat. She turned over each room and found nothing until she got to the foredeck. When she saw it, Caroline covered her mouth and gasped.

On the floor before her, the remains of the plastic carrier

aquarium lay strewn in shards. Loose aquarium gravel littered the deck. Water was everywhere.

"Gary!" she said. "Oh my God!"

Stupid, stupid girl.

She combed through the gravel. She sifted through the other wreckage on the floor of the foredeck. But there was no sign of him.

She raced up the stairs to the sundeck to find Woody. He was working, lying on the floorboards, on his side, shirt off, his sweat staining the teak floor beneath him. Tools were scattered like land mines. Cords everywhere. He was covered in yellow dust and perspiration.

"Morning, Rip Van Caroline," he said.

She was on the verge of crying. "Woody."

"What's up?" He swung the hammer a few times. "Sorry about all the noise. But it's nine o'clock, and I thought, screw it, if you can sleep that long, I officially hate you."

"Woody. Something's happened. Have you seen Gary?"

He obviously sensed the anxiety in her voice and sat upright. "Gary? What do you mean?"

"I mean his little aquarium, the one that was on the windowsill." The tears started; she couldn't stop them. "It's shattered, and I can't find him." Her eyelids squeezed together tightly. "I've had him since I was six," she moaned.

The smile lines around his eyes wrinkled. "I want you to see something."

Confused, she followed him as he moved toward the other side of the boat until they were standing before the aft deck door. Woody opened the sliding doors and told her to go onto the deck.

"What?" she said.

"Go ahead."

There were two chairs on the aft deck. They each had otto-mans. Sitting between the two chairs was a massive aquarium, bubbling happily with an aeration system, filter pump thrum-ming. The bottom of the aquarium was lined in blue gravel. There were plastic boulders inside, phony seaweed, a tiny pirate's trea-sure chest spewing out bubbles, and Gary was regarding Caroline with a happy glare.

She touched her nose against the aquarium. "What in the world?"

Gary wasn't moving his mouth nearly as much as he usually did. Which meant he was oxygenated.

"I thought Gary looked cramped," Woody said. "I didn't mean for your other aquarium to break. I don't know how it fell. I guess it was all the hammering."

She wiped her face and locked eyes with Woody.

"I hope I did it right," Woody said. "I used distilled water and everything. I was kind of trying to surprise you. I didn't mean to freak you out."

Caroline slammed into her father with a full embrace. She fell into Woody so hard he almost fell over backward into the drink.

"You did it right," she said.

Chapter 29

FAIRVIEW RETIREMENT HOME SERVED THE WORST BREAKFAST known to human civilization, outdoing even the excrement-on-a-shingle breakfasts common to gulags, prison camps, and US Army mess halls. Fairview's eggs were cholesterol-free. The coffee was decaf. The sausage was made of turkey and chicken. There was no bacon to speak of. The biscuits were made from some kind of whole grain business that caused them to have the same texture and weight as a regulation hockey puck. None of the residents, no matter how desperate, would touch them. Everyone in Fairview had theories about where the uneaten biscuits went every day. One theory was that the leftover biscuits were used to sand down the hulls of fishing boats.

Eighty-one-year-old resident Clarabelle Anne Walker of room 411 operated a thriving black-market breakfast trade out of her room. Business was booming and would put three of her grandchildren through college. For nine bucks a pop, you could get a Styrofoam to-go box containing real bacon, a whole-fat white-flour biscuit (albeit a frozen one), two eggs fried any way you wanted, toast, and a paper cup of orange juice that was sugary enough to foster a mouthful of cavities. One of Clarabelle's boyfriends usually collected your money at the door.

Today the boyfriend of the week was Eugene.

Eugene sat in a chair outside Clarabelle's door working a crossword puzzle. His US Marines hat sat high on his head. His windbreaker was unzipped to reveal a pocketed polyester shirt that clung to Eugene's belly like Polish sausage casing.

"Good morning, Amos," said Eugene without looking up from his puzzle.

"Mutual, I'm sure," said Amos.

Eugene sniffed his nose. "What's on your mind?"

Amos and Eugene were from different worlds. Eugene was a marine and always seemed to be reminding Amos of this. Amos often reminded Eugene that God invented marines so sailors would have someone to dance with. It was a wonder the two hadn't killed each other.

Amos leaned on his cane and whispered, "Swordfish."

Eugene turned his good ear toward the old man. "Sorry, pal, I used to shoot guns for a living."

"I said, *swordfish*."

Eugene smiled. "You want butter and jam for your biscuits, or gravy? She's got tomato gravy today."

"Jam and butter."

Eugene went back to his crossword. "You sure? She uses real tomatoes."

"Tomatoes give me indigestion."

"Poor baby. How you want your eggs?"

"Scrambled on toast."

"How about coffee? Does the army drink coffee?"

"The army runs on coffee."

Eugene nodded. The old devil dog lifted his iPhone to his

mouth like a walkie-talkie. "Mother, this is Rawhide. Do you copy?"

Static.

"Copy, Rawhide. Go ahead."

Static.

"Gimme Adam and Eve on a raft, and wreck 'em. One cup of shoeshine, throw in one heart attack on the rack, but hold the gravy; add grapes and skid grease to his shoes."

The iPhone squawked in reply. "Does he want orange juice?"

Amos nodded.

Euguene spoke into the mic. "That is affirmative, Mother. Go ahead and squeeze one for the army."

Amos dug into his wallet and removed the appropriate amount of cash. He placed the pile of ones into Eugene's hand.

"You going to the library this afternoon?" asked Eugene.

"Does the pope go in the woods?"

Fairview offered outings three times each week. The bus frequented various places in town each Monday, Wednesday, and Friday such as the supermarket, Cracker Barrel, the civic center, and the library. The library was by far the most popular of all outings.

Namely, because there was no supervision at the library. At the supermarket, staffers followed you around to help you shop. At Cracker Barrel, the nurses sat beside you and wiped your chin. But at the library, the residents were loosed. Some enjoyed reading the paper. Some preferred listening to music. Many snuck into the library's multiuse conference rooms and engaged in carnal activities.

After breakfast, Amos sat in the van, looking at Gulf Beach go by. Eugene was next to him, talking about something related to the Battle of Inchon. Amos was not even pretending to listen because Eugene told the same war stories, in the same words, and followed the same chronological progression of world events every time. He had never—not even once—asked Amos a single question about himself. The bus pulled up to the library somewhere around the Battle of Lake Changjin, and everyone shuffled inside, and there was an immediate line to the bathroom.

Amos waited in line for twelve minutes as his male constituents groaned before their urinals, dribbling on their shoes. After going to the bathroom, Amos began walking out of the bathroom when Eugene called to him.

Eugene was standing at the sink. "In the marines, they teach us to wash our hands after urination."

Amos did not even pause his journey out the door. "In the army, they taught us not to pee on our hands."

He left the bathroom, then took the elevator to the main floor to call dibs on one of the chairs in the reading area beneath the atrium. When the elevator arrived at the main floor, he shambled forward through the daylit atrium, adorned with its million books. And that was when he noticed the young woman with the shock of violent red hair sitting before one of the computers.

• • •

"No, don't get up," said Amos, plopping his body into the office chair next to Caroline's.

His granddaughter looked half stunned. "What are you doing here?"

"What? I read."

Caroline said nothing.

"Nice to see you too," he said. "But try to contain yourself, darling. We're in public. Where's your dad?"

"I came by myself."

"Woodrow released you on your own recognizance? Did he let you borrow the truck?"

"I walked."

He glanced at the computer screen, but before he was able to see anything, she turned the screen off.

"It's just something I was looking up. I'm done now."

He waited for more. But there was no more.

Her eyes were scanning the room like she wasn't paying attention to what he was saying.

"Okay," he said. "This isn't suspicious at all." Amos maneuvered himself so that his prodigiously large head was in her line of vision. "I might be old, but I'm not stupid."

Caroline drew in a huge breath.

Amos just raised his eyebrows and waited.

She looked around the room again. Craning her neck. Twisting her body.

"Can you keep a secret?"

He shrugged.

"I need to know that you won't tell anyone."

"And I need to know why my son gouged a man's eye in a hotel laundry room."

She nodded.

Then she turned on the computer monitor.

• • •

THE CALL CAME EARLY AFTERNOON. WOODY WAS WORKING ON THE sundeck, using a reciprocating saw to cut rotted boards. Anything to take his mind off the events of the last few days. The radio was playing the Braves' first spring training game of the season. He was drinking an IPA that was cold enough to hurt his teeth. But it made his nose ache less. He planned on having a few more beers and polishing the last one off with a hamburger for supper tonight. Forget veganism. Forget yoga. Forget no alcohol.

The phone was lighting up on the floor. He released the trigger of the saw, wiped the sweat from his forehead.

"This is Woody."

"Hello, Father Barker, my name is John Grader. Federal Bureau of Investigation."

Woody turned down the radio. His mind was jolted out of its current state of overactive thinking, and he didn't know what to say. Working with his tools was almost contemplative. In the days since he got out of prison, it was such menial tasks that kept his brain engaged.

"You still there, Father?" the voice asked.

"I'm not your father."

"Sorry. Catholic. What should I call you?"

"How about you start with why the FB of I is calling me at all?"

"This is a follow-up call about the man we arrested, the guy who assaulted you. Peter Tabares. I believe you remember him."

"Rings a bell."

"Yeah, well, he'll be lucky if he ever sees out of his left eye again."

Woody looked at the work he'd been doing. The teak floor was 50 percent new wood. He still had a long way to go. The myth about Brazilian teak is that it never rots. The truth is, if the teak is neglected long enough, it will rot just like pretty much everything else on planet Earth.

"Tabares was released by Birmingham PD three days ago," Grader said.

"You have to love the American justice system."

Silence.

"Anyway," said Grader, "that's why I'm calling. It was the bureau who initiated Peter's release because we can't follow him if he's locked up. And Peter Tabares is the subject of a high-security investigation. He was involved with your ex-wife, Melinda Boyer, briefly. They were part of a local neofascist militant organization that considers themselves patriots. They live off-grid, crap in buckets, Don't Tread on Me, that kind of stuff."

Woody took a swig from his bottle. "He was definitely her type."

"Well, here's the thing . . ." The guy on the phone paused.

The pause lasted a little too long. Woody could hear the guy sigh.

"If I were you, I'd be ready for One-Eyed Pete to come knocking. What has your daughter already told you about him?"

"Nothing. She lied to me."

"Did she say whether she knows Tabares at all?"

"It was kind of hard to hear past all the lies."

The phone went quiet for a while.

"Still there?" asked Woody.

"That's interesting. Don't you wonder what she's hiding?"

"I wonder a lot of things."

Woody heard the rifling of papers on the phone.

"I really shouldn't be disclosing any of this. Is this a secure line?"

"I'm a Verizon customer."

"I have to be careful what I disclose here, Father. This is sensitive information, what I'm about to tell you."

"I'm a sensitive guy. I'm still not your father."

The agent paused again. This time for longer.

"Listen, I don't know what Tabares's involvement is with your daughter, but I know this has everything to do with some sort of disagreement between him and Melinda. This guy is top tier. He's the wrong guy to bring home to meet the fam, if you catch my drift. This guy's pals have been convicted of some pretty horrible crimes. In Canada they are classified as a terrorist organization."

"How nice."

"Birmingham PD wouldn't have known anything about Peter because none of his history will show up on their system. Right now the bureau keeps this information firewalled for federal eyes only. The police thought he was a disgruntled boyfriend or some thug."

Woody set his longneck bottle on the teak railing.

"And what is he?"

"A dangerous guy. That's what he is. And if he's after your daughter, my guess is that it's because she has something he wants. Maybe something Melinda stole from him. Do you know what that might be?"

Woody's alarm bells were going off. "How about you tell me."

Sigh. "It's classified. I'm not at liberty."

"Lucky me."

"And my colleagues aren't going to tell you any of this either, because this would compromise our investigation. But I'm a dad. You're a dad. And from one dad to another, I thought you should know that your daughter's involved in some pretty scary stuff."

"Thanks. Now I can rest easy."

The guy cleared his throat again. "I'll be in touch. And remember, this conversation never happened, totally off the record. Surely we understand each other here, right?"

"We do. And don't call me Shirley either."

. . .

THE GULF BEACH LIBRARY COMPUTER CONSOLES WERE LINED UP IN a long row. Most of them had users.

Amos watched Caroline reach into her pocket and withdraw a small tin box with the yellow Gadsden flag on it. The timber rattler was coiled. Tongue out. Christopher Gadsden designed the flag based on a political cartoon drawn by Benjamin Franklin in 1754. The rattlesnake was a popular symbol representing the American colonies. There were regiments in the military that used the flag. The Third Infantry used it. The marines. The navy.

"Don't tread on me," he said.

"What's it mean?" she asked.

"It means don't tread on me."

Caroline flicked on the monitor, then closed her internet browser, which was showing all sorts of Google maps with routes outlined in blue.

"Taking a trip?" asked Amos.

She removed the flash drive from the box and plugged into the port on the computer. The machine took a few seconds to recognize the drive. Amos donned his reading glasses so he could see better what she was doing.

The drive showed up as *Samsung* on the finder bar. She clicked to open the contents, and inside was a single folder icon entitled 04071865–05101865. She clicked on this thingie. A large subdirectory of files and more thingies appeared. She told him the thingies were all image PDFs, whatever this meant.

Caroline clicked an icon, and the screen was instantly filled with an image of a scanned photocopy of an ancient handwritten page. An extremely high-resolution image, fully zoomed in, with one stroke of the cursive letter taking up the entirety of the monitor. Caroline zoomed outward until the page fit the screen like a tattered piece of yellowed paper.

"What am I looking at?" he asked.

"I don't know. That's the thing, I can hardly read it." Caroline squinted at the screen.

"What do you mean you can't read it?"

"I don't read cursive."

Amos almost passed a gallstone. "You're joking."

But she wasn't. The ornate script was almost illegible to someone from her generation. Caroline was a Gen Z kid, belonging to that curious and unfortunate group that was prohibited from learning cursive in school but was given detailed lessons on proper care and maintenance of their iPad tablet.

Amos leaned in close. The lines were impossibly straight, but the calligraphic letters titled so far to the right, with so little to distinguish one letter from the other, that the page looked as though it were full of scribbled hieroglyphs.

Reading the document took concentration until the word usage and sentence syntax finally opened themselves up to him. The sentences were difficult to put together because of the archaic language. Also, the author used few commas, if any, and every couple of words were marred by oxidation on the page. The letter went:

My dear wife,

I am now permitting myself to write to you under one condition viz: that my letter shall be not examined by my Atty. Genl. or any subsequent members of my cabinet before it is sent to you. Your eyes and your eyes solely are to see the following words. This will sufficiently explain to you the omission of subjects on which you would desire me to write. We shall converse of family matters later and see to the present matter of importance I presume it is however you know of which subject I am to write.

To-morrow it will be two months since we were suddenly and unexpectedly separated and many causes prominent among which has been my anxiety for you and our children have made that quarter in seeming duration long, very long. I sought private solitude to write to you that I might make some suggestions as to your movements and as to domestic arrangements but I have been occupied as I am sure you know while I flee U.S. military forces who pursue us.

Amos shifted in his seat and leaned closer to the monitor. "What in the . . . ?"

Caroline did not respond.

He read onward to the bottom of the page.

You will realize the necessity of extreme caution in regard to our correspondence. The quid nuncs if they hear you have received a letter from me will no doubt seek to extract something for their pursuit and your experience has taught you how little material serves to ignite their flames and this material should result in nothing short of mania among them. Therefore I wish to leave you with a forthright and evident pathlight within the following letters to guide you onward to a gilded reward.

I desire strongly for you to burn these correspondences upon reading and do pray such letters shall not survive one moment of daylight lest our foes certainly locate the tonnage of the treasury which is lawful property to the Confederate States of America. And in the following correspondences shall I disclose to you where such gold and silver is presently hidden.

—Jeffn Davis

Amos removed his glasses and looked at her.

Caroline was clasping the gold pendant on her necklace tightly.

"Where did you find this?" he asked.

"It was my mom's."

Chapter 30

———

ELIZABETH KNOCKED ON THE SLIDING GLASS DOOR OF THE foredeck. The door was locked. She yanked on the handle a few times, but the door didn't move. She beat on the door with the flat of her hand, but there was no answer.

"Where's Daddy?" asked Rachel. Elizabeth's daughter was carrying a pink overnight backpack. She was holding her plastic Tupperware box of toys beneath her arm. It was Friday; she would be staying at her dad's for the weekend.

"I don't know, sweetie. But he's around here somewhere. I can see his truck in the parking lot."

Elizabeth beat the glass again. *Boom! Boom! Boom!* "Hello!"

After a few minutes of knocking, the sliding doors unlatched and parted slowly. Just a crack. But it was not Woody. Behind the glass was Caroline. The young woman was wearing a blue maternity blouse with white daisies and jean shorts. She smelled like sunscreen.

"My sister!" yelled Rachel.

Rachel wedged herself through the cracked doors and hugged Caroline as though they had not seen each other in a few millennia. Caroline hugged her back.

"Where's Woody?"

"I don't know," Caroline replied. "I think he had to go to the store, and he told me to lock the doors."

"Lock the doors? Why?"

"I don't know. He just told me not to let anyone inside."

Elizabeth shouldered her way past Caroline. She had not been aboard since Caroline moved in a week ago, and the place was already cozily disgusting.

"This place is a wreck."

Caroline cleared her throat and put her hands in her pockets.

The den was a mess—more so than usual. The sofa sleeper was pulled out, the bed unmade. There was an overturned five-gallon bucket serving as a makeshift nightstand. The place smelled like a frat house and pizza boxes were piled up. Elizabeth lifted one of the boxes, which contained part of a Canadian bacon and olive pizza.

"Those were for me," Caroline said, pointing at the boxes. "He won't eat them. He says you wouldn't want him to."

Elizabeth tossed the box onto the floor and looked at the clothing hanging all over the place, secured with clothespins. Girl's clothes. Elizabeth removed one of the garments from the ceiling's hanging lamp. It was a pair of pink maternity panties, and they were still wet.

"Why are these hanging from the ceiling?"

"He doesn't have a dryer," said Caroline.

"That's not what I asked."

"He said hang them somewhere out of the way."

"The marina has a laundry room. You can wash and dry your clothes there."

"He won't let me leave the boat today."

"Why not?"

Rachel was jumping up and down. "I like your daisies," she

said, pinching the fabric of Caroline's shirt. The little girl's hands were all over Caroline. There was a magnetism between the two of them that Elizabeth did not want to understand. They were sisters but strangers. Children are more willing to expand the boundaries of family than their adult counterparts.

Elizabeth turned to Rachel. "Get off her."

"What?" asked Rachel.

"I want you to go wait outside in the car."

Rachel's little face broke. "What? Why?"

"Do as I say."

"But I thought I was staying with Dad tonight?"

"Car, right now. We'll talk about that in a second."

Rachel sulked off and flung herself on the foredeck outside the glass doors. It wasn't exactly the car, but Elizabeth would deal with that later.

"Didn't he remember that his daughter was coming over today? Why is he gone?"

Caroline shrugged. "I'm sorry. Why do I feel like this is all my fault somehow?"

Elizabeth marched into the back bedroom on the main deck. When she opened the door, she discovered that the room had been girlied up considerably. Pink bed spread. Multicolored lights dangling from the ceiling. New clothes in the closet with tags still on. Magnetic phone charger by the bed. Expensive items. All Elizabeth could see was money Woody didn't have, being channeled toward expenses he couldn't afford, to support a child he did not need in his life.

"Where did all this come from?"

"All what?"

"All this stuff."

Caroline looked around the room. "Target?"

Elizabeth shut the door. "Okay, whatever."

She went into the bathroom and clicked on the light. There were beauty items all over the counter. The gray cat was eating from a small bowl. There was a litterbox that needed changing next to the shower.

"So did he say where Rachel is supposed to sleep tonight?" asked Elizabeth. "God knows, there's no room on this boat. Is she supposed to sleep in the engine room? Or maybe she's going to sleep cuddled up next to a power saw?"

"Where did she sleep before?"

"In the bedroom."

"She can still sleep in my room."

Elizabeth flipped off the bathroom light. "*Your* room?"

"I mean, his room. I mean, *that* room, the one back there."

Elizabeth thundered into the galley. The sink was overflowing. The counters were littered with chopped onions and dirty knives. A slow cooker was going. The whole place smelled like garlic and spice. She lifted the lid. It was hamburger chili. She searched through the garbage and found a foam tray of 80 percent lean ground beef. "I thought you said he was still vegan."

"The chili is for me," said Caroline.

Elizabeth slammed the lid onto the Crock-Pot. "Sure it is."

The lid fell off the pot and onto the floor, splattering beef juice everywhere.

"We're done here."

She started to leave the boat. On her way toward the door, she kicked a stack of books from a side table. She watched the pyramid of volumes pertaining to meaningless historical things fall to the floor. Elizabeth almost tripped over a book about the antiquity of Chinese Han art.

"I'm really sorry," said Caroline. "I can tell you're upset. I feel like this is all my fault somehow. Have I done something wrong?"

Elizabeth pigeon-stepped over the fallen books and began gathering empty pizza boxes into her arms.

"Is there something I can do to make this better?" asked Caroline.

"I'm not mad at you," said Elizabeth, peeking over the stack of boxes. "This is just really bad timing. Woody's only been out for three months, he's in bad health, and he's not ready for a teenager in his house. It's nothing personal; this is just a bad idea."

The room went quiet.

"*Three months*?" Caroline repeated. "Been out of where?"

Elizabeth dropped the pizza boxes in the corner near the overflowing trash receptacle, then punched them to crease them in the middle. "I'm sorry, what are you asking me?"

"You said he's only been out for three months. Out of what?"

Elizabeth stopped. She turned to face the young woman. The kid's eyes were the same color as Woody's, and her skin was deeply freckled. She really was a striking girl.

"You mean he hasn't told you?"

Caroline shook her head.

"Woody just got out of prison for killing a woman."

Chapter 31

———

WOODY'S TRUCK PULLED ALONGSIDE CAROLINE. SHE WAS walking on the sidewalk at a medium clip, clutching the gray cat in her arms, her backpack on her shoulders. She was wearing her old clothes. The Snoop Dogg shirt and the stretched-out yoga pants with holes in them. He pulled the truck beside her, riding the wrong lane with hazards flashing. Cigar in the corner of his mouth.

"May I be of some assistance, ma'am?"

She did not speak. She kept pace. He could see that her skin was reddened from the sun. Her nose was burnt too. The bruises on her face were clearing up.

"Tennessee's the other way," he said.

No reaction.

"Okay. So now you're not going to talk to me?"

Caroline's shoes made loud flopping sounds on the pavement. They edged on another few feet. Woody following. Traffic passing them by.

"I'm an inconvenience," said Caroline. "This isn't working."

"You aren't even close to an inconvenience."

"Then you really need to talk to Elizabeth."

He threw the truck in Park and stepped onto the sidewalk to follow her. "Elizabeth's problem is me. Believe me, you have nothing to do with this. Where are you going?"

Caroline stopped walking. "Actually, I don't know."

"Then how will you know when you get there?"

"All I know is that I don't belong here."

"This is precisely where you belong."

She shook her head. "I just don't think it's going to work out."

Caroline resumed walking, adjusting the cat against her shoulder.

Woody resumed following, but he was out of breath. "You have to understand Elizabeth. She's just . . . Well. She's Elizabeth."

"Right."

"There was a lot of bad blood between her and your mother."

"My mother had bad blood with everyone."

His truck was a long way behind them now, parked in the road. Traffic angrily weaved around it. Motorists were giving him dirty looks as they passed.

Caroline met his eyes. "Did you really go to prison?"

"Yes."

"Why didn't you tell me that?"

His chest was heaving. "I don't know. I guess I didn't want to scare you away. People don't exactly invite ex-convicts to barbecues."

"You killed a woman?"

He said nothing. The roar of traffic punctuated their conversation.

"What happened?"

"It was an accident."

She turned onto an intersecting sidewalk. "You can quit following me now."

"No, I'm not going to quit. We need to talk. You don't know what you're doing. Your life is in danger, in more ways than I think you understand. Your mom was hanging around with some bad people, and I think you're wrapped up in it."

Caroline was not fazed by the information. She just kept walking.

"Did you hear what I said?"

"I heard you."

A semitruck rolled past, shifting gears loudly. The booming draft blew her hair sideways across her face. She came to an intersection and stopped to look both ways. He fell in beside her, panting. She reached into her pocket and withdrew her phone in a pink case. Caroline handed the device to him.

"What's this?" he said.

"It's yours. You bought it."

"I don't want it."

Woody tucked the iPhone into the pocket on her backpack. "This is yours. Don't you get it? I care about you. And I want to help keep you safe. I'm still the same guy I was when you met me. I haven't changed."

"But see, that's just it. You haven't changed. To me, you're still just a random person. Someone who didn't want anything to do with his own kid. A donor."

"That might be the meanest thing anyone's ever said to me."

"Then you've led a pretty charmed life."

Caroline looked both ways and crossed the street.

He trotted beside her. "So are you going back to your boyfriend now?"

"I don't know."

"Let me at least give you some cash."

"I don't want anything from you, least of all money."

Caroline turned left and followed another sidewalk, which

headed northward. This time he watched her leave without following. Namely, because he didn't have the stamina to walk another step. His heart was racing, he was salivating, and his ears were ringing. The spirit was willing, but the cardiac tissue was weak.

"I'll just keep following you," he called out. "I'll find you, Caroline."

"No, you won't," she said. "You're going to let me walk away."

"How do you know that?"

"Because you let my mother walk away too."

• • •

The clerk at the Gulf Beach Greyhound station counter took Caroline's cash, mashed a few buttons on the register, then slid change back to her. Caroline placed the handful of quarters and the ticket receipt into her pocket, then headed for the restroom. When she exited there was an old man waiting for her at the door. He was leaning on his cane, wearing a thick canvas jacket and cowboy boots.

"What are you doing here?" she said.

"It's a free country." His eyes went to the cat in her arms. "He don't look happy."

Caroline readjusted the cat against herself.

"Your dad called me."

"He's not my dad."

"Would've been pretty hard to be born without him."

Amos draped an arm around her, then guided her to the waiting area, where they sat on plastic bucket seats. He eased into a chair beside her, moaning upon his descent. "Let's talk."

"How did you know I'd be here?"

"Welcome to the age of cell phones."

Amos took the ticket from her hand. He looked at it, nodded, then handed it back to her.

"What's in Georgia?"

"You can't stop me. I'm sorry. I've already made up my mind. I know it's not safe. I know someone is after me. But you saw what was on that flash drive. I think we're the only ones who know where it might be."

Amos was quiet. Contemplative. Staring at the clock on the wall almost as though he were looking through it.

"I think we've had a misunderstanding. I'm not going to stop you."

Chapter 32

———

THE FIRST USAGE OF GOLD CAN BE PINPOINTED TO THE FIFTH millennium BC. The Paleolithic era, back when humans were still hunting in the nude. Gold was the first metal to be manipulated. Before iron. Before bronze. Before anything. The first metal to be valued. The first metal to be used in religion. Gold shows up everywhere throughout religious epics in human history. The gospel story of the magi. In Hinduism, with offerings to deities for healing. In Islam, the five thousand golden plates that adorn the Dome of the Rock.

Gold is as close to everlasting as a physical object can get. Theoretically, eternal. It does not react to oxygen or water; neither will it corrode, rust, or tarnish. Fire cannot harm it, so it cannot be destroyed. If you want to get technical about it, the only way to get rid of gold is to dissolve it. And even then, this doesn't destroy the element. Fact: The world's oceans contain twenty million tons of dissolved gold.

For centuries, gold had no utility. You couldn't do much with it. Too malleable for weapons. Too soft for tools or tableware. So somewhere along the way gold became currency. And ever since, human civilization has been paying the price. Both literally and emblematically. All the wars in recorded history—modern and ancient—have been financed, centralized around, and waged over gold-backed currency.

Amos was thinking about all this when Caroline fell asleep in the Greyhound passenger seat beside him. A library book was resting in her lap, with her index finger marking the chapter on gold.

The old man found himself watching his granddaughter with deep affection. It was hard not to find this child so magnificent that it made his insides ache. He reached out to touch her violent red hair. Just to know what it felt like. It was smooth. Like silk.

The Greyhound plunged through the night carrying ten passengers. The lights were dimmed for sleeping. Outside the scenery darted past the windows, swallowed by the sea of inky darkness. The drone of the diesels was hypnotic, an oddly comforting sound. Most passengers wore earbuds, watching videos, tapping away on laptops, staring at screens, endlessly scrolling the opiate realm of social media, seeing the entire world from only six inches before their nose, using only their thumbs to guide them. Behold your God, America. The Almighty Phone. The future of the human race. Amos Barker had seen firsthand what this glowing device could do to a family. It could tear the whole thing apart.

He looked out the window and wondered what Woody would do when he found out that his eighty-seven-year-old father (almost eighty-eight) had left Fairview under the cover of darkness without alerting anyone but his widow neighbor, Jill, who was feeding his cats.

Woody would not realize Amos was missing for a few days. He was too busy with Rachel right now to notice a missing old man. Because it was a Friday; Woody babysat on Fridays and Saturdays.

Amos watched the hinterlands of rural Alabama roll by. Little towns. Complete with water towers, high schools, football fields, baseball diamonds, YMCAs, and VFWs. Happy places. Places where people lived real lives with real families. He could almost remember what a real family felt like before his wife died, before his only son was locked away in a federal prison.

He closed his eyes and thought about the pages he'd seen in the library. The collection of letters was not exhaustive. There were only ten or eleven of them. And it was evident from references in Davis's correspondence that there were letters missing from the anthology. One of the final letters in the collection was a geographical drawing, with symbols littered across the pre-Reconstruction area in the Southeast. Amos had printed it out at the library along with the rest of the letters. The geographical drawing wasn't a map by any stretch; it was too cryptic.

He pulled the printout from Caroline's backpack. The drawing had been surprisingly well done. Jefferson Davis must've been a skilled draftsman. The symbols, however, didn't make any sense unless you were Varina "Winnie" Davis. They were seemingly unrelated to any information contained in the letters.

This was all probably a waste of time, of course. A fable. The gold had likely been discovered decades earlier—if there truly had been any gold to begin with. This could have been an elaborate hoax, designed to mislead and thoroughly waste the time of hell-bound Yankees.

Then again, the threat to Caroline's life was real. The Major had been around long enough to know that there were only two things mankind considered worth killing for on this planet. And this didn't have anything to do with romance.

He unfurled the pages he'd printed at the library. Davis's final letter to his wife. The only noncryptic letter in the collection. Amos slid on his reading glasses.

Dearest Winnie,

On this day my heart untravelled turns most longingly to you. Many years and very many sorrows lie between this day and that which made you mine in law but did not make you more mine or me more yours than before the ceremony was performed of exchanging before witnesses the vows we had exchanged before God and which were registered where neither destroying elements or thieving Yankees could obliterate or remove the record. What would I not give for one kind embrace from my beloved Wife?

I will not now enter on recitals which may wait for to-morrow. On Saturday I hope the steamer will be in and bring me a letter from you. None has arrived since you left New Orleans and you need not be told that my anxiety is great to know how you are.

I fear my traveling company is about to be captured by surrounding forces making this perhaps a final letter from your beloved husband. If I shall not be seen by you again I pray you memorize the advices I have sent and foremostly I pray you guard yourself against the forces of evil which desire to thieve, kill and destroy. May your life be protected in the name of God.

—Jeffn Davis

The bus began to slow. Beneath his haunches, Amos felt the diesel pusher downshift. The vehicle decelerated rapidly, causing passengers to lean forward in their seats. Everyone on the bus became agitated. Their speed dropped to a crawl on the interstate. Soon they were easing toward the shoulder with the hiss of hydraulic brakes.

"Why are we stopping?" asked one passenger across the aisle.

Another passenger stood in her seat. "Hey, what's going on?"

"Sit down," said the bus driver.

And the interior of the bus filled with red and blue lights.

Chapter 33

WOODY WAS DOING NINETY ON I-20. HE KEPT GLANCING AT the iPhone in his mounted dashboard holder. The GPS tracking app showed a blue dot on the map. Caroline's dot. Her dot had been moving along I-20 East, averaging sixty-five miles per hour.

Rachel sat cross-legged beside him, eating a turkey sandwich, sitting on her "height adjustment apparatus," a device Woody was prohibited from calling a "booster seat" because such implements were for babies. She liked riding in Woody's truck because there was no back seat. Rachel had been asleep for the first leg of the journey but awoke with new vigor, empowered by the knowledge that she was up *way* past her bedtime.

Rachel was watching the double yellow line streak past the windshield. "Where is Caroline going?"

"I don't know."

"Why are we following her?"

"Because I don't have anything better to do."

He unlatched the phone from the holder and passed it to Rachel. "Tell me what her blue dot is doing. I can't watch and drive at the same time."

Woody had been following the blue dot through the darkness, pushing the RPMs of all four cylinders into the red zone. He was slowly closing in on her, which was a good thing, except that he hated speeding and hated it even worse with a child in the car.

"Is she still going sixty-five?" said Woody.

"That's what the app says."

The blue dot, and the bus she was likely on, was heading for Georgia. What was she going to Georgia for? Did it have anything to do with that suspicious FBI guy? He wondered just who exactly was keeping tabs on Caroline.

The nine-year-old pinch-zoomed on the screen and brought up Caroline's location. She held the phone directly to her face like she was solving the Riemann hypothesis.

"What's going on?" he asked.

"It stopped."

Woody decelerated. "What stopped?"

Woody leaned over to look at the phone. The dot was still on I-20, several miles outside Douglasville, Georgia. Sitting right in the middle of the interstate. But it wasn't moving.

"Says zero miles per hour," said Rachel.

Woody jammed the accelerator to the floor. His speed crept up to ninety-five. Then ninety-eight. His little truck sounded like it was going to explode. They were forty miles from Douglasville.

• • •

THREE FBI AGENTS BOARDED THE BUS. ANOTHER GUY WAS WAITING outside. They were wearing windbreaker jackets with big yellow letters, body armor, and badges dangling from neck chains. They were all guys. Clean-cut. A few of them had tattoos on forearms and on necks poking from beneath collars and tactical vests. Two of the men moved through the aisles reminding bus passengers to remain calm.

One officer was speaking with the driver. The driver was upset about the delay, and the officer was trying to calm him down as they questioned him. But the driver was not calming down. The driver was getting agitated, communicating with his interrogator using sentences made up entirely of expletives. Amos quietly hobbled to his feet, then made his way to the bathroom at the rear of the bus.

One of the officers was addressing the passengers. He instructed everyone to get their IDs out and be ready to show them. Everyone began digging for their wallets, and the agents, stoic-faced, resting hands on the hilts of their weapons, watched the audience of drones follow instructions.

Amos exited the bathroom, still drying his hands on a paper towel.

"What in heaven is this about?" whispered Caroline as Amos slid into the seat beside her again.

"Don't play ignorant," said Amos. "It doesn't suit you."

They looked at each other. A cold wave rolled down her spine.

"What do we do?"

"I'm working on it."

The officers began walking through the aisles, checking IDs against the faces who owned them. The passengers on the bus were looking around, floating eyes from passenger to passenger, trying to find the villain. It was as though everyone on the bus were playing Where's Waldo.

"Can someone tell us what's going on here?" shouted one passenger.

An agent barked at him, "Sir, please sit down."

"We have rights," said the passenger. "I don't have to consent to a search of my stuff."

"We're not searching anyone," said the agent. "If everyone will just calm down, this will be over soon, and you can be on your way. IDs out, please."

The agent was already making his way to Amos and Caroline, zeroing in on the girl.

"Evening, ma'am," the agent said. "ID?"

The cat in Amos's lap was becoming restless, emitting a low growl. The agent's eyes were fixed on the cat.

"He's nervous," said Amos, stroking the cat's head.

The agent did not move a facial muscle. The man held his hand outward. "IDs, please."

Caroline and Amos both handed the guy their IDs. The agent glanced at the IDs, then to Amos and Caroline.

"I know," Caroline said. "It's a terrible picture. My hair was awful."

The man gave a polite smile. "What year were you born, sir?"

"I'm not trying to buy liquor."

"Year, please?"

"I was born under the presidency of Franklin Delano Roosevelt in 1937, the year of our Lord."

The agent looked at the ID for a few beats longer.

"What about you, miss?" the agent said.

Caroline recited her birthday. The agent gave a slight nod. Then the agent summoned his coworkers. The other officers soon joined him in the aisle, until all the agents were standing before Caroline. The agent was still scrutinizing Caroline's ID.

"Miss Boyer, we'd like to ask you to come with us, please."

The other passengers were gawking at Caroline now.

"What? Why?"

"Miss, if you'd gather your things."

Amos stood and wedged himself between her and the agents. "How about you tell us what's going on."

The guy glared at him. "Sir, she's not in any trouble. This is a security measure, for her own protection. If she'll come with us, we can explain everything."

Amos kept his body in their way. "You're not taking her off this bus."

The bus driver was now joining the action. He was getting upset. "Man, I got a [expletive] load of passengers that needs to be in Atlanta by nine. For [expletive's] sake, can we hurry this [maternal expletive] up?"

Everyone was glaring at Amos as the source of their delay.

"Sir, if she won't come with us, we'll have no choice but to arrest her, and you."

"You just said she's not in any trouble."

The agent drew in a breath.

Another agent took the lead and spoke to Caroline directly. "You have five seconds to choose, ma'am, or I'll be forced to make a choice for your own safety. We can either do this nicely or less than nicely, but your well-being is what's at stake here."

Amos took a step toward the agents, but Caroline held him back.

"It's okay," she said to her grandfather. "I'll go with them."

She lifted her backpack and threw the strap over her shoulder. Caroline began walking down the aisle, and Amos followed a few steps behind, carrying the cat in his arms.

One of the agents placed a hand on Amos's chest. "You'll have to stay on the bus."

"The hell I will. That's my granddaughter."

The officers all looked at each other with tired expressions.

The lead agent said, "Family members aren't allowed in law enforcement vehicles with detainees. It's regulation. I'm sorry, but I don't make the rules."

"Yeah, well, I want to talk to the person who does. Because

when I go into a diabetic coma without my granddaughter to administer my medication, I want to know who's to blame for my untimely and unfortunate death."

The officers once again exchanged exhausted looks. Dealing with hypoglycemic, type 2 diabetic octogenarians evidently wasn't in the bureau training manual. After a few shrugs and nervous sighs, the agents all nodded at each other.

"Bring him," said the agent.

Chapter 34

———

THE TRAFFIC JAM LOOKED LIKE THE WORLD'S LONGEST STRING of Christmas lights snaking to the horizon. Woody was riding in the grassy median, bypassing the gridlock, driving over drainage ditches and sewer grates, which limited his speed considerably. When the grass got too high in the median, he switched to driving along the shoulder's rumble strip, leaning on his horn.

Rachel held on to the chicken bar, at times being tossed whole inches off her elevation correction apparatus.

"Hold on tight!" he said.

"I'm holding!"

"Are you okay?"

"Yes, but you know Mom's going to kill you, right?"

"Literally."

Woody sounded the horn when his truck came to a Land Rover that was blocking the shoulder. There was no way around the Rover because the highway shoulder dropped off into a grassy ravine.

Woody punched the horn again. "Look at this guy."

"Can you go around him?"

He looked out the window at the drop-off. "Not unless you want to join the ranks of Socrates."

"What's that mean?"

He leaned on the horn again. "Come on! I can't *believe* this guy."

But the Rover was not moving. Instead, the motorist rolled down the window. Slowly, a hand emerged from the open window. The hand gesture that followed indicated that Woody should perform an immoral act upon himself.

Woody rolled down his window. "Get off the shoulder! Move forward! Let me through!"

The Land Rover did nothing. The guy's brake lights remained illuminated. So Woody got out of the truck.

"What are you doing?" asked Rachel.

"I'm going to pray with him." Woody slammed the door.

He marched across the uneven shoulder, reaching into his shirt pocket and removing the tiny nitroglycerin tablet cannister. He let one tablet dissolve on his tongue.

Woody rapped on the Rover's glass. The window did not open. So Woody used his heel to kick the side of the vehicle. The Rover's steel panel was surprisingly flimsy. It dented without effort. Chinese steel. They just don't make them like they used to. The loud noise got the driver's attention.

The man inside staggered out of the vehicle. The guy was wearing a pink polo shirt, seersucker shorts, penny loafers without socks, and a smartwatch. He looked like he'd just left the eighteenth hole. The man was wobbling on his feet, slurring his words, and you wouldn't have wanted to light a match within ten feet of him.

"Don't kick my car!" the guy shouted. Then he called Woody a name not fit for print.

"You're blocking the road," said Woody.

"You kicked my car!"

Woody watched the man shift his weight from foot to foot, struggling to remain upright and erect. The man was about to slither back into the driver's seat.

"Sir," said Woody, "do not get back in that car."

"What did you just say to me?"

"I said step away. You're under arrest."

The guy laughed. "You're not a cop."

"And *you're* not driving."

The man laughed. "You can talk to my lawyer."

"Good idea," said Woody. "Let's get the law involved. In fact, let's call the cops right now."

"Who are you?"

Woody stormed back to his truck and removed zip ties from his toolbox. Zip ties and duct tape were what held half his boat together. The guy watched Woody thread the ends of his zip ties into themselves to get them started.

"Turn around, sir."

"I'm not turning around. You turn around."

The line of traffic began to creep forward ahead of them. Woody was losing precious time. The chain of red taillights began to blink as hundreds of people released their brakes.

"You have three seconds, sir. Turn around or I will disable you."

The man declared loudly that Woody should go straight to a realm where the worm dieth not. Then the man came at Woody. Woody dodged the man and watched him fall to the gravel. He spun the man around and snapped the zip ties onto the man's wrists. He guided Pink Shirt into the back passenger seat of his own Land Rover.

"You can't do this to me," the guy shouted.

"You can trust me, sir," said Woody, between wheezing to

catch his breath. "You don't want to go to the place where they put drunk drivers."

Then he shut the door.

· · ·

THEY HANDCUFFED CAROLINE AND AMOS. THEY SAID THE CUFFS were for their own safety but that they weren't under arrest. Although it felt a lot like being under arrest in Caroline's book. One of the agents told Caroline to watch her head as he helped her into the back seat of the unmarked black vehicle. Another agent guided Amos into the other side of the back seat.

"Where's my cat?" said Caroline.

"He's still on the bus. They'll bring him soon."

She turned in her seat to look behind the vehicle. The agents were still on the bus, doing a sweep of the interior. They wore Latex gloves and used flashlights.

Amos and Caroline sat quietly. Through the windows, she could see that traffic was moving again. The long chain of headlamps inched forward. Behind her, she could see the officers flagging traffic.

Amos's eyes were sober. "These guys are not FBI."

"How do you know that?"

"Because I used to get a paycheck from the US government too. You can smell government workers. These ain't them."

"But we're in a police car."

Amos shook his head. "This is a Crown Victoria."

"So?"

"They quit making Crown Vics when you were still making mud pies in the backyard."

"What's a mud pie?"

He held out his bound hands. "Where's the computer thing?"

"The flash drive?"

"Whatever you call it. Give it here."

She contorted herself, dug through her pocket, and handed Amos the tin box. He opened it, then removed the tiny flash drive.

"What are you going to do?"

"Cooperation only lasts as long as the status quo is unchanged."

"What's the status quo?"

"Soon as this guy gets what he wants, he won't need you or me anymore. We've got to find a way to make sure the status quo stays in our favor."

"How do we do that?"

The old man opened his mouth. He placed the flash drive in his mouth, closed his eyes, and swallowed. "Status quo."

"What about the pages we printed out?"

Amos darted his eyes to the bus in the distance. "Those documents currently reside at the bottom of the bus latrine."

They waited in the idling car for what seemed like hours while the agents searched the bus. She could see one of the men emptying her backpack onto the ground. When they were finished, they flagged the bus on, then split off into groups of two. Two agents went toward one car. The other two agents walked toward them.

The door to the vehicle opened. The driver was sturdy looking. He wore a ball cap and an earpiece. He turned to deliver a silvery smile to Caroline, peering through the cage divider.

He was wearing an eye patch.

"Miss me?" he said.

Chapter 35

WOODY WAS SEATED BEHIND THE WHEEL OF A SHOWROOM-READY, top-of-the-line, factory-upgraded, leather-upholstered, tricked-out Land Rover Defender, MSRP $110,305. He was riding through the median in style. You could hardly feel the bumps in the road.

"Are you all right?" he asked Rachel, who was sitting in the passenger seat, snuggly secure in her elevation modification mechanism. She gave her dad a thumbs-up.

Woody looked into the rearview mirror.

"How about you, back there?"

The drunk guy in the back seat was cussing and hollering as the vehicle bronco-bucked over the swales like a coaster ride at Busch Gardens. The guy had apparently unbuckled himself and so was bouncing around like a metal ball in a can of spray paint.

Without warning, Woody slammed the brakes. The Rover's bumper almost slammed into another vehicle that had un-expectedly moved in front of the vehicle.

The guy in the back seat shot forward. "You son of a—"

"Dad!"

Woody weaved around the car and hit the gas.

"Talk to me, Rachel."

"Something's changed," she said.

Rachel held the phone for both of them to see. The dot started blinking.

"What's blinking mean?" said Woody.

"Means they're changing directions."

"Are you sure that's what it means?"

Rachel looked at him flatly. "Dad. I literally use this app all the time."

In the meantime, the guy in back was spitting venom. "You're going to get in so much trouble. My lawyers are going to put you under the jail. You don't even know who I am, you low-down—"

Woody mashed the gas.

The guy was sucked backward into his buffalo-leather-upholstered seat. But the acceleration was short-lived. Woody hit the brake pedal and came to a skidding stop. He could feel the man collide into the backs of their seats.

"She's turning around now," said Rachel. "She's coming toward us."

"Turning around?"

"I want your full name, you sorry sack of elbows. Because when my lawyers are through with you, you won't even be able to brush your own—"

"Hold on to your butts," said Woody.

Woody spun the wheel and stamped the pedal. He made a two-point turn in the median, and the innards of the Land Rover went flying against the windows. Rachel held the overhead bar. The guy in back made contact with the vehicle ceiling on more than one occasion.

The Rover was positioned on the highway shoulder of the

oncoming lane, ready to join the flow of traffic. In the distance, they could see a vehicle approaching. A law enforcement vehicle, about half a mile away. The car had a light bar, but it wasn't flashing.

"Is that them?" Woody asked.

Rachel zoomed in on the screen. "Pretty sure that's her."

"You're in so much trouble. When I tell my dad about this, it's over for you. If you knew who you were dealing with, you'd be—"

Woody hit the gas.

All eight cylinders howled for mercy. The Rover had more getup than a NASA Falcon 9 on its way through the exosphere.

In a few seconds, Woody was tailing the vehicle. It was a Crown Vic. Plain black. No identification. Side-mounted spotlight. Light bar on top. A push bar on the front bumper. The plates were civilian. He kept a steady pace behind the vehicle, staying a few car lengths back.

Woody looked into the rearview mirror. The man was currently puking onto the floorboards. The whole car was beginning to smell. Woody rolled down the back windows.

In the car ahead, he saw the back of his dad's head.

Chapter 36

———

"WHERE ARE YOU TAKING US?" ASKED AMOS.
After a long drive, the agents' vehicle veered off the highway. Tires crunching on gravel. They had long since shed their ballistic vests and false badges. They had started talking differently too. Less officially. More swear words.

"Hey, spitwad," said Amos. "I asked you a question."

Nobody responded.

"Hello?" said the old man.

The cat was growing restless on Caroline's lap. Growling so that his rib cage was vibrating. His claws were digging into Caroline's thighs.

"Excuse me?" said Amos. "Someone start talking to me or we're going to have a problem back here."

The men up front were talking but not to him. So Amos started beating on the caged partition. The partition was flimsier than it looked.

The men stopped talking and looked back at him. "Stop doing that," said the guy with the patch.

Amos used his palms to smash the cage divider again. This time the grating looked like it might give way.

"I said stop it." The man with the patch was remarkably calm. "Tell me what you need, please? Use your words."

"I have to go to the bathroom. *El baño, estupidos.*"

"I'm sorry. You're going to have to hold it."

"You don't look very sorry. And I've been holding it an hour. I have a prostate as big as a watermelon. The upholstery back here is about to get baptized if you don't let me out."

The two men sighed and traded looks. Amos gyrated his hips so that his rear made squeaks on the upholstery, scooting around in his seat to drive his point home.

But the men in the front seat ignored him.

Amos used his boots to kick the cage divider this time. The grate rattled loudly. One of the brackets came loose and one side of the cage disconnected from the vehicle.

"I said . . ."

Kick. Kick.

"I have got . . ."

Kick.

"To go . . ."

Kick.

"Pee!"

Kick, kick.

Eye Patch turned in his seat to face the old man. He shouted so loudly Amos could see the veins in his neck bulging. He removed a pistol and trained it on Amos. Before Eye Patch could say anything, the other guy interjected.

"Watch the road," said the other man. "Just pull over and let him use the bathroom. He can't run off anywhere out here. He can't even run. Look at him."

In a few minutes, the car pulled into an abandoned gas station with an unlit parking lot. There was nothing around for miles but vacant highway, tall pines, and a spotless night sky.

The vehicle eased to a stop. The car's headlamps illuminated the abandoned filling station so that it looked almost haunted in the darkness. The station's front windows had been covered with plywood. The tall gas station sign, once a Texaco, was leaning downward. There were no lights around for miles. No traffic on the old highway either. They were in the sticks. The roads twisted and turned like giant eels.

The driver turned the pistol on Amos again. "You'd better make this quick or you're going to be very sorry."

"Yeah, yeah." Amos said. "We get it. You're the silent, brooding type. Now let me out of this car."

Eye Patch stepped out of the car and slammed the door behind him. The loud slam of metal on metal caused the cat to grow uneasy in Caroline's lap. Caroline groaned in pain as the cat sank its claws deeper into her thighs.

Eye Patch yanked open her door and pressed the pistol to the old man's temple. Hard steel rested against Amos's hairline.

The man shouted, "Get out! Both of you!"

But the cat had embedded its claws into Caroline's thighs. "I can't!" Caroline said. "I have a cat in my lap."

Amos crawled out of the car on shaky legs.

"You too," the man said to Caroline.

"I don't need to go to the bathroom."

"I said get out!" Eye Patch swore, then reached into the car and grabbed Caroline by the hair. The cat hissed wildly and clung to Caroline's body, clawing at the fabric of her clothes. Caroline screamed.

"Let her go!" shouted Amos.

"Shut up!"

The guy attempted to remove the hissing cat from Caroline's body by grasping the cat's tail.

Grasping an angry cat by the tail teaches a man something he can learn in no other way.

Chapter 37

Woody's vehicle came screeching into the abandoned gas station. His headlights were aimed on the Vic, all its doors slung open. What he saw mystified him. One man was stumbling around, screaming, with something attached to his face. Whatever was clinging to his head had a tail. The man was shouting in agony.

Another man was racing back to the Vic and removed a short-barrel shotgun from the front seat. He steadied the weapon atop the hood of the Vic and took aim.

Woody put his hand on Rachel's head. "Get down!"

The deafening blast took out the windshield of the Land Rover as glass shards filled the vehicle.

"Daddy!" shouted Rachel.

"Get on the floor, sweetie! And stay in the car!" He looked at the drunk guy. "And you, do not let her leave this vehicle."

Woody threw the car in Park and leapt out. He commando crawled through the weeds until he was behind a gas pump. Commando crawling was harder in real life than in Hollywood. Every part of his body was killing him. His chest felt like it was about to implode.

The gun fired again.

The metal casing of the gas pump exploded. Woody made himself as small as he could, crouching behind the innards of the pump.

Another blast.

Woody could hear buckshot whizzing past his ears.

The next discharge took out the front tire of the Land Rover.

"Daddy!"

Woody raced to another gas pump, moving closer to the gunman, and crouched behind it. He was doing mental math. Most police vehicles carry a .33 caliber. The range is only about fifteen yards—at best. Typically, six to ten rounds. Then again, this was not a police car, at least not anymore. Anyone could buy a used police cruiser at an auction.

Another blast rang out.

Woody was hoping this one only held six.

Boom!

Woody closed his eyes, drew in one deep breath, and crossed himself. He shot to his feet, and with all the strength he had left in his weary body, charged the man. Head down. Shoulders square. He collided with the gunman and tackled him to the dirt, and their bodies went rolling in the dust.

Woody wrestled the weapon away from the man. It was a hard-won victory. Then Woody used the butt of the shotgun like a Louisville Slugger, laying the stock against the man's skull. The guy went down but not for long. He used his boot to kick Woody's legs from beneath him. Woody fell to the earth, landing squarely on his tailbone. Then the guy, gunless, leapt up and rushed back toward the Vic. In a few moments, the Vic engine was roaring. The other man crawled into the car, clutching his face with both hands.

"Daddy, watch out!"

Woody heard the V-8 cry out as he watched a push bar rushing up at him doing at least thirty-five. Woody lumbered to his feet and faced the oncoming car. He trained the shotgun on the windshield and fired once.

The hood exploded.

So the gun held more than six shots.

He fired again.

The windshield of the Vic disintegrated.

He fired again, and the sound of buckshot slamming into Detroit steel was like trash can lids crashing together. But the car was still coming toward him. Woody threw the empty gun aside and dove out of the way. The Vic squealed into the outer darkness, fishtailing onto the highway, howling into the night.

"Caroline!" Woody called out.

Amos was on the ground, holding Caroline against his chest. In the glow of the Land Rover high beams, he could see that her skin was pale and her lips were turning blue.

"She's not breathing!" Amos shouted. "Call 911!"

Chapter 38

THE HUMAN BODY NEEDS AN INCREDIBLE AMOUNT OF OXYGEN and minerals and nutrients to survive. Your brain gets first dibs on all nutrients. The other organs get the leftovers. The body's veins and arteries are the plumbing system, controlled by a very big public pool pump in your chest, which is always running. Always churning. Always moving product down the line.

Your heart must continually pump tons of blood across approximately sixty thousand miles of blood vessels, twenty-four seven. But if your pump doesn't have enough pressure, you're in trouble. Nutrients don't get to the brain. Oxygen doesn't reach the organs. Things start shutting down. Low blood pressure can kill you. You learn all this when you have a bad heart.

Shock is just low blood pressure. Very, *very* low pressure. The layperson's misconception about shock is that it's not all that dangerous. You turn white; you get dizzy; you pass out. No big deal. But shock is fatal. One in five people with shock die from it.

"Caroline, stay with me, honey!" Woody shouted.

He held Caroline in his arms, her pulse so weak he couldn't feel it in her wrists or neck. He used his ear to listen to her heart. It was still beating.

The owner of the Rover staggered out of the vehicle. "Is she going to be okay?"

Rachel was kneeling in the dirt beside Caroline, holding the phone toward Woody's face while he kept an eye on her airways. Amos was holding Caroline's head in his hands, using his jacket as a pillow. The cat was curled up beside Woody's dad.

An emergency worker was on the line; the phone was on speaker. A female voice was talking back to him.

"We need an ambulance!" Woody said.

"Sir, calm down. Where are you, please?"

Woody looked around. "Where are we, Dad?"

"Outside Douglasville," said the Major. "About three miles off I-20, not far from the eleven-mile marker."

"Sir, be patient. I'm trying to get a fix on your location."

"I just told you where I am!"

"Please hold on, sir."

After Woody's first heart attack, he learned that when you call 911 from a cell phone, the dispatcher can't see your location. Dispatch centers must first ask your wireless carrier for this information. After a lapse of time—sometimes a long time—the information is eventually disclosed to 911 from a cell tower in your area. But it's only an approximation of your location. The location dispatch sees can sometimes be miles away from your true location.

"She's still not breathing," said Amos.

"She's not breathing," Woody said into the phone.

"Sir, I've almost got a fix on your current signal. I need you not to panic, sir."

Woody wasn't panicked. He was watching his daughter die. Her chest was no longer moving. He rolled up his sleeves and began chest compressions. He placed both palms atop Caroline's sternum, and he was counting in rhythm.

"One, two, three, four, five . . ."

"Sir, are you still there?"

"We're here," said Amos into the speaker. "He's doing CPR on her."

Woody sealed his mouth over Caroline's and exhaled until her chest rose. He started compressions again and felt his own insides turn into bile.

"Come on, Caroline."

It all felt too familiar. The chest compressions. The 911 call. The fear. Woody had done the same thing ten years ago when a young woman stepped in front of his truck on a Saturday night.

"Please, Caroline."

"Sir, I have your location fixed. I'm sending someone to you right now."

"They're sending someone!" said Amos.

"One, two, three, four . . ."

"An ambulance is on the way, sir. Should be there in eight minutes. Stay on the line. Can you tell me if the victim is breathing?"

"Eleven, twelve, thirteen . . ."

Chapter 39

————

THE MAN IN FOREST-GREEN SCRUBS WAS LOOKING RIGHT AT Caroline, shining a penlight into her eyes. Clashing with the bubblegum pink walls of the hospital like bits of cilantro in a puddle of melted bubble gum. Then the guy in scrubs checked one of the monitors.

"Hi," Caroline said.

Her words were weak. Her throat was dry. She sounded like a fifty-year smoker.

The young man smiled. "Huh?"

He was cute. He was blondish. His face was round like a little boy's. He wasn't skinny, but he wasn't fat. He was just substantial, and it worked for him. He brought to mind a blond surfer who was very active but also liked Little Debbie snacks.

"What's your name?"

"I'm Chad," the male nurse said.

"You're cute, Chad."

"Um." He moved the penlight to her other eye. "Thanks?"

Chad did not seem to know how to interpret her exaggerated wink.

He turned to address whoever else was in the room. "Those

are just the meds talking. We've got her on some pretty stiff stuff."

"No," said another male voice. "She is right. You really are very cute."

Chad took her pulse. Then he touched her forehead and looked into her eyes. Chad had imperfect teeth. She loved imperfect teeth. Imperfect teeth were so real. So honest. Such a wonderful thing. She had imperfect teeth too. Imperfect teeth were great. Who cares about nice teeth. What was the truth of perfect teeth?

Chad was gazing at her. "Honey, I need you to say your name."

She smiled. "Your name."

Chad grinned back. "I'd say she's going to be okay."

"I like your teeth," she said.

"My teeth?"

She nodded. "They're all screwed up."

Chad raised his eyebrows.

She bared her teeth at him. "See?"

Chad edged away from her as though she were a carrier of plague. That was when she noticed the other people in her room. One of them was Woody. The others were Amos, Elizabeth, and Rachel.

Elizabeth was sitting by the room's only window drinking from a Starbucks cup, wearing the same green scrubs Chad wore. Rachel was curled up in a chair, sleeping. Woody was standing beside Caroline's bed. Amos was sitting beside her, holding her hand. She hadn't noticed the old man clasping her hand until now.

It took her whole seconds to work up the fortitude to speak again. Her throat hurt too badly.

"I'm sorry," were her first words.

Woody shook his head. "Nothing to be sorry about." He moved closer to her and took her other hand. "But there's something important we need to tell you, sweetie. Some news you're going to need to prepare yourself for. Do you understand what I'm saying?"

"What news?"

"It's about your baby," said Amos.

Caroline sat up fully. "What about my baby?"

"You went without oxygen for a long time," said Elizabeth.

The male nurse came back into the room with a knock on the door to announce his arrival. Chad showed her another warm face. But she could no longer find the motivation to smile back, even in her drugged state. Right now she just felt nauseous.

"I quit breathing?"

"Try to calm down," said Woody.

"Just relax," said Amos.

The heart monitor was beeping faster.

Caroline touched her stomach. "What happened to my baby?"

"The doctor's two rooms down," said Chad. "He should only be a couple minutes now. He'll be in here shortly."

Amos squeezed her hand.

• • •

SOMETIMES YOUR WORST FEAR OVERTAKES YOU. IT JUST HAPPENS. Not *fears*, plural. *Fear*, singular. The one fear. The one thing you have been most worried about . . . It finds you. A fear so terrifying that your brain never lets you think of it in advance. It's a safeguard of the subconscious. Because you wouldn't be able to tolerate even thinking about your fear for very long without cracking. But then one day it happens. No forewarning. No preamble. No indication that your life is about to change. The fear becomes real. And there's not a thing you can do about it except let it happen.

This was one of those moments for Caroline.

This was that fear.

The doctor said he had not been able to hear her baby's pulse. He told her that if a baby goes without oxygen for ten minutes, the child could sustain brain damage. It was simple biology: no air, no life.

The news hit Caroline where she lived. Caroline had been born with physical maladies due to a mother who used narcotics. To see her own child grow up the same way she did. With poor vision. Poor hearing. Poor everything. It was a nightmare. Her great fear.

They wheeled Caroline down the hall. They rode elevators to a lower floor. It was just her and Woody and a medical tech. Caroline wasn't even sure why she had asked Woody to be there. He was still somewhat of a stranger to her. But she needed someone right now.

Soon, Woody and Caroline were in the ultrasound room. Woody sat in a chair in the corner. Hands in his lap. Eyes closed. His head was down and his mouth was moving slightly. No sound came from his lips, but it looked like he was whispering something to himself.

The female tech came into the exam room with an overtly chipper attitude, designed to put everyone at ease. That wasn't working either.

Woody raised his head and opened his eyes when the woman entered.

"Were you praying?" Caroline asked.

He just touched her hand.

The tech with the fetal doppler wand made passes over her belly, staring at a screen. The conductive gel on Caroline's tummy was cold. The tech kept glancing at Caroline's abdomen, then back to the monitor. And all Caroline could think about in this moment was a memory from when she was a child. Sitting on the living room floor. In her foster parents' house. A strange house that had never felt like home. She had always been a guest in that house. Nothing inside the house was hers, so she was always just passing through.

In this memory, she was watching TV. She was eleven. She had just lost most of the vision in her left eye. The vision loss had happened suddenly. Nearly overnight. Doctors could not explain it. Nobody could figure it out. They chalked it up to aftereffects of fetal alcohol syndrome. All she knew was that the world was now black on one side of her head. Not dim like before, just black. She was almost blind in her left eye. They might have to enucleate her eyeball someday. Maybe remove it altogether.

That evening she remembered staring at the television in a state of near numbness. Because she had lost vision in one eye, her other eye was having a hard time focusing. Her brain was trying to compensate, and her vision was blurred. *SpongeBob SquarePants* was on the screen, but she wasn't really watching. It was just a mass of colors. Shapes. Moving bits of light. She wasn't really seeing the colors or the shapes on the screen. She was grieving her dead eye. Grieving for the old Caroline who had two good eyes. And wondering who the new Caroline would be and where she would go from here.

She asked Woody to hold her hand.

He took her hand into his own. His fingers were cold but not colder than hers. He used his other hand to warm hers by rubbing them together as though building a fire with two sticks. He was still moving his lips.

On the fetal doppler screen was a mass of blue swirling around in a black background. Just colors. Shapes. Moving bits of light. The woman with the wand wasn't saying anything. She was just looking at the monitor, staring at the screen with a kind of intensity that made Caroline nauseous.

Bad things happen every day. That was what Caroline was thinking. They happen more to some than to others. Some people just attract bad things. It's in their genes, somehow. These people are magnets for catastrophe. They can't help it. They can't change it. The world is simply against them. End of story.

Woody squeezed her hand between both of his, his lips still forming unspoken words. The lady tech was staring at Caroline with a half smile Caroline didn't know how to interpret.

"Tell me what you found," said Caroline.

"I'm sorry," the tech said. "That's not my job. The doctor will have to be the one who tells you. It's policy."

"How long will that be?" said Woody.

"Shouldn't be long."

The tech put down the wand and snapped off her rubber gloves. She turned off the monitor and the screen went black. The room went quiet. The woman flipped on the overhead lights.

"Can't you tell us anything?" Woody said.

The tech took in a breath. Then she turned to face the machine and flipped a switch. The monitor's speakers began to radiate a noise. A loud noise. The rhythmic sound was unmistakable. Like a washing machine. She cranked up the volume.

"Do you know what that sound is?" the tech said.

Caroline's head fell backward onto her pillow as a throbbing sound filled the room. She squeezed Woody's hand so hard she almost broke it. Hot tears fell down her cheeks and saturated her neck and gown.

"That's the heart," said Woody.

Chapter 40

———

PETER TABARES AND JESÚS PARKED THEIR VOLVO IN FRONT OF the run-down home in the wilds of the unincorporated community of Black Creek. The Volvo was an old model but in good shape. And they had needed new wheels. Jesús had driven the Crown Vic into the lake since most of it was peppered with buckshot. Easy come, easy go.

The place had a caved-in roof covered in the obligatory blue tarp, a popular exterior home decor choice in Eastern Kentucky. The porch contained half the contents of the known universe, including not one but two sofas, one deep freezer, an artificial Christmas tree missing branches, and a female blow-up doll.

Peter and Jesús walked up the steps. Peter stood at the front door. There was a gap at the top and at the bottom of the door, letting heat leak through. There was a wreath of sunflowers on the door. Behold, Jesús stood at the door and knocked.

And if he would have knocked any harder, his fist might have penetrated the rotted door and plunged inside the home.

They heard footsteps.

The door opened a few inches, a little chain preventing it from opening all the way. Behind the opening was a young woman. Her hair was white blond with dark-green frosted tips swishing across her face and falling into her eyes like seaweed clinging to the face of the drowned. She was wearing a T-shirt that didn't come down very far. Her face was so pierced it looked like she'd fallen head-first into a tackle box.

"Is Taylor home?" Jesús asked.

"You mean Tater?"

"Is he here?"

"Who are you?"

Jesús smiled. "We'll just wait inside."

Jesús pushed past her. They both walked inside a home that smelled vaguely like a male dormitory after a very long semester.

"Tater's sleeping," the girl said.

"Go wake him up."

"He doesn't like to be woken up."

Jesús nodded. "How about I go do it then?"

She just stared. "No, I got it."

The girl walked back to the bedroom. She was painfully skinny. Her knees were like pine knots on a dying tree.

Peter sat at the kitchen table and drummed his fingers while Jesús stood tall behind him, hands folded against his lap. His arms were covered in white gauze to cover the needle-thin, bloodred claw marks all over his forearms and biceps. The cuts on his face were even worse.

A quarrel was going on in the bedroom. Then Peter heard stumbling around. Finally, a kid walked out of the bedroom wearing boxer briefs. His face was creased like he'd been sleep-ing directly on it. The girl stormed past them. She gathered her things, shoving them into a plastic grocery bag, then slammed the door on her way out but was blocked by the large man stand-ing in her way.

Peter did not stand to greet him. "Taylor Bunson?"

The kid wore a hard glare. "Who wants to know?"

"Me."

The kid took a few seconds to look at Peter's cat-scratched face and eye patch. "What happened to you?"

"Are you Taylor Bunson?" asked Jesús.

There was a long pause.

"No," the kid said.

"Too late, Taylor," the girl said, "I already told him it was you."

Tater looked right at Peter without blinking. "Don't listen to her. She only thinks that's my real name. That's my alien name. My real name's Pat."

"I think you mean alias," said Peter.

"Exactly."

"What's your full name, Pat?"

"Pat. Um. Roberson."

"Sit down, Pat Roberson."

Taylor did not sit. Instead, he folded his arms across his tiny chest and seemed to be aiming for his most intimidating stare. "Are you going to start talking? Or am I going to have to kick you two out?"

"Yeah, that's not going to happen," said Jesús. Jesús unclasped his hands and took one step toward Tater to communicate his physical size to the boy.

"This is Jesús," said Peter. "He used to play ball for Illinois State. He was a safety."

Jesús outweighed Taylor Bunson by at least a hundred and fifty pounds. He had more than eight inches on him. Jesús had passed kidney stones bigger than Taylor Bunson.

"You're a baby daddy now," said Peter.

"What?"

"You have a kid on the way, don't you?"

Peter removed a pistol from the back of his trousers and

placed it on the table. He kept the Colt between them but kept his hands off it. Sometimes a gun on the table says more than a gun in the hand.

"Sit down," said Peter. "I'm not here to argue. I'm here to make a proposition."

"That's illegal," said Taylor. "I am not a sex worker."

Peter sighed. "I'm *making* a proposition. I'm not *propositioning* you." Then Peter used his foot to kick a chair from beneath the table. The chair slid a few feet across the kitchen and landed against Taylor's shins.

"Sit down before you hurt yourself thinking."

Taylor sat.

"If you play ball with me," said Peter, "you stand to benefit."

Taylor nodded.

"Now, this is not going to be fun, I'm going to be honest. But there's really no way around it. I'm going to take you as a hostage."

Tater's whole body tensed.

"Do you understand me? I'm going to kidnap you. You'll be coming with us. That's how a kidnapping works."

"What?" Taylor was looking at the gun.

Peter held his hands out to calm the kid down. "All I ask is that you cooperate with me and Jesús."

"Why are you and Jesus kidnapping me?"

Jesús got in his face. "It's not Jesus. It's *Hay-SOOSE*, whiz kid."

"You said benefit, if I cooperate," said Taylor. "What kind of benefit?"

Peter leaned forward and folded his hands on the table. "The benefit is, I won't kill you right away."

Before Taylor could respond, Jesús came from behind Taylor and placed a burlap sack over his head.

Chapter 41

———

THE SUNDECK WAS NEWLY OILED AND VARNISHED LIKE A SHINY basketball court. You could almost make out your reflection in the floorboards. Twelve partygoers mingled on the topmost deck, eating oysters, feigning interest in forced conversation, stage-laughing at each other's jokes, relaxing on the axis of the Wheel of Life. Some loitered on the docks below or out on the marina's lawn, appreciating the boats in the slips. Woody was gazing out the window of the *Happens*, watching everything and nothing at the same time.

The Land Rover's owner's lawyer called earlier this morning. The owner was declining to press charges, given his state of inebriation. He already had one DUI on his record. He didn't need another. Woody felt nothing but deep sorrow for the guy. He also felt bad for the guy's upholstery.

The *Happens* shined tonight. Not metaphorically, but worse, allegorically. The upper deck had three fifty-foot strands of twinkly string lights stretching across the length of it, suspended by tall bamboo rods. Elizabeth wandered aboard with a drink in her hand, looking for Woody. She found him on the main deck, in

Caroline's bedroom. He was sitting on the bed, in the dark, nursing a beer. He was wearing his khakis. All by himself. Looking out at the black water and tiny lights on the bay.

"Hello, Mr. Antisocial," she said, sitting beside him.

"I don't like crowds."

"You love being around people."

Shrug. "Not anymore."

"Randy is about to tell everyone supper's ready."

On cue, the boat's bell rang. The note sang out an open G across the still water. Within moments, Elizabeth could hear the footsteps of partygoers, all tramping upstairs, topside. The footfalls on the companionways and stairways sounded like livestock. She felt a sharp sense of anger with Woody for involving their nine-year-old in what had almost been a multiple-victim homicide. Rachel seemed unfazed. The kid saw it all as some grand adventure. But Elizabeth was shaken. She was struggling to forgive him.

Woody looked at the ceiling at the source of the noise.

"They're going to be wondering where you are," she said.

His eyes traveled out the window again, to the dark horizon. "I wonder the same thing."

Their shoulders were almost touching. She could feel the warmth radiating from his body being so close to hers. She wanted to be furious with him. But it was hard to hold a grudge against someone who already held a grudge against themselves.

"Do you ever think about you and me?" he asked.

"What do you mean?"

"I mean that I think about you. About us. All the time."

Their eyes were locked. She stared at his mouth.

Knock! Knock!

"There you are," said Jason. "They're announcing dinner, and they're all asking for Woody."

• • •

WOODROW BARKER STOOD BEFORE PEOPLE DRESSED IN COASTAL cocktail attire. A lot of linen and gladiator sandals. They asked him to say a few words to the small crowd. Most of them were former parishioners. Church members from long ago, before they had scattered to the four winds because of publicized tragedy. Everyone was holding their glasses chest high, like they were about to toast, but Woody found that he could not speak. He could give them no reason to toast. There was nothing to toast to.

At least a minute of silence went by. Then all he was able to get out was, "Thank you for coming."

Everyone looked around at each other with big eyes. Disappointed. Full of pity. Unsure how to react. Talk about anticlimactic. He could see it all over their faces. *What happened to Woody? He used to be so warm and fuzzy. How truly sad.*

A light applause broke out. Which was even more awkward than silence.

Woody turned, said something about needing to check something downstairs, and returned to the obscurity of the lower deck. He made his way down the companionway, dodging handshakes and well-wishes. Elizabeth caught him by the elbow. Her white, simple linen dress contrasted with her obsidian hair. Her dark eyes a tonic to a tired soul.

"What the hell was that?" she asked.

"I don't know."

"Why are you trying to run away? Why aren't you talking to your guests?"

"These aren't my guests."

She laughed. "This is *your* party."

"This is Randy Jernigan's party. He's just using my boat."

"He's throwing this whole thing for you. They're celebrating what we've all been praying for. So go out there and say something to them."

"I can't." He looked at his new floor.

The few guests found their way to the two round tables on the sundeck. The votives lit the tableware as people emerged from the galley to deliver plates of food.

Randy Jernigan approached Woody. Randy and his wife had been Woody's biggest supporters at Saint John's back in the day. And when the proverbial excrement hit the fan, Randy had helped with legal fees on Woody's behalf. He was a good man. But he was like a lot of high-powered attorneys: You always knew he was in the room.

Randy hugged Woody's neck from behind. He must have been a tad tipsy, because he squeezed a bit too tightly and almost choked Woody.

"It's good to have you back, Father Woody."

"Thank you, Randy. But don't call me that."

Randy replied with a small shoulder touch. "You'll always be my priest."

"No, I won't, Randy."

Randy seemed confused by this, maybe a little hurt even. He drifted away to talk to other guests.

Woody's small family sat at one table. Elizabeth sat with Jason. Caroline and Rachel were positioned on either side of Woody. The Major sat in a chair next to Jason, who was forced into listening to an octogenarian explain the subtle albeit essential differences between an M48 Patton and an M60 tank.

Elizabeth insisted they bless the food. She looked to Woody and asked him to do the honors. Everyone joined hands and waited for Woody to speak, but Woody declined. He passed the honor off to Rachel. The child closed her eyes and uttered a prayer her father taught her a few weeks earlier.

"Bless this food, oh Lord, and bless it some more. We know this food needs extra blessing, Lord, 'cause we've eaten this crap before."

Elizabeth wore the face of an anesthetized surgical patient.

Woody low-fived Rachel underneath the table.

The subsequent conversation was pinched but polite. Strained but pleasant. Oddly, Jason had the most to say out of anyone. Maybe it was social anxiety, or that he was trying to fill the sonic space between everyone. Elizabeth also tried to offset the weirdness by engaging Caroline in conversation.

"How are you feeling, dear?" she asked Caroline.

Dear.

One of the caterers was placing a salad plate before Caroline when she said, "I feel better. A little more rested."

"That's good," said Elizabeth. "What about school? Do you think you'll want to go to school eventually?"

It had been four days since Caroline had gotten out of the hospital. And already Elizabeth was ready to plan the rest of the girl's life.

"I mean, you're seventeen. You can't just bum around on this boat all day, right?"

Elizabeth was currently involved in cutting Rachel's chicken as though her nine-year-old were incapable of feeding herself.

"No," said Caroline. "I won't be going back to school."

Elizabeth looked profoundly saddened by this. "Don't you want to graduate? At the very least you could go to a trade school. Learn to cut hair or something."

Caroline looked around the table. "I think you're misunderstanding. I mean to say, I'm not going back to high school because I already graduated."

Silence.

Woody bit his lip and looked into his lap because he'd already had this same conversation with Caroline before.

"At sixteen?" asked the Major.

"No kidding?" asked Jason.

Elizabeth said, "That's very impressive, Caroline."

Woody watched Caroline use her butter knife to negotiate a spoonful of butter beans. In the glow of the lamplights, he could see the difference between her two eyes. He'd never noticed it before. The way the left one caught the light made it look black. The other looked like a regular eye.

"What do you want to be when you grow up?" asked Rachel.

"I don't know. I thought I wanted to be a teacher, but I think I've changed my mind."

"Teaching can be fun," said Woody. "Rewarding if you do it right."

The people at the table broke into splintered conversations. They talked about random stuff until it was time for dessert. When the caterers brought plates of blackberry bread pudding to each table, Woody noticed Jason was conversing with Elizabeth intensely, as though they were communicating about something crucial. Swapping glares with each other, as though something was about to go down.

Eventually, Jason tossed his napkin on his empty plate and addressed the table. "I guess this is as good a time as any to share the great news."

He had everyone's attention.

"Do you really think we should do this now?" whispered Elizabeth.

Jason gave her a look of reassurance and clasped her hand in his. "Why not? This is a celebration, and I can't think of a better time to share some good news." Jason kissed her hand. "Elizabeth and I are eloping."

The reaction around the table was one of shock, but everyone congratulated the happy couple with smiles and hugs.

"What's eloping?" asked Rachel.

"It means your mom and I are going away to get married," said Jason.

Nobody really knew what to say.

"We'll be leaving town," said Elizabeth in a quiet voice.

Woody was staring at Elizabeth. Remembering the animated twenty-three-year-old who first walked into his office. Full of ambition and character. Full of drive. And heart. A woman who had fought for his sentence to be commuted. Who had never missed a visiting day. It was impossible for anyone who met her not to love her deeply.

"When are you leaving?" Woody asked.

"Next Friday."

Chapter 42

TAYLOR BUNSON SAT IN THE BACK SEAT, BOUND IN DUCT TAPE at the hands and ankles, with a big strip over his mouth, forcing him to breathe through his nose. Which was difficult inasmuch as one side of his nose was clogged.

The burlap sack was still over his head. It was dark outside. That much he knew, for no daylight was penetrating the sack anymore.

His captors had been mostly silent throughout the drive, communicating in one- or two-word sentences with each other. Sometimes they would whisper. But never for very long. And any time Tater spoke, they ignored him. And so Tater had been listening to the world around him, hoping for any indication of what was happening to him, or where they were heading, or what time of day it was. Tater hadn't figured out much. He did know they were heading south because he heard one of the men say something about Alabama.

Also Tater had figured out that the vehicle he was riding in was a Volvo. He knew this because beneath the opening of the sack, he could see the Volvo logo imprinted on the floormats. The car was definitely a four cylinder. Two liter, at least. Judging from the high-pitched whirring noise the engine made at high RPMs, it was probably an overhead camshaft, since it lacked the valve-train noise of a standard pushrod. So that meant it was a redblock engine. Maybe the B200 or the B230. Likely, it was a Volvo from the 200 series.

The vehicle began to decelerate.

He made his senses as sharp as he could.

The whir of the tires lowered their pitch.

They were pulling over.

In a few moments, the engine was off. The Volvo was quiet for a few moments. Then he heard the men get out. Tater's door opened. Jesús ripped the bag off his head.

"Merry Christmas," said Jesús, who was lighting a cigarette. He cupped his hands and flicked his lighter.

Tater screamed from behind the tape.

"If you shut up," said Jesús, "I'll take the tape off so you can breathe."

Tater went silent. He nodded.

Jesús peeled the tape from his mouth, and it felt as though Tater's lips had been stripped cleanly off his face.

Tater drew in a deep lungful of air and lightly moaned in pain. He licked his lips and tasted the sour duct-tape adhesive. It felt so good to breathe freely.

"Can you untie me for a few seconds too?" asked Tater, pleading.

Jesús stared at him. "Hey, great idea. How about I give you the keys and you could drive for a while?"

"Why have you kidnapped me?"

"Leverage."

Tater wrinkled his face. "I don't even know what that means."

"That doesn't surprise me."

"Bite me."

"Happy to. Just show me where."

"Where are you taking me?"

"Spoiler, kid. We're not going to Legoland."

When the gas tank was full, Jesús put the tape back on Tater's mouth and the bag over his head. In a few minutes they were back on the road.

And it was definitely a 240.

Chapter 43

———

THE MORNING AFTER THE PARTY, A MOTORCADE OF BLACK Chevys pulled into Saint John of the Cross Episcopal Church. There were three of them. The vehicles met at the far edge of the parking lot, huddled together like the cool kids in *Grease*. They were Tahoes. Civilian plates. Lots of antennas. The government must have gotten a deal on Chevys. The FBI was setting up its temporary home base at Saint John's because it was central to town, and Woody had connections with Saint John's. If Peter Tabares was making an appearance, they were going to be ready.

Saint John's had agreed to headquarter the agents, which was ironic. Woody found it surreal that Saint John's would aid in the security of his family when they had been the ones who helped tear it apart.

Woody's asthmatic Ranger pulled into the church. He looked at the old building. White clapboards. Bell tower. Red front door. The more recently built brick elementary school was attached to the wooden building. The architect did a poor job of blending in the old with the new. Woody had been disappointed in the school plans when the architect finished them so many years ago. He had been even more disappointed when the construction crew finished. But, in the words of Doris Day, "Que será, será."

He stepped out of his car and made his way toward the church with a sinking feeling in his soul.

Father Le Roux was waiting by the door. He waved at Woody when he saw him striding across the parking area. He was a tall, muscular Frenchman with a pronounced French Guianese accent. He wore spectacles, and his thinning silver hair was combed and greased to the side. He looked like a math teacher on 'roids. The man had always been a little too powerful for Woody's taste. Clergymen were supposed to be meek. They weren't supposed to be able to bench-press multiple congregational members at once. Then again, priests weren't supposed to go to prison either.

"Brother," said Le Roux. "Welcome."

Le Roux shook his hand so hard Woody could've sworn he heard his fingers crack.

"Thanks for letting me on the premises," Woody said.

Le Roux made a face of disapproval. Then he pulled Woody in for an awkward bear hug. The man's arms were the size of most grown men's thighs. He swatted Woody's back so aggressively that he was surprised he wasn't spitting up bits of bronchial matter. Why did guys do this?

Le Roux had been on the disciplinary committee to get Woody inhibited, which was like mandatory administrative leave for priests, only worse. It was Le Roux who first motioned for Woody's administrative leave. And although Woody was never formally charged with a DUI, it was Le Roux who convinced the committee that he was likely intoxicated and that he should have been charged.

They walked inside. Memories tumbled onto Woody's head like building blocks from the sky. He had not been here since being laicized. Not since before his highly publicized trial.

Saint John's forever lived in his mind. It always would. He walked these hallways in his dreams; he sat in the pews; he stood at the altar. Whether he wanted to or not.

"You grew up in this church," said Le Roux, "didn't you?"

"Since the day I was born."

"This must be a special place for you."

Woody looked at Le Roux. "Must be."

Father Le Roux led him into the choir room. The place was filled with people in FBI hats and shirts. A few Gulf Beach PD officers were present as well. The morning began with a formal briefing. Woody sat beside Le Roux in a brown folding chair that was usually reserved for potlucks and Alcoholics Anonymous meetings.

Woody had gotten a call that morning from an FBI agent asking him to attend a briefing at Saint John's. He'd almost choked on his coffee. There wasn't a place Woody wanted to avoid more than Saint John's. Except for maybe Wallace Correctional.

The call sounded legitimate. More so than the last person who claimed to be FBI. This time, the caller ID showed a Virginia area code and even said "Federal Bureau of Investigation." Which, for all Woody knew, could be a simple technological deception. Still, after all that had happened to Caroline within the last seventy-two hours, he needed information. And since neither Caroline nor the Major was spilling the tea, he was going to have to figure out what the hell was going on from someone else.

Woody was lost in thought, looking at the bookshelf full of choir books. It was the little things that were coming back to him. Things he'd forgotten during his time away. The smell of stale coffee emitting from the choir room walls. The rattle of a window-unit air conditioner. The scent of old carpet.

An agent approached the lectern and began to speak at length about Peter Tabares and the organization he was a part of. A small terrorist group dedicated to defending patriotism, ultranationalism, traditional masculinity, and Western chauvinism. He explained that Tabares had been romantically involved with a woman from this town. The slideshow flipped to a picture of Melinda. It was a police mug shot. Her dyed-blond hair was askew. Her face was covered in the telltale scabs of a meth user. It was not the woman he had been married to so long ago. The agent did not speak of the sensitive information they suspected Caroline was in possession of, but they implied that it was of national importance.

After the briefing, Woody made his way through the choir room toward the main sanctuary. Agents and marshals were scattered throughout the room, charging phones, tapping on laptops. They were all just kids. The oldest among them was maybe late twenties. They all wore trendy haircuts, skinny jeans, designer shoes. He expected former marines and Navy SEALs. Eastwoods, Stallones, and Schwarzeneggers. But Gen Z ran the world. Today's agents were college kids with computer engineering degrees.

When he entered the nave, it was mostly empty, save for an agent on a laptop sitting in the front pew. The vaulted sanctuary was all wood, except for the floor, which was smooth stone. A series of stained glass windows depicted the life of Saint John of the Cross. The scenes illustrated excerpts of poetry from Saint John's *Dark Night of the Soul*, a book Saint John composed in his head while in prison, memorizing it word for word, then reciting it verbatim to the nuns who saved him.

Woody sat in the front pew. He looked at the altar's wooden scrollwork. The little bits of gold. The massive flue pipes of the organ jutting upward into the timber rafters.

Footsteps.

Woody could hear her before he even saw her.

The sound of Elizabeth's nursing shoes was unmistakable. Her soles were squeaking on the stone floor like a high school volleyball player midcourt. The rhythm of her gait was entirely her own song.

When he turned, he could see her outlined by the spears of sunlight coming through the red and gold windowpanes. Green scrubs. Black hair pulled back, swishing behind her. Her backpack slung over her shoulder. Aluminum water bottle on a carabiner clip. The diligent medical staffer. The working girl.

She sat beside him in the pew.

"Father Le Roux told me you were in here."

He stared at the altar in perfect quiet. Hands in his lap. Head slightly bowed.

"You okay?" she asked.

"I don't know."

"Anything I can do?"

"Yes."

She touched his shoulder. "What is it?"

His gaze met hers, and his eyes were burning. "Can you hold me?"

Elizabeth held him as he buried his head into her shoulder and chest. She squeezed him tightly and kissed the back of his wizened head, kissed the sides of his aged face, as he sobbed into her. She pressed her temple against the crown of his head. Woody could feel his lungs heaving and his shoulders bobbing as painful moans exuded from his core like the sounds of a wounded animal. His eyes leaked. His nose clogged.

"I thought you'd never ask," said Elizabeth.

Chapter 44

———

T HE DANK MOTEL WAS SEVERAL NOTCHES BELOW A MOTEL 6, adhering to the strict design style loosely referred to as Early Postmodern Crack House. The wallpaper was floral. Or at least it had been sometime around the mid '60s. Although currently the paper was peeling off the walls to expose a green fungus that had probably been wallpaper glue at one time but now represented a rare genus of subtropical mold. The carpet was brown but did not appear to have started off its career that color. It was not the cheapest place in Gulf Beach, but it was third, according to Jesús.

"This place got three stars on TripAdvisor," Jesús explained, turning on the room lights.

"Wow," said Peter. "Three whole freaking stars?"

"It's a smoking room," added Jesús.

"No way," said Peter in faux excitement. "Score, brah." Then he dropped his bag onto the floor, marched out of the room, and slammed the door behind him.

Jesús shoved Tater onto one of the queen beds. Then the big man hovered over Tater and grinned. "Let's get you dressed for the ball, Cinderella."

Jesús muscled Tater into the bathroom and propped him

against the corner of the tiled shower-tub. He got out his phone and took a picture of Tater. "Say cheese, kid." The flash went off several times. Jesús checked each pic, presumably for composition, then reposed Tater.

Peter entered the bathroom. "No, not like that. Have him kneeling in the shower. It'll be more effective. Kneeling looks helpless."

"What if we had him curled up in the bathtub, you know, on his side?"

Peter crossed his arms like Kubrick. "That could work. Fetal position is scary."

"Yeah, that will scare her."

The two men positioned Tater in the bathtub, adjusting him until he was in an embryonic position. And he kept trying to figure out who they were trying to scare. And why. His mom? Did they think his mother was loaded or capable of paying a ransom? If so, they were in for a huge shock. His mom might have been able to pay them off in porcelain clown figurines but not with actual cash.

Finally, Jesús peeled the tape from Tater's mouth. Tater drew in a cool breath of air through his mouth. His lungs filled and he felt his stomach expand.

"Thank you," Tater said. "Oh God, thank you."

The big man asked him, "How much do you think you're worth?"

"What?"

"In dollars and cents."

"I don't know."

"Guess."

"Probably not much."

The big man smirked. "Better hope it's a lot more than that."

Jesús helped him back to one of the beds and gave him a

bottle of water. Tater drank thirstily, clasping the bottle with his two bound hands while Jesús was working on a laptop, editing the pictures.

"Who are you sending these to?" asked Tater.

"Questions, questions," said Jesús.

Chapter 45

Amos and Caroline sat in Ellen Simmons's room, using the old woman's computer. Ellen Simmons was originally from Senoia, Georgia, the widow of a State Farm salesman and a two-time national champion knitter. She had a hopeless crush on Amos. The feelings were not reciprocated. And although Amos did not like leading Ellen on, he didn't own a computer, so he took one for the team. He and Caroline had decided that using a public computer in the library wasn't prudent ever since they had been kidnapped by terrorist asshats.

Caroline manned the keyboard and mouse while Amos was constantly pausing to look over his shoulder to keep tabs on Ellen. The gray cat sat in the Major's lap. In the short amount of time he'd been living with Amos, Caroline could swear the cat had already gained significant weight. The Major would glance at the screen quickly, then rise from his seat, head popping up, surveying the room like a whac-a-mole.

"Quit doing that," said Caroline. "You're making me nervous."

"You need to hurry," said Amos. "She's about to come back. I can feel it."

Presently, Ellen was in her kitchenette, making tea. He could hear the kettle squealing, and he could see Ellen standing before three teacups and saucers, arranging silverware, napkins, and cookies on a platter. The woman was not just making tea; she was preparing a full-blown tea service for the queen.

"I don't know why you're so afraid of her. She's sweet."

"The woman is a competitive knitter."

"She's nice-looking."

"She looks like Barbara Bush."

Amos glanced behind himself once more, then returned his attention to the seventeen-year-old at the computer. "You have one more minute, tops."

"I need more time."

"You don't have more time."

"This is an old computer. It's moving really slow."

Amos whac-a-moled for another look. "Hurry. She's coming this way."

"What's the big deal? She's probably not even going to know what we're doing. I don't think she's going to care."

"You don't know Ellen. Telephone, telegraph, tell-an-Ellen. She keeps the Gulf Beach rumor mill in business."

Caroline clicked the mouse a few times and closed the open windows on the computer. Then opened a new one.

Ellen was already placing the tea service onto the coffee table in her living area.

"Lucky, do you want sugar in your tea?"

"Yes, please!" said Amos. "Lots and lots of sugar. And take your time putting it in. I like my sugar fully dissolved."

Caroline looked at him oddly. "Lucky?"

"Long story."

"I thought you couldn't eat too much sugar, Lucky," said Ellen. "What about your diabetes?"

Amos patted his right upper arm where his continuous glucose monitoring apparatus was mounted. "I'll just give myself some more magic juice."

Ellen spooned sugar into his cup and looked at them from across the room. "Lucky, what are you two doing over there?"

"She's teaching me how to check my email. Be right over."

Caroline maneuvered the mouse and clicked a few more times. "I got it," Caroline whispered. "The flash drive still works."

Amos let out a monstrous sigh. The USB-C drive had been trapped in his stomach for almost twenty-five minutes. Stomach acid, he'd heard, was powerful enough to dissolve a license plate. And from the looks of the flash drive, this was true. In only twenty-five minutes, the plastic portion of the drive had been semi-digested and the metal portion oxidized. And it probably would have been worse if he hadn't been taking his stomach-acid inhibiting medication. He had been keeping the flash drive in his sock ever since. Surgically taped to his ankle.

"How about cookies?" said Ellen. "Would either of you like any cookies?"

Amos removed the flash drive and slipped it into his pocket.

"Yes, ma'am," said Caroline, rising from the chair and powering down the computer. "I know I'd certainly like some cookies. What about you, Lucky?"

• • •

This was not home. Not to Elizabeth. If it had been home, everyone would have been dressed differently. The invitation to the small lunch at Jason's house had said "snappy casual," but everyone disregarded the "snappy" part and went straight for the "my kid plays lacrosse" motif. Pastel colors, seersucker, Vineyard Vine's ten-dollar polo shirts with the eighty-dollar whale embroidered on the chest.

This was supposed to be an intimate lunch among friends, but

it had turned into a coed wedding shower among Jason's friends
and family. This was exactly the kind of thing Elizabeth had been
trying to avoid by eloping. But Jason's family had other ideas.

Six couples sat in Jason's living room watching Elizabeth
open gifts. A small card affixed to a plastic-covered basket was
adorned in curlicue handwriting, citing the list of the contents.

>*A jigsaw puzzle piece, because you fit together.*
>*A stick of gum, so you'll always stick together.*
>*A pack of seeds, to help love grow stronger every day.*
>*A single tissue, to wipe away the tears, good or bad.*
>*A matchstick, because you are a perfect match.*
>*Glitter, so you'll never forget to sparkle.*
>*A candle, for a bright future together.*

All that was missing from the kit was the barf bag.

Elizabeth hugged the woman who gave the gift, then said,
"I'll just go get a pair of scissors to open it." She left the room
wearing a slightly insane, albeit well-bred 1950's housewife smile.

She walked into Jason's newly repainted kitchen, which still
smelled of low VOC paint. Elizabeth searched for the scissors,
digging through various drawers and cabinets to no avail. Her
search reminded her that this space was not hers. And it never
would be hers. This was Jason's home.

"Which drawer are they in again?" she called out.

"They're not in a drawer," said Jason from the other room.
"They're hanging on a hook in the pantry."

On a hook in the pantry? What kind of deranged human kept
his scissors on a hook in the pantry? God made scissors to go in
drawers. This was the natural order of things.

Elizabeth flipped on the light to the pantry and collapsed
against the wall. She listened to everyone's happy voices coming

from the other room. They all seemed to be having a gay old time, sipping fruity drinks, eating tiny crustless sandwiches. But Elizabeth wasn't fully here at all. Not in spirit. Right now she was still in Saint John's nave. In the pew . . . with him.

Elizabeth shut the pantry door and leaned against it with her head in her hands, the fluorescent light above flickering ever so slightly.

She was startled by a knock at the door behind her. The knob jiggled.

"What are you doing in there, sweetie?"

She couldn't bear to look at him. She didn't even want to be here. *Who are these people?* And more importantly, *Who am I?* And why wasn't she with her own family? These people were not her family. Right now, Woody was babysitting Rachel. They were in his den, Woody and his two girls, eating lunch, sitting on his ugly couch, amid his books and junk and his colossal mess. And Elizabeth would rather have been there.

Knock, knock.

"Liz?"

"I'm fine."

"Why are you blocking the door?"

"I just need a minute."

"Why?"

"Just give me a second, Jason." Her voice was harsher than she intended.

Elizabeth could hear his footsteps as he walked away. She could hear mumbling voices from other partygoers in the kitchen. Concerned voices. "What's she doing in the pantry?" "I always knew she was a weirdo." Voices discussing what might be wrong with Elizabeth. That was what everyone had always wanted to know. What *was* wrong with Elizabeth? She wished she knew.

She plucked the scissors off their little pantry hook. And that was when the reality sort of landed on her. The awareness had always been there, of course. But sometimes awareness lies buried beneath the mountains of sand and dust of daily life. Sometimes you're so busy being who you should be that you forget who you are.

Elizabeth exited the pantry quietly and turned off the light. Jason was waiting for her on the other side of the door.

"What's going on?" he asked.

"I just have a really bad headache."

He came to her and kissed her forehead. "Do you want some water? Some aspirin?"

"No, it's okay." She was smiling but not fully. "I just want to go home, Jason."

"Home?" he asked.

Home.

Chapter 46

———

PETER PULLED THE BAG OFF TATER'S HEAD.

"Wakey, wakey."

Tater's eyes snapped open. It was evening. He was disoriented because he'd been sleeping on and off all day.

"Phone call time," said Jesús. "How's that sound to our guest?"

Although it wasn't really a question since Jesús was holding a knife to Tater's throat.

Jesús presented Tater with a phone. Tater told them where they could shove their phone, and the knife was pressed harder against his throat.

Peter spoke in a calm voice. "You're going to talk to your girl, Baby Daddy. And you're going to keep her on the phone for at least three minutes."

"Who? Caroline?"

"How many baby mamas you got?"

Tater struggled against his bound wrists. "Caroline ain't got no phone."

"She does now. Caroline's got a lot of things now."

"What the hell's that supposed to mean?"

Peter leaned into Tater's line of vision. "If you don't quit asking questions, I think I'm going to kill you just to shut you up."

Jesús pressed the knife tighter into his Adam's apple. "Let me kill him right now. He's not going to cooperate. I don't like this little turd."

"Wait! What do you want with Caroline?"

Peter shook his head. "Get a load of this kid. More questions. What did I *just* say?"

The knife dug deeper.

"Please!" Tater was screaming. "What's Caroline got to do with any of this? What do you want from me? What's this all about?"

Neither of the men replied.

Peter sighed, then looked at Jesús with a frown. "All I hear are questions. Kill him."

"You just can't reason with some people," said Jesús.

"No! Wait! I'll do it. But she don't want to speak to me. I can promise you that. You're wasting your time."

The bald man smiled and patted Tater's cheek. "That's a brave little potato."

Jesús plugged the phone in with a cord that was connected to an iPad and a bunch of devices with lots of blinking lights. He positioned the phone before Tater's mouth, and a satellite map appeared on the screen.

"What do I say to her?"

Peter said, "I don't care. Just keep her talking. If she hangs up on you, I will have Jesús cut off your tattoos, one by one, and we will mail them to your mother. Do you think your mom would like that?"

Jesús was grinning at him.

"No," said Tater. "My mom hates my tattoos."

The phone was ringing.

"I'm telling you," said Tater, "Caroline's just going to hang up."

Jesús moved the blade from Tater's neck to the tattoo on Tater's chest.

"Chill out with the knife! I'm cooperating."

"I just don't want you saying the wrong thing," said Jesús.

"What are you afraid I'm going to tell her? That Professor X and a college football player are holding me hostage at the Motel Craptastic?"

The phone kept ringing.

"Why three minutes?" said Tater.

Peter was still clicking on icons, typing numbers into a keyboard. "Because it takes three minutes to break into her phone. And if you can't give us three minutes, it's bye-bye Buzz Lightyear."

Tater waited for a voicemail greeting. He *prayed* for a voicemail greeting. Maybe if it went to voicemail, they'd let him live for another few hours. But there was no voicemail. Only a click. Then a long pause. Then the noise of someone fumbling with a phone came through the console.

"Caroline?" Tater said. "Caroline, are you there?"

The voice was female. And young. Like a kid.

"No. This is Rachel. Caroline left her phone on the counter."

Tater looked at Peter. The satellite map was zooming in.

"Is, um, Caroline around? It's important. I need to speak with her."

"Who's calling?" asked the girl. "Your name isn't showing up on her ID."

"Um."

Peter gave Tater the "keep rolling" gesture.

"Uh. Just tell her it's her boyfriend."

"She doesn't have a boyfriend."

"Tell her it's Tater."

"Tater? Pretty sure she said you're a giant butthole."

"Please. You have to get her. I mean . . . tell her I miss her." Tater nearly started crying. "Tell her I really need to talk to her and that this will probably be the last time she'll ever hear from me again, I swear."

Long silence.

"Hold on. I'll get her."

. . .

TALKING TO CAROLINE WAS WEIRD. HEARING HER VOICE ON THE phone brought up bad memories. Which surprised him. He didn't realize how terrible he felt about the way he'd treated her until now.

"What do you want?" she asked.

"Nothing. Um. What're you doing?"

"Why did you call?"

Taylor let it all go. He told Caroline about his abusive father and about how his dad kicked him out when he was sixteen. About dealing drugs and sleeping in his car. He said he was sorry for how cruel he had been. How sorry he was that he had treated her so badly. He did all the talking while Caroline did all the monosyllabic responding. He lost all track of the clock that was running and forgot all about Peter's iPad.

Caroline finally barged in, "What do you want from me? Why are you telling me all of this?"

"I don't know. I'm just . . . I don't know."

"Are you done?"

He wiped his face. "I guess."

"Okay, well, then I'm hanging up now."

He glanced at the clock. Two minutes and fifty-three seconds.

"No, wait. Oh my God. Caroline, please don't hang up the phone. I'm begging you."

"I don't need this right now," she said. "You're probably high. You'll get over it when you sober up. Goodbye, Tater."

"No, Caroline." He was crying now. "Don't. Please don't hang up. I am not in a good place right now, and I need you to listen to me."

"I have to go."

"No, please—"

"Don't hang up just yet, Caroline," said Peter.

There was a long pause.

"Who is this?" said Caroline.

"An old friend of Melinda's."

Silence.

"Stay on the line," Peter said. "I'm about to text you some pictures."

Chapter 47

———

Woody's truck came to an intersection where a flock of young albino tourists waited to cross the street. That was what the locals called the herds of white-bodied teenagers and college students who before the week was finished would either die of sun poisoning or wish they had.

Spring breaks in the US occurred at varying intervals, ranging from February to mid-April. Thus, the waves of spring breakers were always changing. One week it was Jayhawks, Razorbacks, Cornhuskers, and Badgers. The next week it was Go Dawgs, War Eagle, and Roll Tide. This week the spring breakers must have belonged to Auburn. Because there were enough tigers in town to film a Frosted Flakes commercial.

Woody stamped on the brakes and flashed his high beams, signaling to the tourists that they were safe to cross. He and Rachel watched the spring breakers move across the street en masse. Woody removed a cigar from the plastic sheath and clipped the end while he waited.

"Can I ask you a question?" Rachel asked.

"Shoot."

"Are priests allowed to smoke?"

"I'm not a priest."

"I know. But when you were?"

"Priests are human, just like you. Are you allowed to smoke?"

"No. I'm nine."

More tourists crossed his path. Young women wearing bathing suits that looked like they were made of dental floss and strategically positioned bottle caps. Young men behind them, bowed out. Were these kids planning on swimming tonight, this early in the season? The water was cold enough to kill. Fact: The most common causes of tourist death on the Gulf Coast is hypothermia.

"I thought God didn't like for people to smoke and drink."

"Ever notice how everybody seems to know exactly what God *doesn't* like."

When the crosswalk was clear, they were driving again.

They arrived at Elizabeth's house on Filmore Avenue. Woody yanked the parking brake and Rachel slid out of the truck. Woody kept the truck running. He got out and carried all Rachel's bags up the sidewalk to the front door. She had only stayed at his house for less than twenty-four hours, and she came with four bags. Four big bags.

When Woody got to the porch, Elizabeth was on the swing. She held a longneck bottle in her hands. She was staring off into the night. Rachel said goodbye and rushed inside.

Elizabeth never drank beer. She was a white-wine person.

"Hey," he said.

"Hey yourself," she said.

"Catching up on some solo drinking, I see."

Elizabeth glanced at the truck, idling at the curb. Then his ex-wife turned her eyes to him, and they did not have their normal spark. The last time they had been together, he had lost his composure and wept. It was a hard thing for two people to forget. A great exchange of emotion like that.

"I want to apologize for what happened earlier," he said.

"I don't want you to," she said. She leaned forward, her eyes earnest now. With perhaps a touch of the old spark in them. "How are you doing?"

Woody sat beside her. The swing rocked back and forth.

"I don't know," he said with a sigh. "How about you?"

"I don't either."

Chapter 48

———

TATER JOGGED THROUGH GULF BEACH TRAFFIC, HALF CLOTHED, barefoot on the pavement, beneath the high-pressure sodium lamps lining the highway. His wrists were badly burned and bleeding. Bits of duct tape were clinging to his ankles. Jesús was on his tail, racing behind Tater, matching him step for step.

"You're dead!" shouted Jesús.

Tater had no reason to doubt the man.

In high school, Taylor Bunson had been on the track team, but he was not a gifted athlete. He had only signed up for track because he had been a big fan of the girls' track uniforms. His days of running the four-hundred meter had long since passed. Since then, he'd plowed through a few freighter loads of vape cartridges, and right now his lungs felt about as healthy as two dried figs.

"I'm gonna kill you!" shouted Jesús.

He glanced over his shoulder. Jesús was only a few hundred yards behind him. Running wide open, like a fullback. The guy was superhuman. Knees pumping in the air. He didn't even look tired. It was only a matter of time before he caught Tater and turned his body into a heavy bag.

Tater dug deep. He put as much distance between himself and Jesús as he could.

Jesús was screaming profanities, which only gave Tater more incentive to run harder. Tater's bare feet were striking the grit and gravel with loud slaps. His chest burned like an inferno. They were running through the commercial district. Past all the T-shirt shops, tattoo parlors, and chain restaurants beside the busy highway.

"You hear me!" shouted Jesús. "You're dead!"

There were a bunch of tiny-house businesses ahead. All colorfully painted like miniature beach bungalows. Tater took a series of turns, weaving through each of the small buildings and finally landing behind a dumpster and waiting until he saw Jesús fly past. It took a while, but he heard Jesús trot by. He could hear the big man's heavy breathing.

Tater emerged from the dumpster and began running the other way. He ran through a run-down apartment complex, fast-food parking lots, and a Publix supermarket. A gas station parking lot was where he finally hit the energy wall. Tater was so breathless that he lost the contents of his stomach in the grass. For a few minutes, he squatted outside the station, tucked between the thrumming ice machine and a display of bundled firewood, trying to catch his breath.

A pile of rags beside him rattled a paper coffee cup of coins. "Spare change?" the pile of rags asked.

Tater asked the guy if he knew where the Bald Point Marina was.

The man's glassy eyes were almost yellow. His words were garbled and mostly incoherent, but that didn't stop him from barking a few colorful obscenities at Tater. "Man, I just want some food. Don't ask me no questions."

"Listen to me. I don't have any money. But I need to know where the marina is."

That was when Tater saw Jesús standing in the gas station parking lot. Jesús was screaming into his phone, waving hands in the air, having an animated conversation. But he had not seen Tater. Not yet.

"Hey, I'm talking to you!" shouted the homeless guy. "I just want a little food, man."

The guy's shouting drew Jesús's attention. The big man locked eyes with Tater and his face broke into a smirk. Within a millisecond, Tater was running through traffic again. He had no idea where he was going or which direction to run.

The running seemed to last forever. His feet were cut to shreds on stray bits of highway gravel. He could feel hot blood on his toes.

He found a Home Depot with a monstrous parking lot full of cars and trucks. He checked over his shoulder. No signs of Jesús.

What he needed was a break from running. What he needed was to breathe. With staggering steps, he curled himself behind the tires of a semitruck tire in the parking lot. He clutched his bare torso with both arms and found that he was shivering from cold. He was covered in a film of clammy sweat.

He kept checking for Jesús from beneath the wheelbase of the eighteen-wheeler. Every couple seconds he would glance under the truck, prepared to see Jesús striding up. But he never did.

After a few minutes, Tater caught his breath. He was about to leave the parking lot when he heard the sharp noise of a loaded weapon behind him. The unmistakable *ka-click* was deeper and louder than expected.

"Gotcha," said the voice behind him.

• • •

WOODY AND CAROLINE ENTERED THE RESTAURANT. IT WAS YOUR typical all-American diner. A neighborhood restaurant. The kind of hole-in-the-wall joint you could only find in the older section of Gulf Beach, a part of town where real estate developers had not found any fiscal value. Yet. The kind of place where a steady stream of loyal customers had been keeping an old family business afloat despite the Alabama Department of Health's low opinion of the establishment.

There was a bell over the café door. Twin fiddles and a steel guitar played overhead. A thick layer of patina that looked like one part nicotine and two parts grease coated everything. The walls were lined with autographed black-and-white headshots of has-been celebrities whom nobody had ever heard of, from minor TV shows nobody ever watched, adorned with sloppy signatures nobody was able to read.

They got a booth. The waitress was older. Her hair was more purple than white. Woody had gone to high school with her. They ordered coffees. The waitress gave them a couple menus.

"Are you really going to eat a hamburger tonight?" Caroline asked.

"Yes, I am."

"It's late. Almost ten o'clock.

"Receiveth what cheer you may, the night is long that never findeth the day."

"But what shall Elizabeth saith, Shakespeare?"

"Elizabeth is going to be a married woman soon. She won't have time to worry about the condition of my arteries anymore."

Woody glanced out the café window at his truck. And he remembered bringing Elizabeth to this same café when they were dating. It was their place.

"What does that tattoo on your hand mean?" Caroline asked.

He looked at the five purple dots between his index finger and thumb. Like markings on a die. He touched his hand. "Four corner dots represent four walls. The inner dot is me."

"Where'd you get it?"

"I used a BIC pen and a guitar string."

"Is that a prison thing?"

"It is." He glanced at her sunflower marking on her forearm. "Now you show me yours."

She turned her forearm over. "A sunflower isn't actually a flower. A sunflower's actually a whole bunch of flowers. See, each sunflower head is made of thousands of teeny-tiny flowers, and the disc florets in the middle have both male and female sex organs; they produce seed. They can self-pollinate or receive pollen that's in the wind or pollen by insects. They can live in a drought. They can take harsh sunlight."

"I'm afraid you lost me, Teacher."

"A sunflower needs nothing to survive but itself." She used her finger to trace the letters imprinted on her arm: *Survive*.

He was still looking out the restaurant's window when he noticed the green Volvo pull up next to his truck. The motorist was sitting behind the wheel but not getting out of the car. Like he was waiting to pick someone up. He was wearing sunglasses even though it was dark. He wasn't slouching. He wasn't looking around. He wasn't fiddling with a phone, or a radio, or a book. This guy was just looking into the restaurant windows.

"What are you not telling me, Caroline?"

She stared at him.

"Why won't you turn it over?"

"Turn what over?"

"You're endangering yourself. You're endangering everyone who loves you."

She did not answer this. They sat in silence for a few moments, staring into cups.

"Can I ask what made you want to be a priest?" she finally asked.

Woody took a sip and drew himself back into the conversation. "Hard to explain, really. Happens differently for everyone. I was twenty-seven when I first knew. I thought I had gone insane. But I wasn't crazy. It took another eight years to finally enter a lifestyle of true medical insanity."

The waitress came with their drinks. She asked what they wanted to eat. Caroline ordered a burger with fries and two sides of ranch. Woody ordered a bacon burger on white and asked the waitress to give him as many onion slices as she could without losing her job.

He looked out the window. The Volvo was still there. Idling.

"What's a vocation?" she asked.

"Marching orders from God."

Caroline nodded. She was silent for a long time, looking into her coffee. She looked like there was something she really wanted to say but didn't know how to say it.

"Can I be honest with you?"

He just waited.

"I don't believe in God," she said.

He nodded.

"Does that bother you?"

"Why would it bother me?"

"Well, you're so . . . you know."

"I don't care if you believe in God. Your biology believes, and that's all that matters."

"What do you mean?"

"Doesn't matter."

After a long moment of silence, Woody spoke again. "Consider the birds. A bird cannot comprehend the idea of God. Probably can't comprehend anything beyond the idea of food and shelter. A bird just flies around, randomly pooping on people's heads all day. They can't help it. They have brains the size of Tic

Tacs. And yet your heavenly Father feeds them. Now I ask you, do you think God cares whether a bird's little brain *believes* in him? And aren't you worth much more than a bird to God? And yet not one of these birds falls to the ground without God's care."

"You make it sound so easy."

Shrug.

Caroline was playing with a sugar packet on the table. She thought for a long time. Then she spoke using a soft, almost indiscernible voice.

"I was raped," she said.

The words hit him like a bullet. Like being slapped. He was unable to respond at all. And from all his years listening to confessions, he'd found no response was often the best.

"I think that's when I quit believing in God. When it happened. I mean, how could I keep believing? You know? Why would he let that happen to me?"

"I'm sorry."

"Not your fault."

The waitress delivered their food. The meals came on big blue plates. Haystacks of french fries. Mountains of onion rings.

He looked out the window again. The Volvo was still there.

"How old?"

"Thirteen."

Silence.

"It was one of my foster dads," she said. "He was a big-time Christian. Really active in his church. I never told anyone."

The plate resting before him looked appetizing, but he was undergoing a sudden loss of hunger.

"If your God were real," Caroline said, "all the bad stuff that happens in this world wouldn't happen. So it just doesn't make sense. Why would God sit back and watch bad things happen? I mean, how do you explain why God lets all this crap go down? If

God is real, why doesn't he change anything? Why does he just sit there and do nothing?"

Woody had still not touched his burger. "Who says God did nothing?"

"Well, it happened to me. So obviously he did nothing about it."

"What about me? Am I nothing?"

She gave a slight eye roll. "Come on."

"And Rachel. Is she nothing too?"

"Of course not. You're missing the point."

"How about the love you feel for the miracle in your womb, and the fact that even after all you've been through, you're going to bring life into this world? Real, pure, innocent life. You're going to get a chance to set the record straight with your own infant. Is that nothing?"

"No."

"I don't know much about God, Caroline. I wish I did, but I'm too dense. But here's one thing I know. In life, every person is given one adventure. One big, scary, horrible, awesome, incredibly alarmingly, disturbingly beautiful adventure. It doesn't look like an adventure when it's happening, and it sure as hell doesn't feel like one. But when you reach the end, something happens.

"All the ups and downs, the peaks and valleys, the agony and the ecstasy, the moments of beauty interlaced with suffering—you realize it all meant something. It wasn't a test. It wasn't a trial. It wasn't punishment. It was an adventure. And you only get one, so you'd better make the most of it. Because one isn't nearly enough."

Caroline was staring at him. "No offense, but that sounds like a load of crap to me."

"Maybe it is."

"Is this what got you through prison? Your belief in some big adventure?"

"No. What got me through prison was Psalm 119:86."

She wrinkled her brow.

"Shortest prayer in the Bible."

"What prayer is that?"

"'Help me.'"

Woody looked out the window again. The guy was still in the Volvo. Looking straight at them.

Chapter 49

———

THE OLD COWBOY HAD A HOME DEPOT BAG IN ONE HAND AND A pistol in the other. Tater's hands were in the air. He was still crouched with his back pressed against the twenty-four-inch truck tire. The old man was moving toward him, boot heels clicking on the blacktop. He was bowlegged and tall. Broad-shouldered but old.

He told Tater to get to his feet.

Tater stood.

His eyes landed on Tater's Buzz Lightyear tattoo above his nipple.

"Who are you?" the man said.

The guy was clad in denim on denim. He did not wear a cowboy hat, but he might as well have. The pistol he carried was the only thing wrong with the cinematic picture of a cowhand. The gun was smaller than a man his size ought to be carrying, at least by movie standards. This was a tiny weapon that looked almost comical in the man's big hand.

"State your business, son," the old man said.

Tater stammered. "Y-you . . . you have to help me."

The man spit.

"Please, I need your help."

"Why were you crouched like that?" the man said. "Why were you hiding under my trailer?"

Tater tried to think of the best way to explain his situation, but he kept coming up short.

The man was growing impatient. He stepped forward, gun first. "I saw you peeking beneath my truck just now when I come walking up. Are you waiting to rob someone? Are you fixing to rob me? Talk, kid, or I got a right to self-defense."

"I'm not going to rob anyone, sir. I was just watching for someone, that's all. Someone is after me."

"After you? Cops?"

"No, sir. Nothing like that. Please, just listen to me. I can—"

"You on drugs?"

"No, I swear—"

"You hitting the bottle?" The man waved the gun downward. "Get on the ground. Hands behind your head."

Tater began to kneel on the pavement, hands behind his head, supplicating for mercy. "Please, sir. If you'll just listen to me, I'll explain."

When Tater's hands were above his head, the man's eyes traveled to Tater's burned, mangled wrists. And Tater felt the dam inside him begin to break. He was about to die tonight; he could feel it. And he couldn't shake the feeling that there was nothing anyone could do about it.

Tater sobbed. "Help me, sir. Help me. I don't know what to do."

The man's hard face seemed to soften. "Help you do what? Tell me why you're running, boy."

Then the tears started pouring. The pent-up emotion from the past few days just gushed out.

The cowboy took a step closer. "Son, I can't help you if you don't tell me who you're running from."

Tater sniffed. "His name is Jesus."

The cowboy lowered his weapon. He engaged the safety and secured the firearm in its holster. There were fresh tears in the old man's leathery face. "Hell, son. If there's one thing I've learned, it's that you can't run from Jesus."

Chapter 50

——

Woody's truck was approaching a four-way stoplight downtown, across from the high school. The driver of the Volvo was behind them. The motorist was making no attempt to hide that he was following them now. He followed at a normal distance. He wasn't annoyingly close, but he wasn't staying a few cars back to blend in either. He still wore the shades.

"Why do you keep looking in the rearview mirror?" Caroline said.

"Because someone's following us."

Caroline fell into her seat and buried her face into her hands. She made a self-defeating grunt. "Oh my God."

"Mine too."

"What should we do?"

"You act like I'm supposed to know."

He could see anger all over Caroline's face. It reminded him a little of the Major, the way her face turned into a complete snarl. She turned around in her seat and looked through the rear windshield, staring right at the Volvo driver, then gave him the one-finger salute.

"Pretty sure we shouldn't do that," he said.

Woody ran a stop sign, just to see what would happen. The Volvo tapped his brakes at the sign and ran it with him. Woody drove through random neighborhoods, off the main highway, taking a series of twists and turns through an impossible onslaught of McMansions. He drove through industrial areas, residential areas. The Volvo followed. After about fifteen minutes the Volvo was still eating their bumper.

"I hate to say this," Caroline said, "but I have to go to the bathroom."

Woody glanced into the rearview mirror. "Sorry, you'll have to file a complaint with customer service."

He yanked the wheel left. Then right. He pulled into a neighborhood and hit the accelerator, taking a serpentine route through all the terracotta-stucco-style homes that pepper the Gulf Coast from the tip of Texas to the Straits of Florida and are wholly indistinguishable from each other except for their differing shades of antiseptic pastels. He spun the wheel over and over again until they launched into a random driveway.

It was a nice house. Big lawn. The only house without enough landscape illumination to signal a 747. Woody parked behind a guesthouse and turned off the truck lights.

"What are we doing here?"

He shushed her. "I'm pretty sure I lost him."

Woody was watching the mirrors. No Volvo. Woody waited to make sure the Volvo was gone. In a few moments, they were on their way again. Seemingly no cars following them now. Woody let out a mock sigh of relief.

Caroline was still bouncing her knees. "Can I go to the bathroom now?"

Woody glanced in his side mirrors. It was the Volvo again.

"He's back," said Woody.

Chapter 51

─────

TATER ARRIVED AT THE BALD POINT MARINA RIDING SHOTGUN
in a Peterbilt 579EV, listening to the Gaither Vocal Band
sing of a "yonder city" while he watched a crucifix swing gaily
from the truck's rearview mirror.

The semi pulled into the marina, and Tater asked the man
to wait here for him. But the driver said he couldn't wait; he had
to be in Orlando by tomorrow morning. So the trucker got out
of the vehicle and God-blessed Tater, prayed for him, and gave
Tater a small vial of water from the River Jordan he'd ordered off
the Home Shopping Network.

They embraced for a final time, and Tater stood in the marina
parking lot wearing the man's rubber flops and a XXL T-shirt
and carrying a brand-new Dollar General Bible beneath his arm,
along with a Joel Osteen book titled *Whatever You've Done, That's
What You Did*.

"Go with God, son," said the trucker shortly before climbing
into the Peterbilt.

The marina was old. Long past its heyday. There was an abandoned restaurant with faded wood-shingle siding. A lopsided patio

with sun-bleached umbrellas and picnic tables, way past their prime. There was a light on in the marina office.

He went inside, where he found a clerk who was a middle-aged lady with bottle-blond hair watching cable news and playing sudoku. Tater asked the lady if a girl named Caroline lived here. The clerk smacked her gum and looked him over.

"Caroline?"

"She's got red hair and she's, um, pregnant."

The woman scrutinized him, head to foot. Then she pointed nonchalantly out the window to the wooden boat with paddle wheels.

"She lives there?"

The woman smacked her gum. "Yep."

Tater walked along the docks until he reached the boat. It was big, run-down, and it had paddle wheels. He made his way along the gangway until he was standing on the deck. He knocked on the sliding glass door. Nobody answered. A motion-sensing light came on. Then it clicked off.

He knocked again.

In the distance, a few boats trolled by. Their motors, gurgling quietly, reverberated across the dark water.

Behind him, a woman came walking up the gangplank. "Can I help you?" the woman asked.

She had short dark hair and wore a windbreaker.

"Uh," he began, but no other words came out. "I'm Taylor Bunson," he finally said.

The woman raised an eyebrow. "Okay?"

The woman waited for an answer. She put a hand on her hip.

"I'm a friend of Caroline's," he said. "Is she here?"

The woman's eyes went to Joel Osteen, who was smiling at her from beneath Tater's arm. Then her eyes went back to his. "I don't know where they are. I'm just a neighbor. How do you know Caroline?"

"I'm her boyfriend, actually. I mean. Was. I was her boyfriend."

The woman nodded. Looked at his wrists. "Why don't you just call her?"

"Don't got no phone."

The woman eyed his burns again. "You're bleeding. Do you know that? Your feet are bleeding too."

He placed his wrists behind his back.

"Do you have any proof you are who you say you are?"

Tater removed a picture from his sweat-stained leather wallet, chained to his belt loop. It was a photograph of himself and Caroline. They were in a Disney-themed photo booth. Caroline was kissing his cheek, but Tater was looking at the camera like he was either angry or severely constipated.

"It's important," he said. "I really need to see her."

The woman folded her arms and looked at the books beneath his arm again. "You're not a Jehovah's Witness, are you?"

"No, ma'am."

And two FBI agents tackled him to the ground.

• • •

THE DRIVER OF THE VOLVO WAS STILL WEARING THE SHADES. THEY were being pursued by Roy Orbison.

"I hate to keep reminding you," Caroline said, "but my bladder is reaching the red zone."

Woody glanced in the mirror. "How long can you hold it?"

She bounced her legs. "I don't know."

Woody finally pulled into a Walmart. Lots of cars around. It was the only safe place he could think of. If anything sinister was going to happen, better it happened around witnesses.

"Shouldn't we call someone?" Caroline asked.

"I think that would be prudent. You'll have to use your phone. I left mine at home."

Caroline got out her phone. "Who should I call? Police? The FBI people?"

"I don't think it matters."

Woody drove around the parking lot in big circles. Stopping and going. Making loops. The Volvo kept close behind him, matching him turn for turn.

"Something's wrong," she said. "My phone doesn't work." She slapped the screen of her device. "Nothing is working at all."

"You tried restarting it?"

They drove around the parking lot some more. She rebooted her phone. In a few moments, after the Apple logo disappeared, the screen went completely black.

"It's not working. Something's definitely wrong."

Woody looked into the rearview. The guy was still riding his tail.

"What are we doing?" she asked.

"We are not going to be afraid," said Woody. "That's what we're going to do."

He spun the wheel and found a parking slot. He threw the truck into Park. On cue, the Volvo pulled into a parking space about twenty feet away from them. The guy did not get out of the Volvo. He only sat there. Sunglasses on. Staring forward.

"Oh my God," Caroline said, still bouncing her knees. "What are we going to do now?"

"You wait here. I'm going to have a talk with Hank Junior."

Woody got out and slammed the door as hard as he could.

Chapter 52

WOODROW BARKER APPLIED TO THE DISCERNMENT COMMITtee when he was a twenty-seven-year-old pup whose ears hadn't dropped. They did not make it easy to become a priest. You *really* had to want to be one if you were going to make it. You had to meet with committees. Parish priests. Bishops. Go through a series of hard interviews before you were even allowed to apply to the diocese to become a postulant. Postulants were studied. Analyzed. Then you had to gain acceptance into seminary, which wasn't easy. And then, somehow, you had to manage to pay your way through school while (a) tying down a full-time job, (b) not filing for Chapter 11 bankruptcy, and (c) not dying from repeated consumption of ramen noodles.

But truthfully, admittance into any candidacy program boiled down to a simple list. They were looking for the same qualities and talents churches have been looking for since Peter, James, and John were breathing. Kindness. Compassion. Humility. And just the right amount of ignorance.

Woody had plenty of the latter.

He beat on the Volvo's window hard enough to break the glass.

The guy rolled down the window. He had scratches all over his face. The guy looked at him from behind the glasses. He leered at Woody, showing teeth. It was the first time Woody had a chance to study his face while not in the throes of a wrestling match. The guy was in his thirties. The mustache was gone. Fresh white T-shirt.

He removed the sunglasses and Woody saw he was wearing an eye patch. The man lifted the patch to reveal an eye that was all screwed up and bloodshot. The eye was not facing forward but sideways. The guy was perfectly calm. Which was even more unsettling. He blinked his eyes a few times.

"I've got my eye on you, Father," said Peter Tabares.

And that was when Woody's truck exploded.

• • •

THE FLAMES ROSE HIGH INTO THE NIGHT. A SHOWER OF AUTO PARTS rained onto the Walmart parking lot. There were bits of metal everywhere. Little pieces of upholstery. Splintered falling glass. Flecks of smoldering steel and ash rained down like hail, spreading like snow all over the pavement. Christmastime in the Walmart parking lot.

For a fleeting second Woody was paralyzed.

The driver of Volvo was still wearing a flat face. No change in expression. Woody was looking at what used to be his truck but was now a smoking automotive skeleton. His rear tires melted on the pavement. Flames were cracking loudly like popping hickory logs. The tailgate was disconnected from the truck. The hood was somewhere in the next county.

Woody's first instinct was to assault the man responsible. To drag him out of the vehicle and turn the man's body into a sack of bone fragments. To make him pay.

But a greater instinct made him race to the truck.

He screamed her name.

"Caroline!"

He ran across the parking lot, his thighs burning and his chest aching. But when he got to the truck, there was nothing to see. The doors had been blown off. The windshield was gone. Inside the cab was an inferno. The truck didn't even *look* like a truck.

"Caroline!"

He removed his shirt and beat it at the fire. But his actions were almost laughable. He could feel the pavement heating up beneath his soles, almost as though he were walking on a skillet.

He continued swatting his T-shirt. He found it nearly impossible to breathe. There was no oxygen in the air. The flames were consuming it all. He ran to the other side of the vehicle and tried to see inside, but the cab was mangled and twisted. So he went around back and muscled open the tailgate. It was like touching a potbelly stove. He tried kicking in the rear windshield, but his heel wasn't strong enough to shatter the glass at first. Finally, after several attempts, the window exploded.

"Caroline!"

But there was no Caroline.

Chapter 53

CAROLINE WAS IN THE WALMART STALL VOMITING. STRESS AND worry had overtaken her like a virus. A sense of dread surged over her. She thought of the pictures of Tater, lying in a bathtub, tied up like a branded calf. Caroline flushed the toilet and went to the sink to wash her hands.

A great booming noise shook the bathroom.

The vibration resounded so sharply it made the mirrors distort. Caroline watched her reflection morph for a few moments and felt more fear growing in her stomach.

She left the bathroom, still moderately out of breath from sprinting into Walmart. No sooner had she exited the bathroom than she saw customers and employees inside the store running toward the doors. Abandoning carts. Leaving their cash registers. Jogging toward the exit to see what had happened.

Caroline followed the herd of customers. Elbowing her way forward. Pushing her way toward the front of the pack. The sinking feeling in her gut was getting stronger as she shoved her way past the cluster of bodies and buggies onto Walmart's front sidewalk, still clutching her backpack against her shoulders.

And that was when she saw it. In the distance, a large red

fire climbed high into the night. It was tall and well fed. The fire was mounting quickly, gaining height with every few seconds, as though the monstrous inferno was finding more fuel to feed itself.

She weaved through the spectators and jogged toward the flaming vehicle, waddle-running through the parking lot, moving as quickly as a pregnant woman could.

The fire was raging brightly, reaching toward the stars above them.

And she saw Woody charging into it.

• • •

A BLAST OF FLAMES EXITED THE OPEN CAVERN OF WHAT USED TO BE the truck cab. The heat was so intense it blurred Woody's vision. Bigger conflagrations were erupting from where the engine well used to be. Flares were coming from the cab. Then he heard a strange groaning sound. Like a belch getting ready to release. He could feel the tension building beneath him.

Woody hit the ground and rolled as a second explosion thundered behind him and shook the earth. The boom was so loud he couldn't hear himself cry out in pain.

Through the haze, he could see people in the parking lot standing around gawking. Shoppers held bags in spellbound awe. Fires hypnotize people. In olden times, people used to attend house fires and hangings. Like going to a Broadway musical. There's something morbidly entrancing about a fire.

Woody stumbled to his feet and looked back at the Volvo. The passenger door was open. And there was no sign of a body in the car. When Woody turned, he saw the man in sunglasses parting through the onlookers. The guy walked toward Woody, unhurried. Relaxed. He had something in his hand.

"Everyone get back," the bald man said to the crowd. Then he brandished a badge. "Police."

The man reached into his back waistband and removed a pistol. He held it with a double-handed grip. More onlookers were pouring out of the Walmart doors. He could see people's mouths open; he could tell they were shouting, although he couldn't hear their voices. The explosion had left him with nothing but a shrill ringing in his ears.

That was when his eyes fell on her. She was at the forefront of the multitude. Woody felt relief sweep over his entire being, like he'd been submerged in a warm bath. They locked eyes.

"Everyone get back!" shouted the guy with the weapon.

He aimed at Woody's chest.

And he squeezed the trigger.

Chapter 54

——

A FEMALE MEDIC WAS PATCHING UP TATER'S WRISTS IN THE BACK seat of the Chevy Tahoe. Several SUVs were gathered in a semicircle in the marina's gravel parking area, with people milling around the vehicles wearing FBI polo shirts and ball caps, probably drinking from official FBI thermoses and coffee mugs.

Beneath the Tahoe's bluish dome light, the medic worked from a massive medical kit that was spread out on the back seat. She was a young woman, early twenties. Maybe a few years older than Tater. Nice looking. Dark eyes, dark hair. He felt grimy and disgusting before her.

Another agent was sitting in the driver's seat, his pen poised over a legal pad. He was trying to conduct an interview between Tater's gratuitous usage of expletives.

"And how did the burns happen, exactly?" the man said.

"I used a lighter."

"A cigarette lighter?"

"Is there another kind?"

The lady medic's gloved hands gently probed his wrist burns. The injuries were badly blistered, covered in sticky black and gray adhesive material.

"I can see the traces of duct tape all over his wrists," the medic said.

The agent in the front seat kept on questioning. "How about telling me how you escaped?"

The lady medic said, "This is going to hurt, really bad, actually, but I need to use wound-cleaning solution to get this sticky stuff off."

"I stole their lighter when they weren't looking. I burned through the tape on my wrists. I don't know what else to tell you. It took longer than I thought. I could feel my skin burning."

The medic doused his wounds with the cleaning solution. It hurt like holy hellfire. She used gauze to remove bits of duct tape that were married to his skin. Tater bit his bottom lip so hard he thought his lip might be bleeding. He wanted to cry, but he didn't want to blubber like a baby in front of a woman.

"I don't get it," said the agent. "How did you get away if they were watching you in a closely confined motel?"

"They cut my feet loose so I could go to the bathroom. When I was in there, I used the lighter to burn through the tape, and I crawled through the little window behind the toilet."

Tater sat erect, lifted up his shirt, and showed the scrapes on his bare torso with a note of pride.

"That's why I'm all cut up, see?"

The male agent inspected Tater's torso, and his eyes lingered on Buzz Lightyear flying over his left nipple.

"'To infinity and beyond,'" said the lady.

"So then what happened?" asked the guy agent.

"I ran through the parking lot and got the heck out of there."

"Any idea where Tabares might be going now? What was he up to?"

"I don't know. He was trying to break into Caroline's phone. I don't know why."

The agent rubbed his eyes. "Can you think of anything that might help us? Anything at all?"

Neither the agent nor the medic said anything for a little bit.

"What's wrong?" asked Tater. "Did he already find her?"

"We can't get in touch with Caroline or her father. Haven't been able to reach them for a few hours. So anything you can tell us will help. Can you remember anything else that might be pertinent?"

Tater shrugged. "Not really."

Both agent and medic wagged their heads, and Tater felt disgusted with himself.

The agent sighed before turning to leave. "Just try to get some rest."

The medic cleaned his wound again, and Tater watched the man walk away. He felt hot tears fill his eyes. His whole world clouded over with water.

"I could tell you what they're driving," he called to the agent. "Would that help?"

The agent stopped. "Might. What kind of car you think it was?"

"Volvo 240, hunter green, a '93 or a '94."

"How do you know that?"

"Because it couldn't have been a '95. Volvo phased out the redblock engine in '95 in the US, and this was definitely a redblock. The timing belt was so quiet I couldn't hear it from the back seat. My guess is they were running a B230 under the hood, straight four, overhead crankshaft."

Then Tater recited the tag number.

Chapter 55

———

RUMACK RIVERS HAD NOT SET OUT TO BE AN UBER DRIVER. FEW men ever do.

Driving for Uber was a decent job. Not great but not bad. It was not, for example, as rewarding as working at Best Buy, a job he started when he was sixteen. He knew the Best Buy store backward and forward. He was a demigod at Best Buy. He did well at Best Buy. Very well. They promoted him to manager after only nine years. With a half-finished associate's degree, still living with his mom, still making payments on the Jetta he bought as a junior in high school, Best Buy was a win-win.

So when the Best Buy he worked at closed, it was like losing his identity. If he wasn't Best Buy Guy, who was he? He went through a short period of unemployment. About three years. Then his mother insisted it was time to get a job.

At first he started supplementing his income by doing food deliveries for a meal-delivery app. That was a joke. Food delivery prices were too high for customers. Customers ended up paying seventy-five bucks for a twenty-five-dollar meal. By the time their food arrived, they were so annoyed over the long wait, the price hike, and the cold food, they wouldn't tip the driver more than a few bucks for their delivery.

On his last delivery, he screwed up and delivered a two-hundred-dollar order to the wrong house. Instead of the customers reporting the botched delivery to the app, the recipients at the wrong address accepted the food. Rumack had to pay the courier service the entire cost of the bill *plus* the cost of the customer's inconvenience, and then he quit.

At which point he signed up to be an Uber driver.

It just made sense. He got to choose his own hours. Got to be his own boss. Got to call his own shots. Each day he woke up and decided whether he wanted to work a full day, a half day, a few hours, or stay home in his underpants and watch Disney+. He was twenty-eight years old, six three, a Capricorn, and he could play the national anthem on his armpit. Uber just felt right.

When he did work, which was about three days a week, he liked his job. Namely, because he got to meet people. He was a people person. He did a lot of pickups at Gulf Beach Regional Airport. He picked up a lot of elderly people at assisted living facilities and took them to CVS or Walgreens. Sometimes they asked him to take them to a drive-thru. But he never charged extra for that; all he asked was that they get him a milkshake.

The only Uber shifts he avoided were Friday and Saturday nights, when all the drunks wanted rides downtown. Two drunk people once puked in his back seat. It was a mess. He thought his mom would never get the smell out.

But otherwise, he was basically pleased with his career choice. He spent the day around interesting people. He listened to good music. He smoked Delta-9 pre-rolls, popped CBD gummies, and talked to friends on his Bluetooth gaming headphones. Most of whom were former Best Buy employees.

Tonight was a slow night.

He had picked up four guys from the airport, all in business attire. All wearing earth-tone suits. They were too important to have a conversation with him. They just sat in silence, lost in their screens. So he had called his friend Brad, whereupon they embarked on a conversation debating the actual birthday of Superman, which is widely recognized as February 29 but is also listed in *Action Comic*s #655 as June 18, since June 18 was the day the infant who came to be known as Clark Kent landed on Earth in a tiny spaceship.

Rumack dropped off the businessmen at a hotel and was deeply involved in this conversation when he received a ride request notification on the Uber app. He hit Accept, then headed to Walmart. The app said the passenger was named Cherr, like the singer, but with two *R*'s.

The Superman conversation began to heat up. Brad called him an ignorant idiot. And Rumack stated that Brad was full of a substance common to most barnyards and hog pens. When he arrived at Walmart, he was still on the phone, practically shouting into the headset mic.

"No way!" Rumack yelled. "Martha and John Kent specifically chose to celebrate Clark's birthday on the *precise day that he arrived* from outer space, and they were his *parents*!"

He saw his ride standing just outside the Walmart entrance. At least he assumed it was her because she was waving her arm at him. A crowd of people were gathered in the parking lot, screaming. A large column of smoke was rising from the remains of what looked like a flaming vehicle. Just another night at Walmart.

He pulled up in front of the woman, who had several enormous bags of Ol' Roy dog food loaded on the bottom rack of her buggy. Rumack sighed. He did *not* feel like lifting heavy bags tonight. But in the end, he decided to do the truly masculine thing and, like he'd done so many times before, fake recent spinal surgery.

"Are you Cherr?" he called through his window.

"That's me," she said.

He put the car in Park, unlocked the doors, and popped the trunk.

"Furthermore, Bradley," Rumack went on, "if you will recall, the DC Comics calendar, *originally published in 1976*, clearly confirms that the birthday is actually on June 18, so we can see—"

His passenger door was thrown open so violently he thought it was going to pop off the hinges.

"Hey," he said. "Take it easy with my car, lady."

The person now climbing into his car was not his ride. It was someone else. A pregnant girl.

"Hey," he said again, "you can't sit in front. You have to sit in back."

Cherr was not happy. She started shouting in a voice capable of giving headaches to the recently deceased, "She's trying to steal my Uber!"

"Whoa," said Rumack. "Lady, I'm sorry, but you can't take her ride. You're going have to call your own Uber."

The girl slammed the car door and shouted, "I'm in labor. Start driving!"

Rumack looked at her for a beat. She was not panting. She did not seem to be in distress. She pointed through the windshield to a green vehicle across the parking lot that was driving toward the exit and said, "I need you to follow that car. Right now."

Rumack drew his eyebrows together. "You don't look like you're in labor."

The young woman removed a pistol from her backpack and pulled the slide. "How do I look now?"

"I'll have to call you back, Brad."

Chapter 56

——

CAROLINE WAS SQUINTING THROUGH THE WINDSHIELD OF THE Volkswagen Jetta, trying to draw a bead on the Volvo ahead of them.

"Do not let that car get away!" she said, shoving the weapon deeper into the driver's rib cage.

The driver turned to look at her with a long, hard glare.

"What?" she asked.

"You don't seem like you're in labor."

The Volvo ahead flashed its turn signal.

"They're turning," she said. "Left. Get in the left lane."

He flipped on his turn signal. "You're probably an insane person. You're going to chop me up with an axe and leave me on the side of the road somewhere, aren't you?"

"It looks like they're heading to the interstate."

The driver moved into a turn lane full of flashing blinkers. The man looked at the gun pressed against his ribs. He wore the face of a skeptic. He clearly didn't buy it. "You're not going to shoot me."

"I need you to stop talking."

"The safety is on."

He kept both hands on the wheel and both eyes straight ahead. The light turned green. The line of cars began creeping forward. The Jetta gently accelerated toward the intersection. Once his turn was completed, he started to slow down and moved into the right lane.

"What are you doing?" she said. "Stay in the left lane!"

"I'm not doing this. And you're not going to shoot me. You probably don't even know how to use that thing."

Caroline unlatched the safety, assumed a doublehanded grip, pulled back the slide to arm the weapon, then pressed the muzzle into his shoulder.

"I am asking you nicely to keep driving."

"Oh my God. You *are* crazy."

"I'm not crazy, I'm pregnant. Now follow that Volvo and do not let it out of your sight."

He mashed the pedal, and the Jetta sped onward into the night, rocketing onto the highway at a breakneck speed, catapulting over the shallow slopes as they raced to catch up with the Volvo several cars ahead. Then the driver reached forward and turned up the radio. The car interior immediately burst forth with music, playing at a volume loud enough to crack plate glass.

"What're you doing?" she said.

"If I'm going to get shot tonight, I'm going to do it while listening to some Dead."

. . .

WHEN WOODY AWOKE, HE WAS UNABLE TO MOVE. ACTUALLY, HE wasn't totally paralyzed; he just had little control over his movements. There was an ineptness to his muscles, like they had minds of their own.

It took a few minutes to realize he was bound. His hands were tied behind his back. His feet were tied. He was seat-belted in the rear of the car. And he was confused. Profoundly. But the confusion was wearing off, little by little, and he was slowly becoming aware of his surroundings.

He felt as though he'd just awoken from one of the deepest sleeps of his life. Which wasn't altogether unpleasant. He hadn't slept well since leaving prison.

He could see the bald driver looking at him in the mirror. He could only see the man's eye patch and his good eye. He wasn't wearing sunglasses anymore. Apparently the Ray Charles look was over.

"Long time no see," the man said.

"Hello, Peter."

The guy laughed. "You know my name. I'm flattered."

The feeling was coming back into Woody's muscles. He could sit upright without using as much effort now. He propped himself against the seat.

"You're probably a little foggy," Peter said. "Totally normal. It wears off. It's all part of the fun of getting tazed."

Woody didn't reply. He had no memory of being tazed. He was disoriented. There was a gap in his recall of events. He remembered a flaming car. He remembered the lump of soot where Caroline's body had been. He did not have any memory of how he'd gotten here or why he was so sore all over.

"Trust me," said Peter. "I know what you're going through. Your ex-wife tazed the crap out of me. Surprised she didn't stop my heart. She was a hell of a woman."

"You have no idea."

Peter did not react to that.

Woody fell back into his seat. There were stars outside the window. They were on the interstate. He saw exits passing them by, one at a time. His brain was too hazy to figure out where he was. Still, he was trying his best to calculate mileage. Which wasn't difficult. Calculating interstate mileage didn't require brain power. Interstate exits are one mile apart. Count the exits; count the miles.

"If it makes you feel any better, this wasn't supposed to happen," said Peter.

"What wasn't supposed to happen?"

"This. *You* are supposed to be *her*."

"Caroline?"

"That was the plan."

"Would you like me to talk in a high-pitched voice?"

"She wasn't supposed to die. You were. A lot has gone wrong tonight."

Woody thought back to the moment he saw Caroline exiting the store. He felt the wave of relief all over again.

The guy let his good eye rest on Woody. Woody could see his face, lit blue by the light from the dashboard. Despite the patch, Woody could see that he was nice looking. Melinda always dated attractive guys.

A highway patrol cruiser was passing them by. Peter wasn't fazed. He kept pace in the right lane. The man was nothing if not relaxed.

"You're probably disoriented," the guy said, "trying to get a fix on where you are."

Woody was silent.

"But don't worry about it. You won't be alive long enough to tell anyone where you are."

"You think so, huh?"

Peter gave a small laugh. "Sorry, Padre. It's nothing personal."

"Oh, well, in that case . . ."

Woody's brain was clearing up a little, but he didn't recognize this section of interstate even though it was probably familiar, since they weren't that far out of town. His brain wasn't putting images together correctly. By the terrain, he was guessing they were heading northeast. But that's all he could figure out in his current state.

"Aren't you supposed to put a gag in my mouth?" asked Woody.

"You watch too many Chuck Norris movies."

"Actually, I've never seen one."

"*Missing in Action*, 1984. Great movie."

"I'll be sure to add it to my Netflix."

Woody leaned back into his seat and tried to will his brain into normal working order. The driver kept checking his side mirrors. Little flicks of his head.

Peter hit his blinker and passed a few cars. Woody glanced out the back window. A few vehicles behind, another car was mirroring their movements.

"Apparently you've got a friend," said Peter.

• • •

CAROLINE'S UBER DRIVER WORE A GRATEFUL DEAD T-SHIRT CIRCA 1979. The inside of his dilapidated Jetta smelled like Nag Champa and sweat. The radio was playing music that the touchscreen display was identifying as David Grisman. The car was a wreck inside. There was a mashed banana on the floorboard beneath Caroline's feet that had become brown with maturity and oxygen exposure.

He had told her his name was Rumack, and he had been speeding down the interstate breaking every traffic law in existence. Now they were doing an even eighty.

"Shouldn't we be going to the hospital if you're having a baby?" he asked. "The hospital's the other way."

The Volvo ahead changed lanes.

"Just keep following that car."

Rumack gave her an appraising glare. He nudged the wheel left and shot past cars in the slow lane. Caroline was impressed at the man's driving ability. Although he was large and gangly, he had the reflexes of a caffeinated squirrel. He turned the wheel with remarkable ease and athleticism.

"You're a really good driver," she said.

"Thanks. PlayStation. *KartRider.*"

"Why am I not surprised."

• • •

THEY WERE DEFINITELY HEADING NORTHEAST. WOODY COULD TELL by the foliage. A great rural chasm lies between Alabama and Georgia, just off the American interstate. Metropolises with names like Milton, Florala, Geneva. They were tiny towns, with more acres of farmland per capita than they had capita. They were approaching the Donalsonville exit (pop. 2,826).

Woody's wrists were hurting. The man had secured his hands too tightly. He could feel the duct tape digging into his bones. He stared out the windows. The gentle rises and falls of hillsides, the copses of pines, lit blue by the glow of a waxing full moon.

"How you doing back there?" asked Peter.

Woody's mind was becoming clearer with each passing mile. He was starting to feel like himself again. Whatever the Taser had done to him had miraculously made his heart feel stronger. He'd read about medical interventions involving shock treatments for the cardiac muscle. Then again, maybe it was just adrenaline.

"Having the time of my life."

The wilds of Georgia flew by like a blurry smudge. Peter glanced at him in the mirror again. "You need to use the bathroom or anything?"

"Aren't you supposed to be the bad guy?"

"Doesn't mean I have to be inhumane. You want something to drink? I have bottled waters."

"Pass."

"I'm sorry. None of this was supposed to happen."

"If you really feel that bad about it, you can let me go."

A chain of semitrucks passed them by. Peter followed the draft of the great vehicles.

"Sorry, Padre. You've seen a little too much for your own good."

"This is all because of what I did to your eye, isn't it?"

Peter didn't reply. He kept his eye on the side mirror. The car was still behind them.

"Can I ask you a question?" Peter finally asked.

"I'm a captive audience."

"You ever seen gold?" he asked.

"Never."

"I'm not talking jewelry or little wedding bands. I'm talking *gold*. Pure gold. The stuff the conquistadors were after. The largest force Spain ever sent to North America; that's how important gold was back then. That kind of gold."

"So that's what this is all about? Gold?"

Peter looked at his side mirror again. "Oh, I think you know that already, Padre. I think you know a lot more than you let on."

Woody was silent.

"You never expect gold to be as heavy as it really is. And you aren't prepared for the reflectiveness. If it's polished, it's like looking into a yellow mirror. Plus, it's stable. Physically speaking. The only existentially stable money in the world, really."

Woody didn't feel like listening to a history lesson. He tried to tune him out, but Peter waxed on.

"America has 147 million ounces of gold in the treasury. They keep it at the United States Bullion Depository, big golden bars that weigh about twenty-seven pounds each. This gold used to represent, more or less, the entire US economy. But that gold doesn't mean nothing in today's world, not really. Our currency isn't backed by gold anymore. No country has used gold-backed currency since the 1970s. It's a shame, if you ask me. America has fallen so far."

They rode in silence for a while. The miles were heaping up behind them, but the scenery never seemed to change.

"Where are we going?"

No answer.

Woody used his bound hands to itch his nose.

"You believe in free will, Padre?"

"I thought we were talking about gold."

Peter laughed quietly.

"You believe in the freedom to choose your own path, Father? Freedom to change your own eternal destiny?"

Woody shrugged. "Not in your case."

"You think I'm evil, Father?"

"Probably not." Woody stared at the man. "I think your problem is that your mom dropped you on your head."

Chapter 57

—

PRETTY GIRLS HAD ALWAYS HAD A WAY OF MAKING RUMACK DO stupid things. He had dated a pretty girl once. Once and only once. And that was enough. Dating her was a mistake. Namely, because knockout women already knew how pretty they were. And this made them biologically willing to accept offers from the highest bidder. You couldn't hold on to a pretty girl when you looked like giant ball of hair wearing a Jerry Garcia T-shirt and your mom still did your laundry. There was no reason this girl in his passenger seat should be any different from the pretty girls who had come before her. Yes, she had a gun. But he probably would have done whatever she asked even if she was brandishing a toothpick at him.

They sped along the highway heading eastward as "I Need a Miracle" pumped through the stereo. They had been in this car for a long time, driving heaven only knew where.

"You're a liar," he said.

Caroline was still holding the weapon on him but not as aggressively as before. She was trying to get her phone working using one hand, the phone balanced on her knee. But the device wasn't cooperating.

"I said you're a *liar*."

"I heard you."

"You're not in labor."

She did not respond.

"I knew it. You lied to me."

"Get over it."

Rumack slammed a hand on the wheel. "What are we even doing? I've turned down, like, fifty pickup requests. I have no idea where we're going. Are you even pregnant?"

"Oh my God, stop talking."

The car ahead got into the exit lane. Rumack eased the wheel right. They took the off-ramp onto a rural highway route.

As she held the pistol against his shoulder, she explained her entire situation to him. The girl seemingly held nothing back when she told the story. Rumack hoped she remembered that the weapon was armed, because she was getting awfully involved in her monologue right now, and sometimes she would get so animated she would begin talking with her hands and waving the weapon around.

The young woman delivered an elaborate retelling of a complex situation involving car bombs, terrorists, a priest, a nurse, gold, a big boat, and a green Volvo. It sounded like the plot of a truly poorly written novel. It seemed the most unlikely story he had ever heard, and that was what bothered him. It was so unlikely that it had the outlandish ring of truth to it.

"So you're not really going to have a baby?" he asked.

She looked at him flatly.

"I mean, you're not in labor?"

She was staring at him now as he drove. He could see her from the corner of his eye. She was arrestingly lovely. And when she looked at him, he felt his insides turn into Jell-O.

"I just need you to help me," she said.

"That's hard to do when you're pushing a gun into my shoulder."

"I know."

"Are you really going to shoot me?"

She sighed. "I haven't decided yet."

"I really don't want to die tonight."

"I know," she said in commiseration. "It really would be a shame."

He looked at her. "I think you're delusional, Caroline."

"No, I'm crazy. Not delusional. There's a difference."

"Well, this has certainly been one of the craziest nights I've ever had. I'm surprised the cops haven't pulled us over yet. I've been doing ninety in a sixty-five zone, following some random car. How do I know you're not going to lead us out into the middle of nowhere and leave me for dead?"

"That's actually not a bad idea."

He could smell her perfume filling his car. Or maybe it was her soap, or whatever it was that girls used to smell like that. And whenever she looked at him, it was as though her eyes were fracking for oil beneath the coarse and battered bedrock of his interminable soul.

Rumack watched her in the glow of his dome light. "What's wrong with your phone?"

"It just quit working."

He nodded. "Welcome to AT&T."

The Volvo was two cars ahead of them on an old two-lane. Rumack clicked his blinker and moved up one car length. His Jetta engine began to scream as he changed lanes.

And that was when the blue lights started flashing behind him.

Chapter 58

———

THE VOLVO PULLED OFF THE INTERSTATE ONTO ANOTHER TWO-lane, this one dark and twisty. The car that was tailing them was no longer behind them. Woody had lost track of the vehicle when he began drifting in and out of consciousness. He had awoken when he felt the Volvo lose speed. He had been napping. For how long, he couldn't say. A short time, he guessed. Maybe thirty minutes. He looked at the clock, but he couldn't remember what time it had been before he fell asleep.

He looked out the windows and didn't recognize anything. Wherever they were, they were deeper in the hinterlands than they had been. No houses. No headlights in the oncoming lane. No lights anywhere. No nothing.

The Volvo rode through a long, twisting, winding set of meandering curves that seemed to go on forever. Rises and falls. Hairpins and ditches. Dirt roads and rocky gravel. They loped over shallow creek bridges, cantered down narrow roads made of top-dressed gravel with a rooster tail of dust behind them, rising into the night.

On each side of the car were walls of suffocating longleaf

pines passing them by like old spirits. Like the ghosts of loved ones, standing tall in their memories, cemented in time.

The ride reminded him of the drives his dad used to take his family on when Woody was a kid. There was a time in this nation when the Great American Family went out for Sunday drives. When did those days disappear? When did we get so busy that we quit enjoying the drive?

Peter rolled down the windows. The cab was filled with the scent of pine, damp earth, and farmland.

"Can you smell that scent in the air, Father?" said Peter.

Woody didn't answer.

Peter made a big show of drawing in the scent. "Can't you smell it?"

Woody stayed silent.

"It smells like you're about to die, Father."

"That's funny," said Woody. "Smells like bull manure to me."

• • •

RUMACK WAS PULLED OVER ONTO THE SHOULDER. HE COULD SEE the cop in the side mirror exiting the vehicle. Light bar flashing. The officer was approaching the passenger side of their car, keeping away from traffic.

Rumack pressed his forehead against the steering wheel. "I'm going to jail."

Things never went well with the cops. Not for him. He got too nervous, and they always thought he had an attitude. And he was always afraid that, even though he wasn't high, they would think he was. Which made him act high. A lot of police officers saw the Grateful Dead stickers on the backs of Jettas and started writing citations for misdemeanors before they even got out of the car.

The officer rapped on Caroline's window.

Which wasn't good. Rumack already should have rolled down both windows in the spirit of cooperation. But he'd been too busy hiding a loaded firearm with a filed-off serial number in the back seat. Strike one.

The passenger window whirred downward. The cop hunched over and stuck his flashlight into the vehicle. The beam of light traveled to the Jerry Garcia and Bob Weir bobbleheads mounted on Rumack's dash.

Rumack smiled. "What seems to be the officer, problem?"

Strike two.

The police officer was so heavily muscled that his neck seemed not to exist.

"You're not going to make me tell you how fast you were going, are you, sir?" said Officer Schwarzenegger.

"No, Officer. I know I was speeding. I'm sorry."

At that point Caroline started breathing heavily. The breathing got louder, and things became awkward all over again.

The cop watched her, and so did Rumack. She was really putting on a great show. Caroline clutched her stomach and squealed in agony. The scream was so loud it hurt Rumack's ears. Rumack stared at her in disgust. She was a liar. A beautiful liar. But a liar, nonetheless.

It wasn't that he didn't appreciate the effort. It was sweet; in a way, it was even noble. And he would remember her effort with fondness when he was in the prison cafeteria line getting stabbed with a sharpened toothbrush handle. But her idea was juvenile and misguided. The cop would never buy it. Rumack himself hadn't even bought it, and he was an idiot.

Rumack rested a hand on her shoulder. "Please, Caroline. You'll just make things worse."

The police officer arched his brow. "Is your wife okay?"

"We're not married," Rumack said.

"He's an Uber driver," said Caroline between breaths, as though this explained the reason for their non-marriage.

The officer shined his flashlight on her. "What's going on, ma'am?"

Caroline was obviously in too much fake pain to answer. She let out another howl. This time Rumack was so embarrassed he could feel his face turning colors. He wanted to disappear.

He leaned over and spoke into her ear, "Caroline, please. You're going to get us into a lot of trouble."

The cop kept the light on her. Caroline screamed.

"She's fine, Officer," Rumack explained. "She's not really in labor. She does this sometimes. She's only—"

"Something is happening!" Caroline shouted.

She gripped her belly. Suddenly Caroline's moaning stopped for a few moments. She seemed to be holding her breath. This was followed by the sound of splashing liquid on Rumack's rubberized floormats. Like someone had just overturned a gallon of Pepsi.

The cop shined his Maglite on the soaked floorboards.

"Uh-oh," the cop said.

· · ·

THE ROAD TURNED FROM GRAVEL TO MUD. THEY WERE OFF THE highway now, in the sticks. The turns were tighter and coming more often. Peter was traveling painfully slow. The effects of the Taser had totally worn off. Woody felt clear-minded. He felt charged, even.

The car slowed. The vehicle pulled off the main road onto a kind of frontage road. Ahead of them, at the rise of a tall hill, was a little church. It was a small clapboard building. Two stories. No steeple. It was a primitive church. It looked like a house from a Grant Wood painting. All that was missing was a guy with a pitchfork.

Peter parked at the top of the hill.

"Don't read too much into the symbolism of it," Peter said. "I take a lot of my people to churches."

"Your people?"

Peter shrugged. "Cemeteries are perfect spots to hide a body."

Woody nodded. "How do you know about this place?"

"I've done business here before."

"Business?"

The man got out of the car and removed Woody from the back seat, non-gently. Peter used a flashlight to inspect his prisoner. Woody stood before him and leaned against the car.

"You doing okay?" Peter said.

"I'm confused by this question."

He clapped Woody's shoulder. "At least we understand each other. If I unbuckle your feet, will you be a good little priest and not try to run away? I've had some bad experiences with prisoners in the past few days."

Woody did not answer.

Peter shined the light in Woody's face. "Are you going to try to do something brave if I untie your feet? Answer me."

"Where would I go?"

"Don't know. You're the one with all the free will."

Peter removed a pistol. It was an M1911, Colt, .45 caliber. A lot of the old-school correctional officers carried them. Single-action. Recoil operated. The original semiautomatic. Built like Fort Knox. Kicks like a mule. The army used to carry them in his dad's day, but they replaced them with 9 mm Berettas. The Colt made quite a hole.

Peter kept the gun on Woody. Then he removed a knife, flicked it open, and cut the ties around Woody's ankles while keeping the pistol trained on him.

Woody felt relief when the tight bands were gone.

"Don't make me sorry I did this."

The cemetery stood behind the old-time meetinghouse. Overgrown in weeds. Rusted iron fence, falling apart. The church looked even worse. It had long since been abandoned. The building was constructed on block pilings, some of which had crumbled with age, so the whole structure was leaning left. The early Americans were all Episcopal. After the Revolution, when Americans disbanded from the Church of England, they took the name *Episcopal*, which translated, literally, as "rich, white, liberal Democrat." But this church looked like it was Presbyterian. The Scots built their chapels a certain way back in olden times. More like houses. Strong and sturdy and stout.

Peter popped the trunk and got out a shovel. Gestured toward the cemetery with the gun.

"Keep walking, Father."

"Where are we going?"

"We are going to visit your grave."

Chapter 59

TATER SAT IN THE FRONT SEAT OF THE CHEVY TAHOE admiring the primally raw power of a 355-horse, 383-pound-feet of torque, 6.2-liter V8 manufactured proudly in the US of A. Just being in the seat was a privilege. The only way this scenario could have possibly been better would have been if the Tahoe had been a turbo-diesel. Tater might have had to change his shorts.

The lady medic was driving, only she wasn't a medic. She was an FBI agent. And her name was Maria. He was sitting in the seat beside her as red and blue lights flashed from the rear windshield and front windshield. The whole highway was colorfully lit around them, and the resplendent 355 horses were operating at max capacity, with RPMs reaching into the red zone whenever the agent passed another car. He had never been in an FBI vehicle before. He was sure he'd never be in one again either. And he had never seen a law enforcement officer this striking before. She looked like she could star in her own Netflix drama. One where she would kick a lot of ass.

"How you doing over there?" Maria asked.

"I'm okay."

"How are the burns?"

He looked at his wrists. "Fine, I guess."

She changed lanes without signaling and passed a throng of vehicles that were crowding the left lane.

"Shouldn't I be sitting in back right now?" he asked.

Maria's eyes were dark. "I don't know. Should you be sitting in the back right now?"

"I mean, isn't it the rule or something?"

"Are you a threat?"

"No."

She tapped the computer console. "Then help me read this GPS and be a team player, Taylor."

"Most people usually just call me Tater."

"I'm not most people."

He looked out the window at all the cars passing by. Traffic on the interstate was all moving to the right lane to let the motorcade of Tahoes pass. It was a curious feeling to be in a vehicle to which all highway motorists instantly showed deference. It was a feeling of power. The agent was able to travel ninety-six miles per hour as easily as if she were traveling thirty. Without obstruction.

"Where are we going?" he asked.

She flipped on her siren to pass a few semitrucks; then she glanced at her console screen. She sped down an off-ramp and onto another highway, blowing through stop signs and yield signs. Behind her, a cavalcade of Tahoes was following. They had just covered sixty-odd miles in record time.

"You know what ALPR cameras are?" Maria asked.

"No."

She pointed out the window at a road sign. "Like that?"

A small camera was mounted to a speed-limit sign. He'd seen them before but hadn't really paid attention to them.

"Automatic license plate recognition. There are hundreds and hundreds of thousands of these cameras all over the US. Millions in the world. They're everywhere. Traffic lights, road signs, police vehicles, in the windows of storefronts, mounted on the dashboards of semitrucks."

"And, what, they read your license plate?"

She turned to look at him. "They do more than read it. They are connected to a vast network all over the nation. They upload each car's plate to the system instantly, and we can follow the plate almost anywhere. Right now the computers know where nearly every single car in this nation is located. Each year ALPR cameras help American law enforcement solve about seven hundred thousand cases."

Tater nodded. "Then you know where they are?"

"Plates get a little bit harder to find in the rural areas."

Tater looked out the window at a cow pasture going by. "So if you know where they're going, why am I here?"

Maria smiled. "I didn't have time to find a babysitter."

Chapter 60

———

CAROLINE WAS IN THE BACK SEAT OF A SHERIFF'S CRUISER ON the side of the highway with the rear passenger door open. The officer and the Uber driver stood on the highway shoulder, watching traffic, talking, trying to figure out something to do but being about as helpless as mammary glands on a proverbial boar hog. The contractions were coming close together now. All she felt was fright sweeping over her.

Caroline thought cops were supposed to know how to deliver babies. They did it on TV all the time. But this cop was apparently not one of those. He looked like he could power squat a Buick but had no neonatal experience.

She was lying on the back seat of the police cruiser and shouted in pain. The agony was like nothing she had ever experienced. The muscles of her stomach would harden, and the contraction would build and build until it felt as though something was going to rip inside her body. Slowly, the spasm would subside. Then the contraction would come again, even worse than the time before.

"Someone help!" she said.

Strings of vehicles shot by like streaks of red and white lights.

The officer was speaking into his chest-mounted radio, using his official voice, trying to do anything but be involved in the birthing process.

Rumack came and sat down beside her. "How are you doing?"

"How's it look like I'm doing?" she screamed.

He held her hand. "Um. Not good?"

"Great guess."

The officer removed the microphone from his face. "How far apart are the contractions?" he shouted to Rumack.

Rumack leaned toward her. "He needs to know how far apart the contractions are."

"Do I look like I have a stopwatch?"

Rumack translated. "She doesn't know."

Rumack was a great middleman.

The cop relayed this message, then said, "Can you give me a ballpark?"

"Take a guess how far apart they are, Caroline."

"Not freaking far enough!"

The pain was intensifying. Although she had no baseline to compare the pain to, if she had been forced to describe it, she might have said it was like someone was beating her belly with baseball bats. There was also a stabbing, knifelike pain in her lower back, as though someone were repeatedly kicking her lumbar muscles.

"Help me!" she said to Rumack, squeezing his hand.

"What can I do?"

"I don't know."

"Tell me what to do. I'll do it."

"I don't know."

She had watched childbirth videos on YouTube in preparation for this moment; she had watched TikTok birthing videos; she even followed Hearth Home and Midwifery on Instagram.

But this was nothing like the sterilized content on the internet. She was not ready for this. She was thoroughly unprepared.

Stupid, stupid girl.

"How bad does it hurt?" Rumack asked. "On a scale of one to ten?"

"Four hundred and eighty thousand."

Rumack pushed a strand of hair from her face. "You're doing great, Caroline. Just hold on a little longer. He's calling the ambulance."

"I think it's happening."

She screamed.

"You're doing great," he said.

"Stop saying that. I'm the opposite of great right now."

"From where I'm sitting, you're pretty awesome."

Her body was overtaken by the abrupt urge to push. This reflex overwhelmed her entire being. Her muscular system was operating on autopilot now.

Caroline leaned forward and pushed so hard she felt pressure in her eyeballs. The pushing seemed to bring her a modicum of relief, even though it didn't seem to be producing any result.

She pushed again. Harder this time.

"Doing great, Caroline."

"If you say that again, I'm going to punch you in the throat."

"Got it."

Chapter 61

WOODY HAD BEEN DIGGING HIS OWN GRAVE FOR NEARLY AN hour.

The sign on the little graveyard fence read "Meadowland Presbyterian Cemetery." The name was etched on a tall stone pillar with a pointed top. Like a miniature Washington Monument. The whole cemetery was engulfed in weeds. None of the graves were visible in the tall grass. The dates on the only gravestones he could see were all eighteen hundred and something. Most of them had the same last names as the others. McCall. McCollough. McConnel. And most of the McDeaths had occurred young.

In this moment he was thinking about how, throughout life, everyone forgets how brief life really is. It had been especially brief before the advent of specialized medical care, advanced nutrition, and Jane Fonda aerobics videos. But if you read history, you are confronted with the fact that there was a long period in American when a fifty-year-old guy was an elderly man. It was no wonder people back then got married in their teens. No time to wait.

The large hole was only up to his knees. He still had a long way to dig. He was sweating badly. His heart was pounding. He was surprised he hadn't died already by the overabundance of adrenaline coursing through his vascular system.

Peter was sitting on a nearby tombstone, legs crossed. Ankle balanced on his knee. The pistol was resting on the man's thigh, trained on Woody.

"You're doing pretty good for a guy with a bad heart."

Woody stopped and leaned on his shovel.

Peter said, "You know how in old Westerns, a guy digs a grave and it only takes him a couple minutes? Hollywood's full of crap, don't you think?"

Woody wiped his face. It felt better to keep moving, so he kept digging. He stepped on the shovel, inserting it deeper into the earth. He could hear the heaving sounds of his own breath. His chest was aching. And he was violently thirsty. But he was hanging in there like hair in a biscuit.

"You've been awfully quiet, Father."

"You don't have to call me that. I think we're past that now. I think we both know I'm not a Father."

"So it's possible to stop being a priest?"

Woody stopped digging. He mopped his brow. "Yes, it is absolutely possible."

"You're not a priest forever, inside your heart?"

"Not if you get fired, no."

"But who fires you, man or God?"

Woody looked at the tombstone at the head of the grave. It was made of rough-hewn, pockmarked stone. The name of the grave's resident was listed as Something Seetin Something. Born in 1821. Died in 1842. The person, whoever they were, was only twenty-one when they died.

Peter used the barrel of the gun to scratch his chin. "So must've been a pretty big mistake you made, to get fired by God."

"It was."

"What happened?"

"I killed someone."

Woody resumed digging violently. He stamped on the shovel as hard as he could.

"She was the beautiful mother of two. The prime of her life. And I took her from this world."

"They convicted you of manslaughter?"

"Womanslaughter."

He could feel his pulse in his hands. He felt his heart beating in the back of his neck and behind his rib cage.

"Did you ever reach out to the family?"

"I wrote them, yes."

"Did they ever write you back?"

"No."

Peter frowned and looked off. "So it looks like I'm doing those kids a favor then, don't it?"

Woody touched his chest. "Looks like."

• • •

THE TAHOE EASED ONTO A GRAVEL ROAD. RED DIRT. NO SHOULDERS. Cavernous ditches. The trees shrouded the sky, making the evening so black that it engulfed everything it touched.

The lady agent looked at her watch. The vehicle's low beams barely cut through the murky nightscape.

"Jeez," said Tater. "Those are dim lights."

"All part of the experience."

"I'm afraid you're going to run off the road."

But Maria was all business now. She did not pay attention to him; she was too busy talking on the handheld. She spoke quietly, communicating almost entirely in some kind of verbal shorthand that sounded like code.

Tater was reclined in the passenger seat, staring at the console's digital map that showed them wheeling through rambling backwaters. A single gray highway on the glowing map cut through a vast green wilderness, far away from any highways.

The woman turned onto a road so narrow there was barely room for the Tahoe's wheelbase. They could hardly see the road before them it was so dark. There were no little green signs marking the streets. Come to think of it, there were no signs anywhere. No stop signs. No slow-down signs. No nothing. He did not see any ALPR cameras. The motorcade of headlamp-less Tahoes was behind them, kicking up dust in the night.

They came to a fork in the road.

"Where to now?" she said into the radio. But the radio was silent.

"I asked, where to now? Over?"

Static.

No answer.

She fooled with the radio dial to no avail, searching for service, before finally plopping the radio onto the seat beside her with a sigh.

The others behind her veered right.

Then she veered left.

Soon they were headed through wilderness even more remote than before. The road became less evenly surfaced. Until now, the path had been gravel, but now it was just dirt ruts, washed out from years of rain and neglect from the Alabama DOT.

"Why aren't they answering?" said Tater.

The woman was noticeably on high alert. "Must not be many radio towers nearby."

When the SUV tires ran over the huge, canyon-like patches of road where earth had been eroded by floods and time, she and Tater bounced entire feet into the air.

"I think you should go a little slower," said Tater.

"Excuse me?"

"You don't want to wreck your suspension on these roads. Chevy struts are crap. Doesn't take much to ruin them."

Maria glared at him. Tater shut his mouth.

"I'm gonna need you to stay in your own lane tonight," she said. "Can you do that for me?"

He nodded with a little too much enthusiasm. "I'll do whatever you tell me to do, Maria."

Chapter 62

THE AMBULANCE ARRIVED WITH A WAILING SIREN. RUMACK WAS amazed at how long it had taken the ambulance to get there. Nearly thirty minutes.

Two EMTs jumped from the cab. One was tall and lean; the other was older and heavyset. In seconds, the paramedics had unfolded an aluminum stretcher. They covered Caroline's lower body with a blanket and lifted her onto the stretcher, then examined her.

Rumack had no idea what they were doing or saying, but by their tones, something was very wrong.

"What's going on?" said Rumack.

"We need to hurry," the older medic said to his partner.

"Where will you take her?"

"The hospital. It's a breech."

"What's a breech?"

"It means your child needs to be born in a hospital."

Caroline was on the stretcher, grunting and moaning. The veins in her forehead and neck showed with each contraction.

"Ma'am," the younger EMT said, "do you want your husband to come with us in the ambulance?"

"We're not married."

"Ma'am, what I need to know is, do you want your boyfriend to drive and meet us at the hospital, or come with us?"

Caroline was still squeezing Rumack's hand.

"He's not my boyfriend either. He's just an Uber driver."

"I'm between jobs," said Rumack.

The younger medic said, "Ma'am, I just need to know if you want him here with you or not."

They were already rolling Caroline toward the ambulance.

Rumack was following the stretcher, jogging alongside it. More specifically, *being dragged* by Caroline. She would not release his hand.

"He can come with us."

Before Rumack could say anything else, everyone was loading up into the back of the ambulance.

"Sir, get in."

"I don't think I should," Rumack said. "You heard her, I'm just a driver."

"Hey," the young medic said, clapping his shoulder. "You're here for her. That's what matters."

The medics slid the stretcher into the back. Rumack found a seat in the corner of the ambulance. The paramedics slammed the doors behind them, and the engine roared.

• • •

WOODY OPENED HIS EYES. HE WAS ON THE GROUND. LYING IN THE dirt. There was dirt in his mouth. Clinging to his teeth. The fall had gone harder than he'd anticipated. He hadn't been fully braced for it.

"I think you had a heart attack," said Peter, standing over him.

The nighttime insects were screaming. So it was difficult to distinguish sounds from one another with the constant white noise of the crickets. Woody was in the pit. His body was growing cold in the night air. And his joints hurt. But he was okay.

"Must've been a small attack or else you wouldn't be looking at me right now." Peter squatted next to Woody and took his pulse.

"Here." He gave Woody a bottle of water. "You're making this too easy for me, Father. Maybe I should just leave you here for a little bit and come back to throw dirt on top of your body."

"You're a real gentleman."

Peter wrapped his arms around Woody's chest. He heaved him out of the pit, dragged him through the tall grass, and propped him against a headstone, feet splayed before him.

Woody was breathing heavily and holding his chest. He retched as though he were going to vomit. Peter removed his shirt and picked up the shovel. Then the man started digging.

His captor was in excellent shape. His arms were like pillars, coiled with serpents beneath the skin. Each shovel stroke was easy for him; Peter moved as easily as though he were simply putting in time at the gym.

"You don't have to dig," said Woody. "I'll be okay. Just give me a few seconds to recover."

"I don't have a few seconds."

Woody could see the Colt tucked in the back of the man's jeans. Woody sat deathly still. He was still in a state of shock. Namely, because he had not expected this guy to fall for a fake heart attack.

• • •

SPECIAL AGENT MARIA LOPEZ TURNED OFF HER HEADLIGHTS. THE Tahoes behind her did the same. She had a feeling they were getting close. They were on their own now, caught within the far-flung backwoods of the Cotton State.

"We can't see without lights," said Tater.

She held up a finger. "I'm hearing your voice again."

"Why aren't they radioing you back when you call them? They're literally right behind you."

Her face was severe now. "There you go again, talking."

She drove on rural dirt roads in the ink darkness. The black of night ate and digested everything it touched, leaving only void in its wake. Ahead of the Tahoe they saw the Volvo, parked alongside the culvert. The agent eased onto the brakes.

"That's the car," Tater whispered.

"Thanks for the update," she said, squinting into the darkness. The car was parked a long way from a distant church that sat perched on a hillside, forming a silhouette against a purple sky.

"What are you going to do?" said Tater.

"Why are you whispering?"

Tater had watched a lot of crime dramas on Amazon Prime. And in such dramas, they always whispered. The characters whispered even in daily life, like when they went to the coffee shops, the police station, or the dentist.

Maria spoke into the radio again. When no responses came, she fumbled with the dial again. The agent was visibly aggravated. After giving up on the radio, the woman took a few moments to stare out the windshield, like she was thinking long and hard about what to do.

Without saying a word, she unfastened her seat belt and stepped out of the car. She marched around to the back of the Tahoe, outfitting herself with various ballistic vests and artillery.

Tater got out of the car and followed her. "What are you doing?"

She was curt and biting. "I feel like this doesn't need to be stated, but you need to get back in the car right now."

Tater had never been very good at following directions. He didn't move.

She strapped her vest around her tiny waist and buckled it. "If you don't get back in the vehicle, I will disable you."

"But I can help you."

"You are already endangering an agent's life. Do you know what they do to cop killers in prison?"

Tater made no moves.

Maria checked her weapon, then holstered it. "I'm counting down from five, and then you will be classified as a threat to my safety."

Tater let go a big sigh.

"Five, four . . ."

He sulked back to the SUV and climbed inside. He did not shut the door. He gazed out at the night. The old church in the distance was the only structure around for miles, leaning slightly off plumb. Tater faced a brief crisis of conscience. From the cab, he watched as she crept toward the Volvo, handgun leading the way. She peered in the windows of the Volvo and inspected the interior.

Maria dropped to the ground and used the Volvo as a kind of shield. She peered from around the rear fender.

She began crouch-walking up the hill toward the church. There were people up there. Their silhouettes were visible against the night sky. And there was the glowing dot of a lantern; a flashlight, maybe. And Tater realized he did not even know this woman's last name.

Within the solace of the cab, Tater pouted. His heart was beating harder than it ever had before. He inspected the shotgun scabbard mounted on the center console. He slowly placed his hand on the gun. Examined the chamber. They were short-barrel shotguns. Like the kind Tater and his cousins used for shooting Ken dolls off fence posts at his grandmother's house back when he was a toddler.

Tater watched as Maria climbed up the hill under the cover of night, keeping low to the ground, and he knew he would likely go to prison for the rest of his life for what he was thinking. But, again, Tater had never been very good at following instructions.

So he got out of the car and followed her.

Chapter 63

———

The inside of the ambulance was lit far too brightly, with LED lights that were probably capable of causing epileptic episodes. The LEDs were flickering slightly so that they were giving Caroline a headache.

Both medics were men. And the younger one was cute. Caroline was caught in the throes of child labor. This was not her best look, lying in an ambulance with her pants off and a belly that was roughly the size of Texarkana. She was mortally embarrassed. This wasn't the side of herself she would have chosen to present to a couple of males in uniform. To make matters worse, her legs were spread and one of the EMTs was looking right at her business.

"How are you doing?" the older EMT said.

"Living the dream," she said.

Rumack was beside her, holding her hand. And the poor man looked like he was about to pass out. His face was bedsheet-white. He kept telling the EMTs that he had never seen so much blood before. This had become his mantra. He could not quit saying it.

"Wow," said Rumack. "That's a lot of blood."

"It's totally normal for her to discharge that much blood," the EMT said. "If you're feeling sick, turn your head away, sir."

"No, I'm fine."

"Please, sir. Look the other way."

Rumack shook his head. "I'll be okay."

The older medic was moving to Caroline's other side. The other was shoving Rumack out of the way.

"She's almost fully dilated."

Rumack seemed as though he was about to lose consciousness. But he held a valiant face. She could see the muscles in his forehead tensing, trying so hard to look normal.

"Sir, do you need to put your feet up?"

Rumack was holding Caroline's hand. "No, don't worry about me. Just take care of her."

"Are you going to be okay?" asked Caroline.

Rumack's face was as white as a ghost.

"I'm here for you," he said. "You're doing great, Caroline."

Chapter 64

——

TONIC IMMOBILITY OCCURS A LOT IN THE ANIMAL KINGDOM. IT'S called thanatosis. In layman's terms: playing possum. But possums aren't the only ones who do it. The hog-nosed snake plays dead when threatened, rolling on its back and releasing a foul odor from its body, mimicking the smell of rot. Predators lose interest in the snake quickly.

A lot of spiders resort to thanatosis after being shaken from their webs. Think about it. You see a spider curled up on the floor and your instinct to squash it disappears. Black house ants play dead—they even do this with each other during conflicts. Frogs play dead. Wild ducks play dead. Domestic chickens play dead. Quail. Badgers. Grasshoppers. Even a shark will go belly-up when it senses a challenge it cannot win.

Feigning death isn't always about defense. Some species, such as the female nursery spider, will play dead to find a mate. Think: damsel in distress. *("Can you help me change this tire, sir?")* On the other hand, the female tree frog's instinct is to play dead to *avoid* mating. *("I have a headache, honey.")*

Woody's captor was still digging his grave, still standing in-side the hole, and the man was already up to his shoulders in earth. The guy was a much faster gravedigger than Woody. Of course, the man was considerably more motivated than Woody had ever been too.

The man was steadily talking, having a philosophical conversation with himself. Woody had no idea what he was going on about. He was too busy lying inert, holding his bottle of water.

Finally, the man crawled out of the grave. Woody tossed him the bottle of water, and the man guzzled down the rest of the water, then threw his shovel on the ground.

He walked over to Woody and stood over him. Woody propped up against a grave marker, still holding his chest.

"You're taking all the fun out of this, Padre."

"Sorry to be a spoilsport. I'll try harder next time."

The man stooped and took Woody's hand. He took his pulse again, looking at his wristwatch.

"Almost two hundred."

"What do I win, Johnny?"

"Kind of funny, isn't it?"

"What's so funny?"

"How you're going to end up killing yourself without any of my help. Surely this must be destiny, don't you think? Surely this means you were meant to die."

"Don't call me Shirley."

The man didn't register a reaction. Instead, he grasped Woody's ankles and dragged him by his legs to his grave.

"You're not missing anything, you know," the man said. "This country's been going to hell for decades. There's no telling where it will be in five years when the hard times come."

"What hard times?"

"They're on their way. This country is worse off than it's ever been before. You can't trust the media. You can't trust local judges. Police officers. The military. You can't trust anyone. In a way, I'm doing you a favor. This is not the America you or I grew up in."

"Remind me to thank you when this is all over."

When Woody neared the deep hole, he was eye level with the shovel lying on the ground, the handle only a few inches from his grasp.

Woody reached outward. Slowly. With both hands. If he was going to do this, he only had a few seconds to get it right. Woody wrapped his hands around the shovel handle and squeezed it tightly.

And prepared to make his move.

• • •

THE AMBULANCE WAS STUCK IN TRAFFIC. CHAINS OF TAILLIGHTS stretched backward toward the Mobile skyline. They were not getting through. There had been an accident, the medics said. So the ambulance sat parked on the shoulder. The emergency vehicle's red lights were glaring. The yelping sirens were sounding.

The medics were in the back of the ambulance prepping Caroline for what was coming next. The epidural was taking effect, but the pressure was still intense. It felt like her insides were rupturing. And the bright lights were giving her a headache. They told her the baby was breech. That the baby's bottom was coming out first, which made a vaginal birth risky. Normally a breech baby would be delivered via C-section, the older medic explained.

"So that's what you are going to do?" she asked the older guy.

"Ma'am," he said, "we can't do an emergency cesarian section in an ambulance. That's a surgery you don't want done in the back of a van on the highway."

"What's going to happen to my baby?"

The cute one told her to calm down. It was their go-to phrase.

Calm down. Try to relax. Breathe deeply. And of course, *You're doing great.*

The older EMT examined her, then moved to speak to his partner in a quiet voice. But she could hear them. There wasn't much privacy in an ambulance.

He was telling the other that he had learned to do a breech delivery in school. The younger medic was insisting this was no place to experiment. The older was insisting they didn't have a choice.

"I think her body can handle it," he said.

"No way. We need to call aeromedical."

"We don't have time. It's happening now."

On cue, Caroline was seized with a contraction. She had the urge to push for all she was worth. The pressure in her head was so intense she thought her skull was going to burst open.

"This baby can't wait." The older medic was already changing his gloves. "We're going to have to do this here."

"What's going on?" Rumack said.

"We are going to deliver this baby, sir. And that means I'm going to need your help."

Rumack swallowed. "My help."

"Sir, if you just do what I say, everything will be fine."

"But . . . I've never done anything this . . . this important."

The medic placed a hand on his shoulder. "Tonight is your chance to change that."

Chapter 65

———

SWINGING A HEAVY INSTRUMENT, SUCH AS A SHOVEL, IS AN IN-efficient way of using it as a weapon. Woody learned this in prison fights. Swinging a long-handled heavy object takes too long. The swing requires a windup. Then you have to factor in the time it takes for the actual swing itself. A baseball bat, for example, weighs about three pounds and takes hundreds of milliseconds to finish making contact with the ball. But a shovel weighs a lot more. To swing a shovel would be to give your opponent ample time to counterattack you, kill you, and go grab a Starbucks latte before your swing ever makes contact.

No, the correct way to use an instrument like a shovel is to jab it. You could jab a shovel handle quicker than swing it, and you could do more damage too, if you did it right. Woody once saw a man almost get paralyzed during a prison fight in Wallace when his opponent used a mop handle. The man jabbed the handle into the guy's spine.

Woody had already worked it out in his mind. He had only a few microseconds to strike first.

His limp body was nearing the grave as Peter dragged him. Woody took a few steadying breaths. Using every bit of energy reserves he had left, Woody kicked himself free of the man's grasp. Peter released his grip just long enough for Woody to jab the blade of the shovel at the man's crotch.

But he missed.

Peter was younger, more limber, and quicker. The guy sprang left. So Woody thought, *The hell with it*, and swung the shovel like a bat. It worked. Hey, you learn something new every day.

The wooden handle hit the man upside the head, but the blow only knocked him backward a few steps. Peter clutched his face and blinked a few times. He was grinning.

Woody stood poised, holding the shovel like a batsman.

"You shouldn't have done that, Father," said the man, touching his bloody lip. "I owe you for that one."

"Put it on my record," said Woody.

Then Peter reached into his waistband and removed the Colt. He moved closer to Woody, aiming the handgun at Woody's chest, using a double grip.

"I should've done this to begin with."

Woody dropped the shovel.

The man smiled. He pulled the trigger, and a shot rang out.

Chapter 66

——

STEVE McCROSKEY WAS FIFTY-TWO. MARRIED. TWO KIDS, ONE IN college. A Boston native. Go Celtics. He'd been a professional Band-Aid slinger for longer than his patient had been alive. But he had never done anything like this. Which was why he was taking deep breaths, trying to gather his courage.

McCroskey's instructor at the EMS academy had talked about delivering a breech baby. His instructor was a grizzled, chain-smoking, foul-mouthed paramedic. An old-school guy. He was a million years old, and he'd seen everything twice.

Which was why his instructor made his students become familiar with all kinds of childbirth scenarios. The students had to be at least conversationally familiar with basic birth complications like uterine ruptures, shoulder dystocia, umbilical cord prolapses, fetal macrosomia, and chorioamnionitis. And they had been required to practice breech deliveries using a rubberized model.

"Can you do this?" asked the Uber driver.

"Yes."

"You sure?"

McCroskey nodded, feigning a level of confidence he did not have. "What's your name, man?"

"Rumack."

"Rumack *what*?" asked Caroline.

"Wattle Rumack Rivers."

"Your first name is Wattle?" she asked.

"Family name."

His partner, Atkins, was next to Caroline's head, administering anesthesia. Young Wattle Rivers was next to the patient, serving as a second set of hands, watching McCroskey and waiting for further instruction.

"Are you ready?" he asked Rumack.

"Um. Yes. I think."

A breech delivery wasn't complicated—in theory. It was a little like doing gymnastics with a baby. You had to move quickly. And you needed another pair of hands to assist you. That was the hardest part: working in tandem with someone else. And while he had never performed a breech in real life—McCroskey had never birthed a baby at all in real life; ambulance births were a rarity unless you were in a made-for-Hulu drama—he knew how . . . technically.

"Let's do this," he said.

"Okay," said Rumack.

The meds did not seem to do the patient much good. She was screaming with the next contraction. "I don't know if I can do this!"

"You've got this, Caroline," said Rumack.

McCroskey barked out instructions every step of the way:

"I need your hand, right here."

"Okay."

"No, right here."

"Right."

"And I need pressure, right here."

"Okay."

"More pressure. Use your whole hand. Do it like this."

"Yes. Okay."

"How are we doing?"

Rumack nodded. "So far so good."

McCroskey performed a maneuver to change the position of the baby. The baby's legs emerged from the birth canal.

The Uber driver was hanging in there. He let out a sigh of relief. It may have looked like they were almost there. But looks were deceiving.

"Are we almost done?" said Rumack.

McCroskey was sweating all over himself. "No. Not even close."

"Really?"

"I need more light."

Rumack held the light closer. "What're you doing now?"

"We can't use any traction during this part of the process. No pulling on the baby. Not until I can reach the umbilical cord. Understand? I need you to apply gentle pressure to the abdomen. But that is all. I don't want you *moving*, do you hear me? Don't even breathe."

Rumack nodded.

"If we exert *any* traction, we'll have an injured baby, a broken neck, or a lifetime of cerebral palsy. Got it? Gentle pressure. Nothing more."

"Got it."

"I also need you to relax."

"Right."

"Mr. Rivers, you can do this."

Caroline shouted, "Are we sure about that?"

After a few minutes, the baby was halfway out. Now it was technically okay to start pulling the baby, but this had to be done very, *very* carefully, with almost *ridiculously* gentle pressure.

McCroskey spoke in a half whisper. "Okay, we can start to pull the baby, carefully. Apply just a little bit of pressure, Mr. Rivers."

McCroskey was gently removing the baby.

"Careful, Mr. Rivers. Easy."

The anterior arm came next, but only up to the elbow. He paused the birthing process.

"What's wrong?" said Rumack.

McCroskey wiped his face with his sleeve again.

"That was the easy part."

"We're good over here," said Atkins, checking the baby's heart monitor on the other side of the ambulance. "I still have a pulse."

Sweat was pouring into McCroskey's eyes. "Now we have to turn him one hundred and eighty degrees to get the other arm out. And I need you to support his body while I rotate him, Mr. Rivers. I need both your hands and complete focus from you."

"Me?" asked Rumack.

"Yes. You."

"Him?" asked Caroline.

"Yes. Him."

"Can we get someone else?" asked Caroline.

McCroskey ignored her and spoke directly to Rumack.

"I need his back to be facing the other way. And we have to keep the head flexed just right. We need to keep the body un-elevated or we'll end up breaking his neck."

"Oh my God," said Caroline.

"Wait," said Rumack. "Do you really think I can do this?"

McCroskey wiped his face. "I picked the wrong week to quit smoking."

• • •

THE BULLET HIT WOODY IN THE COLLARBONE. HE FELT IT RIPPING through his flesh and muscle. He felt the resistance his body offered against the slug. The fact that Peter had only one good eye was probably the only reason the bullet didn't land squarely in Woody's forehead.

The impact stunned him. He lost his balance and fell into the grave.

His face was pressed into the cool soil.

The bare earth was moist. Cold against his flesh. He felt himself coughing, but he could do nothing to control it. He wasn't sure what the coughing was from. The bullet might have punctured his lung. His breaths felt hot. He tasted warm liquid filling his mouth.

He'd been stabbed before. By a fellow inmate. It had been over changing the channel on the television in the recreation room. The first thing you learn is that a puncture wound does not feel like you think it would. It does not hurt, per se. At first, it just feels as though you've been punched by a very, *very* big fist. Soon the affected muscle stops working. That's when your brain tells you something is wrong. But weirdly, the pain doesn't set in for a while.

There was sticky, hot blood everywhere. There was the tightness of his chest. And now he truly couldn't breathe.

When he opened his eyes, he could see Peter standing over him. The man trained his weapon at Woody. The black hole of the gun barrel was staring right at him.

"Should've done this a long time ago."

A loud voice broke in. "Drop the weapon!"

It sounded like a woman's voice. He could hear her getting closer. It was authoritative. Professional. Angry.

"I said drop it!" the voice shouted. "Drop the weapon."

And that was when a crazed, tattooed young man smacked Peter's head with a shovel.

. . .

THERE ARE MOMENTS IN YOUR LIFE WHEN EVERYTHING SEEMS TO converge. The good and the bad. The beautiful and the ugly. The unimportant with the paramount. The past, the present, the future. Your dreamworld and reality. And when this happens you rapidly realize that truth and imagination, material and make-believe, significance and insignificance, they're all kind of the same thing. That might sound like a bunch of woo-woo. And maybe it is. But in the split second when your life changes, it all makes sense.

The person you thought you were is not the person you actually are.

You are not your body.

You are not your mind.

You are something altogether different.

But what are you? Who are you? And why?

The fact is, you represent the entirety of life's possibilities. You are the greatest expression of God's artwork. And if none of that makes sense in your brain, well, that's how it's supposed to be.

You can't understand because in order to understand, you have to have all the information. You would have to see your life from all angles, all perspectives, all points of view. This would be impossible. There's no way you can see the symphony of your own life. Too many moving parts. Too many cogs and wheels behind the clockface.

Sometimes, however, maybe once in a lifetime, you get a flashing glimpse of everything at once. Usually during a trauma. But when it happens, you see life in its entirety. You see the whole enchilada. Past, present, future. This vision only lasts for a fraction of a nanosecond. But it's enough to change you. If you let it.

Caroline was experiencing such a moment.

The years she spent in foster care as an orphaned child. The large swaths of life spent in the hospital with nobody beside her but a state volunteer. The rejection on the playground. The broken hearts from selfish lovers. The pain of life. It all made sense. It was a collage. A mosaic. In a flash she was able to see the entirety of God's tapestry.

The medic placed a child into Caroline's arms.

Rumack was weeping. Tears freely flowed down his cheeks, saturating his full beard.

Caroline held the infant against her chest.

Her son.

She was surprised at how warm his little body was. She pressed her face against the infant's head.

"Is he okay?" she said.

"Looks like a perfect score on the Apgar."

The tsunami of relief washed over Caroline, and she began to weep.

The medics threw open the doors to the ambulance. The night air in the back of the ambulance was hot and sultry.

Caroline's eyes were full of light and water. "Would you like to hold him?"

Caroline wanted to share this moment with this Uber driver who had risen to the challenge offered by his fare.

"I don't know," he said. "I'm kind of a mess."

Caroline asked him once again if he wanted to hold her son.

"Are you sure?" he asked, wiping his hands on his shirt. "I'm not really a baby guy."

She watched Rumack cradle the baby in his arms. He seemed

to be marveling at the child's hands and feet. He smiled when the baby cried. He kissed the little face.

"What're you going to name him?" Rumack asked.

"Sunflower," she said.

"You can't name him that. Oh my God. That's weird."

"Weird? Your first name is Wattle."

Chapter 67

———

WOODY WAS WEARING A BLACK SUIT AND A CLERICAL COLLAR. He had been driving through town on a summer evening. There were tourists everywhere. Hundreds of them. No, thousands. Hardly clothed. Girls in skimpy dresses. Muscled young guys in swim trunks. Families of ten, twenty, thirty tourists, lazily walking down the sidewalk, licking ice cream cones, slurping milkshakes. Clusters of teenagers moving tightly together in packs. Guy packs. Girl packs. Mom-and-dad packs. Like platoons, marching as to war.

You could hear conflicting music from a million stereo systems filling the air. And the music from local clubs that left doors open to draw customers. Screaming electric guitars. Dueling drum kits booming across the street. Thumping electric bass lines. Each playing their own uniquely bastardized version of "Mustang Sally."

There were lights everywhere. Colorful lights, illuminating the darkness. Illuminating the new Ferris wheel that had just been installed at Captain Joe's Seafood Shack. And the new zipline course they recently erected at TJ's Bar. Strobe lights pulsed from dance clubs.

Traffic had been reduced to a crawl. Woody was on his way home. He'd just finished dinner with Randy Jernigan at Mama Mia's Italian Bar & Grill. Jernigan was getting divorced from his first wife. Randy was a big donor to the church, a cradle Episcopalian, and a well-known attorney. He was going through a hard time. He wanted to talk about it with his priest. They had a few beers. Woody listened to him complain about his future ex. They prayed about it.

After a long dinner, Woody had gotten into the truck to leave. He was totally sober. The beers had been spaced over the course of three hours. Two beers for an Episcopalian was like popping two aspirin. He had no buzz. No glow. No nothing. He could have piloted the NASA International Space Station. He was well within his legal limits to get behind the wheel. Though lawyers would argue it differently. Never let the truth get in the way of a good story.

Woody had been driving toward home. Stuck in gridlock as multitudes of tourists found their way along the sidewalks of Sodom and Gomorrah. Traffic was moving ultraslowly. Motorists were on their phones. Woody was no exception. He was answering texts that had accumulated over the last three hours. Whenever he looked up from his phone, he would see hordes of tourists crossing the street illegally. *Crosswalk? What's a crosswalk? We're paying good money to be here; we don't need no stinking crosswalks.* Tourists just crossed the street wherever, whenever, and however they felt like it.

Woody kept one hand on the wheel. The other was holding his phone down by his lap so nobody would see. They weren't important texts he was answering, just random conversations he was chiming in on.

It had been a long day. He was dog-tired. He'd been on his feet for over twenty-four hours. He had visited the hospital three times for various sick parishioners. He had attended one vestry meeting, a police chaplain meeting, and somehow found time to deal with the air conditioner repair guy at Saint John's to the tune of forty-one thousand bucks.

Of course, he was not actually thinking about any of this when the young woman came rushing up in his windshield.

He was just texting.

Woody slammed the brakes. A scream exited his mouth. But by the time he'd stopped the vehicle, it was too late. She was lying beneath his front tires.

She had been crossing the street. Jaywalking. In the middle of the busy highway.

Woody huddled over her body, trying CPR. "Please stay with me, sweetie!" he shouted. "Stay with me!"

Traffic was speeding around him as he cradled her body.

Her rib cage was already crushed. Her face was battered. He had never been more afraid of evil than he was in that moment. Evil he had created. Evil of negligence. Which is the worst kind.

Woody held the woman in his arms. He called 911. He begged her to open her eyes. He pleaded and sobbed. He could smell heavy alcohol on her breath.

"There's been an accident," he shouted into the phone.

Her name was Lindsey Holcomb Allen. She was thirty-one. Dressed in a glittery dress like she was going out dancing. Mother of two. A seven-year-old and a ten-year-old at home. Boy and a girl. Townes and Katy were their names. She lived in Gulf Beach. But she had friends visiting from Mississippi, so they were all going to go out dancing. She was on her way to meet them. Her hair was brown. Eyes green. Disarming smile. Five foot six. Loving husband. She was a second-grade teacher. She volunteered at the library. She headed up the local Angel Tree ministry at the Methodist church every year. Her kid played Little League. Third base.

When the police arrested him, they questioned him. Woody heard his own voice replying to law enforcement with all the usual clichés.

I don't know where she came from.

I just looked up and there she was.

I never even saw her in the street.

Pick one.

Over the years, Lindsey's face never left him. Her features were seared into his memory like grill marks on cooked meat. He had rocked her dying body in the highway for nearly an hour before the police and ambulance could get to him. It was enough time to memorize every line of her face. The curves of her mouth. The redness of her lips. The liquid color of her eyes. He prayed over her as she exited this world. And he just kept saying, "I'm sorry! I'm so sorry!"

Woody visited her face every night before he drifted off to sleep in Wallace Correctional. She was always with him. She was perpetually beside him. Her spirit. Her essence. During his first year inside, the guys in his devotional support group talked Woody through the process of tattooing her name on his abdomen. Woody stood in the mirror while a guy used a grease pencil to outline the letters on his stomach. He spent three days finishing the job in his cell, using a guitar string dipped in the ink from a ballpoint pen.

And right now, as Woody Barker lay dying in the dirt, as federal agents lifted him from his filthy grave, he saw Lindsey. Her face was no longer dim and hazy. She was clearly visible. Young and lovely. Tall and lean. Vibrant, healthy, and whole. Aiming her electric joy at him. Except their roles had been reversed. This time Lindsey was the one cradling his body in her arms.

"You," he said.

She gave a maternal smile. "You need to wake up, Woody."

"I can't," he said lazily. "And I don't want to."

Lindsey touched his face. "You have to. It's not your time."

She rubbed his cheek. Her hand was warm. And soft. He could feel her love. Her joy. Her youthful energy, radiating from her entire being.

"Open your eyes, Woody. Open up."

Chapter 68

———

WOODY'S EYES WOULD NOT OPEN ALL THE WAY. HIS LIDS WERE crusted shut and they were sore. Like he had sand in them. And he was thirsty. His throat felt as though it was filled with razor blades so that anytime he tried to speak or swallow he wished he hadn't.

He finally managed to get his lids open, but all he could see were cloudy shapes in the room. He knew people were talking to him, but he couldn't tell where their voices were coming from or who they were.

There was a broad plastic tube in his mouth. Taped to his lips. Breathing for him. He felt his chest expanding and contracting without any effort on his part. They told him he had vomited in his breathing tube twice. The doctors said the vomit had gone into his lungs, unbeknownst to medical staffers, and this had caused pneumonia. His oxygen was lingering at 83 percent. Not good. He was on a feeding tube and he could feel the plastic hose in his nostrils.

Elizabeth was beside his bed. She was touching his face.

"Open your eyes," she was saying. "Open up, Woody."

His weary eyes brought her into focus.

"There he is," Elizabeth said as though playing peek-a-boo with an infant. "You're going to be okay, Woody."

He wasn't sure who she was saying it for. For herself or for him. She kept repeating it. "You're going to be okay."

He had undergone three blood transfusions and was awaiting a fourth. The bullet had passed clean through him, leaving an exit wound near his shoulder blade the size of a tennis ball. He kept slipping into congestive heart failure. They were just trying to make him comfortable now.

"Mr. Barker," a nurse said, speaking directly into his eyes, her voice loud and strong. "Do you hear me? Blink if you can hear me."

He blinked.

Rachel held his hand. She was squeezing it tightly. Elizabeth was holding his other hand, pressing it against her face. He wondered where Caroline was. He prayed she was safe. He would have liked to see her just one more time. Then again, he couldn't see anyone clearly; his eyes were too blurry. But he knew the way their hands felt. And he knew they were there. This was enough.

"She's okay," said Elizabeth. "Caroline is okay." Elizabeth could read his mind. She always could. The woman knew what he was thinking. "She's had her baby. And the baby is okay too."

"We need to take him back now," said a nurse. "They're ready for him in the OR."

"Woody, you're going to be okay."

"Ma'am, you're going to have to let go of him."

He tried to speak, but the only thing that came out was a garbled mumble.

They wheeled him away.

He could hear Elizabeth's squeaky shoes on the floor beside him.

"You're going to be okay. Do you hear me?"

You're going to be okay.

• • •

WHEN AMOS WAS SIXTY-SEVEN, HE GOT HIS FIRST CAT. MARILYN WAS recently deceased, and he was drinking too much. The animal just showed up one afternoon after work, crouched in the corner of his truck bed, hissing at him. He used cat food to lure the cat from the truck, but the cat was not leaving. After an hour, Amos said the heck with it, slammed the tailgate, and went home. The cat came with him and never left. Within a few months, he had three cats. A year later he had nine. He had no idea where they came from.

Animals were just attracted to him. Kids and dogs always followed him around. He had never wanted children of his own. He and Marilyn tried *not* to have kids. But the universe had other plans. Woodrow Amos Barker came into the world one summer afternoon and changed the foundations of Amos's world. Woody had softened him. Woody had given Amos purpose. The only real purpose he'd ever known in his life. And now that purpose was laid open on an operating room table.

A seventeen-year-old grandchild was in the room across the way, talking to a group of FBI agents. And he was holding his great-grandchild in his arms. Ironic for a guy who never wanted kids.

He could see Caroline behind the wire-glass windows, explaining things like a pantomime, as he rocked his great-grandchild and said, "Shhh," even though the baby wasn't crying. Why do adults always say this to babies?

Finally, Caroline came out of the room and made a beeline for the baby. The officials left the hospital in a whoosh of windbreakers.

"It's over," Caroline said quietly, falling into the seat beside him. It was as though she were saying this more to herself than to him.

"What's over?"

"It's all over," she said, and then she started crying. She used the baby's blanket to dab her face. "They've got them in custody. All of them."

"Who's *all of them*?"

"The guy who tried to kill me. Who tried to kill Woody. The man who blew up his truck. The whole terrorist group, they said. It's over."

Amos looked at the tightly closed eyes of the baby in his arms.

"And the computer thing?"

"What computer thing?"

He cut his eyes at Caroline. "The thing for which we almost expired."

"Oh, *that*."

"Yes. That. Did you give it to them?"

"They never asked about it." She shook her head. "I don't think they know about it."

They were silent for a long time, considering what all this meant. They watched the dervish of nocturnal activity within an American ICU swirl around them. Lots of professionals half jogging. Lots of nurses half shouting. It was a terrible place to be.

Caroline placed a hand on the Major's hand.

The old man looked at both hands. One young, supple, and warm. The other cold and knobby, with veins and spots.

"Do you think he's going to be okay?" she asked, tears on her cheeks.

"Shhh," he said to the baby.

• • •

I<small>T WAS NIGHT</small>. T<small>HE</small> M<small>AJOR SAT NEAR HIS BED, STARING OUT THE</small> window at the tops of the palm trees outside. The fronds were eye level with the window. So were the lit rooftops of the Gulf Beach skyline, all spread out like a topographical puzzle.

The Major hadn't even noticed that Woody was looking at him, and Woody was too weak to get his attention.

Eventually, his father figured it out.

"Heaven's sake," said Amos. "It's about time you woke up."

"Dad," came Woody's raspy reply. "What are you doing here?"

"What am I doing? I'm getting sore from sitting here all ding-dang day, watching you drool on yourself. That's what I'm doing." Amos's eyes were rimmed red, glassing over with tears.

"Dad."

"You never move; you never open your eyes. You just lie there, and I can't even tell if you're breathing or not." Amos used his sleeve to wipe his nose.

The old man reached out his liver-spotted hand and placed it atop Woody's. His hand was meaty, twice the size of Woody's. Cobby fingers and a beefy slab of a palm that swallowed Woody's hand whole.

Woody's dad had not been known for his affection. At least not toward other males. Masculinity did not permit the display of fatherly affection toward one's son, save for the occasional Little League coach butt swat. The vision of their two hands touching was foreign to Woody, and so very humbling.

They were interrupted when someone cleared their throat.

Standing in the doorway was Elizabeth.

"Can I join the party, or is this a boys' only club?"

Amos stood onto shaky legs. "I was just leaving, Colonel."

He gave Woody's hand one final squeeze and something passed between them. Something uniquely paternal. A feeling Woody had seldom experienced from the receiving end.

Elizabeth collapsed in the seat beside Woody's bed. She wore jeans and a T-shirt. Her sable hair still wet, like she'd just gotten out of the shower. The lovely woman grasped his hand in both of hers.

His mouth opened, and he winced beneath the pain of speech. "How are you doing?"

"How am I?" She laughed. "You want to know how I am?" Whereupon she buried her head into her free hand. He could see her shoulders bobbing. When she raised her head to look at him, her face looked like it had been busted apart.

"I'm not well, if you must know."

It took all the effort he had. He lifted his iron-heavy arm from the bed and moved himself closer to her. Woody placed the arm on her arm, then entwined his grip around her hand, interlocking their fingers.

"I'm not marrying Jason," she said.

It hurt too badly to speak, so he just squeezed her hand.

"I'm not doing it for you," she said. "I'm doing it because I will not get over you. And I don't ever want to get over you. Not for as long as I live."

Elizabeth wept into him, almost like a little girl. She moved his hand to her face, rubbing her salty tears against his smooth skin, kissing his knuckles.

"Liz."

With that, Elizabeth stood, lowered the bed's guardrail, and crawled into the bed beside him. Her body was warm and firm beside his, as close to him as she could get. The majestic woman kissed his face, clutching his head with both hands. She kissed vigorously, bathing his chin, his forehead, his eyelids, and his lips in her passion, chewing on his lower lip. He could taste the salt of her tears. And he was pleasantly unable to breathe.

She curled beside him and stayed that way until she fell asleep. With his hand, he petted her hair. Listened to her breathe.

"You were my big adventure," he whispered.

Chapter 69

F ATHER LE ROUX STOOD AT WOODY'S BEDSIDE ALONG WITH HIS family. The Major was holding Rachel's hand. Elizabeth and Caroline were shoulder to shoulder. There was a baby in a carrier resting on the chair beside a nurse. They brought the baby to him so he could see him. There was nothing so remarkable as a shock of red hair on a baby's head.

Next, Le Roux approached the bed. The man looked like a mountain. Clad in black. White clerical collar. His hands were the size of supermarket chickens. His shoulders were tight in his sport coat. He was looking down at Woody like a mythical figure from ancient lore.

"How much do you bench-press?" Woody asked. His voice was a muffled whisper. His voice felt stronger than it had before, but it still felt like he was talking around a throatful of razor blades.

Le Roux did not crack a smile. "Three fifty."

Woody closed his eyes. "Show-off."

The funny thing is, Woody thought he had only closed his eyes for a moment, but when he opened them, everyone in the room had shifted positions. He had been out longer than he realized.

But Le Roux was still there, although no longer standing next to Elizabeth, Caroline, Rachel, and his dad. He was on the other side of the bed now. Sitting in a chair.

Woody closed his eyes again, then opened them. Now the room was empty and it was nighttime. He realized he'd been out for a full day.

He closed his eyes once more, then reopened them. This time it was daylight, and all he saw were doctors. They were having a tribal council of some sort.

Blink. This time all he saw was Elizabeth, lying in the bed with him. Curled beside him. Her face was pressed against his. He could feel her hot breath on his neck.

Blink. Woody opened his eyes and saw Father Le Roux was there again, with Woody's whole family. They said it had been a week, and he'd been intubated twice during that time. Which would explain why he could hardly speak. His vocal cords were barely hanging on.

Father Le Roux was holding the sacraments.

The bread and the wine.

A feeling of total warmth washed over Woody. Almost like beach water in the middle of summer.

"Oh my God," he said.

"Woody," said Le Roux.

"Oh my God."

Caroline was standing in the corner with the baby in her arms. She was huddled against Elizabeth and Rachel. The Major was standing by himself, looking at the floor. They were all standing there like something important was about to take place.

"Oh my God. It's my turn."

Nobody spoke for a whole minute or more.

The sacraments were sitting on a hospital roller table, atop a pink cafeteria tray. The bread. The wine.

Elizabeth came to the bedside. Her face was puffy. Her eyes were rimmed pink. She used her palm to wipe her cheeks before she spoke, and she could hardly get words out. "Woody, I've asked Father Le Roux to bring Communion."

Woody nodded.

"Do you want to receive Communion?" Elizabeth asked.

He nodded again. But the movement of his head was too imperceptible for anyone to notice. They kept waiting for his answer.

"I do," he finally grunted.

Woody had been on the other side of this ceremony so many times that he had never stopped to think about what it might feel like for the dying person. To see a clergyperson standing over you with the species of Holy Communion in their hands. To know that death is on the horizon before you can see it. To know there is no turning back.

Le Roux stepped forward with the tray of bread and the wine.

"Don't worry about sitting up, Woody. We'll do it lying down."

"No," said Woody.

"You have to lie down," Le Roux said. "The doctors say you're in no condition to sit up. Just stay like that."

"No."

Woody's voice came out louder than he had intended.

"Woody. What do you mean by *no*?"

"I mean no, I don't want you to do it."

Le Roux stopped.

Everyone looked at each other.

Elizabeth seemed surprised. He could tell by the look on her face she was embarrassed.

"Woody, Father Le Roux has offered to be here for you. You don't want him to do it? Who would you like? Do you want the hospital chaplain?"

Woody shook his head. "No."

Elizabeth touched his face. "Woody, who then? There is no-body else."

Woody used his eyes to speak.

His gaze landed on the tall, beautiful redheaded young woman in the corner.

Chapter 70

IN ANCIENT ROME, ABOUT A HUNDRED YEARS AFTER JESUS, A LOCAL Roman governor wrote a letter to Emperor Trajan. It was an annual report kind of deal. He talked about the weather. About current events. And he also bragged about how many Christians he had killed. He bragged particularly about the torture of two slave girls who were deacons in their church. The governor imprisoned the women, who were then ravished by the guards and brutalized in their cells. The young women were interrogated to reveal the practices of the church. Their responses became the first documentation of what early churches actually did when they met.

Turns out it was simple. There were no smells and bells. No robes and funny hats. The girls said that everyone simply gathered in a home. They sang hymns. They promised to be moral. And they ate a lot of food. In fact, food was one of the most important parts of their meetings. The early Christians didn't eat wafers and drink thimbles of Welch's grape juice. They called the meals "love feasts." Someone began by breaking bread and pouring wine.

Woody walked Caroline through the administration of last rites. Step-by-step. The remnant of an ancient ritual that ties all

Christians to their forebearers. His voice was a weak whisper. And each vibration of his throat sent stinging pain through his body. But somehow he summoned the strength he had left to speak. After all, there was nothing left to save his energy for.

Caroline's hands trembled. Her voice quavered.

"I can't do this," Caroline whispered.

Woody muttered words of encouragement.

She touched his arm with her warm hand. "I don't know what I'm doing."

He used all the fortitude he had to touch her hand. "I love you."

She began to weep. "Thank you for loving me." Caroline mopped her face with her sleeve. "I love you back."

She recited the Lord's Prayer. Everyone "amened" in response. Then Caroline placed the bread into his mouth and Woody closed his eyes. He had said the words before, a million and one times before, but he said them now only in his mind.

The body of Christ. The bread of heaven, keep you until everlasting life.

Le Roux passed Caroline a chalice wrapped in white cloth.

Caroline lowered the cup and touched the rim to his mouth. Wine spilled onto his chin and gown. His daughter continued to weep, and her tears mingled with the wine.

The blood of Christ. The cup of his grace, his salvation, and his mercy unto all. Unto you. And unto me.

The alcohol burned his tongue and throat so badly he thought it was going to burn a hole through his throat.

Depart, O Christian soul, out of this world.

He faded in and out of consciousness. He felt as though he were getting lighter.

In the name of God the Father Almighty who created you.

Everything in the room seemed so vibrant. And filled with air. Like a mighty wind was purging the world.

In the name of Jesus Christ who redeemed you.

He was thinking about all the people he'd met in life. About the guys in prison. So hopeless and forgotten. So rejected and alone.

In the name of the Holy Spirit who sanctifies you.

And there was light too. Just like all the near-death stories said there would be. It was warm light. A kind of serene happiness. Like sunbathing on a summer day. Like the kiss of a loved one. Like cuddling with a lover in the early hours of morning. Like standing next to a window with a baby in your arms.

And there were people around him. Lots of people. A roomful of humans, in fact. Hundreds of them, maybe. He wondered where they had all come from. He didn't recognize them all. But they were there. Too many to fit in one room, and yet somehow they all fit. He saw people like his grandfather. Standing over him, smiling. He saw his mother; she looked like a teenager again. He saw Melinda, healthy and strong. And happy. He saw Lindsey Holcomb, dressed in a white linen dress. Her hair pulled back in a ponytail. She was whole.

Caroline remained at his bedside. Elizabeth was also next to him, her warm hand resting against his face. Rachel was holding his hand. The Major was smiling at him with tears in his eyes as he rocked the baby on his hip. He could not hear what anyone was saying, but they were all talking to him in soft voices.

People everywhere. Both living and not. All around him. And in the end, it came down to people. Life did. It wasn't about what you had done. It wasn't about what you had accomplished. It wasn't about how much fun you had, how much money you made, or whether you left your family with a great life insurance policy. It was about who you loved. Love was the only thing you could take with you.

May your rest be this day in peace.

"I'm losing his pulse," a nurse said.

"We need to bag him."

May your dwelling place be in the paradise of God.

"It's okay, Woody," said Elizabeth, speaking through tears. "We're going to be okay. You can leave us. We're going to be okay."

He squeezed her hand. "*Mizpah*," he said.

"*Mizpah*," Elizabeth said.

And Woody Barker died of a massive heart attack.

Epilogue

───────

"MOM! YOU'RE GOING TO BE LATE!"

Gary was shouting from the bottom of the staircase. He was thirteen. And at this age, he was already a stickler for being on time. He was a stickler about everything, actually. He was cocky. He was smart. He was a know-it-all. All teenagers are know-it-alls, which makes life considerably harder on those of us who actually do.

"Mom! We're supposed to be there in fifteen minutes!"

"Get your panties out of your crack!" Caroline shouted. "I'm still getting ready!"

Caroline was digging through the sock drawer. She was only wearing her bra and jeans. Her husband was sitting on the bed, playing on his phone. Probably fantasy football or whatever in God's name it was he did whenever he wasn't taking care of the house, coaching Little League games, or preparing chicken divan for three.

"Have you seen my T-shirt?" Caroline asked.

"T-shirt?"

"I keep it in the sock drawer."

"And you're looking at *me*?"

"Mom! Hurry!"

"I don't know where you keep *anything* in this house," her husband said. "I can't step foot in your office without causing an avalanche."

Caroline slammed the drawer and collapsed on the bed.

"This is so stupid. I don't even want to go do this. It's not like I don't have enough to do today."

Rumack came behind and entwined both arms around her.

"Get dressed. Go downstairs and do this for your son. Forget about that shirt. Anything you wear will be great. You don't need it."

"Yes, I do. It's important."

Caroline allowed him one kiss. One kiss turned into four; then she shoved him onto the bed.

When she went downstairs, she found Gary sitting on his backpack. Waiting. When he saw his mother wearing only her brassier, Gary rolled his eyes, then tapped his smartwatch.

"We're officially late, Mom. Thanks."

"Avert your eyes, child, I'm not dressed."

"Are you serious?"

She ignored him and dug through a pile of clothing in the laundry room. Over the past week, dirty clothes had piled up to form a miniature Mount Shasta of crap. She found the shirt in question. It was clean. It smelled like Gain.

"Thank you, thank you, God," she whispered to the ceiling.

She donned the Willie Nelson 1989 T-shirt. It was still a little big on her. She adjusted the shirt on her shoulders, then stuffed her mother's necklace into the collar.

"You're going to do great," Rumack said as he handed her a cup of steaming hot coffee, black, just the way she liked it.

She kissed her husband goodbye, and mother and son left the house. They sprinted through the garage, which was crowded with mountain bikes, three kayaks, power tools, fishing gear, and various other garage-related effluvia that was a prerequisite for any respectable suburban American existence. She shooed the army of cats out of the garage before shutting the door, most of them inherited from her late grandfather.

They jumped in Caroline's Passport and rode through Huntsville traffic, breaking the speed limit. Huntsville traffic was no laughing matter. It was a lot like driving through Dante's Fifth Circle of Hell, only slower.

Gary didn't say much on the car ride. He was too busy texting the girlfriend du jour. Lydia was her name. Or maybe it was Laura. Or Lana. It started with an *L*.

They pulled into the middle school on Bob Wallace Avenue (*Go Panthers!*). And Caroline noticed how nervous and eager Gary was. He was already jumping out of the car before it had—technically—stopped moving. He was checking his phone again.

"Come on, Mom! Let's go!"

"Hold on," said Caroline. "I haven't even put the car in Park."

But Gary was already jogging toward the doors.

Soon Caroline was trotting through the parking lot, chasing her son.

"I swear," Caroline yelled. "If you don't slow down and wait for me, I will choke you with your phone charger and bury you in the backyard!"

At this exact moment the school principal happened to be exiting his car.

Caroline smiled at the principal.

"I was just kidding, of course," she explained. "I could never do that to my son. His phone charger isn't nearly long enough."

The principal didn't smile back.

Gary and Caroline rushed to the classroom, sprinting up the

steps. Elizabeth met them on the staircase. She embraced Caroline, pecked her on the forehead, and stared at the T-shirt with warm eyes.

The three of them rushed past the band room, where brass music was thrumming from the walls. They passed a laboratory where one of the teachers was wearing safety goggles and working with Bunson burners. They passed classroom after classroom until they arrived at a door at the end of the hall.

Gary opened the door quietly.

The teenage boy crept inside, then motioned for Caroline and his grandmother to follow. Gary clutched his backpack in both arms and found a place for them at the rear of the room.

At the front of the classroom was a man in a NASA jumpsuit uniform standing before a silent class. The spacesuit was the color of a traffic cone. He spoke in a loud, sturdy, TED Talk voice, describing something about "atmospheric reentry." He used words nobody understood. And in his hand he was holding a model of a rocket.

Gary whispered, "That's Chase's dad."

"An astronaut," said Caroline. "Great. I'm going after a spaceman."

"Well," said Gary, "I could've asked Dad to come instead. He could have given a riveting speech about his graveyard shift at the Amazon shipping center."

Caroline gave Gary the stink eye.

"He couldn't have come," she said. "He has group therapy on Mondays."

"He would've canceled."

"Yes, he's very good at canceling."

Neither of them moved a facial muscle.

Caroline was standing with all the other parents who kept

their backs against the wall like wallflowers at the senior prom. The parents all watched Rocket Man's presentation, silently comparing their own flailing professional careers with the Buzz Aldrin of the eighth grade.

One of the students raised a hand. The student asked Rocket Man which planets NASA was going to explore next. The guy in the spacesuit got really excited about this question. For the next ten minutes, he used a professorial voice, drawing engineering schematics on a whiteboard, delivering an answer to the student's question that lasted longer than a public recitation of *The Brothers Karamazov*.

When he finished, everyone gave a round of applause.

"I am *not* going after him," said Caroline to Elizabeth.

Then the teacher looked at Gary.

"Gary, is your mother ready?"

Gary said, "Someone else can go in front of us. It'll take a minute for my mom to get ready."

Caroline was astonished at her son being so thoughtful. This grubby teenager. This sweet, handsome, optimistic, innocent, brilliant, talented little wiseass.

So someone else's mom got in front of the class and talked about her home renovations company. In the meantime, Caroline was digging into her backpack and removing her vestments.

Gary helped his mom get dressed. She wore her white chasuble and multicolored stole, which was made of dozens of patches sewn together. The stole had come from Caroline's very first group of unwed mothers, who met at the YWCA. Long ago, the pregnant single mothers had all pitched in and sewed the stole for Caroline, using T-shirts from their own wardrobe. Each colorful patch represented a person to Caroline. Their group affectionately called themselves Upcycled Trash. She stayed in touch with each of them even after all these years. She maintained contact with many unwed mothers.

Caroline Rivers was the founder of a chain of homes for unwed mothers: the Sunflower House. They had started with one home in Mobile, Alabama. But over an eight-year span, they had expanded to forty-three locations, stretching across twenty-one states, from Maine to Texas; Oregon to Florida. Rachel worked at the home in Pensacola. The homes were privately funded. Nobody knew where the money came from, but they always had what they needed.

Finally, it was Caroline's turn to present.

She adjusted her stole. Gary squeezed his mother's hand.

"You know what I wish?" whispered Elizabeth. "I wish your dad was here to see this."

Caroline's eyes pinkened.

She walked to the front of the class, all eyes on her. Her son was snapping photos in rapid succession with his phone.

The teacher said, "Let's give Gary's mother a warm welcome."

Everyone clapped half-heartedly. Except Gary and Elizabeth, who clapped like they were trying to break their wrists.

When Caroline got to the front of the room, the teacher leaned in to speak to Caroline. "I'm sorry," the teacher whispered. "I don't really know what to call a female priest. Am I'm supposed to call you Mother or Reverend or something?"

Caroline smiled.

"I don't care what you call me, just don't call me Shirley."

Discussion Questions

1. How does Woody's accident impact all of his relationships?
2. Did you think Elizabeth's response to learning about Caroline was realistic? Would you have responded differently?
3. What role did religion and faith play throughout the novel, positively and negatively?
4. Peter was a vicious criminal, but did you find him likeable at all? Why or why not?
5. How does the author's use of multiple points of view add or detract from the impact of the story? If you had to chose one character's story to reflect the events, which one would you chose and why?
6. What do you think it felt like for Woody to conduct the last rites for Melinda? To hear them conducted later by Caroline?
7. Were you rooting for Tater to turn his life around, or do you think he had done too much damage?
8. What did Gary the goldfish provide Caroline?
9. Who was your favorite character and why?
10. "Woody believed that every person was given one adventure in their lifetime." Do you think this is true? Have you had a significant adventure in your life, one that "makes you more human than you ever thought you could be"?
11. Amos and Woody had a complicated relationship, but how

did their love and affection for one another reveal itself throughout the novel?

12. Were you satisfied with the ending of the novel? With how Caroline ended up using the Confederate treasure? Her marriage to Rumack? If not, how would you have concluded the novel?

About the Author

Photo by Sarah Dietrich

Sean Dietrich is a columnist, humorist, multi-instrumentalist, and stand-up storyteller known for his commentary on life in the American South. His work has appeared on *The Today Show* and in *Newsweek*, *Southern Living*, *Garden and Gun*, and *Reader's Digest*. His column appears weekly in newspapers throughout the US. He has authored eighteen books and over four thousand columns. He tours his one-man show throughout the US, makes appearances on the *Grand Ole Opry*, hosts the *Sean of the South* podcast, and he's a really nice guy.

• • •

Visit Sean online at seandietrich.com
Instagram: @seanofthesouth
Facebook: @seanofthesouth
X: @seanofthesouth1

LOOKING FOR MORE GREAT READS? LOOK NO FURTHER!

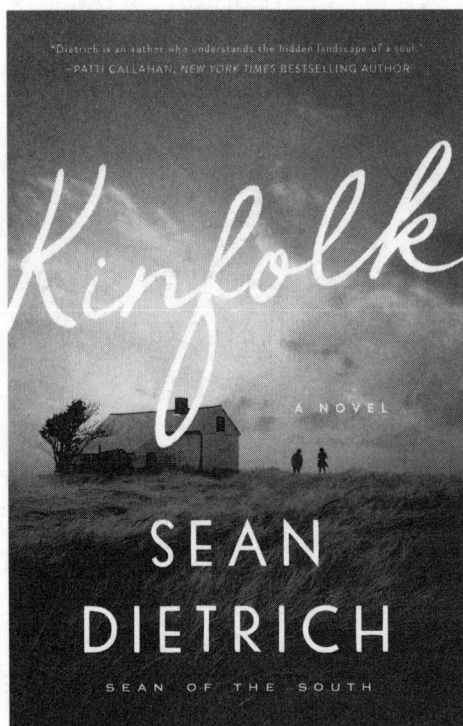

Beloved writer Sean Dietrich will warm your heart with
this rich and nostalgic tale of a small-town sheriff,
a mysterious little girl, and a good-hearted community
pulling together to help her.

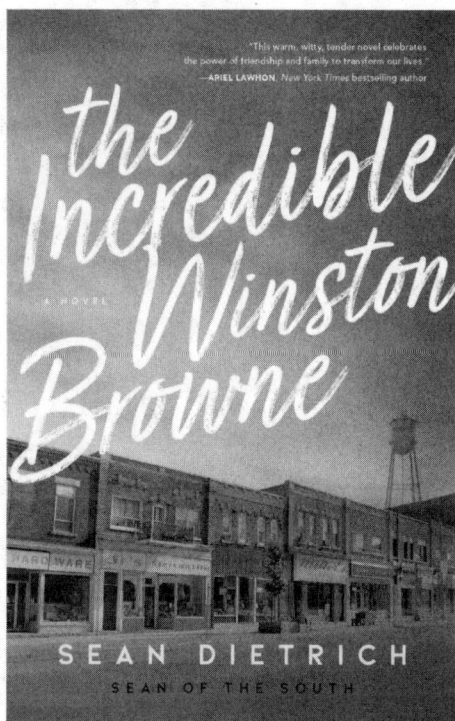